Praise for the novels of Jean Meltzer

"A delightful romantic comedy that
reminds us to follow our hearts."
Brenda Novak

"Wise, witty and warm."
Sarah Morgan

"Meltzer lovingly highlights Jewish Modern Orthodox
life using rom-com tropes people of all faiths
love… An accessible, adorable romance."
Publishers Weekly

"*The Matzah Ball* had me laughing out loud. It's
witty, funny and an all-around terrific read."
Debbie Macomber

"Funny, bright, and lovingly crafted! *The Matzah Ball*
healed a piece of me I didn't know was hurting."
Rosie Danan

"The perfect blend of funny and magical but also
tender and thoughtful. It lit me up like a menorah."
Jenny Bayliss

"A warm, heartfelt ode to self-acceptance, honesty, and
tight-knit Jewish communities… A true pleasure to read."
Olivia Dade

"Delightful."
PopSugar

"A sparkling holiday romance told with
both honesty and heart."
Kirkus Reviews

Also by Jean Meltzer

The Matzah Ball

Mr
Perfect
on
Paper

JEAN MELTZER

PIATKUS

PIATKUS

First published in the US in 2022 by Mira Books, an imprint of Harlequin
First published in Great Britain in 2022 by Piatkus

1 3 5 7 9 10 8 6 4 2

Copyright © 2022 by Jean Meltzer

The moral right of the author has been asserted.

A CIP catalogue record for this book
is available from the British Library.

ISBN 978-0-349-43008-9

Printed and bound in Great Britain by
Clays Ltd, Elcograf S.p.A.

Papers used by Piatkus are from well-managed forests
and other responsible sources.

Piatkus
An imprint of
Little, Brown Book Group
Carmelite House
50 Victoria Embankment
London EC4Y 0DZ

An Hachette UK Company
www.hachette.co.uk

www.littlebrown.co.uk

Mr
Perfect
on
Paper

☑ Mr. Perfect on Paper

September

(OTHERWISE KNOWN AS
THE START OF THE
JEWISH HIGH HOLIDAYS)

1

DARA RABINOWITZ HAD AWOKEN, AS SHE DID EVERY
morning of her life, with a plan.

Sitting on her couch in her warehouse loft apartment in
Hoboken, she stared at the gray concrete walls in front of her.
She had been up since 4:00 a.m., running through a ritual
of to-do lists and carefully constructed patterns to keep her
anxious thoughts at bay. There was showering, meditation,
candle-lighting, deep breathing. And when those didn't work,
she turned to the miracle of modern medicine: benzos.

Otherwise, the early wake-up was unnecessary. Dara never
slept well on days when she would be doing publicity.

Pulling her Bergdorf Goodman dressing gown taut against
her body, she attempted to breathe through her anxiety. Her
mother, along with a dozen other therapists over the years,
had taught her the value of positive self-talk. Closing her eyes,
Dara breathed in the scent of the patchouli candle burning
precariously in the center of her coffee table. She could do
this. It was just an interview on national television with her
beloved bubbe. What could possibly go wrong?

The buzzer on her front door rang. Dara opened her eyes,

grateful for the intrusion. Rising from the couch, she hid any overt sign of stress behind the cool veneer of a high-level executive. Naveah, her executive assistant, was standing on the threshold.

"Morning!" Naveah said, her hands full of items. "You ready for us?"

Dara returned a wide smile. "Of course."

Naveah clicked her teeth in open delight. "So much fun!"

At twenty-four years old, Naveah was a full decade younger than Dara. With golden skin and dreadlocks decorated with tiny shells, she gave the impression of being one of those people who was born instinctively cool. She was also a damn good executive assistant. Three outfits, each covered in protective plastic sheeting, hung delicately over one arm. A large backpack, like she was planning to spend the month hiking through Peru, was slung over her shoulder. In her right hand she held two cups on a biodegradable tray.

Behind Naveah stood the full entourage. Bobbi and Simi, her hair and makeup people, in addition to Cameron and Alexa, Naveah's assistants. The group headed upstairs while Naveah made her way toward the kitchen.

"First," she said, placing two disposable cups down on the counter between them. "Large macchiato coffee, made with almond milk, no sugar and a dollop of caramel sauce on top. Plus, one venti blueberry-and-lavender tea, non-caffeinated, just in case we're not in the mood for coffee this morning."

"Thank you." Dara smiled. Naveah knew her so well.

"Second," she said, reaching down into her backpack, pulling out a pink box wrapped up in white twine, "black-and-white cookies for Miriam and the ChallahBack Girls."

"You are the absolute best, Naveah."

"I know." Naveah beamed before lifting up her plastic bags on hangers. "And finally, the pièce de résistance. Three fabulous new outfits for you to review!" She hugged all three items against her *boobelahs*. "But first, how are you feeling?"

"Fine."

"Really?" Naveah asked, squinting suspiciously in her direction. "Because Janet says I'm supposed to text her immediately if you, you know—" Naveah glanced around the room, dropping her voice to a whisper "—are about to have one of your panic attacks."

Janet was head of marketing and publicity at Dara's company and, after ten years of working together, a close personal friend. Alas, Naveah did not need to whisper—Dara's diagnosis was not a secret.

"You can use the term, Naveah." Dara grabbed her tea. Opening it up, blowing on the piping hot liquid, she breathed in the comforting scent of blueberry and lavender. "Generalized anxiety disorder. They're not dirty words, you know."

Indeed, Dara had lived with the diagnosis of GAD since she was sixteen years old. It was a part of her. Inherent to her nature. For this reason, it didn't feel unnatural or wrong.

"So…" Naveah asked again, cautiously. "You're not going to freak out?"

"You can tell my handler that I am the picture of composure this morning."

"Wonderful!" Naveah beamed, dropping the topic. "Then shall we go upstairs? I'm dying to show you what I picked out."

Dara pointed toward the industrial steel staircase. "After you."

Her condo sat on the exclusive Hoboken waterfront. As such, it overlooked the Hudson River and offered expansive views of the Manhattan skyline. With three bedrooms, it spanned over four thousand square feet, and was a true testament to her success in business over the last fifteen years. She had bought the stylish apartment at twenty-eight years old—

outright and in cash—while it was still being developed. She was also able to specify with her developer any upgrade she wanted in order to make her living space perfect.

Landing on the second floor, Dara passed the long line of magazine covers she had appeared on over the years—*Insight Tech*, *Venture Magazine*, *American CEO*, *Young Entrepreneur*. Glancing up at the images, she considered the woman on the covers. Sitting on a stool, chin on her fist, smiling knowingly at the camera. In a black business suit, arms crossed against her chest. In every image, she looked fierce. Powerful. She was someone firm in her decisions, sharp, unafraid to fail. It wasn't a lie, exactly. Though, like all things in marketing, it was a carefully constructed image that she sold.

Dara entered the last bedroom at the end of the hallway to find that Bobbi and Simi were already in the process of getting set up. Makeup palettes and hairstyling tools littered her expensive vanity, which sat to the side of the room. She had originally planned to make the third bedroom her office, but after falling in love with the floor-to-ceiling windows that overlooked the Hudson River on her main floor, she moved her desk downstairs and turned the third bedroom into a fully decked-out closet instead.

Shelves of designer purses, shoes and accessories hung from handcrafted oak shelving. It was the type of closet that would make a Real Housewife squeal in outright jealousy. It gave the impression of someone who lived a fabulous life, full of high-end dates, epic parties and world-class travel.

In reality, Dara never got a chance to wear many of the items. Her three-hundred-plus-person company functioned almost entirely remotely. Aside from a quarterly get-together, like most of her staff, she worked from home, spending her day braless and in a variety of loungewear. Granted, it was expensive loungewear—the very best loungewear money could buy—but sweatpants nonetheless.

"Before we begin," Naveah said, pulling up a chair beside her, "I was wondering if I could ask your opinion on something."

Dara smiled knowingly. "Let me see."

Reaching into her bag, Naveah pulled out a phone. After turning it on and tapping the screen, she handed it over to Dara.

Glancing down, analyzing the image before her, Dara found a profile for a man named SenatorAcid69 smiling back at her. His head a sweaty mess of curls, his arms loaded down with tattoos, his profile picture was a shot of him singing on the stage of some grimy-looking dive bar.

"Senator Acid?" Dara asked, raising one eyebrow suspiciously.

"We matched on MeatCute," Naveah squealed, excitedly. "Anyway, I was wondering what you think of him."

The rest of the team leaned over Dara's shoulder.

Dara came from a long line of well-known and highly successful *shadchaniyot*, or matchmakers. In her youth, she had learned all the tricks of the trade. She knew what to look for in a partner in order to make a match successful. But while most matchmakers considered their job an art, Dara relied firmly on science.

Dara scanned the young man's profile. Senator Acid was forty-one, never married and childless. He had been raised on the West Coast but moved to New York in his late twenties to pursue a career in music. Now Senator Acid made the majority of his income by playing in dive bars throughout New York. His life, like those leather pants and tattoos he was sporting, was exciting, but also...terribly unstable.

"It won't work," Dara said definitively.

"Really?" Naveah sighed, disheartened. "But we have so much in common. We both love music and tacos. Plus, he looks incredible gyrating in a pair of leather pants."

Dara rubbed her forehead. She had a good idea where Senator Acid was heading.

As a matchmaker, Dara had been taught to never bite her tongue. It was far better to tell a singleton the truth than let them spend unnecessary amounts of time drowning in a wrong match that would never lead to marriage. As a boss, however, she needed to be more delicate.

Dara handed Naveah back the phone. "Your perfect match is someone committed to their family, with strong Catholic values, who is close to their parents. Ideally, they should be from the tristate area and make more money than you, as you will likely want to stop working once you start having children."

"But I love working," Naveah defended herself.

"Naveah," Dara said pointedly. "In love, people tend to repeat the patterns and examples set by their parents. Let's consider the facts of your life. You went to Catholic school. You live for your nieces and nephews. Almost all your vacation time is taken up with holidays, and weddings, and christenings. More telling, your mother doesn't work. Senator Acid might be fun now, but his entire lifestyle stands in stark opposition to the values you were raised with. Are you going to want to go to work while Mr. Acid is traveling from nightclub to nightclub? Is your musician going to be content giving up his dream of being a rock star and settling down with a house in suburbia full of children? It might be fun now, but you and Senator Acid are not looking in the same direction."

"I know," Naveah said, finally. "I know you're right."

"Of course I'm right," Dara quipped. "I'm the expert, remember?"

The entire room nodded their acquiescence. Indeed, it was Dara's knowledge of successful love—the tips and tricks that had been passed down from her mother and grandmother—that formed the basis of her career. Dara was not only a third-generation matchmaker, she was creator and CEO of J-Mate, the world's largest platform for online Jewish dating.

"Now," Dara said, glancing down at her watch. "If you don't mind, we're on a tight schedule here. I need to get out of here before the coming of *Moshiach*."

With that, the entire room jumped into action. Dara took a seat at her vanity. Bobbi laid out the makeup palettes, flipping on two nearby lights to mimic the high-intensity lighting of a studio. Simi took the clip out of her hair, allowing Dara's thick black corkscrews to fall free around her shoulders.

Naveah moved to the center of the room, by the built-in island that housed an impressive array of shoes, and began unzipping the plastic packaging. Hanging the outfits up on a mobile rack, she worked hard to carefully display each item.

"Okay, we have three looks for you to choose from this morning."

Dara analyzed her choices. There was an elegant pleated skirt and tight cashmere sweater. It was Jewy, which went with her brand, but possibly too Jewish for a nationally syndicated televised event that needed to appeal to a broad audience. She glanced over to her next choice, a pair of smart silk pants and a floral blouse. Finally, there was the casual tech look. A pair of tight blue jeans, Converse sneakers and a Patagonia vest.

"Number two," Dara said.

"Fabulous," Naveah swooned, hanging it up on the room divider screen.

Dara stepped behind the screen, tossed off her robe and changed into the outfit. After a few moments, she returned to the center of the room, taking her usual place in front of the full-length mirror to analyze the final look.

The black silk pants, cinched at the ankles, gave her more curves than usual. The dramatic blouse, made from the most luxurious of fabrics, was imprinted with stunning large white orchids. It achieved the right type of look for her interview. Professional yet feminine. Assertive without feeling aggressive. It was all the things she needed to accomplish as a powerful female executive—often held to a different standard than her male counterparts.

"What do you think?" Naveah asked, looking over her shoulder.

"It's perfect."

Everyone applauded. Dara sat back down at the vanity. Simi ran her fingers through her curls, while the rest of her staff gathered round, peering down at her with tablets and makeup brushes in hand.

"And what's the look we're going for today?" Cameron asked.

"Professional," Dara instructed.

"Got it," Cameron said, moving to pick out a pair of maroon heels. "A pop of color to go with all that black and white!"

"And the hair?" Simi asked.

"Just put it up." She smiled. "A stylish bun, nothing too sexy."

Bobbi and Simi began working on her hair and makeup.

Meanwhile, Naveah pulled up a chair and turned on her tablet. "Now, I know you're taking this afternoon off to be with your grandmother, so what do you need me to work on in your absence?"

"I sent you a list this morning."

Naveah tapped on her screen. Moments later, she had the to-do list that Dara had sent her at four o'clock in the morning.

"'Grocery,'" Naveah said, reading the items aloud, "'laundry, check with caterers for Yom Kippur Break Fast, confirm travel for all executives attending October J-Mate sales conference, confirm all of Miriam's oncology and radiation therapy appointments for September…'"

Dara was always making lists. Always trying to figure out how to turn her chaotic and extremely busy life into something manageable and organized. In truth, her to-do lists, like her obsessive planning, helped her control her anxiety.

She was certain that her nonstop list-making drove everyone she worked with—including Naveah—straight-up *meshuga*. Janet had even once jokingly referred to Dara as the *Good List Dybukk*, a dislocated soul who appeared without warning and sprinkled to-dos on every person who crossed her path. Fortunately, as Dara paid her staff extremely well for their efforts, they kept the majority of their criticisms to themselves.

Dara heard the familiar refrain of an incoming Skype call. "Got it!" Naveah said, snapping at Cameron to grab Dara's phone. "It's Janet."

Dara waved Simi away from her face. She asked everyone to give her a minute, and her entourage left the room. Dara waited for the door to shut firmly behind them before continuing.

"Good morning!" Janet beamed from her home office in Colorado.

"What time is it there?" Dara asked.

"Early." Janet laughed. "You got the whole crew with you today, huh?"

"You know it," Dara said, glancing at her half-done makeup in the mirror.

Just as Dara's generalized anxiety disorder was well-known among those she worked with, so, too, was the fact that she genuinely despised all types of public appearances. Alas, that didn't stop her from doing them. She had learned early on that selling herself on television, in interviews and on Instagram was a necessary evil. Everybody wanted a face, a real person to support, behind the brand. Over the years, Dara had devised all sorts of systems for handling her anxiety regarding these appearances.

"And how are you feeling this morning?" Janet asked, getting right to the point.

"Oh, you know me," Dara said. "I'm only nervous for the three days before and the six days after...so in terms of the actual interview, I imagine it will go just fine."

Janet laughed. "You're going to do great, Dara."

In truth, she always did great. She was a perfectionist, after all. She always had a plan and always said all the right things. She smiled in all the right places. She was never caught off guard, and therefore, never floundered. Though the glam squad and to-do lists may have seemed overkill to some, her obsessive-compulsive tendencies worked. Her business was thriving. Her reputation in tech, and the Jewish world, was flourishing, too.

"Like we already discussed," Janet continued, "there shouldn't be any surprises, okay? Everything has been worked out between our publicity people and their producers. You want to run through the script one more time?"

"No," Dara said firmly. "I got this."

Janet nodded. "Then I hope you have a blast with your bubbe today."

The camera shut off. Dara put her phone away, catching sight of her reflection in the mirror. Her hair had been arranged into a sophisticated bun. Her angular features had been softened with light contouring. On the surface, she was the picture of poise and finesse. And yet, her hands were shaking.

She cracked her knuckles, took a sip of tea. She knew it was ridiculous, being this nervous about going on *Good News New York*, a show that nobody even watched…but she couldn't help herself.

Dara watched it.

Religiously.

It was a habit of hers to keep the television running in the background while she worked. She liked the noise, the hum of familiar voices. It helped her anxiety. She especially liked the deliciously handsome head anchor of *Good News*, Christopher Steadfast, and the easygoing way he ended every episode with the words, "I'll be waiting for you."

Unfortunately, it had a weird time slot. Midafternoon, during the week, squeezed between the morning talk shows and the soap operas. Plus, it was an oddity in the world of live broadcasting in that it only focused on positive stories. Good news and human interest tales, like the two kids who donated proceeds of a lemonade stand to a homeless shelter, and Bucky, the vegan golden retriever.

Dara adored the segments on Bucky. She watched all of them, often on repeat, staying up late into the night, scrolling through all his reposted videos on the *Good News New York* Facebook fan page. In fact, the only reason she had even suggested going on *Good News New York* to begin with was for a chance at meeting the King of Aww himself. Though she was far too mired in her own busy schedule (and anxiety) to ever own a pet herself, she had adopted the quirky golden retriever in her heart.

As for Christopher Steadfast, it could never happen. And the reason it could never happen was right there in his name. Christopher Steadfast was not Jewish. As such, and thanks to a very clear rabbinic prohibition against interfaith marriage, she regarded the man the same way she would some beautiful non-Jewish Fabergé egg you passed by in a museum. Something to gaze upon and admire…but never, *ever* touch.

She couldn't believe she would be meeting him today.

The dog, obviously.

Not the man.

She had no interest at all in some sexy Southern heartthrob with a voice that could melt schmaltz and the pectoral muscles of a Norse god.

Dara shook the thought away. Then, as her own ema, or mother, had taught her, she focused all her energy on dealing with practicalities.

She had Simi and Bobbi come back to the room, finish her hair and makeup. She did one final run-through of her schedule with Naveah. She had Cameron and Alexa double-check her bags at the front door, packing up her phone and tablet. Eventually, with well wishes and air kisses, Naveah and the entourage departed for the day. Normally, she would have someone from her staff accompany her to her events. But today, she wanted to focus on spending time with her grandmother.

Dara found herself alone in her apartment once more.

She glanced down at her watch. She still had fifteen minutes left before she needed to head out to her bubbe's. *Fifteen minutes.* It was a long time to sit around staring at the concrete walls of her apartment. Quiet was dangerous for Dara. It left her open to obsessing.

She moved to fill the space. She brushed her teeth *again*. Double-checked the bedroom, making sure the bed was made and everything was neat and tidy. She turned off her computer monitors and all the lights. She unplugged her coffee maker and double-checked the third bedroom for any hair straighteners or curling irons left plugged in. She made sure all the knobs on the oven were turned off, and that the patchouli candle was blown out. She pulled out her phone and snapped a photograph of both. Just in case her brain started obsessively worrying that she had left something on by mistake, and she was single-handedly responsible for burning down all of Hoboken.

Dara landed at the front door. Her eyes wandered down to her red high heels. She hated wearing heels in the city. Not for any practical reason, or because they gave her blisters. But because in case of emergency, the zombie apocalypse or another mass casualty event, she was worried about having to traverse sixty city blocks—or, God forbid, a bridge—to get back home.

She debated her options. She could pack her heels and wear sneakers for the commute, but that would require yet another bag for the simple day trip into Manhattan.

She hated that it had to be that way. That she couldn't just be judged on who she was and what she created. Sadly, Dara was a realist. A huge part of her success in life had been understanding how the world works, and the way people interact with each other. Whether she agreed with it or not, first impressions were important. Like a *shidduch* sheet, or a profile on J-Mate, everybody went to the photo first.

Otherwise, she looked perfect. The house looked perfect, too. Perfection was the layer of armor she wore to protect herself from the swings and swipes of an uncertain world.

She reminded herself of the positive. She was going to be spending the day with her beloved bubbe. They would be making important memories together. Necessary memories. Any anxiety she felt—any sense that something terrible was about to happen—was simply the neurons in her brain misfiring. Her feelings could not be trusted.

Forcing her shoulders back, and her chest upward, she projected confidence. And then, slinging her messenger bag over one arm, she grabbed that box of black-and-white cookies from the kitchen counter and headed out.

2

CHRISTOPHER STEADFAST WAS CERTAIN THAT OF all the mornings he had managed to ruin breakfast, this was the worst. Standing in the minuscule kitchen of his two-bedroom apartment in Brooklyn, bent over a skillet with a spoon, he attempted to dig a chunk of shell out of the scrambled eggs.

"Come on," he grumbled. "Don't do this to me this morning."

The edge of the spoon made contact with the shell. Slowly and methodically, he began easing the tiny piece of white to the side. He was just about to lift it out of the pan when the strangest scent floated past his nose. Something acrid and off. Something burning. Chris dropped the spoon.

"No," he said, turning his attention to the skillet of bacon. "No, no, no, no!"

Leaving the eggs behind, he grabbed the pan, shaking it back and forth. In response to his efforts, the oil splattered. A blotch in the shape of Massachusetts landed in the center of his work shirt.

"Shiii—" Chris stopped himself. "Shinoozle."

Glancing down the hallway, he made sure that his eleven-year-old daughter was not within earshot. Thankfully, the coast was clear. He sighed, relieved to have done one thing right this morning, before grabbing a paper towel and attempting to wipe the oil stain away.

"Lacey," he shouted down the hallway. "Hurry up, kiddo!"

He stopped wiping his shirt long enough to inspect the damage. Once again, all his good intentions were for naught. Massachusetts grew in size, and quickly morphed into California.

Chris threw the towel down, frustrated. The shirt was new—and ruined, just like breakfast. Glancing over to the small counter and stove top, he took stock of his best efforts. The bacon was burned beyond recognition. The scrambled eggs had two large chunks of shell sitting inside. The bread, still waiting in its bag on the counter, hadn't even been toasted. It seemed that his morning could not get any worse.

And then the smoke detector went off.

"Oh, come on," he groaned aloud. "Seriously?"

He attempted to swat at the machine with a dish towel, jumping in place repeatedly to reach the off button. It was no use. Despite being six feet tall, he couldn't reach. Finally, he grabbed a chair from the dining area, dragged it back to the kitchen, and used the extra height to reach the alarm and shut it off. He stepped down just in time to see Lacey. She was still in her pajamas.

Chris forced a smile. "You ready for breakfast?"

Lacey crossed her arms against her chest. Her eyes wandered over to the bacon pan, where the meat was now an unrecognizable shade of tarry black.

"We normally just have cereal for breakfast."

"You want cereal for breakfast?" he said, twisting toward a cabinet.

Chris moved to grab milk from the fridge, when he realized they were out. He closed the fridge, quickly pretending like cereal was never an option.

Lacey sat down at the table and blinked her green eyes, tired and listless, in his direction. He could tell that she was still half asleep. "Why are you making eggs? You never make eggs and bacon on a school day. It's weird."

Chris didn't know how to answer her.

"You know what," he said, throwing that pan of bacon into the sink, "I have a better idea. Why don't we stop for doughnuts on the way to school?"

"Doughnuts?" she asked, incredulous.

"Yeah." He beamed. "As many as you want. We'll make it a special thing, just for today, before school. What do you say, kiddo?"

She considered his offer. "I guess."

"Great," Chris said, relieved. "Then hurry up and get dressed. We don't have much time before school starts."

Lacey rose from the table. When she turned, the morning sun, streaming through the windows of the living room, kissed her freckled cheeks. For just a moment, one smiling instant, he thought he saw Claire.

He breathed through it. It was funny how grief could sneak up on you. How it was always there, lingering in the background, like the ambient noise of a bustling city. Sometimes he noticed it more than others.

Two hours later, after Lacey was fed and dropped off at school and Katie, the nanny, was texted a message regarding groceries, Chris arrived at the studios of NBS. He beamed as he entered, a bounce in his step, offering a hearty good morning to each person he passed.

He was a champ at this. Faking it. Looking happy. Smiling through whatever pain was threatening to drown him. When faking it didn't work, he simply avoided the conversation entirely. As his own father had pointed out as Chris packed up the car, and Lacey, leaving Virginia forever, he was someone who ran away.

Chris headed to the fifth floor, where the production team for *Good News New York* had their offices. Like always, it was busy. Producers handed off notes to cameramen and directors. Interns raced back and forth, shuttling coffee and helping set up equipment. It took a large and devoted team to make live television happen.

Chris made his way toward his office and took a seat at his desk. Moments later, Eleanor Cohen, his executive producer, appeared at the door. She grimaced in his direction, and her eyes wandered down to the large oil stain on the center of his shirt. "Jesus Christ," she said. "You go to war with a deep fryer this morning, or you just finally giving up on life?"

It took Chris a minute to remember what she was talking about. Glancing down at his shirt, he quickly rose from his desk. "I tried making my kid breakfast. Bacon, eggs...the whole works."

Eleanor squinted, confused. "Why?"

"Long story," he explained. Chris moved to the side of his office where he kept a few spare suits, wrapped up in plastic, for just such an occasion. "Which one?" he asked, holding up two pastel shirts.

"Pink," she said succinctly. "I always liked you in pink."

"Pink it is, then," he said.

Eleanor waited for him to change, taking a seat across from his desk. After a few thoughtful minutes, she answered the question for herself.

"Oh, crap," she said, cocking her head sideways. "It's the anniversary, isn't it?"

Chris returned to his seat. "Two years today."

"Well." Eleanor sighed heavily. "That freaking sucks."

Chris couldn't help but laugh. What else was there to say, really?

There were only two people in the Northeast who knew about Claire. Jensen, his best bud in New York, because it had come out early on, one morning while they were working out together. And Eleanor, because she had demanded to know the real reason why anyone would give up a "perfectly respectable position in a DC bureau for a crap gig like *Good News New York*."

Of course, *Good News* wasn't a total disaster. It was still a nationally syndicated show on daytime television. It paid decent. At least, decent enough to rent a two-bedroom apartment in Brooklyn and afford a full-time nanny.

More important, it got him and Lacey out of Virginia. Away from the nonstop reminders of their family tragedy. It was a win-win in that regard. What it lacked were ratings, professional accolades and personal fulfillment. But Chris didn't care about any of that. All he wanted was to give his daughter some stability. He wanted to see her laugh again. Perhaps, deep down, he wanted to find a reason to laugh again, too.

"So—" Eleanor leaned forward, her hands steepled under her chin "—you thought that eggs and bacon would somehow make up for the death of her mother?"

"Seems pretty stupid now, doesn't it?"

She shrugged. "You've always been kind of a softy."

"Thanks?"

"I'm just saying," she said. "You have a soul. You have, like…a good heart and annoyingly decent intentions. I just want to make a ton of money and spend two weeks a year vacationing someplace really expensive."

"At least you know who you are."

"Damn straight," she said, lacing her fingers behind her

head. "It also helps that my womb is made of concrete. I don't have to complicate my life with...spawn."

Eleanor wasn't trying to come off as harsh. It was simply that the woman had the emotional sensitivity of a Mack truck. Born and bred in Staten Island, she was street-smart with a no-nonsense attitude and a desire to get firmly down to business. Eleanor wasn't the type of EP to cut someone slack simply because they had a sob story and some talent.

"Truth be told," Chris said, considering his morning with his daughter, "I don't even know if Lacey realized it was the anniversary. She looked at me all weird...and then we just wound up getting doughnuts."

"Well, maybe you think about it more than she does?"

Chris sank lower in his seat. "I doubt that."

The car accident that had robbed them of Claire had changed the course of their lives. He didn't expect Eleanor to understand. Most days, he couldn't even understand the pain that sat between his shoulders like an anchor. The only thing he knew for certain was that every moment since she passed felt like he was breathing underwater.

Claire had been the center of their world. She had been the sun around which they circled. Life couldn't just go on without her.

Chris moved to change the topic. "So, what's on deck for today?" he asked.

Eleanor got right down to business. "We're going to start the episode with Can-Kid," she explained, pulling out the production notes that she had brought with her. "Jason already has all the footage shot and edited, so all you need to do is open and introduce."

"Can-Kid," Chris said, scribbling down a reminder. "And then?"

"After that, we'll cut to the segment on the motorcycle club that delivers roses to the old-age home. Lisa will be handling that one outside. That'll be live—four minutes, tops—then a cut to commercial break."

"Sounds good."

This was how Eleanor and Chris began every morning. Running through the production schedule. Noting last-minute changes or cancellations to the segments. It took a full team of camerapeople, producers and crew members to make *Good News* happen. But when all was said and done, the final product rested on Chris's shoulders. He was head anchor, after all. He was the face, and voice, of *Good News*.

Eleanor continued, "Next will be the gecko that prevented a nuclear attack, the car company working to reduce global emissions, Bucky, and finally, the matchmakers."

Chris looked up from his production schedule. "Matchmakers?"

"Last-minute addition," Eleanor explained, handing him a write-up to review. "With Rosh Hashanah coming up, we thought we'd do a little something heartwarming and Jewish. Plus, *Good Day* already nabbed the Upper West Side honey sale *and* singing rabbis...*freaking sharks*...but whatever, we'll make it work with the matchmakers."

Good Day was their rival in their time slot. No matter what Chris did to try to match them in ratings, they took every decent story. Poor Eleanor. All she wanted was to prove to the bigwigs on the upper floors of NBS-7 that she was capable of executive producing a television show in a prime-time slot.

Chris skimmed the notes. At least, it was an interesting story. According to the write-up, they weren't just any match-makers, but three generations of matchmakers within the same family. The business had begun with the grandmother. The mother had died ten years back. But the youngest, Dara Rabinowitz, was some sort of tech genius zillionaire.

"She created J-Mate," Eleanor said.

Chris looked up from his pages. "You're kidding me."

"I hold her personally responsible for every terrible date I've ever been on."

Chris laughed. "So they want me to talk about J-Mate?"

"Apparently, the company is expanding into new territory," Eleanor said, pushing another write-up his way. "The deal was we would give Ms. Rabinowitz some airtime to talk about how J-Mate is changing, updating their app for a modern age, in exchange for an exclusive on their three-generation matchmaking story. The grandmother will be accompanying her. You'll wrap the show from the interview."

"Simple enough." Chris shuffled the pages into a neat pile. He assumed this conversation was done, and he would shortly head to makeup. Instead, Eleanor remained in his office, tapping on the edge of his desk. It was so unlike her—she often spoke without any filter. Something was wrong.

"What is it?" he asked.

"I don't know how to tell you this—" Eleanor shifted in her seat "—but the ratings on *Good News*, they haven't been that great."

"In fairness, they've never been great."

"We're drowning next to *Good Day*."

"So, bring in more Bucky," he said, unconcerned. "Everybody loves the vegan golden retriever."

"Bucky would need to start cooking his own meals to get us to where we need to be in terms of numbers."

Chris leaned back in his seat. "What are you trying to say?"

"The higher-ups, the network executives, they're giving us warning. Either we get the ratings up and start being competitive in our time slot…or they're canceling the show."

It couldn't be worse news.

"How much time do we have?" Chris asked.

"I don't know," Eleanor said honestly. "A month, maybe two, maybe more. Only thing I know for certain is that we need to find *something* that can start pulling in numbers. If not, we'll all be out of work come Christmas."

Christmas. His mind went straight to his young daughter.

Still, Chris was not the type of man to crumple in front of others. Swallowing any feelings of trepidation, he forced a confident smile.

"Well, then," he said, meeting Eleanor's gaze with a strong lift of his chin. "Guess I'll have to figure out a way to blow these ratings out of the water."

Eleanor nodded. "I hope so. For all our sakes."

Moments later, she was gone, shutting the door behind her.

Chris dropped the smile. Despite his bravado, he was panicking. He couldn't afford to lose *Good News*. It wasn't just a professional blemish that would likely follow him for the rest of his career. He couldn't bear the thought of uprooting Lacey again for the sake of a new job. How could he rip her away from New York when she was just beginning to get settled?

She had already lost so much.

Folding his head into his hands, he knew something had to be done. But with the ratings the way they were, Chris had no idea how to save the show. People loved Bucky, but he didn't pull in the numbers. *Good Day* stole all their decent segments. He was at a complete and total loss. More than another new beginning, what Chris needed now was a flat-out miracle.

3

DARA EXITED HER BUILDING, TAKING A DEEP AND
centering breath of the crisp fall air. The shifting colors of the
sky, the way the breeze hinted at cooler temperatures ahead,
always reminded Dara of the fall. Even without the Jewish
calendar app on her phone buzzing away with reminders, she
would know that Rosh Hashanah was approaching.

Rosh Hashanah, literally meaning "head of the year,"
marked the start of the Jewish New Year on the lunar calendar. It celebrated the birth of the world and, unlike many
other new year celebrations, was a serious affair. A time for
introspection and reflection. But also, a time for Jews to look
back on mistakes of the past and contemplate *teshuva*—returning and changing for the better. For Dara Rabinowitz, *change*
would be the word of the season.

Dara had created J-Mate when she was just twenty years
old. She had started her company in her dorm room at Bar-
nard College, funneling three generations of matchmaking
knowledge into one carefully coded algorithm, while her
roommate and friends were all out partying.

Over the last fourteen years, she had built that tiny application into an international business. J-Mate was now a fully functional, multimillion-dollar company. Dara had countless *shidduchim*, or marriages, under her pleated skirt.

The problem was, of course, in that anxiety-producing word floating around on the winds. *Change.* People changed. The world changed. Technology, especially—and the way people interacted with technology—shifted on the regular.

In order to keep up with the demands of her audience, Dara was in a nonstop race to stay up-to-date on modern dating trends. Each week, she pored over reports from her sales and marketing teams. Every second, she worried about disrupters.

J-Mate was in no danger of closing up shop, but over the last five years, it had seen its share of troubles. Subscriptions were down. They had been hacked by some foreign government, bringing with them a firestorm of bad press, affecting their reputation in the marketplace. More problematic, Jewish demographics in America were changing.

Intermarriage had become more common. The definition of who was a Jew—and who was not—had become muddied. J-Mate was no longer the likeable modernization of a shtetl tradition, but an antiquated notion. Worse yet, they had stopped being the cool platform. Like Facebook suddenly being the domain of your parents as TikTok took over the youth, competitors were threatening J-Mate's exclusive reach into Jewish online dating every day.

Gone were the days of in-depth profiles listing out hobbies, educational background, and pictures of extended family. Now her audience was far more interested in swiping right, meeting up with someone immediately for drinks or coffee, without wasting time on long get-to-know-you emails.

To Dara, meeting up with a complete stranger seemed like a great way to get murdered. But her anxiety about being killed—or worse, someone using her app being killed—was what had sparked her latest update. It was a simple little idea. A tiny button next to each profile photograph that read *Play Jewish Geography*. But that *"J-eography"* button had taken three years, and six different developers poached from Amazon, to create.

Dara was banking on that update to keep J-Mate a leader in the online space.

Clutching the box of black-and-white cookies, Dara arrived at Adath Israel Senior Living. Opulent columns of gold overlay and marble greeted her. Just the sight of that building, looming large and familiar before her, caused the anxiety inside her belly to dissipate. Dara was often at her best, and most calm, around people and places she was familiar with.

Her personality shifted. She did not have to mask her reality behind the facade of a high-powered tech executive. She was simply a woman, and a granddaughter, visiting her beloved bubbe. Her shoulders relaxed. Her heart opened wide. The smile on her face came authentically.

"Good morning, Dara!" Steven, the doorman, greeted her. "You're looking lovely this morning."

"Thank you so much, Steven." Dara beamed. "Are you going to be watching the show today?"

"Wouldn't miss it for the world."

Dara squeezed his arm and headed inside.

Passing an indoor waterfall, she made her way toward the elevators. A silver tray near white couches offered incoming visitors champagne flutes filled with peach and plum nectar. It was the Rolls-Royce of nursing homes, and not surprisingly, it cost a fortune. Although, at Adath Israel, they preferred the term "Senior Lifestyle Residence."

Getting off on the fourth floor, she recognized the nurse—or "lifestyle adviser"—manning the front desk as Monica. Dara made it a point to check in with her.

"How is she doing today?" she asked.

"Oh." Monica laughed. "You know your grandmother! Doesn't slow down for a second."

Dara was relieved to hear the update. They had a big day coming up, after all.

"Is she in her room?" Dara asked, pointing down the hall.

"Sixth-floor rec room," Monica informed her. "But be careful. The ChallahBack Girls are on a warpath today."

Dara took heed of the warning and made her way back to the elevator, pressing the button for the sixth floor.

There was likely not a finer or more luxurious senior living center on the planet. But even with all its amenities—private chefs and three dining rooms, indoor pool on the penthouse level, a doctor who lived in the building—it had not been Dara's first choice.

No, what Dara had wanted was to purchase a large and extremely expensive mansion somewhere in Rumson, New Jersey. She had the money for it, obviously, and she liked the idea of living in one house together. Plus, moving to the suburbs of New Jersey would put both of them in closer proximity to Shana—Dara's older sister—and her four nieces and nephews.

It seemed the perfect solution for everybody. Dara would have her best friend in the world, her bubbe Miriam, living with her. Shana would have nonstop access to babysitters, a necessity since she often dealt with nannies quitting at the last minute. Alas, and for reasons she still didn't completely understand, her grandmother had vehemently refused the offer.

As it turned out, Miriam didn't want to live with Dara, all alone in a big house in New Jersey. Shana also thought it was a terrible idea, going on and on about the ridiculousness of kidnapping their poor grandmother as an excuse to not have to deal with the world. They had fought about it for weeks, in fact—after her mother had died, and right before her father had retired to a kibbutz in Israel—and then, Bubbe Miriam was diagnosed with brain cancer.

Even now, the words didn't seem real. A brain tumor? It felt like the punch line of some joke, like some poorly plotted cliff-hanger in a soap opera, before the character descends into a coma. But it was real. As real as all those doctors' appointments, medical tests and experts that Dara had sourced in the wake of the news.

There was no other option. One of the selling points of Adath Israel had been an enhanced memory program to help seniors struggling with dementia.

Dara made a decision. She took the money that would have gone into some ten-thousand-square-foot mansion on the water and found the most luxurious "Senior Lifestyle Residence" that money could buy in Hoboken. Then, Dara found a similarly lavish condo—two blocks away and on the water—and bought that, too.

Now Dara visited her grandmother every day. Sometimes for lunch. Sometimes for dinner. Sometimes she would even bring her laptop and work beside that fancy-shmancy indoor pool on the penthouse level while her grandmother and the ChallahBack Girls did laps.

Thankfully, Miriam was still in a place where she was having more good days than bad ones. It was the only reason Dara had agreed to let her beloved grandmother accompany her on television. At least, that was what Dara told herself.

The elevator doors parted, and voices reverberated down the hall.

Most of the ChallahBack Girls struggled with hearing loss in some form. When they weren't screaming to be heard, they were actually fighting. The four elderly women were like sisters that way. Fiercely loving and loyal...but also totally incapable of biting their tongues when they had an opinion on something.

"More rouge!"

"It needs to be fluffier."

"I can only work with what I have, Miriam!"

"Let me see that mirror."

"Stop talking! You want to look like a clown?"

"*Alter cockers*, the lot of you!"

Dara entered the sixth-floor rec room to find her bubbe, Miriam Rabinowitz, holding court. Fawning over her were her three best friends—Ruth Eckelberg, Shira Stein and Arlene Kahn. Clad in polyester loungewear and white orthopedic sneakers, they were a trifecta of trouble that were not to be trifled with.

Dara affectionately referred to these three women as the ChallahBack Girls because of their tendency to stand in the doorways of their apartments and scream into the hallways at each other, much to the chagrin of the overnight staff. (Dara had needed to rectify that situation with a rather sizeable donation.)

There was Ruth Eckelberg, aka the Heartbreaker. Ruth was known for her long hair and gigantic *boobelahs*, which she rested on the table during card games. In her four years since arriving to Adath Israel as a widow, she had never once lost a game of gin rummy, leaving many to speculate if her *joobs* and the winning were related.

Next was Shira Stein, the Comedian. Shira could warm your heart with a smile and an old Yiddish joke…until she got bored. Then, you'd find her sitting in the cafeteria, eating chocolate pudding out of a bedpan, sending the staff screaming while she giggled outrageously at the brilliance of her mad prank.

Last but certainly not least was Arlene Kahn. Known as

the Artiste, Arlene had spent her youth working as a nuclear physicist, before finding her true calling in the visual arts. Now she never missed an opportunity to beautify, redecorate or remodel. She wore her craft in purple hair, a paintbrush swinging from a leather braid around her neck and vibrant shawls she had collected over the years.

The unofficial leader of them all was Bubbe Miriam, the Matchmaker. Having arrived to Adath Israel alone, and knowing no one, she quickly rose through the ranks of the social hierarchy. Meanwhile, someone else—maybe even someone like Dara—would have folded up on themselves completely.

Miriam was a firecracker. She did for her retirement community what she did for all those she met throughout her life. She made connections. She brought people together. She took the loneliness that often came with being elderly, and from that void created families.

In return, the ChallahBack Girls treated her with a sort of sacred reverence. When Bubbe Miriam began to fall ill— when her right shoulder began to slump, and she started having lapses in memory—the ChallahBack Girls responded. They surrounded her grandmother with triple the love and a torrent of nonstop devotion.

Dara would forever be grateful to them.

Dara put her box of black-and-white cookies on one of the tables and watched the four women from a distance. Pulling bobby pins from her grandmother's hair, Ruth fluffed and prodded. Shira held a mirror while Arlene—paintbrush swinging around her neck—applied a bold coral lipstick.

Her grandmother would be beating off men with a stick in that color. Indeed, she got a proposal nearly every day at Adath Israel. Granted, it was from the same man—another resident, a Mr. Meyer Kaplan, who struggled with dementia. Sadly for Mr. Kaplan, Miriam always turned him down.

"Boker Tov," Dara interrupted them. "I brought you all a little nosh!"

The ChallahBack Girls swiveled around on their sneakers. But whatever they were doing to her grandmother was clearly far more important than black-and-white cookies. With barely a second glance toward her box of goodies, they finished whatever project they were furiously working on.

"Oh, Dara," Ruth said. "Perfect timing."

"If you want your grandmother to look like a clown," Shira mumbled.

"Pssssh." Arlene waved away both their comments. "Don't make her nervous."

The three women fell silent, huddled in a half circle around Miriam. Her grandmother remained completely out of view.

Dara smiled politely. Everybody knew about her anxiety. Nothing to be ashamed of, and not a secret.

"Go on," Dara egged the old women onward. "Show me, already!"

The ChallahBack Girls smiled knowingly at each other. Then they parted like the Red Sea making way for Moses. Bubbe Miriam rose from her chair and, like the queen she was and with arms outstretched, tapped a little dance toward Dara. She did one final spin, swinging her hips to an invisible song, before landing with a tiny curtsy in front of her granddaughter.

"Well," Miriam asked, "how do I look?"

Dara swallowed a lump inside her throat. She was overwhelmed, seeing her grandmother looking so healthy. "Perfect," Dara said, biting back tears. "A vision of beauty."

Everyone applauded.

Yes, her grandmother was spectacular. At almost ninety years old, Miriam was a woman of style and substance. She wore dresses in wild prints, the shape of lampshades. She paired her carefully designed outfits with chunky and colorful jewelry—pink flamingos and frog princes, tropical fruit and giant plastic lips. But what always struck Dara as quintessentially Bubbe Miriam were her shoes. Dara's grandmother had the cutest, and most epic, array of vintage-style dance shoes—Mary Janes and prim oxfords in a quilt of colored leathers—which she wore on the regular.

Of course, some would say that Bubbe Miriam was outlandish. But her clothing was simply a reflection of her energy. When Miriam entered a room, she demanded attention. She drew others to her, with her wide-open arms and her refusal to apologize for being unusual. In truth, it was why she had been so damn good at being a matchmaker.

Alas, poor Dara had not inherited this tendency to sparkle.

Oh, she had other talents. Like computers, and writing code, and avoiding everything that made her fearful. She was also genuinely spectacular at making lists, and having a plan, and foreseeing every possible disaster. And when people inquired—if her grandmother or the ChallahBack Girls prodded, wondering why at thirty-four years old, and so very rich, and so very beautiful, that she was also *so* very single—she had the perfect excuse. She was busy.

"It's not too much?" Shira asked, pointedly.

"No." Dara sucked back a well of emotion. "Never."

"Told you." Ruth grinned smugly in the direction of Shira.

"What was that?" Shira screamed, cupping her ear. "I can't hear you."

"You can hear me!"

"You said something?"

Ruth grumbled out one of her famous Yiddish curses. "May all your teeth fall out except one, but may it always hurt."

A fight broke out between Shira and Ruth. Their words twisted into shouts splattered with Yiddish. Rather wisely,

Arlene chose not to get involved. She sashayed her way over to the table, the ends of her silk dressing gown flailing about her, and grabbed a kosher black-and-white cookie.

"Dara," Arlene said, munching on one. "Look at this *meshugas*!"

Dara laughed. She loved the ChallahBack Girls as much as her own family. They bickered and fought, but always showed up for each other when most needed. She would have liked to spend all day basking in a warm cocoon of their support and love, but it was getting late. Dara and her grandmother were on a tight schedule.

"Are you ready to go, Bubbe?" Dara asked.

Miriam frowned. "Well, what about you?"

"Me?" Dara laughed aloud. "I'm all dressed. Glam squad and everything. Ready to go!"

The four old women fixed each other with concerned frowns.

"What?" Dara asked, confused. "What's wrong?"

Perhaps it was a generational difference. Maybe little old yentas could not understand the choices of well-paid glam squads, but the question opened the floodgates. "It's a very special day. Maybe we fix the hair?" "Just a little bit more lipstick." "Arlene—give me that scarf." "Honestly, Dara…how can someone so rich dress so poorly?"

Dara did not have time to respond. Before she could object to an elderly intervention, the ChallahBack Girls were pushing her down into a chair. There was tugging on her bobby pins as Arlene removed her hair from the tight bun, allowing her curls to fall freely around her shoulders. Shira swiped a tube of fire-engine-red lipstick across her mouth before her grandmother violently slapped her right cheek.

"Ouch!" Dara said, clutching her stinging face.

"It's for your own good," Miriam said, and then slapped the left cheek.

"Seriously!" Dara held her face for protection. "What has gotten into you all today?"

"We just want to make sure you look extra beautiful," Arlene explained gently, then knotted that scarf so tightly around her neck that it felt more like a noose.

Finally, after what felt like an eternity, Dara's smart watch vibrated to attention. "Oh, shucks." Dara feigned disappointment. "The car is here. Guess we better get going."

After grabbing their belongings, Dara led her grandmother downstairs, where an executive car service was waiting for them. The ChallahBack Girls followed after them, waving wildly, wishing them mazel. Dara helped Miriam into the vehicle and, taking the seat beside her, settled in for the long drive across New York morning traffic.

4

THERE WERE A MILLION THINGS THAT COULD KILL
you in New York City. Sitting in traffic on her way to midtown Manhattan, Dara couldn't help but obsess over every
single one of them.

There was the statistical probability of dying in an auto-
mobile accident. Which, given the way their driver swerved
in and out of traffic, was increasing by the minute. There
were all those viruses—colds and flus, bacteria and microor-
ganisms—lingering on banisters, exploding from uncovered
mouths in elevators, resistant to treatment. And then, there
was the prospect of some terrifying mass-casualty event. A
random 10.4-Richter-scale earthquake hitting the city right
as they entered the Lincoln Tunnel, sending bucket loads of
water from the Hudson River into their vehicle. Or worse,
some psycho with an axe to grind sending a package stuffed
with anthrax to NBS-7 Studios on the very same day she was
set to give her interview.

"Isn't this fun?" Miriam said, glancing over to her granddaughter.

Dara forced a smile. "The best!"

Her anxiety was spiraling out of control. Still, the last thing she wanted to do was ruin this big day for her grandmother.

She glanced down at her black messenger bag. Dara had brought every rescue with her, just in case. Her lorazepam to dull the constant drumming of fears in her brain. Her work to keep her mind occupied. And, of course, her beloved emergency scanner app on her phone.

She knew it was an unusual remedy, but when she was little and suffered from insomnia, her mother used to leave talk radio on for her to fall asleep to. Now, as an adult, talk radio stressed her out. There was too much focus on bad news. The scanner, however, always managed to make her feel hopeful.

She desperately wanted to pull it out, turn it on and escape into the sound of a million disparate voices. She would have, in another situation, but she worried about looking weird to their driver.

It was the beauty of generalized anxiety disorder. Unlike schizophrenia or psychosis, where a person believed their delusions were real, Dara knew her anxiety was irrational.

She was also logical enough, and tech-savvy enough, to run the numbers. She knew that there was almost no chance in hell of an earthquake in New York City, or someone sending anthrax to *Good News New York*. She could look around at the driver and her grandmother and see that everyone else was calm, everyone else was rational. But knowing her thoughts were illogical didn't stop them from coming.

The driver spun the steering wheel, moving out of traffic. Dara sat up in her seat. "What are you doing?" she asked, worried that they were being kidnapped.

"Traffic," he explained. "I'm going to take the George Washington Bridge instead."

Her heart began to pound in her chest. Her mind started

spiraling. Kidnapping suddenly seemed like the better option. God. How she hated bridges.

There were so many terrible ways to die on a bridge. Her mind ran through a laundry list of them. Car accidents. Earthquakes. A rogue gust of wind, some hurricane-strength anomaly, sending their car cascading off the edge.

"You don't think it's better to take the tunnel?" she squeaked out, trying to sound sane.

"I need to get you there by ten." The driver could not be reasoned with. "Quicker if we just bail now and head for uptown."

Dara's heart settled in her throat. Her mind was racing. Her entire body was suddenly thrust into a battle of flight or fright. She tried to stuff it down, fumbled with papers in her bag, looking for work to take her mind off her anxiety. But it was pointless. When she got like this, her mind and body moved without her. She swallowed hard and, looking at the passing vehicles, considered jumping out of the car.

"Dara-la," Miriam said, gently taking her hand. "It's okay."

"I'm fine," Dara lied through a smile.

The driver glanced back in the rearview mirror. "You afraid of heights?"

Dara grumbled, "I'm afraid of everything."

"Just close your eyes," Miriam said, squeezing her hand a little tighter. Her grandmother began to sing a lullaby from her youth. "My *shayna madela*, my pretty baby-la…"

Dara closed her eyes. The sound of her grandmother's voice, the feeling of her hand wrapped around her own transported her back to childhood. Back to a time where every banged knee and every monster in the closet could be defeated with a kiss. It wasn't enough to squelch the intrusive thoughts running through her brain, but it did bring her some relief.

Dara felt the car slow down. She opened her eyes just in

time to see their car rolling through the tollbooth. They had made it across the bridge. In one mighty exhale, she relaxed, slumping back into her seat. She had survived.

"I'm so glad you're here, Bubbe."

"Me, too," Miriam said.

Indeed, hand-holding—in all its various shapes and forms— was one of the ways she dealt with her anxiety. She had so many carefully constructed systems. A life built entirely from the safety of home. A sick bubbe she visited on the daily. A career where she was just *so* busy. It wasn't her fault she had absolutely no time for stretching beyond her comfort zone.

Her life was organized, controlled and safe. She had a carefully crafted image, cultivated over thirty-four years of life, and in that time, not one single crack had managed to break through her constructed veneer. There was no reason to stop what she was doing, or consider trying something different.

But what would she do without her grandmother?

Dara glanced over at Miriam and found her staring out the window. Her heart ached. For a moment, in the midst of her panic, she had forgotten that her grandmother was dying.

The push and pull of that reality was like an in-between space where Dara now lived. There were good days, days that felt normal. But there were also trips to hospitals and consultations with specialists. Radiation and targeted drug therapy. Prayer.

She would look at her grandmother in the present and find herself asking the same question on repeat. Would this be one of their last times together? Should she move around her schedule—take on less work, delegate more—in order to make more time with her bubbe?

Alas, there was no way to know what the right answer was. Her bubbe's death could be months or years away. Dara couldn't uproot her entire life for something that wouldn't follow a schedule. Even if her heart screamed otherwise. Even though she worried constantly about what her life would look like without her bubbe to hold her hand through all the things that scared her. But maybe this was the point of irrational fears. It was so much easier to focus on all the things that would never happen.

Dara shook off any trace of sadness. "We are going to have the best day ever, Bubbe!" she said, excitedly. "You'll see... I have everything planned."

"Oh, Dara." Miriam cupped her cheek gently. "I know."

Dara and her grandmother arrived at NBS-7 Studios in midtown Manhattan, and made their way to the fifth floor as instructed. The elevator doors parted. Dara gasped. All her positive self-talk went flying straight out the fake cutouts of windows.

She was *actually* standing on the set of *Good News New York*.

"Dara and Miriam Rabinowitz?" A woman with bright red hair came racing forward.

"That's us!" Dara smiled widely. "We're both so—"

The woman cut her off. "I'm Eleanor Cohen," she said, shifting her clipboard to under her arm in order to offer her hand, "executive producer for *Good News New York*. Is there anything I can get you before we begin? Water, coffee, restrooms or Danish?"

She spoke so fast, Dara struggled to keep up. "I think we're okay."

Bubbe Miriam tapped on the giant black pocketbook she was holding. "I brought my own water."

"Great," Eleanor said before waving over a young man. "Then let me introduce you to Eli. Eli is one of our fabulous production assistants here at *Good News*. He's going to give you a brief tour of the studio, tell you what you can expect, then bring you to the greenroom to wait for your segment."

Before they could respond, the woman was off. Miriam turned to Dara, shrugging her shoulders. Their fate was now in the hands of Eli. He was young, Asian, with his hair pressed down around his forehead in a sensible manner. Unfortunately, while he spoke slower than Eleanor, he smiled almost as infrequently.

"If you would follow me," Eli said, waving them forward.

The tour was all-encompassing. There were the production offices, cubicles and paperwork as far as the eye could see. There was wardrobe and makeup. Dara nearly shrieked aloud when she recognized Lisa Lambert, one of the co-anchors on *Good News*, getting her makeup done.

"Now," Eli said, forcing himself to sound excited as they made their way to the studio, "we come to the most exciting part of our tour. This is where you both will be filming your segment today. Many of our segments are pre-recorded and then cut into the show during the broadcast…but you two, you two brave and incredible women, will be going on live television today."

Dara wasn't paying attention. Seeing the set in real life, in real time, made her heart pitter-patter in excitement. She recognized every inch and crevice of the *Good News* studio from her two years of watching the show. The fake windows overlooking a painted skyline. The orange couches where the guests sat. The chair behind the desk where sexy head anchor, Christopher Steadfast, did his interviews with guests.

His butt had been on that chair.

Eli pointed with two fingers toward one of the cameras. "Everything you say, everything you do…broadcast, right there, for the entire world."

"The entire world?" Miriam mused aloud.

"Well," Eli backtracked, "just the United States. Some parts of Canada. Actually, we just got canceled in Idaho. But who really cares about Idaho, right? Anyway…" Eli clapped both his hands together. "Any questions before I bring you two lovely ladies to the greenroom?"

Dara looked at her grandmother. She was staring at the studio, deep in thought, her pocketbook clutched firmly to her chest.

"Great," Eli said, and began walking.

"Actually," Miriam said, bringing both Eli and Dara to a full stop. "I do have a question."

"Oh." Eli turned back to face her. "Okay."

"I was wondering…what happens if someone makes a mistake?"

"How do you mean?"

"Like if one of your fancy reporters flubbed their lines?"

"Are you worried about making a mistake, Bubbe?" Dara asked, surprised.

"Oh no." Miriam waved away her granddaughter's concern. "But you know, I'm an old lady, and sometimes I fart without realizing it. If that were to happen—"

"Ah." Eli nodded, unfazed. "The old farting-on-television fear. No need to be concerned there, ma'am. There is a five-second lag between what is filmed and what is broadcast. So if that were to happen, the people in control would simply edit it out. Does that answer your question?"

"Yes." She tapped on her large black bag. "It does."

"Great. Then I'll just—"

"But what if my mistake is longer than five seconds?"

"Longer than five seconds?" Eli asked.

"It happens." She smiled innocently.

Dara narrowed her eyes at her grandmother. "Are you feeling okay, Bubbe?"

"I'm fine, Boobeleh. I'm just curious, is all. What happens if something unexpected happens and it lasts longer than five seconds? What do the people in the control room do then?"

Eli put one finger on his chin. "Well, the five-second lag time really only functions as a safety net. Once those five seconds are up, the camera goes right back to broadcasting. And once something is broadcast…well, I'm sure you both know this…but the footage lives forever. Does that answer your question?"

Miriam nodded happily. "Yes, it does."

With that, Miriam walked ahead. Dara watched as she departed, sashaying her hips, doing a tiny dance move, before clicking the heels of her red-and-white oxford pumps together. Dara cocked her head, surprised. Also concerned. It wasn't strange to see her grandmother dancing—her grandparents had won all sorts of awards for swing dancing back in their day—but they were in the middle of a television studio.

"I'm sorry," Dara said, turning to Eli. "She's just…she gets these episodes…"

Dara stopped stammering on the truth. *She's dying. She's sick. I don't know how much longer we have together, or what I'll do without her.* The in-between place beckoned her back, pulling her down like quicksand.

"Don't worry about it," he said gently. "I have a grandmother, too. If it helps to alleviate any concerns, Christopher Steadfast is a pro. One of the best in the business, in my humble opinion. Not that anyone cares about my humble opinion around here. But point being, the man can handle anything, okay? Anything you or your bubbe throw at him."

Dara felt instant relief. "Thank you."

Snaking their way through three more studio sets, Eli led Dara and her grandmother down a long hallway toward their final destination. "And this is the greenroom," Eli said, pushing past a crowd of bikers and other guests, huddled like vultures around a food services table. "Unfortunately, this is also where I will be leaving you."

"Oh, boo!" Miriam frowned sadly. "I was enjoying myself so much."

"Well, I promise—" Eli smiled kindly at the old woman "—the fun is only just beginning. You and your granddaughter can take a seat here for the time being, and I'll return when it's time to get you ready for your interview. In the meantime—" he pointed toward the table, where coffee, muffins and fresh fruit were laid out for the visitors "—please feel free to help yourself to any refreshments."

"Come," Dara said, taking her grandmother gently by the elbow. "Let's go sit down and let you rest a little."

"I'm fine, Dara-la. Perfectly healthy!"

"I know," Dara said, pointing toward her red high-heeled shoes. "But my feet are killing me in these stupid heels, okay? The resting is as much for me as it is for you."

Dara and Miriam found an empty couch along the back of the room. Miriam sighed happily, collapsing into the soft cushions of the couch, relieved at finally having a seat. Her large purse resting safely in her lap, she clutched it to her chest like she was guarding state secrets.

"I'm having so much fun, Dara-la."

"Me, too."

"I wonder who all these people are."

Dara scanned the room. There was a scraggly teenager wearing a necklace full of empty cans around his neck. Next to him, a woman in a smart black-and-red pantsuit held a tiny green-and-yellow lizard in a cage on her lap. The majority of the room, however, was taken up by some sort of motorcycle crew. Men in leather vests and jackets, with flowing white beards, flexed their tattooed arm muscles as they lifted cups of coffee up to their mouths.

"Likely other guests," Dara explained. "*Good News* usually has a few segments per episode, each profiling some sort of human interest story."

Miriam leaned into her granddaughter. "Do you think any of them are Jewish?"

"Bubbe!" Dara knew exactly where her grandmother was heading. "We're not here to do matchmaking."

"Nonsense." Miriam tsked in her granddaughter's direction. "Every moment in life is an opportunity to find somebody their *bashert*. You know what they say. A person who makes three matches—"

Dara finished the sentence for her grandmother. "Gets automatic entrance into Heaven."

Dara didn't know where the saying came from, but it was a familiar refrain in the community she was raised in. Indeed, matchmaking was so important to Jewish tradition that it was considered a mitzvah, or commandment, to create Jewish unions whenever possible.

It was a role not limited to professionals. Anyone in the Jewish community could act as matchmaker—including parents, siblings and friends. But when those efforts failed, the task was often handed over to a professional. For this reason, the *schadchan*, or Jewish matchmaker, was born. It was such an important profession in her community that all matchmakers were commanded to be paid for their services under Jewish law.

The tradition had practical applications, as well. Jewish history was rife with stories of expulsion, segregation, prejudice and genocide. Matchmakers ensured that every young and single Jew of marriageable and fertile age would find a Jewish mate. In this regard, and in more ways than one, matchmakers could claim personal responsibility for the continuation and survival of the Jewish people over six thousand years.

Miriam rose from her seat. "I'm going to ask them."

"Bubbe!"

It was too late. Miriam tapped her oxfords fearlessly toward the loud and boisterous group of bikers.

To be a good matchmaker, you had to be an extrovert.

As a young woman, Miriam would often spend her mornings jaunting around Hoboken and Patterson hitting up the various Jewish haunts. She would talk to everyone, inquiring on the gossip, keeping her ear to the ground, finding out which daughter of which butcher was still seeking a husband. Handing out business cards to distraught mothers whose sons seemed hell-bent on rejecting every nice Jewish girl they invited over for Shabbat dinner.

Once a Jewish single who needed help was identified, the next part of the process was the meeting. The matchmaker would sit down with the young person and, along with their parents, interview them on their wants. Sometimes, there would be something called a *shidduch* sheet. A page with the young person's photograph, accompanied by any relevant information. From there, it was the matchmaker's task to begin setting up dates. It was also the matchmaker's job to keep a watchful eye throughout the process, and intervene when needed.

Sometimes the interventions were simple. A young woman needed to be shown how to wear makeup. A young man needed better etiquette skills on a date. Sometimes they were far more complicated. Miriam once adopted a cat after a young man agreed to marry a woman only if she agreed to get rid of the feline. Which may have seemed extreme to many in the modern age, but the goal of the matchmaker was simple.

Seal. The. Deal.

For this reason, and especially among more observant communities, Jewish marriages could happen quite quickly. Dara knew many couples who had gotten engaged after only a few dates. While Jewish marriages were never arranged, there was no point in wasting time if two people shared enough in common to create a successful and long-term union. Dating was always for the purposes of marriage, and love...well, that was something that would develop over time.

As the world modernized and changed, so, too, did Jewish matchmaking. While the matchmaker was still in use among more observant communities, many contemporary Jews preferred to find matches on their own.

They would meet at singles events hosted by Jewish organizations, or around the Shabbat table with friends. They would intermingle at college Hillels and at parties thrown by Moishe House. When those efforts failed, and just like the good old days of the shtetl, they would turn to their laptops and phones, signing up for J-Mate.

The *shidduch* sheet had become the profile.

The matchmaker had become an algorithm.

Still, the influence of the old-world *schadchan* was there. So, too, were the history and culture of her people. Despite living in a modern world, with endless freedoms and boundless romantic choices, Jews often made the decision to only marry other Jews. Dara was one such person. She had never dated a non-Jew. She had never entertained the idea, either.

Miriam found her way to the largest man in the group, tapping him on the shoulder. "Excuse me," she said, interrupting their boisterous conversation. "I'm sorry to interrupt. My name is Miriam, and I'm a *schadchanit*, or matchmaker. I was wondering if any of you lovely young men happen to be Jewish...and single?"

With her question, a great uproar exploded inside the tiny

greenroom. Before long, a young man—skinny and tall, bald as they come—was pushed front and center. Miriam began her quintessential line of questioning. What did he do for a living, what sort of foods did he like, was he religious, did he want children, did he have pets, a plant, how long was his last relationship.

There was laughter, boisterous responses from his friends as they patted the young man on the back, and offered up their own ideas of the perfect wife. Finally, with all his information taken down, Miriam returned to her seat beside Dara.

"Twenty-two," Miriam said, beneath her breath. "Medical student. Secular. Two sisters. Parents are about to celebrate their thirty-ninth wedding anniversary...and this hobby of his, this motorcycle club, they do charity rides for cancer."

Dara considered the young man in front of her. "Amy Glassman."

"Amy?" Miriam practically spit the name. "Amy is completely wrong for him."

It was a game Dara was familiar with. Ever since she was a young child, during Shabbat luncheons with her bubbe, mother and her older sister, they would play it. One of them, having found some new singleton at services, would lay out all the details of their background and wish list. Then, the four women would spend the next hour debating all the potential partners, and why. It was where Dara learned all the tricks of the trade. Tricks she would eventually funnel into a computer code called J-Mate.

"Amy just started residency for psychiatry," Dara said, defending her choice. "She's got two brothers, and no sisters, which means she'll appreciate all the female energy in his family. Plus, I just saw on Facebook that she recently took up rock climbing. Between the motorcycle rides and the mountain climbs, they can risk life and limb together every Sunday. It's a perfect match."

"Dara." Miriam sighed heavily. "This is what I'm always trying to teach you! Matchmaking is an art...not a science. You have to learn to read between the lines. You have to learn to listen to the things they're not saying aloud. Just because something looks perfect on the surface doesn't mean it's right."

Dara put her tablet down. It was something her grandmother and she diverged on frequently. Miriam would often throw away a *shidduch* sheet if she had a sense about a young couple. But Dara had built up her business, and her life, by turning people into numbers.

"Lauren Ngo," Miriam finally said.

"Lauren?" Dara almost couldn't believe her ears. "From Camp Ahava? The pastry chef? The one with the three yappy dogs who lives in Red Bank?"

"Hmm." Miriam nodded.

"I can't imagine her dogs and his motorcycle gang getting along."

With that, Miriam was making a phone call.

Dara settled into her seat, listening with one ear. She knew exactly what would happen next. There would be a series of phone calls and emails to both Lauren and her mother. Eventually, and through the sheer force of parental and community pressure, the motorcyclist and the pastry chef would be set up on a blind date.

Over piping hot coffee, they would blush nervously and fiddle with the edges of their mugs. They would talk about how they had never been set up by a bona fide matchmaker before, and how strange it all was, and what a great story it would make at their wedding...before laughing at the ridiculous improbability that this could ever in a million years work.

In that laughter, they would start to talk. They would finish their coffee and, realizing that they actually did seem to have quite a bit in common, go for a walk. He would ask for a second date. She would agree. Before long, Lauren would be riding on his charity motorcycle tours with her yappy dogs in saddlebags. It was the one thing that Dara had no doubt about, because Miriam Rabinowitz—famed matchmaker of the Jewish community—seemed to have a sixth sense when it came to relationships.

Miriam finished her phone call, then bounced back over to her seat on the couch beside her. Her giant black pocketbook once again settled comfortably on her lap, she met Dara with a knowing smile.

"Don't you look proud of yourself," Dara teased.

"You'll see," Miriam said. "We'll be attending their wedding before the year is out."

Dara smiled. "I don't doubt it."

"Three hundred and thirteen." Miriam sighed, happy. "How many matches do you think it takes for Hashem to throw me a parade in Heaven?"

Dara swallowed hard. She hated when her grandmother spoke about dying. Quickly, she moved to change the topic.

"Bubbe, are you hungry?"

Her grandmother's gaze wandered over to the food services table. "Do you think any of it is kosher?"

"I don't know." Dara rose from her seat. "Shall we go look?"

While Dara kept a kosher home, she compromised by eating hot dairy out. Her grandmother, however, was stricter. She would not eat any food that was not clearly labeled as kosher. Just like Miriam would never in a million years be seen walking around in a pair of pants.

Dara pointed out all the foods that her grandmother could eat. "There's a banana," she said, scanning the items. "An apple. The coffee should be okay, too. I can check about the bagels if you like."

"A cup of coffee sounds lovely."

Grabbing a disposable cup, Dara headed to the two large coffee makers displayed at the end of the table. She was just about to pour when a voice interrupted her task. Forceful, yet freakishly charismatic, it carried throughout the greenroom, muting the voices of the guests wandering around. "I just wanted to stop in and welcome everybody to *Good News New York*."

Christopher Steadfast, head anchor of *Good News New York*, was standing on the threshold.

5

DARA'S HEART STOPPED BEATING INSIDE HER CHEST.
Her hands crushed the cup she still held. She didn't need to
turn around. She would have recognized the sound of that
voice, the smooth intonation and the way he accentuated his
vowels, anywhere. Christopher Steadfast rolled every *r* like
he was born with gravel at the back of his throat instead of
a uvula.

She had listened to that voice for nearly two years. Watched
the handsome head anchor daily, recording every episode,
letting it play out like wallpaper inside her lonely apartment.
She knew every one of his catchphrases and whimsical winks.
She knew his whole deal, too—the charming cowboy-boot-
wearing hottie from Virginia, who loved belting out country
ballads for his guests. He had grown up on a farm and played
football in high school.

Now the same familiar face who had accompanied her
through countless lonely hours appeared in the greenroom.
Making the rounds, offering up handshakes and chitchat to
everyone standing in the small space, he went out of his way
to introduce himself to guests.

"Bubbe," Dara whispered, tugging on her sleeve. "He's coming! What do we do?"

Her grandmother squinted. "What do you mean *what do we do*? We say hello to the man, Dara-la. What else does a normal person do?"

She was right. There was no reason to be nervous. Chris was a consummate professional. Dara was a reasonably attractive multimillionaire, a confident and self-assured woman, CEO of her own company. She could totally handle a simple introduction with the dreamy and delightful head anchor of *Good News*. She was more competent than her frayed nerves.

"And you must be the matchmakers," Christopher Steadfast said, coming around to offer his hand. "Miriam and Dara, is it?"

It was no use. Whatever courage Dara had inside her totally dissipated. In spite of all her best efforts to appear poised, her lower lip fell to the floor. Christopher Steadfast was easily the prettiest man she had ever seen. Dara could not help herself. She fell into the color of his eyes.

Watching him daily, she had always thought they were blue. But standing just inches from the man, and without the lights of the studio obscuring their true color, she could see that they were more of a gray. More like storm clouds gathering across a distant shoreline than the hue of Caribbean waters. It made him look intense, and thoughtful, even as he flashed her the most charming smile.

"Dara is a huge fan of your show," Miriam said.

"Are you, now?" Chris turned to her directly. "Well, that's something we don't hear every day."

She could not speak. She was mesmerized by the row of perfect white teeth sparkling in her direction. She was attracted to him. She recognized those feelings of chemistry inside her body immediately. But the fact that she was so damn attracted to him—when he was totally and completely off-limits—immediately made her nervous.

She shouldn't be thinking this way.

She shouldn't be feeling this way, either.

An intrusive thought. That was all it was. Some free-floating anxiety running through her mind. Something to be noticed but quickly shooed away. Dara was committed to her Judaism, after all. She was someone who had built her entire career and her life around Jewish relationships and marriage. So what that he was, quite impossibly, the prettiest human being she had ever laid eyes on?

No, she had studied this when building her algorithms. His attractiveness was nothing more than a by-product of science. It had nothing to do with the coif of his dirty-blond hair, the rugged hint of stubble or the angle of his chin. It was simply that his face was symmetrical. It was *science* causing her entire body to flush red with heat, demanding that her thirty-four-year-old womb mate and procreate with this perfect specimen of masculinity.

"You're the creator of J-Mate, right?" Chris asked.

"Yes!" Dara finally got out a word. "J-Mate. Right."

"Very cool." He smiled wider. "I'm not Jewish, obviously, so I've never used your service, but I know a lot of people who have. Our executive producer, in fact, Eleanor Cohen, has been on many successful dates thanks to your app."

She could see by the sparkle in those stormy gray eyes that he was waiting for her to say something. It was probably only a few seconds of awkwardness, but it felt like an eternity.

She was messing this up, taking too long to respond to every question. The realization only increased her anxiety. Chris responded by leaning forward, moving his incredibly sexy chest closer to her own.

"You okay?" he asked, with a quizzical smile.

Dara stammered, glancing down at the disposable cup now completely crushed inside her hand. Quickly, she hid it behind her back. "I just…haven't had any coffee yet."

Chris nodded toward the coffee station. "Can I get you a cup now?"

He was so unbelievably charming. She couldn't help but think it. Her heart fluttered in his presence. Like challah rising on the counter, excitement started in her belly and tingled its way up to her chest. She glanced over to her grandmother, head cocked sideways, watching them curiously. Immediately, she felt guilty. Coffee suddenly felt like a gateway drug into something much worse.

Thankfully, a sight at the front of the greenroom appeared to lead her from temptation. Bucky, the vegan golden retriever, had just arrived with his handler. Wearing a tiny red bow, he barked in excitement, and was quickly rewarded with a biscuit. Dara could barely contain herself.

"Oh my God!" she shouted, pushing Chris out of the way. "Bucky! Is it really you?"

Moments later, she was on her knees, rubbing her face against his cheeks, whispering sweet words into his floppy brown ears. She checked off a box on her bucket list. Bucky responded to her clear adoration with a strong wag of his tail.

As for Christopher Steadfast—Dara looked back to see that the handsome head anchor had already moved on. He had sauntered off to speak to the next guest, taking any problematic feelings that had transpired inside her with him.

6

CHRIS ANGLED HIS CHIN UP TOWARD THE CEILING. Dropping three tiny droplets of rewetting lubricant into each eye, he blinked back the bright lights of the studio cameras surrounding him. They were forty-five minutes into their Thursday afternoon episode of *Good News*, and Sheila, the makeup artist on staff, was on hand to do a touch-up.

"Doing great, Chris," she said. Removing a makeup brush from between her teeth, she dabbed it into some translucent powder on the back of her hand before applying it directly to his forehead. "This is going to be one for the record books."

Chris raised one disbelieving eyebrow in her direction. He didn't need to be coddled. He had come from real news, after all. He had cut his teeth creating packages as a one-man band in Missouri, then Illinois, then Washington, DC, the constant din of an emergency services scanner running in the background of his office.

As a younger journalist, Chris had loved the hard-hitting stuff. Murders and domestic violence. Suicides and four-alarm fires. His greatest thrill was waking up at three o'clock in the morning, throwing on a jacket and tie, and racing out the door to be the first journalist on scene.

Alas, and like most of the people in daytime television, Sheila was used to working with princesses, most of whom were hired for their Instagram-worthy good looks and ability to bring in younger viewers, rather than any talent for chasing a story.

"Twenty seconds," Eleanor came through his earpiece. "Camera one, get ready."

"Ready," the operator responded.

Sheila gathered up her tissues and powder, disappearing to the side of their studio. Chris turned in his chair, shuffling his papers into submission, angling himself toward the camera directly in front of him.

"Looking good, Chris," Eleanor said. "Camera four, ready."

"Ready."

"Three, two, one…"

Chris beamed at the camera, "Well, Lisa, I think we can all agree…what a ride. Up next, it's the start of the Jewish High Holidays, and we're celebrating by interviewing a family of Jewish matchmakers. Find out what makes love work—and what doesn't—with this grandmother-granddaughter duo, who between them both have made over ten thousand successful Jewish marriages."

"And commercial," Eleanor shouted before calling out to the team, "Get me the matchmakers!"

"Matchmakers!" someone shouted back, and a chorus of echoes went down the studio, and into the greenroom.

The studio broke into a flurry of activity. A smattering of audience members rose from their seats and snuck out to use the bathroom. The producers checked their cameras and whispered among themselves while Eli raced to get Dara and her grandmother from the greenroom. Chris took a few moments to review his notes for the upcoming segment.

Dara Rabinowitz. He ran his thumb over her name as he considered the woman he had met inside the greenroom. The sharp angles in her features. Her dark curls swinging down to the center of her back. On instinct, he pulled at his trousers beneath the desk.

He was surprised by the reaction in his body. Ever since Claire had died, it was like that part of him had been shut down. He didn't even know those feelings were possible with another woman. Not that it mattered—there was no way he'd follow through on them. Claire had been his one and only.

Chris turned to the next page of his notes, willing any warm and fuzzy feelings about Dara Rabinowitz right out the window. "Eleanor!" Chris spat her name into his earpiece. "What the hell is this?"

"A script," she said succinctly.

He could feel his ire rising. "You didn't mention a script this morning."

"I knew you would freak out."

He threw the papers down. "I'm not using a script."

"Chris," she said into his earpiece. "Don't be a prick. It was the only way we could get the matchmakers."

He fumed. Guests often tried to control their own narrative on television. He wasn't surprised that Dara wanted to do the same for her company. The problem with scripts, however, was that they made for terrible television.

It wasn't just that Chris, who had been trained in the adrenaline-fueled and fast-paced world of live news, did better off script. It was that viewers responded to spontaneity. They wanted the feeling of banter, of two friends having a conversation, of being invited inside an intimate conversation.

None of which was possible when you were reading from a list of approved talking points.

"You wanna know why this show is bombing in the ratings?" Chris said, pushing his papers out of the way. "It's because we keep booking segments with control freaks. Just let me do my job!"

Chris heard Eleanor grumbling at someone in the control room. He glanced up at the large production clock blinking the time in red numbers. They only had two minutes left until the start of their next segment. Dara and her grandmother still hadn't appeared.

"Look," Eleanor said, returning to his earpiece, "I know it's not ideal, okay? But we're down to the wire. Just read the questions and get through this episode *with the script*. We'll regroup tomorrow, okay?"

Putting his notes away under the console, he stared at the words of their preapproved script on the teleprompter, and the questions he was supposed to read off the monitor like some talking monkey. His stomach turned at the thought. He hated this. Staging a segment. Lying to his audience. It was fiction rather than news. It went against every value he had as a journalist.

Trust was the foundation of storytelling.

In the past, he might have thrown a hissy fit, stormed off set and demanded that Eleanor get Lisa, one of the co-anchors, to film the segment instead. Unfortunately, what had always been a compromise between his values and providing for Lacey had now become a full-fledged capitulation. He couldn't afford to lose his job at *Good News*. Whether he liked it or not, it seemed that Dara Rabinowitz was going to win the battle against journalistic integrity today.

A commotion from down the hall drew his attention away.

Dara and her grandmother, escorted by Eli, scurried down the hall together, an argument clearly taking shape between them.

Plopping down on his orange couch, clutching a large black pocketbook to her chest, Miriam waved Eli and Dara away like problematic flies.

"Everything okay?" Chris asked.

Eli explained, flustered, "She insisted on bringing her bag with her."

"Bubbe," Dara said. "Please! You heard the young man. Your purse will be perfectly safe in the greenroom."

Miriam closed her eyes. Shaking her head like a petulant child, she refused to listen to a single word. "I told you," she said, tapping on the purse a few times. "I prefer to keep my bag right here."

Chris moved to offer a practical solution. "Would you feel more comfortable leaving it under your seat?" he asked Miriam directly. "We can just keep the cameras angled above your waistlines."

"That sounds like a great idea," Dara said happily.

"I'm sorry," Miriam said, raising one hand in the air to stop them all. "But I'm afraid I'm going to need this pocketbook to stay right here on my lap. It's a very important thing, you see…very important indeed."

There seemed to be no convincing the old woman.

Chris considered the situation. Maybe it was the fact that he was having one of the worst days of his professional life, but he couldn't help but compare Miriam to his own Southern memaw. She was a stubborn old mule, too. Once she had made her mind up on something, even the mighty waters of the Potomac couldn't sway her from course.

"I'm sorry," Dara said, taking a seat between Chris and Miriam on the orange couch. "She has these episodes."

Chris squinted. "Episodes?"

"She gets confused."

Chris ran one hand through his hair nervously. Jesus. What were Eleanor and their casting department thinking, booking people with *episodes* on live television? No wonder *Good Day New York* was killing them in the ratings. Between the script and the oversized pocketbook, it was full-on amateur hour.

"We can do the interview with just you," Chris offered.

"Absolutely not!" Miriam tsked at both of them.

"Thirty seconds!"

Dara sighed, slinking down onto the couch. Chris chewed on his lower lip, debating his options. Perhaps the bright side of failure was that none of their efforts really mattered. Who cared if the old woman wanted to hold her purse on television? Nobody was watching *Good News*. They were the worst, and most ignored, show on television.

"It's fine," Chris said, making the final call to everybody. "Just let her keep the bag."

"Seriously?" Eleanor snorted through the earpiece.

"What's it gonna hurt, Eleanor?"

Chris shuffled his papers out of view and turned toward camera two. It was a sign to everyone in the studio that Chris was ready to move forward.

"Fifteen seconds!"

Chris smiled, false and forced, in the direction of the camera. And then, with less than five seconds left on the clock, he caught a whiff of a familiar scent. Lavender, with notes of citrus, and the smallest hint of sage.

His mouth went dry in the realization. His heart ached as he wondered if he was hallucinating. He glanced over to the tiny woman with the mound of curls cascading around her shoulders. There was no way this stranger—this Dara Rabinowitz—was wearing the very same perfume as Claire. It was such an esoteric brand. Indeed, it had been created for Claire by a perfumery in France on the occasion of their ten-year anniversary.

"Camera one, ready?" Eleanor said through his earpiece.

"Ready," camera one responded.

"Three, two, one..."

"Welcome back," Chris said to the camera. "This week marks the beginning of the Jewish High Holiday season and the start of Rosh Hashanah. Which means that all over the world, Jewish parents will be asking their single Jewish children, 'Are you dating anyone?'"

It was a disaster. The segment. The show. *His life.* Dara Rabinowitz was the picture of polished charm and perfection. She answered every preapproved question from her stupid script that Chris threw her way with the ease and simplicity of making blue-box macaroni and cheese. Alas, it made for dreadful television.

"So, Dara," Chris read from the teleprompter. "Is it true that you're three generations of matchmakers?"

"That's correct," she beamed. "My bubbe Miriam established her own matchmaking company while a young woman in New Jersey. At almost ninety years old, she's made over three hundred matches."

"Your mother was quite famous, as well?"

"That's right," she said, looking directly into the camera. "Rose Rabinowitz, her maiden name, was both a matchmaker and a cognitive behavioral therapist with a focus on family therapy. Before she died, she was well-known in both the Jewish and secular world for her books on building successful marriages. She even had her own reality show for a time, *Love under Lockdown*."

"I remember that show," Chris said. "Couples were handcuffed together and forced to work out their issues?"

71

"That's right!" Dara faked a laugh. "It was a major hit."

Chris had never even seen the show.

He thought back to the chemistry classes he had hated as a teenager. The way Mr. Polanski would ramble on about the periodic table of elements. All facts. No personality. Boring as anything. The way he felt listening to him was the same way he felt now.

Dara was so rehearsed, so tightly wound. Like that knotted scarf strangling her tiny neck. Even the hand gestures were practiced. Alas, it was her laugh, forced out of her mouth at appropriate intervals, that was the most annoying of all. Chris did a cost-benefit analysis on gouging out his own eardrums.

"Wow." He smiled, shaking his head as if surprised by the answer. "So you took all that experience in matchmaking... and built J-Mate?"

"I saw a need in the Jewish community for modern solutions to old-world problems. I created J-Mate as a space for marriage-minded Jews to find other Jewish people to date. But J-Mate isn't just the antiquated notions of your parents. We're invested in feedback from members of our community, and updates that reflect the changing needs of contemporary Jews. That's why we created J-eography as a recent update to our J-Mate subscription."

"J-eography?"

"That's correct." Dara beamed. "When you first sign on to J-Mate, you'll be asked a whole host of important biographical information...such as where you grew up, went to shul, went to camp and went to college. J-eography then takes all that aggregated data and allows you to see how you know a potential match through your Jewish community connections. It's a way of vetting a suitor without needing to call your best friend or bubbe to provide references."

"That's incredible," Chris lied.

"We're very excited about it, as well."

He felt his eyes glaze over. He was just about to ask Dara her next question, when Miriam—still with that pocketbook on her lap—suddenly spoke up.

"Can I say something?" she asked, raising her hand.

"Excuse me?" Chris said, glancing from the teleprompter over to Eleanor.

Dara immediately jumped in to protest. "You don't need to raise your hand, Bubbe." She laid one hand on her grandmother's kneecap as a warning to be silent.

"But you won't let me get a word in edgewise!" Miriam shouted.

"Bubbe," Dara said, trying to do damage control. She pointed toward the teleprompter, before leaning in to whisper, "Not right now. Your turn comes later, remember? We went through this—"

"Dara-la." The old woman touched her face gently. "I know you worry, but please stop treating me like an imbecile."

Miriam huffed in her seat before drawing her pocketbook closer to her chest. Chris squinted with curious delight at the mutiny happening before him. With four minutes left on the clock, Miriam had gone off script. Judging by the red blotches rising on her cheeks, it was obvious that *Dara-la* was having a conniption.

"My granddaughter," Miriam said, refusing to be contained, leaning all the way across Dara's lap to speak to Chris directly, "is a wonderful woman. You can see that she's smart, and beautiful, and *very* organized. She likes to have everything under her control."

Chris raised both eyebrows in her direction. "I see that."

"But she's a good girl," Miriam said, returning to the comfort of her seat. "Oh, the best daughter, and granddaughter, a

73

person could ask for! Did you know she's throwing me a beautiful ninetieth birthday party, over Hanukkah, on the pier?"

Chris smiled. "I did not know that."

"It's going to have unicorns!" Miriam exclaimed excitedly.

"Horses," Dara whispered again. "It's going to have horses dressed up as unicorns."

Miriam considered the statement. "Well, whatever shows up, I'm sure I will love it…because I love you."

At this, the whole of the production crew sighed. Miriam was quickly becoming the star of this segment. A pause in the conversation followed. Chris made a hasty decision. He would still stay on script as Dara and Eleanor had demanded, but he would direct the questions to Miriam. The decision would likely cement Dara as his enemy forever.

"And is it true," Chris asked Miriam directly, "that, between the two of you, you have over ten thousand successful Jewish marriages under your belt?"

"That's correct." Miriam beamed, taking the cue from him. "Though most of those matches belong to Dara and her J-Mate. I've only made three hundred and thirteen marriages. Her mother—may her memory be for a blessing—made seventy-six when she was alive. All the rest come from my brilliant granddaughter. Dara is very successful, you see. Extremely wealthy. She has more money than anyone I know… and I know a lot of people!"

"Bubbe!" Dara shrieked in embarrassment.

"I'm just saying, it's a wonder that someone so beautiful, and rich—a person who goes out of her way for the people she loves—would still be single. It makes me sad, Chris. It keeps me up at night, fretting with worry. In truth, it's my greatest regret."

Chris knew all about regrets. "Tell us more, Miriam."

"I'm about to be ninety years old," she explained, sadly.

"I've been blessed enough to create hundreds of Jewish unions. Out of those marriages, even more Jewish children and grand-children. But in all those matches, all those unions, there is one *shidduch* I have never been able to make…"

Miriam fumbled with her pocketbook. After a few sec-onds of digging through wadded-up tissues, sucking candies and pens—leaving them all on the couch in a heap of mess—she found what she was looking for. She pulled out a piece of paper with childlike scribbles all over the front, and pro-ceeded to open it up.

Concern punctuated her voice. "I have never been able to find a husband for my beloved youngest granddaughter."

7

DARA WAS CERTAIN THAT HER BUBBE MIRIAM HAD
finally lost it. They were on live television, after all. Smack-dab
in the middle of an interview. It was not the time to be pulling out drawings from one of her many nieces and nephews.

"Can we get a close-up on that?" Chris asked, popping up
from his chair.

It was only when Dara looked past the poorly rendered images of kitty cats and flowers that her heart stopped. She knew
exactly what her grandmother was holding. It was a list she'd
created drunkenly with her older sister, Shana, on the evening of her thirty-fourth birthday. It was also a list that was
never supposed to see the light of day.

Dara quickly surmised what had happened. She remembered Shana taking the list home that evening, stuffing it into
her pocketbook, before joking that she was retaining it for
"safekeeping." Her nieces and nephews—likely handed the
list as scrap paper during some event to keep them quiet—
seemed to have turned it into a canvas for one of their many
drawings. And it was only a matter of time before they show-
cased their artwork to Bubbe Miriam.

Dara's heart stopped at the realization. Time slowed as the heat of the studio lights bore down on her. A cameraman stepped into frame as her grandmother held the crinkled paper high in the air for everyone in the studio and watching at home to see for themselves.

The Perfect Jewish Husband

Christopher Steadfast returned to his seat behind the interview desk. "So, Miriam, tell us what you have there."

Miriam smiled wide. "My beautiful and extremely wealthy granddaughter has created a list of everything she would like in a future Jewish husband. I was wondering if anybody would be interested in hearing it?"

Dara decided to stop this fiasco. "I don't think anybody is really interested in hearing—"

Chris interrupted her. "I'm interested."

Dara swallowed hard. Even though she had just met Christopher Steadfast, she had been watching him for years on *Good News New York*. His outright unwillingness to put an end to this *balagan* felt like a personal betrayal.

Dara quickly considered alternative options. She could tackle the old woman, grabbing the list from her hands, tearing up that stupid piece of paper. On second thought, she decided against it.

Miriam Rabinowitz was not just her beloved grandmother, she was one of the most respected *shadchaniyot* in their Jewish community. Besides, how would it look for Dara—creator of the world's most successful Jewish dating app—to be violently attacking her eighty-nine-year-old grandmother on national television?

Since tackling the old woman was not going to happen, she settled on playing off the misunderstanding. She blushed, laughed it away, tried to explain that the list was never meant to be taken seriously. Much to her dismay, it was all for naught. Her embarrassment only seemed to amp up the hunger of the *Good News* audience.

There was no other option. Dara couldn't appear like some uptight spoilsport. She would simply have to power through this nightmare of a scenario.

She glanced beyond the cameras to find a clock located on the anterior wall. Situated just beneath the control room, it counted down the time left in their segment with blinking red numbers. *Two minutes left.* How much damage could her bubbe really do in one hundred twenty seconds?

"Please." Chris rested his chiseled chin on one perfectly situated fist. "I'm dying to know what the very single creator of J-Mate is looking for in a future spouse."

With permission granted, Bubbe Miriam returned her attention to the crumpled piece of paper in her hands. As she put on the reading glasses dangling around her neck, her hands may have been shaky, but her voice never wavered once.

"Well, obviously—" Miriam fixed an accusatory eyebrow in his direction ""—he needs to be Jewish.'"

Chris smiled, unaffected. "Obviously."

Miriam continued. "'He should be a lawyer or a doctor. Preferably a doctor, though, because it's always good to have someone in the family who can write prescriptions.'"

Chris squinted, amused. "Does it actually say that?"

"Indeed."

Bubbe Miriam held up the list to prove she wasn't lying. Chris considered the words and added his own thoughtful take on the situation. "So, a Jewish doctor or lawyer? That shouldn't be too hard to find in Manhattan."

"There's more."

Dara folded her head into her hands.

It was only going to get worse from here.

"'In addition to being a doctor or lawyer,'" Miriam said, "'he should have the soul of an artist. He spends his Sundays painting bowls of fruit or writing poetry. Either one is acceptable. He has also taught himself a second language, just for fun. Bonus points if he uses that second language to engage more fully with the world, such as volunteering for Doctors Without Borders or lending his legal expertise to Amnesty International.'"

"It was a joke." Dara spit out the words. "All of it! I don't actually expect—"

Her grandmother ignored her. "'He has a swimmer's body, but hates watching sports. He *loves* going shopping and giving back rubs. He orders appetizers on a date, but not appetizers *and* dessert, because he's fiscally responsible. Unless it's a special occasion, of course. Then he orders both.'"

"Of course." Chris beamed.

"'He prefers the pool to a beach, but would never be caught dead swimming in a lake. He is close with his family and calls his mother twice a week. He doesn't have any baggage. No previous marriages. No children. Also, he needs to be taller than me when I am wearing heels, though not above five foot ten. I don't want to have to stand on tiptoe when kissing somebody.'"

"Guess I'm out of the running," Chris jested.

"Finally…" Miriam exhaled. "'He should have a big apartment'—with the word *apartment* in quotes. Actually, I don't know why the word *apartment* is in quotes. Oh wait, there's something else on the bottom here…by the corresponding asterisk. It says—" Miriam brought the paper close to her face "—'but not too big. I'm not a vending machine, you know?'" Miriam put the list down. "I still don't understand what that one means, honestly."

Dara peeked through her fingers to see Christopher Stead-fast biting back a small smile.

"Well, Dara," he said, knowing full well what she had meant by the euphemism, "would you like to explain that one to your grandmother? How big should Mr. Perfect's apartment be?"

The whole world was awaiting her answer. Dara choked out a response. "Between six hundred and eight hundred square feet?"

"Dara!" Bubbe Miriam shook her head, disappointed. "That's a very small apartment."

Dara slunk down into her seat. "Less to clean up?"

A strange moment of silence settled over the studio. It lingered, terrible and pressing, an awful indication that she had just been humiliated by her very own grandmother on national television. And then, all at once and without any warning, Christopher Steadfast exploded into laughter.

It was a rare sight. Strange enough that even some of the crew, cameramen and producers began laughing with him. Dara had been watching the show for years. She had never once seen the seasoned professional lose his composure. But in the wake of her final shameful confession, he turned bright red, unable to speak through his own hysterics, banging his hand against his desk repeatedly.

"I'm sorry," he said. "I just…didn't expect…*less to clean up.*"

Dara crossed her arms against her chest. She was glad someone thought it was funny. She glanced back up at the countdown clock, ticking off the seconds in bright red. *Fifteen seconds left.* She only had fifteen seconds until this nightmare of an interview was over.

Chris did his best in those final heartbeats of television. Looking directly into the camera, he ended the episode, forcing out the words of his signature closing line. "Thanks for watching. I'm Chris Steadfast," he said, sucking back air in gulps and gasps. "Till next time, America... I'll be waiting for you."

8

IT WAS, QUITE POSSIBLY, THE MOST UNCOMFORTABLE car ride she had ever taken with her grandmother.

Dara sat, arms crossed, in the back seat of their executive limousine. Her black messenger bag by her feet, the streets of Manhattan rolling by her tinted windows, she breathed through the fire burning in her chest. She was not the type to easily lose her cool, but her anger felt extraordinary. Palpable. Even their driver seemed to know better than to swerve in and out of traffic or dare honking the horn.

Miriam tapped on her purse innocently. "So I guess we're not going out to dinner?"

"No."

Dara returned to staring out the window. No, they were not going out for dinner. They were not going out to celebrate their wonderful and perfect day together, making memories. Because Bubbe Miriam, her own flesh and blood, had humiliated her on live television. There was no "appetizer and dessert" on that menu that could dissipate the disgust in her belly.

Dara's phone buzzed to attention in her bag. She reached down to grab it—Janet. Not that this surprised her. Janet had been texting and calling her repeatedly since the segment ended. She tapped the screen awake to find yet another text message from her.

You okay?

Dara stared down at the words. No, she was not okay. She felt like crawling into bed, pulling up the covers and never showing her face again. Another text came in a few moments later:

It's not as bad as you think, alright? The segment was SO cute. And it did its job— which was to garner attention for J-Mate!!! YOU DID GREAT!!!!!

It was followed by far too many emojis to feel believable.

Dara put her phone on Silent. She did not have the heart to talk about what happened. Having her perfect Jewish husband list outed on national television was like one of her intrusive thoughts suddenly coming true. It confirmed all her worst fears and realities. Worse still, it had happened because of her own bubbe.

She should have known better. She should have intuited what Miriam was planning. All the signs were there. The way she so adamantly insisted on coming on the show with her. The way the ChallahBack Girls were all up early, prepping her makeup and hair...before turning their scarves and brushes on her.

Oh, and the worst, the most obvious sign of all, was the way Miriam had asked Eli about that five-second lag time. The way she had insisted she bring her pocketbook on set. Dara had brushed all these oddities off to it being one of Miriam's episodes. Now she saw each and every act as the by-product of a criminal mastermind.

She should have known better. She should have learned a lesson from all their trips to buffets when they were little. The way the old woman would pocket the bread rolls and sugar packets for later. Never trust a bubbe with an oversized pocketbook.

Her grandmother had set her up. And for what? Some stupid list, created with her sister as they played a drunken game on her birthday? Now the woman had the audacity to just sit there acting like her actions were totally appropriate. It wasn't right. It wasn't fair. Her bubbe was supposed to be her best friend.

Dara couldn't take it anymore. In one furious explosion of frustration, she twisted in her seat toward her grandmother.

"What were you thinking?" Dara said, the words falling from her lips in a tirade of hurt. "This is my business, Bubbe! My livelihood! What in the world would provoke you to bring that stupid list on television and embarrass me in front of everyone?"

"Dara," her grandmother said, unapologetic, "it's time."

"Time for what!"

"Time for you to find someone!" Miriam met her intensity. "Ever since your mother died, you've been a complete shut-in. It's not healthy, Dara! It's not normal. You're thirty-four years old, and you spend all your time with me. If your mother was here, she would be saying the same—"

"Don't you *dare*," Dara spat back at her. "Don't you use Ema as an excuse for your behavior today!"

The car settled into another round of uncomfortable silence.

Dara couldn't recall the first time she'd experienced anxiety. In some ways, it felt like her fears had always been there, embedded in her DNA, but it worsened around the time that she was a teenager.

Dara would spend all night worrying about something she had said in class, positive that everyone hated her. Tests would bring her to the brink of hysterics. She froze during midterms, unable to think, second-guessing every answer she wrote down. She would redo tasks and assignments—erasing her answers, starting over from the beginning—always struggling to make things perfect. Until finally, Dara would simply collapse beneath the weight of her own self-induced pressures.

Her mother, relying on her background as a cognitive behavioral therapist, saw what was happening and quickly moved to rectify the situation. After sending her to doctors to make sure there was nothing physically wrong with her, she got Dara into therapy. She got Dara medicated. She filled up her schedule with distractions, signing her up for every Jewish sports team and extracurricular activity, loading their house up with books, arts and crafts, and yarn, all in an effort to focus her overactive imagination on something more productive.

It was around this time that Dara began coding.

Writing code required a skill set with which she seemed particularly adept. It necessitated long and solitary hours hunched over a machine with little else in the way of distraction. It rewarded her obsessive attention to detail and her need for perfection. Every letter, number and symbol had to be correct.

Suddenly, she had a healthy outlet for her anxiety. Every website she developed, every app she created, was now a trophy instead of a blemish. She learned to see the difficulties she had been born with as positive. And thanks to her mother, who treated mental illness the same way you would a skinned knee—without judgments attached—she never saw her anxiety as something terrible. Despite her struggles with mental health, Dara knew her worth.

Dara looked up to see the limo driver, his eyes flicking

from the rearview mirror back to the road. Great. Not only had she been humiliated on television, but now all her dirty laundry was getting aired to a livery driver.

"I'm a modern woman, okay?" Dara said, defending herself. "I'm busy."

Miriam scoffed aloud. "Busy."

"I realize you're still living back in the glorious days of the shtetls, but believe it or not, women today can be perfectly happy without a man. They can have lives, and careers, and even children of their own! Not every woman is sitting around singing 'Sunrise, Sunset,' waiting for the tailor Motel Kamzoil to propose to her."

Miriam simply shrugged. "But you don't have children... or a life."

"Because I'm working!" Dara intensified. "I've been building a multimillion-dollar company since I was twenty years old!"

Miriam was not having it. She pointed an accusatory finger in Dara's face.

"Excuses. What you have are excuses! Oh, I'm so busy. Oh, I'm just so perfectly happy the way I am. I *adore* living all alone, in my giant and expensive apartment, never going anywhere without my bubbe to hold my hand! You're afraid, Dara. You've grown afraid of life."

The confrontation floored her. Dara had never heard her bubbe talk so openly, or harshly, before. She didn't know how to respond. She turned toward the window, biting back tears. In the glass, her reflection was distorted.

Of course, her grandmother was right. Ever since her mother had died, Dara had changed. It wasn't that she had given up on life. It wasn't just that her mother, also a sparkler, had been a powerhouse in her life. It wasn't just that she had been there, holding her hand, making her feel empowered. It was that her mother aligned herself in Dara's battles.

There were days when Dara was so exhausted from her struggles that she could barely find the courage to get out of bed. It was then that her mother would show up, standing over her—and sometimes tearing off her covers—demanding that she fight. *Fight, Dara.* Her mother would repeat it like a mantra on her bad days. *You're allowed to be afraid, you're allowed to be anxious, but you have to fight.*

After her mother died, Dara didn't have anyone to pull down her covers. She didn't have anyone to remind her that dealing with mental illness was a lifelong battle. She retreated into her safe little world. Her business. Her bubbe. She spent all her time with people, and in places, that didn't stoke her anxiety.

GAD was treatable. Not curable. One of the ways Dara managed her anxiety was through avoidance.

She avoided getting on planes, and traveling to new locations, because the thought of dying in a horrible and fiery crash was just too overwhelming. She avoided taking the bridges during morning traffic, choosing a ferry if she had the option. She negotiated the safety of situations constantly—crowded synagogues on the High Holidays, a busy subway during rush hour, eating sushi.

She could handle these things if someone was with her. If Miriam was there, holding her hand, relieving some of that pressure. If she had practiced and planned every detail of what she was going to say, and how she would say it, before her arrival at some event. But alone—going out on a limb to try something new or different—filled her with an impossible dread. New experiences simply weren't worth the amount of anxiety they produced, or the obsessive spiraling that came after.

And yet, alongside all her troublesome catastrophizing, was desire. Dara wanted to do more professionally, take on *Ted Talks*, attend the SimCon conference in Singapore. She dreamed of traveling the world, eco-lodges in the Amazon, mountain climbing in Peru, Kyoto for their cherry blossom festival. But mainly—when she thought about her future—her grandmother was right: she longed to fall in love. She wanted to get married.

After all, she had seen for herself the benefit of a strong and happy relationship. Not only in the marriage of her parents and grandparents, which together spanned nearly a century of commitment, but in the ten thousand successful matches she had helped build through J-Mate. Dara often received letters and emails filled with the pictures of happy couples. Images of them going on vacation, standing in front of first homes, holding babies.

"Dos pintele yid," Miriam said, suddenly.

"What?" Dara snapped her head in her direction. "What are you talking Yiddish about?"

Her grandmother didn't answer her. She was too busy staring out the window, lost in thought. But when Dara touched her shoulder, she saw that her grandmother's eyes were wet and red. She was on the verge of tears.

This was an episode. A real one.

"Bubbe," Dara said, gently, laying one hand on her wrist.

"Where am I?"

"You're okay," she said. "You're with me. Dara. Your grand-daughter."

Dara waited for her to return. Moments later, Miriam cupped her cheek with one hand. "Dara?"

"That's right."

"What happened?" she asked. "Were we fighting?"

Dara lied. "No."

Death was a conspiracy of silence. She had learned that from her mother, too.

Dara didn't want to talk about the tumor growing inside Miriam's brain. The one that gave her these episodes and made her right shoulder droop slightly. The one doctors had told her was inoperable, and malignant. Instead, they pretended that time moved forward, stagnant and unchanging. Bubbe Miriam would live forever.

It was a lie, of course. They both knew that soon, surrounded by hospice nurses and weeping family, they would have to say goodbye. For now, however, Dara lived in that in-between place. Her grandmother was dying. One day, choices would have to be made. Terrible decisions. Their time together, crumbs of challah left behind on a Shabbat table, waiting to be swept away.

She would not waste one second of it on anger.

Dara took Miriam's hands inside her own. "I was just explaining that I made reservations for dinner." Dara blinked back tears. "Your favorite place, Arnies."

"Oh!" Miriam touched her heart, surprised. "I love Arnies!"

Arnies was an old-world delicatessen on the outskirts of Hoboken. Miriam particularly liked their matzah ball soup, pickles and pastrami sandwiches. But it was the *gribenes*—fried chicken fat that could only be ordered off their old-world and very secret menu—that brought her back to her Ashkenazi childhood in the Bronx.

Miriam licked her lips, excitedly. "Can we bring some home for my friends?"

"Of course." Dara pushed a white curl out of her grandmother's blue eyes. "Soup, sandwiches and *gribenes* for everyone."

9

"HELLO," CHRIS SHOUTED, OPENING THE FRONT door to his apartment. "I'm home!"

Though Chris could hear the television on in the living room, nobody answered him. Atmospheric music followed by the sound of a woman screaming bloody murder could only mean one thing. Chris made his way down the hallway. Lacey was lying on the floor of their living room, watching a horror movie. Resting her chin on two tiny balled-up fists, she kicked her feet, an open notebook sprawled out in front of her.

"Hey, kiddo," Chris said, laying his keys and wallet on the counter.

Lacey did not look over. "Hey."

The woman on the television screen went sprinting down a hallway.

"You finish your homework?" Chris asked.

"Uh-huh."

"You sure?" Chris asked again. "I'm not gonna ask to see your work and find it half done and the rest of it wrong?"

Lacey responded with a loud and exaggerated huff. Jumping up from her spot, she grabbed her notebook from off the floor and handed it to Chris. Quickly, she raced back to her movie. Chris looked down at her work, double-checking the ten math equations spread out across the page. It was perfect.

"My mistake," Chris said, putting her notebook on the counter.

Lacey didn't respond. She was far too immersed in her movie, which, judging by the maniacal-looking clowns on the television, was yet another R-rated horror film.

Chris didn't like Lacey watching slasher films, but he found that parenting required choosing your battles. Good grades and hygiene were a fight worth having. Horror movies, however, he had managed to strike an uneasy alliance with. The woman on the television got decapitated. Blood and guts splattered all over the windshield of the car she was driving.

Still, and as her parent, he couldn't help but point out the obvious. "Isn't that a little mature for you?"

Lacey twisted in his direction. "Dad," she said, like he was an idiot. "This is *Slasher-Clowns Twelve: Hell-Bent at the Carnival.*"

"Ah."

"It's totally the best out of all of them."

Chris wasn't sure when her obsession with all things horror had begun, but he knew it was sometime after Claire had died. What bothered him the most was not her interest in all things gore but rather that it never seemed to bother her.

Lacey never had trouble sleeping after watching one of her films. She never woke him up in the middle of the night after having a bad dream. But he reckoned that Lacey had learned early on that there were real horrors in life. The truly scary stuff—like losing your mom suddenly at nine years old—blindsided you without warning. Perhaps reality had made getting decapitated by serial-killing clowns feel more like comedy.

Chris looked around the apartment. "Where's Katie, anyway?"

"Right behind you," a pleasant voice called out.

Chris turned to find Katie, his nanny and landlord, standing behind him. Her long black hair pulled into a high ponytail, she was balancing an overfilled laundry basket against the edge of one very pregnant belly.

"Oh, jeez," Chris said, quickly taking the basket from her. "Let me help you with that."

"Thanks." She smiled, and moved one hand to her back.

Chris found a place to drop the laundry. He had told Katie a million times to stop doing the laundry. She was pregnant, after all, and about to pop any day now. Given that she was also dealing with a case of gestational diabetes, she was high-risk.

He despised the thought of her huffing up and down the two flights of stairs to the laundry room in the basement and back to his apartment. But that was Katie…and Jensen. They always went out of their way for him and Lacey.

Chris hadn't had a plan when he left Virginia for New York City. He simply drove, heading north, knowing that a job at NBS-7 was waiting for him.

When he arrived in Manhattan with Lacey, he quickly realized that finding a place to live would be no simple matter. It wasn't just the expense of living in the city—exorbitant condo fees coupled with the costs of renting a two-bedroom apartment—it was that he was now a single parent to a nine-year-old child.

Unlike in Virginia, he didn't have his family to rely on. He didn't have a wife who could help with taking care of Lacey and making decisions about her schooling. He had no clue where to find a trustworthy and reliable babysitter in a city of nine million strangers. He was out of his element, alone. Lost.

Chris had driven for hours. He and Lacey circled Manhattan, looking in the outer boroughs, popping in and out of open houses that he found on his Zillow app. But each place they visited seemed worse than the last. It also amazed Chris that anyone would spend $2,500 a month to live somewhere the size of a closet. Or worse, when it wasn't the size of a closet, it was located above what could only be *generously* described as a crack den. Neither of which was acceptable for a grown man raising a nine-year-old girl.

Finally, after searching for hours, Chris was dejected. Lacey was exhausted. Feeling completely hopeless about the situation—not even sure where he was—he pulled off to the side of some street. He had collapsed into the steering wheel, regretting every decision he had ever made in his life, when a firefighter knocked on his window. Chris hadn't even realized that he had parked in front of a fire station.

Apologizing profusely, he put his car back into Drive, and that was when he saw it. A simple "2 Bedroom—For Rent" sign on the second-floor window of a small brownstone. The building had a certain charm about it. The whole street, with its line of green trees dotting the sidewalks, a large school at the end of the block and a firehouse in the center, felt welcoming.

It felt safe.

Chris called the number below the sign, and Katie met him at the door a few minutes later. It was not a luxurious apartment by any stretch of the imagination. It didn't have recessed lighting or marble countertops, but it had enough space for them both. A decent-sized living room with a kitchen attached. Plus, it was close to the subway, and there was a decently rated school (according to Katie) right down the road. Beyond all those things, Lacey had taken an immediate shine to Katie. At one point during their tour, he had even looked over to see her holding her hand.

Thankfully, Katie didn't seem to mind.

Chris put down a deposit even before he saw the one tiny

bathroom he would be sharing with his daughter. They moved in that very same night.

Later, hauling their many boxes of stuff up the stairs, he met Jensen. The same firefighter who had told him to move his vehicle out of a fire zone turned out to be Katie's husband. The picturesque brownstone that had been broken into two apartments had been in Katie's family for generations. Jensen, however, had been a later addition, the duo having met when Jensen took a position as a firefighter at Engine 46 just next door.

Like so many families in the outer boroughs of Manhattan, looking to make extra income in an increasingly expensive city, Katie and Jensen lived on the top floor and rented out the bottom apartment to tenants.

Alas, and for reasons Chris still didn't completely comprehend, they always had trouble finding tenants. Something about the noise, and how nobody in their right mind wanted to live next to a firehouse, with alarms blaring at all hours of the day and night. But Chris didn't mind the noise. Indeed, he had spent most of his career chasing engines to find the best story. Living next to Engine 46 felt intimately familiar.

When Katie, who had a degree in teaching English as a second language, mentioned that she was in between jobs—that she was looking to stop teaching in order to spend more time on her true passion, running a knitting business on Etsy—Chris offered her a happy alternative. In addition to rent, he offered Katie the job of watching Lacey in the afternoons and being on-call during the day for any emergencies. In return, and while Lacey was at school, Katie could use the time to build her Etsy empire. Katie happily agreed.

Perhaps it was naive of Chris to simply allow any woman, any stranger with a warm smile and never-ending supply of hugs, to watch his daughter. But both Katie and Jensen had a comforting warmth about them. They were the type of people who oozed sweetness, like pulling a tray of piping hot chocolate chip cookies straight out of the oven. You knew they were going to be good.

Katie had been a permanent fixture for both of them since moving to New York. She had cooked meals. Picked up Lacey from school when she was sick and Chris was stuck at work. She did the laundry, even though it had never been a part of her job description. She wasn't Claire, of course, but she took on the role of mom, of sheltering and helping Chris by being the other parent, and he was infinitely grateful to her for it.

He still hadn't dealt with the reality that this was her last day working for them.

Thankfully, Chris had found a suitable alternative. A woman named Mona, who happened to be a cousin of Katie's and came with excellent references. Still, the knowledge that his daughter would be safe didn't dampen their shared loss.

Chris returned to the foyer and found Katie by the front door. As she pulled on an oversized cardigan she had left hanging on a hook, he could see the sadness in her eyes. This was it. Katie was leaving. Even though she would always be right upstairs, their lives were changing once again.

"Thank you again for everything," he said, fumbling to help her gather her bags.

"I'll be right upstairs."

"And…you really didn't need to do the laundry."

She smiled knowingly. It wasn't what he wanted to say. What he wanted to say was *Please don't go. Please, have your baby in our living room and take all my money.* Alas, Chris was far too much of a gentleman to devolve into pleading. He also respected Katie and Jensen too much to take what was already a difficult decision for his friends, and neighbors, and load his own baggage onto it.

Katie was going to be a mommy. Jensen was going to be a daddy. It was a time in their life when they needed to focus on each other, grow together as a family. As much as he wanted Katie to remain a permanent fixture in their lives, it was time to let her go.

"Lacey," Chris called out to his daughter. "You want to say goodbye?"

Lacey kicked her feet, but otherwise did not respond.

Chris sighed, then moved to correct her behavior. Katie laid one hand on his wrist. "It's fine," she said gently, then called out to Lacey, "I'll see you around, okay?"

Lacey, once again, pretended not to hear her.

Even though it was unnecessary, Chris apologized before adding with some effort, "We'll try not to bother you."

He held the door open for Katie, and she departed up the stairs.

Chris sighed, closing the door behind her. Glancing back to his daughter in the living room, he realized that today had truly just been god-awful. *Good News* was failing. Katie was leaving. In truth, the only bright spot in his day had been Dara Rabinowitz and that ridiculous list. Shaking off any visible signs of worry, Chris turned his attention back to his young daughter.

How was he going to do this? How was he going to tell Lacey that there was a likelihood—hell, who was he kidding, an extremely strong chance—that they would be moving again? That he would, once again, be ripping her away from her friends and her makeshift family in New York? He settled on acting casual, breaking the news in the best way he knew how.

Moseying back over to the living room, he took a seat behind his young daughter on the couch. On the television screen in front of them, a clown was getting his leg amputated by a hacksaw.

"How would you like to go out for ice cream?" he asked.

"Why?"

"What do you mean *why*?" Chris scoffed. "I'm your dad. It's Thursday night. Let's celebrate with some ice cream."

She fixed him with a suspicious look. "We only go out to eat ice cream when something is wrong."

Chris made it a point not to swallow. His growing daughter had become far too smart.

He glanced back toward the television, where a man was running through a fun house full of mirrors, and suddenly longed for killer clowns to come bursting through his screen. He could deal with homicidal circus clowns. Telling his only daughter the truth felt impossible.

"Come on," he said, grabbing her pink jacket from the closet. "Let's go."

The ice cream store that Chris would occasionally visit with his daughter was called MilkShAXEs. It rested three blocks from their apartment, and had a giant neon sign in front of a milkshake in the process of being poured, before being struck by an axe. It wasn't actually an ice cream store, but rather a trendy Brooklyn bar that featured adult milkshakes alongside axe throwing.

Honestly, Chris thought it was a terrible idea, mixing alcohol and sharp objects. But they had a large and extensive menu, where Chris could get a burger, and Lacey could get a *virgin* milkshake, while watching axes fly through the air. Given her penchant for horror, MilkShAXEs was an immediate favorite spot of hers.

Chris watched his daughter dig her spoon into an oversized glass of slushy strawberry slurry. In between bites, she rattled on happily, telling Chris every detail of her day, her teachers, her best friend, Jasmine, who liked some boy, Gabe, and how some other friend, Colt, was totally jealous.

His own burger, in the meantime, was growing cold. Listening to Lacey talk, express all the ways she loved her home in New York, filled him with a growing sense of dread. He couldn't bring himself to eat. It had taken Lacey forever to acclimate to New York City. But what choice did he have? Better to tell her the truth now, get her ready for reality, than blindside her last-minute with a move.

"Look, Lacey." Chris cleared his throat, trying to be strong. "There's something we need to—"

"Can I get a bra?" she said, suddenly interrupting him.

Chris cleared his throat. "Excuse me?"

"A bra." She said it matter-of-factly. "You know...for boobs?"

"I know what—" he closed his eyes, stumbling over the words "—a bra is."

What he didn't expect was for his only daughter, his precious baby girl, to ever be wearing one.

A million thoughts ran through his head. He thought back to every book he ever read on parenting. The ones that taught him about brain development, and first steps, and covering electrical outlets. Not one of those stupid books had ever prepared him for this. For being a single father, alone in the world with your eleven-year-old daughter, asking for help buying a bra. He didn't know the first thing about buying women's underwear. But she was changing. Growing. He wasn't ready for it. What the hell was going to happen next? Her period. Dating. *Oral sex*.

He shook that beyond-awful thought away. He wanted to be sex-positive, teach her to respect her body, and demand the same from others. But he felt this tremendous weight pressing on his chest. What if he got it wrong? What if he screwed it up, and her, in the process? She had already been through so much. Now he was going to rip her away from New York *and* screw up her entire adolescence by messing up her first bra.

She couldn't have asked this a week ago? Before Katie quit to go on maternity leave, and might have been able to help? Then again, he looked back at his young daughter, her green eyes filled with hope… Maybe boobs didn't happen on schedule.

Lacey lowered her eyes, embarrassed. "Don't be weird."

"I'm not." Chris sat up quickly. Too quickly. Moments later, he was fumbling for his phone, typing in words. "I think it's great that you need a bra. Bras are awesome. Bras are the best! Just the start of all the wonderful things…that are going to happen for you."

Lacey squinted. "What are you doing?"

"Going on Amazon."

It seemed like a good idea. He bought all his own underwear and socks there.

Chris went to type the word *bra* into his search bar. But when he glanced back at his daughter across the table, he stopped. He could see it in her little face. The way she stared down at her half-drunk milkshake. The way she pressed her lips all the way to one side, biting the inside of her cheek. She was trying not to cry.

Claire.

Her absence was palpable.

And yet, neither of them brought her up. They didn't talk about the terrible day they had lost her in a seemingly impossible car accident. It was the anniversary of her death, and Lacey needed a bra, and nobody said her name aloud.

"We'll figure it out, okay?" he said, trying to make Lacey feel better. "I'll figure it out."

Lacey returned to eating her ice cream. Like most kids,

she had the attention span of a squirrel. With a happy little shrug of her shoulders, she was on to the next topic. Chris listened to her tiny voice, the trills and squeaks of it, and his heart came to life.

He tried to listen attentively to every word, capture every fleeting moment, but in the back of his mind he couldn't forget why they were here. He waited for an opportune moment to tell her the truth. But every time there was a break in the conversation, or the perfect segue into the topic, Chris faltered. He couldn't do it.

Finally, after three hours of hesitating, it was past Lacey's bedtime. Chris paid the bill and took her home. Getting her ready for bed, Chris ran through the motions.

He made sure her face was washed and her teeth were brushed. He made sure her schoolbag was packed and by the door. He picked up all her shoes, stuffed animals and the makeup Katie had given her from the floor of the bedroom, making sure that if she got up in the middle of the night, she wouldn't trip on any hazard. Finally, he poured her a glass of water, putting it on the nightstand beside her bed. An image of Claire, resting in a photo, smiled at him.

He turned his attention back to Lacey. She snuggled into her pillows, twisting beneath her sheets. But she was happy. Safe. The perfect little world he was trying to create for her, the one filled with pink walls and unicorn-shaped lamps—also, occasionally, killer clowns—would remain intact for another day.

"Daddy," she said, and rolled over toward her nightstand. "I love you."

"I love you, too, Lace."

Back in the living room, Chris scanned the shared apartment. They were living in a sty. Even with Katie's help—now something they would both need to do without—it looked more like a frat house than the prim-and-proper home they'd had in Virginia.

He settled on cleaning up the house. He straightened up the living room, picking up strewn-about items like sneakers and backpacks, laying them by the door. He put away the laundry that Katie had so thoughtfully done for them. It wasn't that he was bad at homemaking. Not exactly. It was just the demands of being a single dad, on top of a full-time broadcast journalist, felt nearly impossible. It was like he was always playing catch-up. Like he was forever in some game of Whac-A-Mole, tackling one problem only to realize that three more had popped up in its place.

Now, aside from his failing career and Katie going on maternity leave, Lacey needed a bra.

He needed to relax. Grabbing a nonalcoholic beer from the fridge—because *kids*—he took a seat at the counter in their kitchen, and focused his attention on work. Opening up his laptop, he clicked on his email. Eleanor had sent him production notes.

On Fridays, they always did a weekend cooking segment. Tomorrow, they would be rolling in a grill for a barbecue. His stomach rumbled at the thought. It had been a while since he'd had some decent ribs. Unfortunately, even pork wasn't enough to save *Good News*. Nothing was good enough to save a show that was, from its very inception, faulty from the start.

Chris closed out of his email and opened up his Twitter account, expecting the same old banality of retweets and shares from the studio—and whatever anonymous weirdo happened to want to troll him that day—when his fingers went motionless above the keyboard.

"What the…"

The words fell from his lips. Chris leaned in to his laptop screen to check that he wasn't hallucinating. According to the little heart at the top of his profile, he had over one thousand updates waiting. People—lots of people, it seemed—were sharing the segment he had filmed with Dara and her eccentric grandmother.

His phone buzzed with a text from Jensen:

We meeting tomorrow morning?

Chris wrote his best bud back:

You mean...am I still alive after last week?

You were breathing when I left you.

Eight AM works for me.

Jensen confirmed with a thumbs-up emoji.

Chris turned his attention back to his social media. It was remarkable, really. A curiosity. He'd been far too immersed in filming the segment—and his own issues—to consider how it was received by the audience. But now, in the privacy of his own home, rewatching those five minutes of Dara on camera, he could see why people liked her.

When she stepped away from her obsessive need for control via scripts, she was relatable. There was something about the way she interacted with her grandmother, and the camera. She wore her whole damn heart on her sleeve, and that vulnerability, that honesty, made her likeable.

Her perfect Jewish husband list, however, was just comic gold.

Chris found himself watching her segment several more times. He forgot about his troubles, laughing alongside the audience. She was a terrible liar. The type of person who told you what they thought with their whole body.

Could the segment go viral? It didn't escape him that Dara

Rabinowitz had that certain something—that certain joie de vivre, that unquantifiable star quality—that could propel ratings and fans alike.

He shook the thought away. The chance of any segment on *Good News* charging past ten thousand let alone one hundred thousand shares was unlikely. Even Bucky didn't pull in those numbers. More likely, it would garner a little bit of buzz on the internet, and speedily fizzle out.

10

DARA RABINOWITZ MADE HER WAY DOWN THE
hallway of Adath Israel. She steadied her grandmother with
one elbow while her other arm was loaded down with plastic
bags. She had brought enough food back from Arnie's to feed
her bubbe, all the ChallahBack Girls and half of Hoboken.
Unfortunately, given their late hour of return—nine o'clock—
the majority of the residents had gone to bed. Dara passed by
the doors of the ChallahBack Girls and found them all closed.

"It looks like everyone has gone to sleep," she said.

Miriam tapped Dara gently on the wrist. "Not to worry.
Arnie's only gets better with time. All the fat coagulates, you
know?"

Dara smiled knowingly. Perhaps it was a skill developed
from her many years of being a matchmaker, but her grandmother had always been able to put a positive spin on a nega-
tive reality.

Inside her apartment, Miriam kicked off her shoes by the
couch, then scurried to her bedroom to change for bed. Dara
headed for her kitchen. She put the food away, making sure

it was carefully arranged in the front and fully visible so that her grandmother would not forget it was there.

Then, and as it was her nature to worry, she reached for the junk drawer beside the sink. Pulling out some masking tape and a black pen, she wrote the date on each container. After, she found a piece of scrap paper and scribbled a note, taping it to the fridge:

> *FOOD FROM ARNIE'S IN THE FRIDGE*
> *SHARE WITH CHALLAHBACK GIRLS*
> *THROW OUT BY*
> *THURSDAY, SEPTEMBER 9TH*
> *AT MIDNIGHT*
> *CALL ME IF YOU HAVE ANY QUESTIONS*
> *212-555-6178*
> *I LOVE YOU VERY MUCH!!!!!*

The addition of her phone number was likely overkill. But overkill—like making sure every single detail was perfect—helped dampen Dara's anxiety. Besides, it was better that her grandmother feel offended by her neurotic and over-obsessive helicopter-grandchilding than the poor woman come down with a horrendous case of food poisoning from spoiled *gribenes*.

Miriam was in the bathroom now, the sound of water running behind the closed door. Dara headed back to the living room and collapsed onto the soft cushions, her feet weary.

It was then that she noticed something unusual. Her grandmother's stylish shoes—red-and-white oxford heels with tiny red stitching around the front and back edges—were kicked off and tossed casually beside the couch. Dara sighed, picking them up, and headed to the second bedroom to put them away.

Opening the double doors to the Elfa system that housed nearly sixty-five pairs of Miriam's exquisitely designed shoes,

Dara found an empty spot and settled the red-and-white oxford pumps where they belonged.

Her grandmother had been quite the little dancer back in her day. In fact, and even though it was frowned upon as immodest in Jewish tradition, she would often sneak out on a Saturday night with her second husband, Dara's grandfather, to attend all the latest dance competitions.

Miriam had won all sorts of awards in her younger years, before children. Though Dara had never been privy to seeing one of these wild nights out herself, that big, independent spirit had followed her bubbe into her senior years.

Staring at the shoes, running her fingers over a blue pair that was all glitter and sparkle, she recalled the way her grandparents had sashayed around a synagogue banquet room during their fiftieth anniversary. The image of them forever cemented in her memory. Hands gracefully meeting, feet kicking in time to the swinging music, eyes gazing forward. Looking in the same direction.

The funny thing was that she never saw her grandparents dancing privately. Maybe it was because they were Jewish. Romance was almost a secondary thought to the primary directive of marrying and raising Jewish children. Dara never saw her grandparents kiss. She never saw them hold hands, except for that one time at synagogue when they were dancing. Indeed, what she remembered about Miriam and Chayim Rabinowitz was that they fought all the time. Always in Yiddish. Often, at the most extreme ends of their vocal spectrum, her annoyed by some minor offense, him just as happy to scream right back.

And yet, Dara knew they loved each other. Although they fought constantly—not surprising after fifty years of marriage—their devotion to each other was constant.

Dara grew aware of a presence behind her. She turned to

see her grandmother standing there, staring sadly at her collection of footwear.

"Bubbe, is everything okay?"

"What should I do with them?"

"Hmm?" Dara looked at her grandmother.

"All my shoes," she said simply. "When I die. It seems a waste to throw them all out."

Dara recalled an old Yiddish saying. *It's a mitzvah to wear their clothes, but it's a sin to walk in their shoes.* For this reason, she had always been taught that you discard the shoes of a loved one after their death.

"Come now, Bubbe," Dara said, wanting desperately to change the topic, "let me help you get into bed."

Closing the doors to her closet, Dara led her grandmother to the bedroom. Then, as she always did when she was the last person to see her grandmother for the evening, she cared for the woman she loved. She checked, and double-checked, that Miriam would have everything she needed for a good, and safe, night's rest.

She made sure that her medication was in order, and that her grandmother had taken every pill she was supposed to for the evening. She made sure that there were no items on the floor. She picked up any bits of clothing strewn about, and neatened stacks of papers, even as her bubbe begged her to stop touching her stuff. Finally, with the house in order, Dara lowered the lights, filled a glass of water and helped her beloved grandmother into bed.

Pulling up the covers, she tucked her in tight.

"My *shayna madela*," Miriam said, and cupped her cheek.

"I love you, Bubbe."

Dara kissed her on the forehead. She waited to hear the soft sound of breathing before heading out for the night.

There was nothing quite like fall in Hoboken. The skyline

of lower Manhattan lit up across the waters. The waterfront was filled with couples, arms wrapped around each other's waists, heads pressed close as they whispered secrets. She passed an old couple on a bench, two little white dogs sitting by their feet, peacefully gazing out over the water. Everywhere she looked, Dara saw love. And yet, she'd never felt more alone.

Her grandmother's words—and the outing of her perfect Jewish husband list on national television—had forced her to confront the truth of her situation. Like the shofar blowing each morning in Elul, she was shaken awake from her life of sleepwalking. Dara was lonely. She didn't want to be single any longer. She just didn't know how to overcome her fears.

Returning to her apartment, she threw her black messenger bag down by the door. As she looked around at her expensive gray couches and modern furniture, she couldn't believe how depressingly silent it all felt. All those slate finishes and swirling silver quartz countertops suddenly felt cold and sterile. Like she was standing in a morgue, a place for cold and lifeless things, instead of a home.

There was no warmth in her apartment. No photos of a partner, trips to fabulous places, adventures all around the planet. No ridiculous drawings, like the ones her nieces and nephews had scribbled all over her perfect Jewish husband list. The only things that even denoted a hint of an actual life were the multiple computer monitors on her desk, and the floor-to-ceiling windows overlooking the skyline of Manhattan.

She stared down at the people passing by on the waterfront. Beneath one of the flickering streetlamps, a woman laughed as a man leaned in to kiss her. It was an intimate moment. Gentle and romantic. Feeling guilty for intruding, Dara spun away from the view.

This was how she lived her life, really. Through other people. Through other matches, and happy endings, and marriages.

Dara took a seat at her desk, thinking about the events of the day. Her mind wandered back to her perfect Jewish husband list. Yes, she had created it drunkenly with her sister on her last birthday...but in vino veritas. There was a speck of truth in every scribble of humor.

Besides, she reasoned away the ridiculousness of her actions against firm logic. Dara was someone who always had a plan. If you were heading to a new location, you didn't just get in the car and start to drive. You plugged the address into your GPS. You googled every bathroom, restaurant, gas station and fire department along the way.

It was the same with dating.

Resolutely, she turned on her computer. Ignored the ten thousand email messages from Janet that were sitting in her inbox, with exclamation points screaming IMPORTANT.

Instead, she went to her profile on J-Mate. It was the first profile she had ever created, back when she was still building the nuts and bolts of her code in her college dorm room. Unfortunately, having been so busy with work, the photo that stared back at her hadn't been updated in fourteen years. She grimaced at the realization that she was one step away from going full-fledged catfish.

But just as quickly, she shook away any concerns. Her photo didn't matter. She was just looking. She was just...peeking in as the CEO of J-Mate, making sure everything was working on her J-eography update. Nothing more. Still, she found herself searching for eligible men, never divorced, no children, between the ages of thirty-two and thirty-nine and with a graduate degree.

A stream of photos attached to profiles appeared on the screen. She clicked on the first one. LKCycle1989.

As it turned out, her algorithm was working perfectly. LK-Cycle1989 was a lawyer in Manhattan with a focus on environmental policy. She appreciated a smart man with a focus on *tikun olam*, or fixing a broken world. She also liked his red hair and freckles, but when she continued clicking through his uploaded photographs, she realized that he had far too many pictures of himself biking.

It was a hobby she could never get behind. Not only because she had once fallen off a shoddy mountain bike in the Negev, nearly killing herself in the process, but because biking implied an adventurous sort. The type of man who loved traveling to exotic locations, exploring the world on two wheels. The type of person who pedaled his way through morning traffic and didn't scream aloud in abject horror at every car that zipped past.

Or worse, what if the man actually *enjoyed* going to spin classes?

No, a marriage between them would never work out.

There was a thinner man, very handsome, with fewer pictures of biking and more pictures of food. It was certainly to Dara's liking. The problem was he didn't use any punctuation in his About Me section. Likely he had filled out the form on his phone using voice-to-text, the program not picking up the nuances that came with starts and stops in language. But leaving it that way felt like an unforgivable crime. Dara could not spend the rest of her life with a person who didn't appreciate periods.

Undeterred, she pressed onward. She looked at dozens of profiles, clicking through each and every one in an organized manner, before finding something wrong or lacking with each match. Too short. Too old. Too many teeth in his smile. Not enough teeth in his smile. One man—she leaned in closer to inspect—wore a sports-themed yarmulke. Another was wearing a black shirt with white buttons.

Of course, she was aware of the small, almost infinitesimal, possibility that she was searching for reasons to reject each potential suitor. But awareness of her issues had never stopped Dara from fully swimming around in them.

She was just about to turn her computer off when her eyes landed on the most fantastic-looking creature, and the word in blue just beside his photograph: NEW.

On the surface, he was just her type. Dark hair and eyes, the most glorious smile. But it was more than just general attractiveness. There was something poetic about the way he looked at the camera, not too self-conscious, dignified and self-aware. She laughed aloud at the nickname he had chosen—YourMomWillLoveMe. She clicked on the profile.

Her heart raced as she continued reading. He was a doctor. There were no pictures of him biking. She liked his shoes. He'd included a picture of himself wrapping tefillin. Two tiny black boxes of phylacteries wrapped around his arm and head. There was nothing sexier than a hot Jewish man wrapped up in leather. She loved the way the straps left imprints on their arms in the morning.

Though it seemed wrong to spy on the man for purely personal purposes, she gave in to her curiosity. Using her privileges as creator of the app, she ran a simple R-script to preview his profile from a data science and analytics perspective.

She analyzed his click-through rate, connection and messaging activity. She was pleased to see that he had only ever contacted three women. Though his financial activity and home address were both double encrypted for security, she could tell that his residence was in Manhattan.

He was perfect.

She clicked on the tiny envelope at the corner of the screen. The cursor blinked in the message box.

Her mind began swirling. All she had to do was jot out a simple email, and yet her anxiety was spiraling. What should she say? What if he didn't write back? Or worse, what if he did write back?

A million terrifying scenarios flashed through her brain. What if they hit it off, and he wanted to talk on the phone? She was terrible at chitchat, coming up with the right thing to say on the spot, sounding witty. Then there was the even scarier prospect of going on a date, having to meet a stranger in some coffee shop or restaurant. What if he was secretly some sort of psychopath, a serial killer who would chop her head off and bury her behind a brick wall the first chance he got?

Dara completely glitched out, clicking out of J-Mate.

Spinning around in her chair, she faced the deafening silence of her empty apartment once more. She needed to calm down. She needed a distraction.

She found her phone. Her screen displayed a barrage of notifications. One after another pinged on her phone. They came from Janet and Naveah. They came from her older sister, Shana. They came from her fan pages and business profiles on LinkedIn, Instagram, Twitter and TikTok. Dara began scrolling through the messages:

Dara Rabinowitz, CEO of J-Mate, has been tagged in a video.

Dara Rabinowitz, CEO of J-Mate, has been shared one hundred and sixteen times.

Dara Rabinowitz, CEO of J-Mate, has twelve new messages.

She groaned aloud. It had been Janet's idea to establish social media pages for Dara. Though her accounts were primarily run by other people, she still had access to them. Either way, it was far too late at night to deal with dousing the onslaught right now. She would handle it in the morning.

Crawling into bed, pulling her covers over her head, she found the one thing that always managed to take her mind off the worst-case scenarios. She opened the app for her NYC emergency scanner, pressing it to her ear.

The sound of police and firefighters, EMTs and 911 operators, rang out across her empty bedroom. In a staccato of static and beeps, and voices calling out codes, her breathing slowed. Hearing those voices, listening to the sounds of life beating all around her, her anxious mind slowed.

Outside, there was a world in progress. Outside, there were people confronting all sorts of *real* disasters and catastrophes. Heart attacks. Car accidents. Four-alarm fires and burglaries. Her simple problems—like her lackluster love life, or her embarrassment over her perfect Jewish husband list being outed on national television—paled in comparison to the tragedies of real life, love and loss.

And yet, despite these terrible truths, life tumbled on.

The thought comforted her as she drifted off to sleep.

11

THE FOLLOWING MORNING, CHRIS AWOKE TO HIS typical single-parent tornado. Forcing himself out of bed, he got Lacey dressed and threw on gym clothes. He chugged two cups of coffee while Lacey scarfed down a truly despicable breakfast of microwave waffles slathered in strawberry cream cheese. Finally, Chris rushed her out the door and walked her the half block to school.

"So," he said, nervous. "Mona will be picking you up from school today."

"I know, Dad."

Mona was a middle-aged cousin of Katie's who lived in Queens. Though the woman never smiled, and had told Chris flat-out at the interview that she would not be doing any house-work, she was willing to work part-time in the afternoons.

It wasn't ideal. Mona certainly wasn't Katie. But having a body in the apartment to watch Lacey was the best he could do for the time being.

"I want you to wait for Mona," Chris continued. "No going to your friends' houses. No stopping for ice cream. Also, I want you to text me as soon as you get to the apartment. I'll be home by dinnertime."

"Yes, Dad, jeez. You've told me a million times already!"

Chris would tell her a million more times if it meant keeping her safe.

It wasn't just that he was worried about her getting home. It was all the other aspects of danger that parents had to account for in the modern age. New York City seemed tame in comparison to technology, where any pervert could have access to his young daughter. As a journalist, he was intimately aware of every horrible story.

Lacey was a good kid. Smart as a whip, too. But she was still very much a child.

"Don't forget to text me!" Chris called out.

"I know!" She waved him off. At the front entrance to Hopewell Middle School, Lacey was met by a crowd of her friends. She disappeared into their tiny circle of pink and purple backpacks, not even bothering to look back as Chris waved goodbye.

She was growing up, nearing that place in adolescence where she was far more interested in her friends. It felt wrong to move her now.

His phone buzzed to attention in his pocket. Chris pulled it out to find a message from Jensen:

You coming?!?

Chris rolled his eyes.

Down the block, in front of the firehouse, Jensen was standing on the sidewalk, waving at him with both arms.

"Dude!" He smiled wide as Chris approached. "What took you so long?"

"I know this is hard to believe," Chris said, greeting his

friend with a strong shake of the hand, "but I have a kid who needs to get to school."

"That sounds like a *you* problem," Jensen said, giving Chris a friendly slap on the back, nearly sending him flying face-first into the sidewalk in the process.

Engine 46 was your typical firehouse. It had an industrial-sized apparatus bay where three different fire trucks were stored. Beyond the bay, there was the dayroom, which included a large kitchen and a long table where the firefighters took most of their meals, a conference room and an administrative area where Fire Chief Gunther Radzinski, affectionately nicknamed Rudolph because he oversaw the trucks and crew, periodically did paperwork.

Upstairs, and beyond the hectic noise of the first floor, were the subspaces. Dorm rooms that provided privacy to crews on shift. Individual lockers next to Murphy beds, depending on your rank, hierarchy…and, frankly, how much trouble you got into with Gunther. Jensen knew every squeaky inch of those uncomfortable wall beds intimately.

"Hey, Rudolph!" Jensen called out to Gunther. The old man had taken his usual position in a metal chair in the loading dock of the apparatus bay, with two arms crossed sternly against his chest. "What do you think? You think Chris here can take me in dead lifts?"

Gunther grunted in their general direction, but otherwise did not respond. He came from old Polish stock on his father's side and Okinawan pride on his mother's. In homage to both, he wore an authentic *tenugui* folded around his forehead, and always left two buttons undone on his (always the exact same) green collared shirt, his white chest hairs sprawling outward, fighting to meet the ones extending from his nose and ears.

Alas, Gunther ruled Engine 46 with an iron fist. He could have easily joined in on the banter the firefighters shared. Indeed, Jensen had tried to pull him out of his stern shell on numerous occasions. But Gunther was far too old, and too serious, to ever provide more than a nose wiggle and a sneer.

"Come on," Jensen said, leading Chris through the wide-open doors of the apparatus bay. "I'm planning to love you something awful this morning."

The four times a week that Chris spent an hour in the training room of Engine 46 were invaluable. He loved the brutal workouts that Jensen foisted on him. He found it therapeutic to work through his pain, escape from his mind, after everything that happened with Claire. He especially loved the comradery among the cast of characters who had become his friends in his new life in Brooklyn.

There was probie Don McNamara, who had been born and bred in Staten Island, but skirted family tradition and three generations of battling blazes when he took a position as a probationary firefighter at Engine 46 in Brooklyn.

There was Amerpreet Delmonico, a firefighter of mixed Indian and Italian descent, lauded throughout their house for his spectacular fusion of both cultures' cuisines in the kitchen.

There was driver engineer Lilliana Sanchez. The proud daughter of Mexican-Albanian immigrants, Lilliana rose through the ranks of Engine 46 in record time and served as the company's resident expert on the fire apparatus. When Lilliana wasn't prying the wheel of the trucks away from Jensen, she was often beneath it, checking that every aspect of the vehicle was operating and safe.

Finally, there was Captain Reese Osborne. Reese, born female, identified as gender fluid. Sometimes they let their mohawk hang wildly to one side. Sometimes they slicked it back, binding their breasts and throwing on an oversized tank top. But no matter what Reese wore, or how they identified, one thing was always certain. Reese could out-lift Chris—and toss him across the Hudson—with merely a pinkie.

Over two years, the crew of Engine 46 had adopted Chris as one of their own. But while maintaining appearances and keeping up a good physique was a professional necessity for Chris, it could mean life and death for Jensen, whose job as a firefighter with the FDNY often meant pushing through barricades and breaking through walls.

"Dude!" Jensen said, looking up from the two-hundred-pound bag of sand he was hauling across the training room of Engine 46. "Are you freaking kidding me?"

Chris coughed out the words from the mat. "I'm done."

"How the hell can you be done?" Jensen dropped the bag of sand down by his feet. "It's only been forty-five minutes. We're just getting started!"

Chris clutched his chest, certain he was dying. He knew he wasn't. Workouts with Jensen always ended for him in a pool of tears. Sweat rolled down his forehead and neck as he attempted to catch his breath.

"Why are we friends?" Chris asked, somewhat seriously.

"Because—" Jensen leaned in, booping him on the nose "—you love me. And because I know you got a beast mode *somewhere* in there. You are not just a pretty face, my friend! You are intelligence, and heart, and someone who can dead-lift more than ten pounds."

"Thanks."

"Now come on." Jensen smacked him again. "Give me ten more minutes on weights, and I'll let you go home to lick your wounds."

Chris watched Jensen sashay off, and then, finding that last ounce of strength inside himself, followed. Jensen lay down on a bench, and Chris got into position to spot him.

"I caught your show yesterday, man."

"Oh yeah?" Chris was surprised to hear this. He didn't think Jensen was a fan of *Good News*. No one was actually a fan of *Good News*.

"You sound surprised."

"The ratings haven't been good," Chris admitted sheepishly. "I don't know if Lacey and I will be able to stay in New York."

Jensen furrowed his brow, but otherwise, did not offer any consolations. It was another thing that Chris appreciated about him. People had a tendency to fill in the blanks, or smooth things over, when they heard bad news. Perhaps it was because he was a firefighter, and accustomed to dealing with people in the midst of tragedy, but Jensen always made it a point to listen first.

"I need to tell Lacey," Chris explained. "I tried last night. Took her for ice cream and everything, thinking that would smooth things over...but... Jesus, Jensen. How can I break this kid's heart again?"

"Kids are resilient, Chris."

"That's the problem." Chris pursed his lips. "They shouldn't have to be."

Jensen was just about to say something when his phone buzzed at the side. "Oh, snap," he said, looking down at it. "It's Katie. Let me just tell her..."

"No." Chris wouldn't hear of it. "Go deal with your very pregnant wife."

Jensen nodded. Taking the phone, he skirted off to speak to Katie privately.

Chris returned to his bench. Rubbing the sweat away with his towel, he pondered the state of his life. Maybe he could try to enjoy these last few weeks in New York City. Until he caught his reflection in the mirror. For a minute, he didn't recognize himself. He looked old. Tired. Without the makeup and studio lights, he could see how much grief had aged him.

He could see his loneliness, too. He closed his eyes, tried to breathe through the gurgling, choking spasms that were following him.

A commotion from the dayroom drew his attention. Chris looked over to see half of the firehouse, and even Gunther, huddled in a half circle around the dining table. They were gathered around a cell phone, laughing.

Lilliana attempted to catch her breath. "That list is epic."

"The thing is—" Gunther said to his crew, as if sharing some great wisdom "—she's saying what every woman is actually thinking. Someone who loves shopping and giving back rubs. That's exactly what my wife wants!"

Laughter exploded from the crew.

"Well, I'd date her," Amerpreet admitted. "She's super cute."

"And loaded," Reese added.

"Is there something wrong with wanting to be a house-husband?" Amerpreet sighed dreamily. "Get me some of that Oprah money!"

"Except for the fact that you don't have a chance in hell!" Don interjected.

More laughter spread across the room. Chris felt his mouth go dry as his heart began to race. It seemed impossible. Like something out of a dream, too good to be true. Was the crew of Engine 46 actually watching a clip from *Good News*? Nobody, including his friends and daughter, watched his show.

"Excuse me," Chris said, interrupting them. "What are you watching?"

"Your show, silly!" Lilliana smiled in his direction.

"Don't you recognize the sound of your own voice?" Amerpreet asked.

"Yeah, but..." Chris blinked. "*Why* are you watching it?"

The room exchanged confused glances. "What do you

mean why?" Gunther finally spoke the obvious. "It's freaking hilarious!"

Another round of thunderous hysterics echoed in Chris's ears. He must have been in shock. Either that, or the workout with Jensen had been harder than he thought and he was, indeed, dead. Just to be certain, he waved toward the phone. He needed to examine the evidence for himself.

"Can I see?" he asked.

"Sure," Lilliana said, handing it over.

Chris stared down at the three numbers below the video.

425,000 likes
116,000 shares
3,198 comments

It was impossible. A mistake. *A miracle.* It had more views, shares and likes than any segment on their show had ever managed. The woman had outperformed Bucky.

Right away, Chris knew what this was. He had sensed the same thing after watching her segment in his apartment. Dara Rabinowitz was born to be a star.

Chris didn't return to his apartment, take a shower or throw on clean clothes. He didn't grab the beige suit, pressed and cleaned, waiting by his front door. He simply bolted, sweaty and reeking, toward the door.

"Everything okay?" Jensen called out, just before Chris exited onto the street.

"Great!" he said, spinning around for one last shout-out to his best friend. "Better than great! I'm going to save *Good News*."

12

SOMEONE WAS POUNDING ON THE FRONT DOOR of her apartment. Dara groaned beneath her covers. Sitting up among a dozen throw pillows, she glanced at the clock on her nightstand. It was already ten o'clock on Friday morning. Dara had overslept.

"Coming," Dara called out groggily. "Just a minute."

Throwing on an oversized sweater, she raced down the steps. The knocking and buzzing grew louder. Nearly killing herself on the industrial steel staircase, she made her way downstairs.

She opened the door to find her older sister, Shana. Hands splayed out on both doorposts, her blond corkscrews pushed back and held out of her eyes with a patterned *teichel*, or scarf, her cheeks blushed red with frustration.

"The goddamn nanny quit again," Shana said, fully exasperated.

Dara glanced down to see all four of Shana's children—Ari, Tziporah, Ruben and Chayim—waiting behind their mother with eager and expectant faces. Pushing beneath the arms of their mother, they came racing through the front door, nearly toppling Dara over in the process. Her entire apartment was suddenly filled with loud shouts and uproarious giggles.

"Chayim!" Shana shouted, following them inside. "Get off the coffee table!"

Dara only had one sister. Although they were close in age, they couldn't have been more different. Whereas Dara was shy and introspective, Shana took after their grandmother. She was all chutzpah and force. The kind of woman who knew exactly what she believed, and where her life was heading.

Shana had married young, while still in graduate school. She had taken after her mother, becoming a psychologist, setting up a private family practice in New Jersey. After the birth of their third child, however, she had limited her hours, working part-time in order to focus on the children.

Before Shana could even lay her bags on the floor and get settled on Dara's couch with a cup of coffee, she was in full mom mode. Pointing in the children's direction, she exploded with a torrent of warnings and hypothetical threats. "Tzippy! Keep your brother off that staircase! Chayim! Stop putting things in your mouth! Ari, what did I tell you about touching your *pupic* in public! I swear to Hashem, if you four do not calm down, I will cancel Rosh Hashanah this year! No apples and honey! FOR ANYBODY!"

The threat did little to calm the tiny tornadoes down. The screaming continued. Dara raced to one of the drawers in her desk, pulling out colored pens and computer paper. "Hey!" Dara said, displaying the items. "Who wants to draw me a picture for Rosh Hashanah?"

The children turned from their positions of hanging off the staircase—and playing with the buttons on the stove—to jump up and down in excitement.

Quickly, Dara handed out the supplies. Crayons and markers. Paper and child-friendly scissors. Stickers. Lots and lots of stickers. Until finally, with the children fully occupied, Shana collapsed on the couch. Her eyes rolled from the steel staircase over to the quartz countertops in the kitchen.

"This place is a death trap," Shana said, partly to herself, mainly not.

Shana was a big sister in every sense of the word. As such, she felt wholly in her right to offer up any opinion, good or bad, deserved or not.

Still, she wasn't wrong. This apartment was not built for children. It was all hard edges and dangerous angles. Stylish, but also totally incompatible with the needs of children.

"I saw your segment on *Good News* yesterday," Shana said.

"Ugh, I know. It was a disaster."

"A disaster?" Shana squinted in disbelief. "Dara…it was ah-mazing!"

It was the beauty of having a sister. There was no person in the world who could hurt you more, annoy you more, say more hurtful and pointed things. And yet, when needed, they always came through for you.

"You and Bubbe," Shana continued, "you were totally great! I've never laughed so hard. I sent the video to at least ten of my friends."

"I'm glad you think it's funny."

Shana seemed genuinely surprised. "You can't really be that upset about this? What would Ema say? That you're catastrophizing, that you're blowing it all up in your head as something terrible and awful, something that will destroy your career, when it's not any of that. Besides, nobody even watches that stupid TV show."

"I watch it."

"Yeah, but you're…" Shana searched for the word. *"You."*

"Thanks?"

"I'm just saying." Shana shrugged. "You have a tendency

to catastrophize. It was a funny little segment on a television show that no one watches. Don't blow it up in your head more than that! Besides—" Shana crossed her arms against her chest "—one day, we'll probably be glad to have it to look back on."

Dara's heart sank at her words. Her big sister was right, of course. Years from now, when life had shifted in ways that were irrevocable, she would be grateful for these strange and happy moments captured together with her bubbe on camera.

"Anyway," Shana said, shaking off the thought, "I'm here for a reason. What are you doing for Shabbat tonight?"

"Oh." Dara looked around at her empty apartment. "I don't know. I was thinking of maybe keeping it quiet this week."

"I have a better idea," Shana said, leaning over and grabbing her sister's knees. "You remember Elissa Spitzman?"

"From Camp Ahava?"

Shana nodded, speaking quickly. "Well, she has a cousin, and he's new in town. We're going to their house for Shabbat, and she suggested I bring you. He just took a position as an attending physician at a hospital in Manhattan, and we think it would be an *ah-mazing* idea for you two to meet! He's a *doctor*, Dara…"

Dara played with a strand of her hair. "I don't know."

"What do you mean, you don't know?"

"I just don't want to be a burden on anybody."

Shana squinted. "Why would you be a burden?"

"I just—I have so much going on next week. J-eography has just launched in beta, and with the High Holidays starting, I really should just chill out here and focus on stuff at home. Plus, you know I don't like leaving Bubbe all alone on Shabbat."

"Oh my Gawd!" Shana groaned. "Seriously, Dara?"

"What?" Dara defended herself. "She has no one to visit her!"

"Give Bubbe the day off, okay?"

The energy in the room changed. All four kids looked up in the direction of their mother. Dara knew what was coming next.

"It's your anxiety, isn't it?"

"It's not—"

"No," Shana said, shaking her head. "It was one thing after Ema died, but this has been years now, okay? This *thing* of yours is starting to get ridiculous. You want to be single forever? You want to be lonely, surrounded by computer codes and voices that don't belong to you? When was the last time you even went on a date?"

"Excuse me," Dara defended herself. "I just did a Zoom conference with Tech-Bubble."

"A Zoom conference is not a date, Dara."

"Well, I—" Dara blinked, thinking back on it. She recalled the last time she went on a date. It was three years ago, and a total disaster. "I was just looking on J-Mate last night, as a matter of fact."

"Great!" Shana asked her directly, "Did you contact anybody?"

"I didn't see anyone that suited my needs."

"That's an excuse!" Shana huffed, unhappily. "For your entire life, all you've had are excuses! And don't tell me you like your life the way it is, because I know you. You were playing house longer than anybody. Besides…think about me! Think about your nieces and nephews! You think they want to see you being old and sad?"

"I don't think they see me as—"

"Tzippy," Shana snapped. "Don't you want to see your auntie Dara happily married? Don't you want to wear a pretty dress at her wedding, and have lots of cousins to play with? Wouldn't cousins be *soooo* much better to come visit than sad Auntie Dara in her death trap of a house?"

All four children rose to their feet and cheered. *"Sad Auntie Dara! Sad Auntie Dara!"*

"See?" Shana said, her point made. "Even the children are worried about you."

Dara slunk in her seat on the couch. It was not that her sister was trying to be cruel. It was simply that Shana had no filter when it came to dealing with her family. Shana loved Dara, after all. She wanted the best for her. Her words, and frustration, came from a place of concern.

"I want you to be happy, Dara."

"I know."

"If you want to be single for the rest of your life, fine. But it kills me inside to think that someone as remarkable as you, someone who deserves all the love and happiness in the world, and who *wants it*…is drowning in loneliness."

"I'm not drowning in—"

"And I know it's not as simple as pushing through it, okay? But you have medication! You have me and Bubbe. You have that stupid emergency scanner app on your phone—*STOP EATING THE PRINTER INK, CHAYIM!*—and all the money in the world to hire matchmakers and life coaches and doctors!"

"I know, okay?"

"But if you don't even try—if you can't figure out some way to get over this phobia you have and put yourself out there—then you are never going to get married. *Never, Dara.* You understand what I'm saying? This is real life! Mr. Perfect isn't just gonna float down from the Heavens and knock on your front door."

Suddenly, there was a knock on the door.

Shana and Dara snapped their heads in the direction of the threshold.

"Are you expecting someone?" Shana asked.

"No..."

Dara rose from her seat, heading to her front door. Peering through the peephole, she saw a warped image of a man, sweaty and wet, wearing a T-shirt and shorts. Seconds later, the man stepped back. The blond hair and gray eyes of a demigod came into focus.

"Oh my God." Dara spun back around, hands pressed against the metal door in shock. "It's Christopher Steadfast!"

"What?" Shana said, rising from the couch and making her way over to the door. She pressed her face against the peephole to confirm for herself. "What the hell is he doing here?"

"I don't know," Dara whispered.

"Well, are you going to open the door?"

"Nope."

"So..." Shana said, crossing her arms against her chest. "We're just gonna stand here and pretend nobody is home?"

Dara shrugged. "It's worked for me before."

"Seriously, Dara?"

"Hello?" Chris shouted through the door. "Dara? I was wondering if I could talk to you for a second."

Dara looked to her sister. With her eyes, she begged her not to open it. But Shana—like all big sisters everywhere—had other plans. Pushing Dara out of the way, she threw open the front door.

13

"OH." CHRIS STEPPED BACK. "I'M SORRY. I MUST HAVE
the wrong address. I'm looking for Dara Rabinowitz?"

The woman holding the door open was not Dara. Though
they looked similar. She had tight blond corkscrews, held back
with a scarf. She was wearing a skirt, leggings underneath,
paired with a stylish set of sneakers. Behind her, a small boy
in a knitted kippah and four waving tzitzit was doing zoomies
around the coffee table.

"This is her place," the woman said, nonchalantly, before
adding, "CHAYIM!" The little guy stopped running in circles. Almost as abruptly, the exasperated woman leaned against
the doorpost, running her eyes over the length of his body.

"I'm her older sister, Shana. Can I help you with something?"

There was something about the way Shana was guarding
the door with her whole body instead of inviting him in that
reminded him of interviewing hostile witnesses back in DC.

Chris sucked back any fear and reminded himself that he
was on a mission. Flashing a smile, trying to hide his outright
desperation, he worked to turn on the charm. "I'm Christo-

pher Steadfast," he said, pulling out the smooth intonation of a television anchorman. "I'm the head anchor of—"

"I know who you are," she said, interrupting him. "What do you want?"

Damn. The woman was not at all friendly to him. Chris dropped the charming reporter routine and got right down to the point. "I was wondering if Dara was home. I need to talk to her."

Shana rolled both eyes over his form. "One second."

She dipped back behind the door, leaving it open only an inch, one hand keeping it from closing. Chris could tell she was whispering to someone standing beside her, though he couldn't make out who from his vantage point. The muted voices of arguing grew in intensity before finally the woman guarding the door snapped. "Then put on a bra!" she said, before turning back to Chris. "Dara will be with you in one minute."

She shut the door, and Chris waited. And waited. Finally, after what felt like an eternity, the door swung back open. Dara emerged. Pulling the belt of an oversized sweater firmly around her waist, she stepped out into the hall, shutting the door behind her.

"What are you doing here?" Dara asked.

"I need to talk to you."

"How do you even know where I live?" Her eyes landed on the sweaty gym shorts and T-shirt he was still wearing. "And why do you look like you ran the entire way here?"

"Oh." Chris glanced down at his outfit. "I got your address from Eli. It was on the release forms you and your bubbe signed. And I didn't run here. Not exactly. I was at the gym. Look, I... I apologize for showing up unannounced, but I needed to talk to you about your segment on *Good News* yesterday."

"Oh, God." Dara turned bright red. "Of course!"

"Excuse me?"

"I realize that yesterday was an absolute disaster, but you didn't have to come all this way to tell me I ruined your show."

"No—"

"I get it, alright! Your point is made. I'm a disaster. *Dafka*, I should never go on television again."

"Dara!" He spoke over her, finally, getting her to stop. "You're not a disaster, okay? If anything, it's the opposite."

She blinked. "What?"

"Your segment was a raging success for *Good News*."

Chris scrambled to pull his phone out of his pocket. "Look," Chris said, stepping next to her to show her the video. His arm nearly brushed hers in the process. "Look at all those comments, likes and shares. You're a hit, Dara. You're more popular than Bucky!"

"Oh my God."

"Isn't it amazing?"

"No," she said, her cheeks fading to the color of printer paper. "No! It's not amazing!"

The reaction was not at all what he was expecting.

Most people loved being the center of attention. Indeed, he had interviewed dozens of influencers in his day. He knew how important a social media presence was to building a brand. With Dara launching her app's latest update, he would have thought she'd be thrilled by this news.

Instead, it was the opposite. All at once, she began pacing up and down the hallway, arms flailing about, her breath quickening with every step.

"Take it down."

"Why would you want it taken down?"

"I will sue you and everybody at *Good News* if you do not take that video down right now!"

Chris cocked his head at the threat, unsure of how to respond. For one, she couldn't sue them or make them take down the video. Dara and her grandmother had signed a release form. The content belonged to NBS-7, and NBS-7 could use the footage as they saw fit—in all media, worldwide and in perpetuity.

Most of all, he didn't understand why she was suddenly devolving into full-blown hysterics. The segment was cute. It was fun. There was nothing scandalous enough about her perfect Jewish husband list worth suing people over. People loved it, in fact. They loved her.

He didn't understand the freak-out. And then, Dara slumped against the wall. Chris watched, somewhat confused, as she sank down and pulled both her knees up to her chest. Closing her eyes, she breathed in and out, deeply.

"Are you okay?" he asked.

"I'm sorry," she said through exhales. "I'm just…having a panic attack."

"You have anxiety?"

"Generalized anxiety disorder," she said. "I've had it since I was a teenager. It gets hyped up around social media. Social anything, really. Just…give me a minute to get my cortisol levels under control. I know it's not rational."

It surprised him. She was so open about her diagnosis. Most people tried to hide their mental health challenges. Any challenges, really. He was immediately impressed at her ability to be vulnerable. He also was rather shocked that she had managed to build a successful business from scratch. It must have been terrifying, starting your own company, hiring employees, going on television to build your audience.

The journalist inside of him couldn't help but find her terribly curious. He also began to understand her a little better, too. Chris slid down beside her.

"That's why you wanted a script," he said quietly.

She nodded. "It's hard for me otherwise."

"Is that why you're single, too?"

Dara frowned. "You ask a lot of inappropriate questions, you know that?"

Chris smiled. "I do."

They remained like that in the hallway. Dara breathing deeply, attempting to calm down. Chris sitting beside her, waiting patiently.

He so desperately wanted to help her through it. He debated touching her—putting one hand on her knee, or taking her hand in a show of solidarity—but he didn't want to overstep any professional boundaries. He also wasn't sure how touch affected her anxiety.

He settled on a happy medium. He leaned his head against the wall beside her. Pressing his arm against hers, he let her know that he was there. He could feel the softness of the sweater she was wearing against his bare skin. The thick knots of expensive material bound up in threads. It was the material, not the woman, that made him feel warm.

Finally, after several minutes, Dara calmed down. Turning her head in his direction, she met his eyes directly. Chris took the moment as his chance.

"Dara," he said, getting to the point. "I have a proposition for you."

"What kind of proposition?"

"I want to do a series on you for *Good News*," he said, laying it all on the line. "I'd like to follow you around New York as you go on dates, searching for someone who ticks every box on your perfect Jewish husband list. I want to help you find your Mr. Perfect on Paper."

Dara could still recall the first time she went live with her beta version of J-Mate. She was sitting in her dorm room at college, another night spent alone while her suitemates were off at some party. She had run the algorithm for her site a dozen times. She had checked every link, button, upload and security certificate. But she sat there for days—weeks, actually—waiting to push the button that would make J–Mate available to the public.

There were so many things to be afraid of in that moment. Failure. The fear that all her hours of hard work, her dream of funneling her grandmother's algorithm into a modern-day matchmaking service, would all be for naught. Heck, there was even the very real possibility that someone would use her site for nefarious purposes. Or worse, that her security checks and codes would be out of sorts, and her members would get hacked. But none of that was what kept her awake at night.

The hardest thing for Dara—the greatest difficulty she faced in building J–Mate from scratch—was simply pushing the button.

She felt as if she was standing on a similar precipice with Chris.

"No," Dara said, rising from her spot. "Absolutely not."

Chris seemed ready for a fight. "Just hear me out, okay?"

"Are you out of your mind?" she shot back at him. "I don't have time for this!"

She began to rattle off excuses. She was busy launching J–eography. She was a strong and independent woman. She didn't need some man to complete her.

Chris came back just as hard. "We'll work around your schedule," he said, growing more adamant. "We'll make it work! Whatever you need…my people, your people…you can use it as a vehicle to promote J–Mate and J–eography. And think about how happy it will make your bubbe. She wants to see you matched more than anybody."

Just the mention of her grandmother caused Dara's heart to

feel like it was crumpling inside her chest. All at once, a wave of anticipatory grief flooded over her. Dara turned away from Chris. *Just breathe. Just push the button. Your bubbe is dying.* But every time the word *yes* bubbled up to the tip of her tongue, she found herself unable to speak it aloud.

"I'm a mess on camera!" she said.

"What?" Chris laughed off the suggestion. "You're not!"

"Stop it," she shot back at him. "Stop lying to me."

"I'm not lying."

"Yes, you are." She was getting annoyed now. She had been watching Chris Steadfast on television for years, never missing a single episode. "When you're not being completely honest, your left eyebrow twitches."

"Excuse me?"

Dara gasped, covering her mouth. Had she actually spoken the words aloud? All at once, her cheeks blushed red-hot with embarrassment. *Great.* Chris was totally going to think she was an obsessive *Good News* superfan. She had to downplay her obsession.

"I have occasionally watched your show," she admitted.

"You watch my show?"

"Occasionally," she repeated, with a strong rise of her chin. "And only for Bucky."

"Fine," Chris huffed. Throwing his hands up, he admitted the truth. "You're right. You're a total disaster on television."

"See!"

"But…" he interrupted her. She watched his eyebrow carefully. "It's not for the reasons you think, okay? Look, you came to our show with a script, right?"

"What's wrong with a script?"

"For one, it makes for god-awful television."

"I don't agree with that, at all."

"Dara," he said. "I get it now, okay? You have anxiety. It

135

helps your anxiety to micromanage every detail. I also understand that you have a business to run, and a certain image you want to maintain. I actually really respect that about you, and I imagine that for someone in your position, it's probably an occupational necessity to be a bit of a control freak."

"I prefer the term 'highly organized.'"

"But sometimes…" He pursed his lips. "Sometimes…people are actually better when they go off script."

"I don't understand."

"You know anything about race car driving?"

Dara deadpanned, "I go every Sunday."

"Right." Chris bit back a smile. "So the thing about race car drivers is they all skid, right? They're going around this track super fast, and at some point in their career, in one of those races, their car is going to spin out of control. Now, the instinct for most people when that starts to happen is to look at the wall. They look at the place that they're heading, with their hands on the wheel. They grip down hard and try to correct course. And do you know what happens if a race car driver looks at the wall while skidding?"

Dara shrugged.

"They crash."

"This is supposed to be a pep talk?"

"My point is, Dara—" Chris couldn't help but laugh a little "—if you look at the wall, if you look at the thing you fear while you're skidding, you'll crash. The right thing to do, even though it feels completely antithetical to every human instinct, is to look back at the track. You turn your head around in the vehicle, with your hands still gripping the wheel, and you focus on where you need to go. You focus on the goal. Not the thing you fear."

Dara crossed her arms against her chest. "Wow."

"What?" Chris said.

"Did you get all that from a meme or an inspirational poster?"

Chris bit back another smile. "I interviewed Tony Robbins once."

She rose from her spot, pointing toward the elevator. "You can go now."

"Dara!" He stood, too.

"No!" she stammered, shaking her head. "I can't do it, Chris. I appreciate you thinking that there is some bright and shining light tucked away inside me, but my answer is no."

"Please—"

"It's too much for me, okay?" she said. "Even if I wasn't mired in anxiety 24/7, even if I could somehow get over my all-encompassing fear of dating, I'm swamped. Between work, and my bubbe being sick, and the Jewish holidays, I barely have time to make my own coffee, let alone fall in love! Now, if you don't mind, I've given you my five minutes. I need to get back to work."

"They're canceling my show."

Dara felt her entire body go numb. "What?"

She could tell when he was lying. But she realized, in all her obsessive watching of *Good News*, she had never seen him look outright sad. Her heart broke for him. Then, alongside that feeling of sympathy came another wave of uncontrollable panic. What was she going to do without Christopher Steadfast?

He had been a centerpiece of her day for almost two years. He had been the person she turned to when she was riddled with anxiety, the voice she fell into when she needed to laugh. She adored the segments with Bucky. She loved that silly, quirky dog. *Good News* was her favorite show in the world, and it was going away.

"Are you still gonna be on TV?"

"I hope," he admitted, with a tiny shrug. "Though probably not in New York."

"But...what about Bucky?"

"I'm pretty sure Bucky will be fine without us. He's got one million followers on Instagram."

"He won't be fine, at all," Dara whispered.

"Look." Chris tried to sway her again. "All I'm saying is, give me a few weeks to profile you trying to find your perfect Jewish husband. If people love it and the ratings shoot up, then I was right. It's a win-win for both of us. You get to find your match. I get to keep *Good News*."

"And if you're wrong?"

"Then the show dies in obscurity, and you were single anyway."

The excuses sitting on the tip of her tongue shifted into silence. It was a stupid idea. The worst idea she had ever heard from anyone. And yet, she knew that her bubbe was right. Her tendency to avoid had moved to epic proportions. If she ever wanted to find her *bashert*, stand beneath the huppah with someone, she would have to go on a date.

"What if I mess it up?" she asked.

"You won't."

"I don't have much—" Dara stammered, then tried again. "I haven't really dated a lot."

"Perfect," he said, tackling her fears. "Because I'm gonna handle everything, okay? I'll vet the men. I'll plan the dates. I'll handle all the back-and-forth with your people. All you'll have to do is show up and be your fabulous self."

"Myself?"

"People are going to love you, Dara."

Her racing heart slowed. Dara closed her eyes and breathed through her anxiety. "If I do this—" she said, quietly, pushing through all those intrusive thoughts still racing through her head "—you will agree to feature J-Mate and J-eography on every date."

"Absolutely," he agreed. "Every single date."

"And you'll make sure—" she was searching for the words "—I won't be alone. You'll be with me...every step of the way?"

"I promise." Chris took both her hands inside his own. "I will be with you every step of the way."

A small wisp of air escaped her lips. She might have believed it was his words that comforted her. Or his eyes, gray like storm clouds. Alas, the truth was far more problematic. Christopher Steadfast was holding her hands.

The Fabergé egg was touching her.

Dara knew she should pull away. Everything about Chris was wrong. And yet, her heart slowed at the feeling of his hands wrapped around her own. She could not pull away. Glancing back toward her apartment, she considered her options. She wanted to say no, to give in to that pressing anxiety sitting on her chest, but what would happen after that?

If she turned away, she would lose this opportunity. She could lose Chris, too. Though it had been almost a decade since her mother had passed, she could hear her voice echoing in her ears. *Get up. Fight. Push that damn button.*

"Fine," Dara said, the word exploding from her lips. "Fine. I'll do it! Yes."

"Really?" Chris eased in one giant breath.

"Yes," Dara said, shaking her head, hating herself already. "Have your people call my people to set up something next week. I can see you're short on time, so we'll go over details before the start of the High Holidays. You better know what you're doing, Chris."

"I do." Chris beamed, nearly lifting out of his sneakers. "You'll see, Dara...this is going to be so great!"

It looked like he was going to hug her—or kiss her—but after a few false starts in which she did not return the outright excitement, Chris backed off. Dara took that as her opportunity to finally get rid of the man.

"Is there anything else you need from me?" she asked, all business.

"No." Chris smiled. "I'm so happy you agreed to do this."

"Wonderful." She clapped both hands together. Totally professional. "Then I will see you next week."

Chris bounced off to the elevator. Pushing the button, he was all cheer and excitement. The doors parted, and he disappeared from view.

Dara took a few quiet moments away from her opinionated older sister to compose herself. And then, like any good businesswoman, she settled on figuring out her next steps. She had to call Janet, and Naveah, and her glam squad—let them all know what was happening. She had to move things around on her schedule, too.

Not surprisingly, she was already regretting her decision.

14

CHRIS ARRIVED AT THE SWANKY RESTAURANT IN downtown Manhattan fifteen minutes before his pre-production meeting with Dara was set to begin. He had never eaten at the trendy, sprawling restaurant known as Wheat-Grass before, but with a highly specialized menu of organic ingredients flown in daily from exotic locations around the world, it was a hot spot among celebrities and moguls alike.

Pushing his way through throngs of people waiting for a table, Chris found the hostess, a woman standing behind the front counter dressed all in black and with a streak of pink running through her hair, tapping notes into a tablet.

"Reservation for two," Chris said.

Pinky barely glanced up from her tablet. "Name?"

"Christopher Steadfast," he said. "Though it may be booked under Eleanor Cohen."

The woman swiped around her device. Getting a dinner reservation, and last-minute at WheatGrass, had been nearly impossible. Thankfully Eleanor had been able to pull some strings and gotten them an early seating.

Perhaps the sprawling restaurant with built-in waterfalls

cascading down acrylic glass and an interior garden boasting over two hundred different species of flowers was overkill, but Chris had wanted to impress the young matchmaker. He also wanted to prove to himself that he was capable of handling her dates.

On television, Chris played a character. He was the charming Southern heartthrob, flirting with his audience, belting out country ballads between sets. He kept the camera—like the questions he posed—pointed at somebody else. He never talked about Claire. He never talked about Lacey, either. He especially never talked about his grief.

He considered the omission his right, a way to protect his young daughter, keep her out of the public eye, far from the constant reminder of the tragedy. Just like he had taken on a stage name—from Chris Steed to Christopher Steadfast— when he took the position at *Good News New York*. The pseudonym made it nearly impossible for viewers to google him and find out the truth about his life.

Otherwise, Chris didn't have a ton of experience with women. Claire had been his childhood sweetheart. They had met in middle school, playing by the swings, when he had heroically saved a handful of ladybugs from the shoe of a schoolyard bully. Aside from that one semester in college back in their early twenties, when they both agreed to spend a few months exploring other options, Claire had been his one and only.

They were married straight out of college.

After Claire died, the last thing Chris wanted to do was start all over again. It wasn't that he was afraid of falling in love. Or being hurt. He understood the value in having a partner, especially when it came to the practicalities of raising children. But his grief was so much deeper than his wants. He was like a watch missing some essential part. You could wear it, hear the sound of it ticking, but it was still broken.

The hostess found his name on her tablet. "Right this way," she chirped, leading him to an intimate-looking booth surrounded by violets.

"I'm sorry," Chris said, rubbing the back of his neck. "Do you have a different table?"

The hostess frowned. "I'm afraid not."

"Right," Chris said, glancing at the state of the restaurant. "Of course."

Chris took a seat, pushing a sprig of purple out of the way. Violets had been Claire's favorite flower. They had covered her coffin in them after she died. A sign of spring. A symbol of eternity.

Realizing the time—five o'clock on the dot—he texted Lacey.

> **Haven't heard from you, kiddo. Everything okay?**

Lacey texted him back a few seconds later.

> You are so annoying.

> **Sorry. Comes with being a parent. You want me to bring you back anything from WheatGrass?**

> What do they have?

Chris sent a link for the menu. It was then that he looked up. Dara was being led to his table by the hostess. She was impossible to miss. His fingers faltered on the buttons of his phone.

Unlike half the restaurant, dressed up in swaths of elegant black and pearl, Dara had gone with a casual look. She wore straight-leg blue jeans, Converse sneakers and Patagonia fleece over a long-sleeve white T-shirt. Her voluminous hair was tied back into a tight bun. She wasn't wearing makeup.

The reporter in him wondered if she did it on purpose. Dressed down, tried to make herself smaller and less visible, hoping not to be seen. The dichotomy only amplified his curiosity. There was a powerhouse of a woman behind that tiny fairylike frame.

Dara slunk down in the booth across from him. "Hey," she said.

Chris stammered on the word. "Hey."

She nodded toward his phone. "Am I interrupting something?"

"Oh," he said, putting it away. "No."

Dara removed her blue jacket. Beneath the formfitting white cotton underneath, he could make out the outline of her bra. A bolt of electricity shot through his body as he diverted his eyes toward two tiny hooks at the side of their table. "Can I..." He cleared his throat, cracking his jaw. "Can I hang that up for you?"

"Oh." She shrugged, handing it to him. "Sure."

Chris hung up her jacket and returned to his seat. Silence settled over the table. They were both sitting at the edge of the booth—as far as possible away from each other. Chris pretended he didn't notice.

"Did you have any trouble getting here?" he asked.

"No." She offered up a polite smile. "Super simple."

"For the actual shoots," he explained, "we'll send you a car service."

"I can afford my own car service."

"Right. Obviously."

"I just mean—" she looked toward the ceiling "—it's easier for me to arrange it through my staff. It's too confusing going through a third party. My people know me, and what I expect. I don't have to...worry as much."

She bounced—or shook, he wasn't entirely certain—in the seat across from him. Chris chewed on his lower lip. Why was this so hard with her?

"I didn't have time to prepare," she said suddenly.

"Oh." Chris sat up in his seat. "Well, that's okay. I'm doing all the legwork on this series, anyway."

"Normally, I would have talking points," she explained. "Things we need to discuss, things we need to go over, but I've been so busy with J-eography and prepping for the Jewish holidays... Did Janet send over that non-compete agreement?"

"I don't believe so."

"Well, it should be heading your way."

Another stretch of awkward quiet settled across their table. Dara was beginning to edge into full-blown vibrations. "I'm sorry," he said. "Do you want a glass of wine or something?"

"I don't drink."

He didn't mean to frown. "Well, do you mind if I get one?"

She waved him forward. Chris ordered a beer from a passing waitress. Moments later, he pulled out a small notebook and pen from his inner coat pocket and began jotting down some notes. Dara, curious, leaned over the table to see for herself.

"What are you writing?" she asked.

"I was just making a note that you don't drink," he explained. "When I'm vetting your potential suitors... I'll make it a point to get rid of any social drinkers or heavy drinkers."

"I'm sorry," Dara corrected herself. "I mean... I *do* drink. Just not during business meetings."

"Right." Chris put down his pen. "This is a business meeting."

Dara threw back her head and laughed aloud. "Of course it's

a business meeting. Just a casual business meeting! We're here to save your television show, and promote J-Mate, and find me a nice Jewish husband. Nothing more than that, right?"

Chris squinted. "Are you okay?"

"You know what," Dara said, finally, "I think I will get that glass of wine."

If Dara closed her eyes, she could almost envision them on a date. The charming way he blushed when asking questions. Those perfectly stormy gray eyes, his cute little worry lines that creased when he laughed in her direction. Oh, how she wanted to slide across the booth and move closer to him. She wanted to do a few other things, too. Instead, she brought her wineglass up to her lips with both hands.

The only thing that ruined the ridiculous fantasy she had swirling around in her mind was that he kept pulling out his phone to text somebody. Or rather—Dara grimaced at the realization—somebody named Lacey kept texting him.

She had seen the name come up several dozen times since sitting down. At first, the intrusion hadn't bothered her. Chris worked in television. She understood that he was always on call. But after the umpteenth time, her patience was faltering. She envisioned Lacey as some leggy blonde, the type of woman who could pull off black bodycon dresses when she wasn't wearing Vineyard Vines. Dara instantly regretted choosing the casual look that Naveah had laid out for her this evening.

Chris smiled at her from across the table. "You know what you're getting?"

"Oh." Dara put down her glass of wine. "Not yet."

"Well," Chris said, tapping out another message on his phone. "Take your time."

"Right."

She reminded herself that she was being ridiculous. What

did it matter that Chris has some fabulous and sexy girlfriend waiting for him at home? Even though he had never mentioned it on television. Even though it bothered her to think that he had been lying to his audience—*to her*—all these years.

She shook the thought away. She was being unfair, after all. Just because Chris was in the public eye didn't mean that Dara deserved access to every detail of his personal life. Besides… it was excellent news that he was taken. Chris was in a happy relationship with a demanding harpy. Lacey was yet another fence around all those feelings she was trying to suppress.

Dara breathed a sigh of relief and pulled her menu closer. Her only concern right now was deciding on what to eat.

She scanned the menu. Her options were limited. Glancing back up at Christopher—still on his phone—she realized, once again, how different the worlds they came from were. Chris had found the fanciest and most exclusive restaurant in all of Manhattan, but he hadn't scanned the menu to see if there were kosher options.

The fish came from places she had never heard of. She sighed, trying to figure out which one would come with scales, breathed through its gills, but had no hard outer shell.

Meats were easier, of course. You knew what a giant hock of ham was before you ordered it. But even then, and in places as stylish as WheatGrass, they put meat in everything. Sauces. Soups. She had once even discovered bacon in her salad dressing.

Dara called their waitress over. "Excuse me, I'm a vegetarian. Do you know which items on this menu don't have meat in them?"

The waitress scurried off to check with the chef. Chris looked up from his phone and frowned. "I'm sorry," he said. "I didn't realize you were a vegetarian."

"I'm not. I'm kosher," she explained. "Well, I mean…not

completely kosher. I do hot dairy out. That means I'll eat kosher foods cooked in non-kosher restaurants. I keep a kosher home, though. Every item...with a *hechsher*."

Chris put down his phone. "Why don't you just say you're kosher?"

"Another simple question without a simple answer."

She rattled off the reasons in her head. Most of the world was not Jewish. People didn't know that the laws of kashrut extended beyond things like shrimp and pork. The wine Dara was drinking, for instance, was certainly not *halachically* kosher. Though it fell under her own personal guidelines of consuming hot dairy outside of her home.

But beyond a simple misunderstanding—clam broth in your soup, a seasoning packet derived from animal by-products—there was also this fact. Not everybody liked the Jews. To publicize your identity to a complete stranger always carried a risk.

"You could try me," Chris prodded her. "I'm actually an excellent listener."

She smiled. "Maybe another time."

"Okay," he said, jotting down another note. "So we're only meeting men who keep kosher..."

"Not necessarily."

"I'm confused."

"Two Jews can be a mixed marriage, too."

"I'm sorry." Chris put his pen down again. "What?"

"Small pool," she laughed. "Sometimes you have to compromise."

It was another one of those peculiarities of observant Jewish life that felt impossible to explain to an outsider.

"There isn't one way to be Jewish," she said, finally. "Some people are very observant. Some people aren't. Some people fall in the middle of the spectrum, or have different philosophies behind the reasons for their observance. Some people don't do anything. When two Jews marry, they have to ne-gotiate these religious choices. For example, will they keep a kosher home? Will they observe Shabbat? Will you cover your hair, or go to *mikvah*? Those are some of the big ones…"

Chris nodded. "And what are the little ones?"

"Oh gosh," she said, "so many. *Kitniyot* on Passover, are you going to go to a synagogue with a *mechitzah*, are you going to boil an egg when a Yom Tov day falls before Shabbat. It can get very complicated."

"Right."

"Really," Dara said, trying to keep it simple, "just find me someone who's committed to their Judaism."

Chris settled the matter with a shrug of his shoulders. "Committed…to… Judaism," he scribbled on his notepad, before looking back up at her. "Can I ask you a question about that, then? I don't know if it would be considered offensive…"

"That's probably never a good way to start a question, Chris."

"You're probably right. I guess, what I'm wondering is… considering that two Jews can be a mixed marriage, and you can have *all* these issues with someone of the same faith, what's the big deal with Jews marrying other Jews? Why is it so im-portant? I mean…aren't we in the modern age? People marry people of other faiths, other cultures, other ethnicities, all the time. Doesn't love conquer all, and all that?"

Dara laughed aloud. "Yeah, no." Then, realizing that it was a serious question, attempted to explain. "I can't speak for all Jews. I can only speak for myself. So let's start with the basics. First off…there's Jewish law."

"Jewish law?"

"Halacha," she said. "And according to Jewish law, Jewish marriage can only happen between two Jews. Of course, a Jew and a non-Jew can get married, but they can't *legally* perform the act of *kiddushin*…which is when the man acquires a woman, sets her aside, designates her as separate through the act of marriage."

"A man *acquires* a woman?"

"Obviously, it's a little more complicated than that, and there are variances between movements and denominations— who can be acquired, who is considered a Jew—but the starting point is almost always Jewish law."

"Okay," Chris said, musing on it. "I think that makes sense."

"Then we have all the historical implications." She quoted a line from the Passover Seder. "'In almost every generation, one has risen up to destroy us.' Pharaoh in Egypt. Inquisitions in Spain. Pogroms in Eastern Europe. Six million Jews were murdered during the Holocaust. For many in the Jewish community, intermarriage is a threat to the very existence of the Jewish people."

Chris chewed on his lower lip. "That seems like an awful lot of pressure on one person."

Dara nodded. "It's still a taboo, you know? People don't want to say that aloud—modern age, and all—but in the world I come from, it can still be very hard for intermarried couples and their children."

"But what about you, Dara?"

"Me?"

"I understand what you're talking about on a large-scale level, but what about *you*? If you found someone you loved, and they weren't Jewish, you really wouldn't pursue a relationship with them?"

"No."

"Not even if you knew, in your heart and soul, that they were the right person for you?"

She sighed, trying to explain the nuances of her life and

culture. "Look," she said, leaning across the table, "let's consider the facts of my life."

"Okay."

"First and foremost, there's my career. I have built my life and my brand around Jewish marriage. I'm basically a Jewish professional. How would it look if the person responsible for over ten thousand J-Mate matches suddenly found herself in a relationship with a non-Jew?"

"People might understand," he pressed her.

"What people?" she said, laughing aloud at the thought. "Even if my company didn't take a hit, there's my family. My sister, Shana. My beloved bubbe. We have been Jewish for six thousand years. My ancestors boarded boats to come to this country to escape the pogroms and the Holocaust, for a better life for their future children...so that I could betray them all by putting a Christmas tree up in my living room?"

"Does it have to be so black-and-white?"

"Yes."

"But love—"

"Doesn't conquer all," she said simply. "It doesn't, Chris. Look at the divorce rates in America. Look at the divorce rates throughout the world. Do you know what every single one of those couples had when they got married? *Love*. They all stood in front of an altar and gazed into each other's eyes, and that's the problem with these modern notions of love. There's too much staring into each other's eyes, and not enough looking in the same direction."

"So you're not a romantic?"

"Of course not," she said. "I'm a matchmaker."

Chris laughed. Alas, Dara was being completely serious. Jewish notions of love were different than non-Jewish notions. Love was an ideal, certainly, but it was only one aspect in a cluster of ideals that were seen as desirable within the boundaries of halachic marriage. Romance did not play an exclusive or even primary role in the matchmaking process.

She could point to statistics, show how marriages between people of the same faith—or even arranged marriages—lasted longer. She could also go on and on about the historical notions of love, that before the nineteenth century it was, in fact, almost unheard of to marry for love. Marriage was strictly for the purpose of political unions, tribal safety and rearing of children. Indeed, marrying for love was considered an antisocial phenomenon.

All of which only solidified the belief held deep within herself. True love came over time. It came with raising children, fretting over bills, holding someone's hand during cancer treatments. But you didn't need to be head over heels in love to have a successful marriage. Nor did you have to be passionately in love with someone to marry them.

"What you're talking about—" Chris said seriously "—it sounds like settling."

"You call it settling." She shrugged. "I call it compromise."

He put his pen down. "You would really marry someone you didn't love?"

"I would expect to enjoy his company, obviously."

Chris grimaced. "That's kind of sad."

"I don't think so," she said, somewhat annoyed.

"Well, what about passion?" he asked. "What about chemistry…that indescribable feeling you get when you're kissing someone who makes your entire body sizzle?" He leaned over to whisper. "What about sex?"

"Actually," Dara was happy to explain, "Judaism places a high value on the sexual satisfaction of the woman in the marriage. In fact, she's always supposed to…you know…first."

"Really?"

"Hmm," she said, finishing her wine. "It's good to be Jewish."

Chris laughed and went to scribble down this fact.

There were all sorts of rules regarding sexuality in marriage in Judaism. Most of them were quite open-minded. Indeed, the rabbis of yore actually held a belief that women were more sexual than men. For this reason, the sexual satisfaction of a woman in marriage was both obligated, and protected, under Jewish law.

Dara tapped on her empty glass, the wine clearly beginning to go to her head. Chris wasn't Jewish, but all this talk about lovemaking caused her mind to wander.

She thought back to the day when he had come to her apartment. The way his biceps flexed beneath his cotton T-shirt. The way the sweat glistened on the back of his neck. The man was ripe with unbridled sexual magnetism. Her body shivered at the thought. Perhaps, in another lifetime, in another dimension, they could have had some extraordinary night together. In this lifetime, however, it was never going to happen.

Instead, she considered who would be his perfect match. She thought back to her two years of watching the show.

Obviously, someone Christian. Maybe a blonde. Given his Southern background, he would need a girl with traditional values. The type of woman who dreamed of being a mom, who wore flowered dresses to church on Sunday and who knew how to bake a ham for Christmas. Bonus points if she did things like ride a horse, loved football and knew how to line dance.

Basically, the complete antithesis of her.

Dara didn't know how to line dance. While she had ridden several camels in her lifetime and more than one donkey, she had never been on a horse. She hated football.

Despite her clear attraction to him, a marriage between them would never work out.

"Besides—" Dara emphasized this point "—you're forgetting the most important thing."

"Which is?"

"I love being Jewish. I don't want a Christmas tree in my apartment any more than you probably want to spend fifteen hours in synagogue on Yom Kippur. I'm committed to my faith and my culture, and I want someone who shares that love of Judaism with me. Would a non-Jewish person really share my same level of commitment? Would he care about Judaism just as much as I do?"

Chris swallowed hard. "I don't know."

She shrugged. "It's easier to just marry Jewish."

The waitress returned with a list of suggestions from the chef. Dara settled on a salmon Caesar salad. It was the most boring option on the menu, but it was safe. There was no chance of her slipping up and falling out of line with her carefully held belief systems. Safe choices protected her. They meant no danger to her heart, either.

Over the next forty-five minutes, Chris learned as much as possible about the young matchmaker. He learned that Dara grew up in Hoboken, and had no plans to relocate anytime soon. He learned that her mother had passed away a decade ago, and that her father had retired in Israel. He learned that despite her traditional upbringing, her family was modern and egalitarian. Dara's mother had retained her maiden name, Rabinowitz, for professional purposes. When Dara began J-Mate, she continued this tradition, ensuring that the Rabinowitz family line of matchmakers would always remain unbroken.

He learned that Dara had a big sister, Shana, who was married with four children, and lived in New Jersey. He learned that she was kosher—hot dairy and all that—and that she didn't believe in traditional notions of romantic love.

He scribbled all these facts into his notepad. *Hot dairy. Kosher. Woman orgasms first.* Until finally he wrote one word in big block letters beneath all the rest:

JEWISH

He underlined that word three times.

After which, and over dinner, he focused on logistics. Dara ordered another glass of wine as he explained the process by which he would be vetting potential suitors. They would utilize both J-Mate and J-eography, as well as suggestions from the at-home viewing audience, to narrow down her pool of potential bachelors.

He explained how events would be covered, the use of cameras and angles, all the basics she would need to know about being on live television. He gave her advice, too. To be herself, to be okay with messing up and making mistakes. He warned her, sixteen different times, not to read reviews or look at comments online. Until finally, over a chocolate lava cake, which they shared, he promised her once again that he would be there with her every step of the way. He would not let her fail.

"Otherwise," Chris said, putting down his fork, "the only thing we really need to figure out is schedule."

Dara opened her calendar app. "Well, what does your show schedule look like?"

Chris leaned back in his seat. "I'm eager to get you on as soon as possible."

Dara nodded. He was grateful she already knew about the upcoming cancellation. He was grateful she was going out of her way to help him, too. Unfortunately, and perhaps not surprisingly given her position running a multimillion-dollar company, her schedule was jam-packed. It seemed she spent all day in meetings. The only time she was really available to film was on Sundays or at night.

"Another problem," Dara said, swiping through her phone. "We'd have to work around the Jewish holidays. Rosh Hashanah. Yom Kippur. Sukkot. Simchat Torah. I mean, I don't know when we're going to fit your show in..."

Chris nodded. They could always film the segment as a "look live," filming her dates the evening before—in one shot—then edit it into a live show the next day. It would give the feeling of her dates being live, keep the tension there for the at-home viewing audience, while still working within her busy schedule.

The problem was, of course, the Jewish holidays. Dara was religious. She was going to observe them all, in some form or fashion. And, as it turned out, the month of September had a lot of Jewish holidays. Chris felt his heart sink. To think, he was sitting on a television gold mine, and she was going to be stuck in shul.

It gave Chris an idea.

"Wait a second," he said, nearly exploding with excitement at the thought. "Aren't there singles events that happen around the Jewish calendar?"

"What do you mean?"

"Like Yom Kippur Break Fast or apple-picking for Rosh Hashanah?"

Dara scoffed. "How...how do you know that?"

"Why wouldn't I know that?"

"You're not Jewish."

"I'm not a mole person, either."

"Yeah, but…" She glanced nervously around the room, like she was revealing some dark secret. "You're from the South."

He laughed a little, delighted to prove her wrong. "I play up the Southern thing for television, but if you want to know the truth… I'm from *Northern* Virginia, which is basically a suburb of Washington, DC, and actually quite diverse. I went to more Bar Mitzvahs than baseball games growing up."

"Really?"

"Really. Actually, one of my best friends was Jewish growing up."

It took Dara a minute, but she laughed. "You are full of surprises."

Chris nodded, warmth rushing to his cheeks. He liked seeing her smile. She was so lovely when she relaxed. There were times throughout the night that their interactions felt more like a date than a business meeting. In truth, hanging out with Dara just felt…right. Perhaps she felt it, too, because even after Chris paid the bill, neither of them moved to leave.

"So, that's basically it, then?" Dara said, tapping her fingers on the table.

"That's basically it," he said, scanning his notes one last time. "We'll base the segments around the Jewish holidays, and we'll go until they cancel *Good News*…or we find your perfect Jewish husband. Either way, all you need to do from this point on is show up."

"It sounds so simple."

"It will be," he said, trying to squash any lasting fears.

Finally, Dara rose from the table. Chris rose along with her, reaching for her jacket from one of the hooks at the side and placing it on her shoulders. She glanced back to thank him. She was so close to him now, he could see the edges of her collar bones when he looked down. An image appeared in his mind at the sight. He wanted to run his fingers along the blades, kiss her neck gently. The scent of her, that long hair just begging to be released from its tightly wound bun, caused his body to react.

He cleared his throat and stepped back. "So I'll have my people contact your people with details for our first shoot around Rosh Hashanah?"

"Sounds perfect."

"I'm really looking forward to it, Dara."

"You know what's weird?" she said, beaming back in his direction. "I am, too."

Rosh Hashanah

15

OUTSIDE THE FRONT ENTRANCE TO WILLOW CREST
Farms, Chris waited patiently on the wraparound porch of a
large white farmhouse. Apple orchards and honeybee farms
stretched as far as the eye could see. Beyond the horizon, in
a clearing of land, lay three red-and-yellow tents and an old
farmhouse barn. It was the perfect location for Dara's first date
on Rosh Hashanah.

"How's it going?" Eleanor said, appearing behind him.

"Good," Chris said, staring at the front entrance where a
long road wound its way toward the main driveway. Dara's
limo would be arriving any minute. "Just waiting for Dara to
get here. My understanding is they hit some traffic. Has her
date arrived yet?"

"Situated in hair and makeup," Eleanor confirmed.

"Perfect." Chris nodded. "Make sure she doesn't see him
until filming. I want her first reaction to be genuine."

Chris had worked harder on that first date than he had on
his own wedding. He contacted six different synagogues and
spoke with four different rabbis. He sent Eli, along with Naveah, all across the tristate area to do location scouting. He

ate raisin challah dipped in honey and apple cake and some sort of cinnamon-date noodle dish called a kugel, gaining four pounds in less than a week. He even taught himself how to seed a pomegranate.

When the location for the first Rosh Hashanah date was settled, he focused on finding Dara's Mr. Perfect. It turned out to be a time-consuming task. Since Dara had gone viral, his email at *Good News* had blown up with interested suitors from all over America and the world.

He got emails from men, and women, professing their outright love for her. He was accosted by three different Jewish mothers, and one very determined *zeyde*, or grandfather, on the subway. He also got sent more junk mail than he ever cared to see.

But aside from the nightmares of shaft-shaped challahs dripping with honey, the task was simple enough. Chris searched for men who checked as many boxes as possible on Dara's perfect Jewish husband list. When he found those men, he funneled them into three bins for casting marked *Yes*, *No* and *Call the Police*.

"You really think this is going to work, Chris?" Eleanor asked.

Chris furrowed his brow. "I hope so."

Perhaps it was overkill, spending all his free time narrowing down locations and suitors, but he wanted things to work out for both of them.

Eleanor clapped him on the back and excused herself to go deal with Bucky. Chris saw a black limousine rumbling down the main driveway. Bouncing down the steps, he readied a smile. He knew that his star talent for the day would be nervous. He wanted to be the first person to greet her.

The car rolled to a stop in front of him. Dara stepped out of the black stretch limo, blinking away the early afternoon sun. His smile faded. His mouth went dry. He swallowed a lump at the back of his throat, unable to take his eyes off her.

Dara looked incredible.

She was wearing a dark red dress, cinched at the waist, with little ruffles around the neck and below the knee line. The fabric shimmered against the light and highlighted every curve on her frame. Her onyx curls swirled in an updo of the most epic design at the top of her head. A large silver, gold and black bumblebee barrette held the thick cascade together.

The word escaped his lips before he could bite it back. "Wow."

Dara blushed. Chris blushed, too. All at once, he felt like a tool. Shaking his stupidity off, he mumbled out an apology. It was also totally inappropriate to find your lead story irresistibly attractive. He forced himself to behave like a professional.

"I mean," he regrouped, "you look beautiful."

Dara smiled. "Thank you."

In the distance, Chris could hear leaves rustling. Bucky barking. The production crew hustling. But none of that mattered. Chris was stung.

"I like your bow tie," Dara said, pointing to his neck.

"Oh!" Chris said, looking down. He had forgotten he was wearing a blue bow tie with little red apples on it. "Yeah." Chris blushed again, not meaning to flirt with her so obviously. "I stole it from Bucky."

Dara laughed. "Bucky is here?"

"Of course." Chris leaned in to her. "I know how much you love him. And I thought…well, I thought he may help with your anxiety."

She touched her heart. "He will definitely help with my anxiety."

"Good. Because I want you to have an amazing time today."

He gave her a grand tour of the premises. He started with

the house, explaining how Willow Crest Farms had been in operation as an apple orchard since 1786. He introduced her to Rabbi Adam Evans, shooting some talking-head shots in the lobby with Eli. He walked her through the main house, pointing out the apple cider distillery and the attached farmers market.

"They have over three hundred honeybee hives located on the property," Chris explained. "Any item produced with honey in the market—from candles, to soaps, to the organic and raw honey you'll be eating today on your date—comes from this farm. I couldn't think of a better place for Rosh Hashanah."

"It's perfect."

Finally, Chris led Dara to a golf cart waiting outside the main house. After helping her take a seat in the passenger side, he drove her over to the main tent in the center of the orchards, where they would be filming their segment.

"The good news," Chris said, attempting to alleviate her anxiety, "is that this will be the only live shoot for a while. Since we were short on time, I wanted to make sure we got something for Rosh Hashanah on the schedule. Of course, I appreciate you being so amenable to changes in your own personal schedule."

"Of course," Dara said, like a tried-and-true professional. "After all, this little experiment is designed to benefit both of us."

"Exactly."

The cart rumbled over the muddy pathways, past the honey farm and through the apple orchards, toward the main tent and old barn where they would be filming.

"Speaking of which," she said, twisting in her seat. "You still haven't told me exactly what I'll be doing today."

"It's a surprise," he said.

"You know I hate surprises, right?"

"Dara," he said gently. "It's important that things feel natural. You're the best when you're natural. I saw it that day during our in-studio shoot with *Good News*. Just trust me, okay? I won't let anything bad happen to you."

"Trust is not my strong suit," she grumbled.

Chris smiled, whimsical and relaxed, in her direction. "You're kind of controlling, you know that?"

"I am not controlling."

"Give up control, Dara Rabinowitz!" he said, and then stepped on the gas.

"What!" she shouted back, grabbing the dashboard for dear life. "What are you doing?"

"Taking you to the main tent," he explained calmly.

"You're driving like a madman!"

"Dara," Chris said, biting back a smile. "I'm not even going ten miles an hour."

"No, you're—"

Chris pointed to the speedometer on the dash of the vehicle so she could confirm this herself. They were, indeed, going about eight miles per hour.

Dara smirked, annoyed. "Shut up."

He laughed and continued forward.

They came to a red-and-yellow tent. Chris parked the cart and jumped out, offering his hand. The ground was not solid, after all. The last thing he wanted was for her to trip. She took hold of him, gratefully.

"Thank you," she said, glancing behind her to survey the scene.

The area where Dara would be filming her segment this afternoon was set up in the middle of an apple orchard, and decorated thematically for Rosh Hashanah, which celebrated the start of the Jewish New Year.

Red apples rested on haystacks and two wooden barrels. Mason jars full of honey, and two round challahs, sat near a long shofar, or ram's horn, blown during the Jewish New Year. Above the decor, strung across a rustic-looking stage, was a burlap sign that read *Shana Tova*. Just beneath, in small bowls, sat jars of honey.

It was all the best of the Jewish New Year.

The apples dipped in honey celebrated the desire for a sweet New Year. The round challahs commemorated life and creation, the birth of the world and new beginnings. The ram's horn, blown one hundred times over the course of Rosh Hashanah and Yom Kippur, was meant to serve as a spiritual wake-up call. Chris had learned about all of it in his studies.

Dara seemed genuinely moved. "It's beautiful, Chris."

He was pleased at her review.

Chris helped her inside the main tent. A makeup table and vanity had been laid out by Sheila.

As promised, Bucky was there, waiting with his handler. Dara immediately responded to the sight by squealing aloud, dropping to her knees and rubbing behind his floppy ears. Chris reached for a plate of apple slices.

"Here," he said, holding them out to Dara. "Bucky is apparently a Honeycrisp fan."

"Of course he is," Dara said, grabbing a slice and feeding it to him.

He watched her for a few moments. She was so happy with Bucky. So relaxed. All the fear and anxiety seemed to dissipate at the sight of his happy pink tongue.

"I figured we'd start off with just some talking-head stuff," Chris explained. "Well, get you warmed up with that, a quick interview of sorts, and then proceed to meeting your date."

"My date?"

It was then that Chris noticed that her hands were shaking.

Chris nodded at Bucky's handler. "Would you mind giving us a minute?" He waited for Bucky and his owner to depart before continuing.

"I'm sorry," she said, rising to her feet. "It's my anxiety."

"Well, that makes sense."

"No." She huffed the word. "It doesn't make sense. It doesn't make sense at all. Look at this beautiful location! Look at everything you've done for me! And still, I'm completely freaking out." She sighed, forlorn. "I hate that I can't just enjoy myself like a normal person."

"You know," Chris said, pursing his lips, speaking honestly, "when I first started doing live television, I used to get really nervous."

"Right."

"It's true," he said, meeting her disbelief directly. "I almost quit broadcast journalism, in fact…thinking I was better suited to something out of the limelight. I flubbed almost every segment my first week on the job, sweated bullets on live television. Someone even wrote in suggesting I get my glands checked."

"No way."

"Hand to heart," he said, laying his palm on his chest. "I used to hate doing live television. I was a total disaster. You know what helped me?"

She groaned. "Not another race car metaphor."

"This advice is more practical," he promised, then nodded toward the flap of the front tent. The production team was now fully set up and waiting for them to appear. "When you get in front of that camera, think about one person who makes you happy."

"Someone who makes me happy?"

"Yeah," he explained. "Someone who supports you and cares about you, someone who always makes you feel good every time they come near. Don't think about talking to the whole world, or the viewers at home, or even the crew. Because you're not talking to any of them. You're simply talking to one person…"

Dara was quiet for a long time. "Can it be a dog?"

Chris burst out laughing. Attempting to catch his breath, he ran one hand over his entire face. When he looked up, Dara was smiling, too, angling her body in his direction. Her cheeks matched the red of her dress. Another moment of silence settled between them. Even though he had a zillion other things to check on before they started filming, Chris found himself hesitating. He didn't want to leave her.

"So what happens now?" Dara asked, quietly.

"Now," Chris said, getting a grip on his emotions, "you wait here." He gestured toward the makeup chair. "Relax. Hang out with Bucky. Eat some apples. Sheila, our makeup artist, will be here in a bit to do one final touch-up on you, and then Eli will grab you when it's time to start your date."

Dara forced a smile. "Great."

"Dara," he said, and took both her hands inside his own. "You got this, okay?"

16

SHE DIDN'T WANT HIM TO LEAVE. STANDING INSIDE
that tent with Chris, feeling the heat of his hands wrapped
around her own, Dara was struck with the most tremendous
feeling. She was floating, aware of every sensation. His hands
were so large—she took notice of every callus and scar—and
yet, he held on to her so gently.

Her racing heart slowed in realization. The nervousness in
her belly dissipated with his touch. Chris had an incredible
ability to calm down her anxiety.

"Hey, Chris!" Eleanor said, interrupting their hand-holding.
"We need you for a—"

Eleanor stopped at the sight of them holding hands. Quickly,
Dara and Chris separated. An awkward moment of silence
stretched between the three of them before Eleanor continued. "We need you for sound check."

"Right," Chris said, forcing a smile in her direction. "Be
there in a second."

Eleanor departed.

Dara chewed on her lower lip. The intensity of the moment—that heat in her body—was quickly replaced by a deep

sense of shame. Though their hand-holding had been totally innocent, she couldn't help but feel like she had just been caught red-handed in some crime.

"I should probably go…" Chris said.

"Of course," Dara squeaked out.

He nodded, disappearing from view.

Dara was relieved. Sighing heavily, she closed her eyes, breathing through her confusion. She hated that she was attracted to Christopher Steadfast, that he said all the right things and made her feel so damn extraordinary. It added layers of confusion and stress to what was already an incredibly anxious morning.

Taking a seat at the makeup vanity, she waited for Sheila to appear. It seemed to take forever. Her mind began to wander. She glanced down at her silver high heels and worried about tripping. She analyzed her face in the mirror in front of her, and then became certain—110 percent positive, in fact—that there was a little green booger sitting just inside her nose that she could not, for the life of her, blow or pick out.

When she wasn't focused on her nose, she was focused on her stomach. Her guts rumbled, and she peed more times in an hour—braving the hell that was a porta potty nearby— than was humanly necessary.

All of these concerns were just her anxious mind, running through every worst-case scenario. Her fight-or-flight response, inappropriately attuned to see danger where there was none, causing a physical reaction inside her body.

Finally, Sheila appeared.

"I am so sorry about that!" Sheila said. The woman was a mess of rambling words and too much hair spray. "I had to set up six different stations this morning, and then your date was getting all weird about makeup. I tried explaining to him that this was television makeup, and not regular makeup. I said, 'Hon, I'm not gonna make you look like some—'" Sheila began opening up makeup palettes and removing brushes before turning to Dara. All at once, her rambling stopped. "Oh my," Sheila said, placing both hands on her hips. "You look lovely!"

"The credit really goes to my styling team."

"This hair is incredible!" Sheila leaned forward to inspect the design. "How did they get it so poofy?"

"Poofy?"

"Yeah," she said. "It's like a peach. A big, round, juicy peach...with a bumblebee landing right in the middle!"

"Thanks?"

"Anyway," Sheila said, continuing talking, "since you're already dolled up, I'll just do the basics—some translucent powder to keep you from looking shiny on film, a reapplication of lipstick..."

Sheila went to work, attacking her with a brush full of powder, rambling on about the latest gossip revolving around some actress in Hollywood. Dara was grateful for the noise. She knew that with the final application of makeup, she would soon have to go on-air.

"She almost ready?" Eli said, appearing at the door.

"Yep," Sheila said, putting her brush down and stepping back. "She's all done."

Dara made her way to the filming area. Chris was already waiting for her. She couldn't help but fold up into his smile. For a moment, she forgot that there would soon be hundreds of thousands of people watching her.

"Remember what I told you," Chris whispered, nodding toward the camera. "Just talk to that one person who makes you happy."

Dara nodded. The camera light went on. Chris began his spiel. He talked about Rosh Hashanah, and why it was important to Jews. He talked about Dara and her search for the perfect Jewish husband, and how thousands of people had contacted *Good News*. Dara barely heard a word the man spoke. All she could see beyond the lens of that camera was the light blinking red. The knowledge that she was on-air, the sense of something sitting in her nose, her stomach turning. She considered the very real possibility that she was going to throw up on national television, embarrassing herself for all eternity.

"So, Dara," Chris said suddenly, beginning their informal interview. "How did you feel after your grandmother outed your list for the perfect Jewish husband on national television?"

Dara stammered. Her mouth went dry. All her good intentions flew right out the apple orchard. She found herself unable to move, unable to speak. Chris waited. The production staff shifted on their feet. Dead air filled the space. Chris attempted to save the situation by answering the question for her.

"You must have been really mad at her, huh?"

"What?"

"Your grandmother," he said, still smiling. "Clearly you were never expecting your own personal matchmaking list to go public."

Dara took a deep breath. She knew that she needed to say something. She just didn't know how. Finally, she considered the advice of the man standing beside her. *Just focus on someone who makes you happy.*

She ran through her mental database to find that person. There was her bubbe. Her sister, Shana. Her nieces and nephews. Bucky. God, how she loved Bucky. Her eyes landed back on Chris. Chris, standing beside her, that infectious smile warming her entire body. Chris, and his voice, the deep lulling melody in his intonation. Chris, holding her hands, promising that she would never have to walk through this dating nightmare alone.

Dara found her person.

She forgot about the camera. She forgot about the people watching at home, and even her suitor hiding offstage. She turned toward Chris, speaking to him directly.

"At first I was upset," Dara said, finding her voice. "I work very hard to be seen as professional, and I feel a certain responsibility toward the Jewish community as the most well-known face of J-Mate. But then, I realized that she just wants the best for me. She just wants to see me settled before…"

Her voice trailed off.

Chris took her hesitation as a cue. "Before what?" he asked.

Dara touched a spot at her heart. "My bubbe is sick."

It seemed the leaves stopped rustling to hear her confession. The entire camera crew fell into a quiet trance.

"I'm genuinely sorry to hear that," Chris said.

"She's my best friend." Dara blinked back tears. "I would do anything for her."

"Even go on television to find your perfect Jewish husband?"

Dara laughed. "Even that."

She was surprised at how easily it was coming to her now. The words. The schmoozing. She almost forgot about the camera completely. She was just having a conversation with an old friend, and the more she spoke with Chris, the more she knew that she was killing it.

Her words came out clear and focused. She felt no shame, or embarrassment, about being her honest and authentic self. It was the same Dara Rabinowitz that she brought to the boardroom at J-Mate.

"It's hard for you, right?" Chris asked.

"It's very hard for me," she admitted. "You see, I have generalized anxiety disorder. That means that I sometimes get really nervous about things that shouldn't make me really nervous. Like flying on an airplane, or going to sleep in the dark, or crossing a bridge. Mainly, I manage these anxieties through a combination of lifestyle and medication… but sometimes, no matter what I do, those anxieties get the best of me. I wind up avoiding things. One of the things I've avoided doing is dating."

Chris nodded. "I think a lot of our viewers can relate to that."

"Probably," Dara admitted. "I know GAD is very common, but that's also why I feel it's important to talk about it. I don't think people should be ashamed of a disorder they can't control. I don't think it should stand in the way of falling in love, or getting married, either. I'm here to exemplify that belief in action."

"You are a very courageous woman."

"I don't know about that." She waved away his compliment before turning to speak to the camera directly. "But maybe all the support, having an entire camera crew and staff to hold my hand—all of you at home rooting for me—make it easier for me to be honest."

"Well, then." Chris smiled, turning toward the camera. "I don't think we should wait any longer to introduce you to your date! Dara Rabinowitz, please get ready to meet the man that is hoping to be your very own Mr. Perfect on Paper…"

A young man, holding a picnic basket, came bounding to the front of the stage. Chris introduced him as Avi Levine, a medical resident from Brooklyn.

Dara was pleased. Avi was quite handsome. He was sporting a blue sweater and gray slacks, and she found the way his black velvet kippah sat upon his auburn curls immensely attractive. She appreciated the way he wore his Judaism so proudly, and knew that because of his kippah, he likely kept kosher and observed Shabbat.

But… Dara pursed her lips. Avi was short. About five foot six. She was hoping for someone slightly taller. Being tiny herself, she had an impossible fantasy of one day having children who could reach the top shelf in her custom-made kitchen cabinets without needing a stool.

"I'm so pleased to meet you," Avi said, introducing himself.

Dara blushed. "Me, too,"

"I thought that for Rosh Hashanah—" Avi stammered a bit, his own nerves shining through "—we could pick some apples, and then try them with different types of honey."

"I would like that very much."

The date began. Chris backed off. Avi and Dara moved to peruse the apple orchards. As they made their way through the fields, the cameras trailed close behind them. They discussed their lives, their bubbes and what brought them both to be searching for a match on national television.

It was all quite pleasant. Dara couldn't help but laugh at how bad her own anxiety had been that morning. All her nonstop obsessing over what could go wrong paled in comparison to the agreeable and easygoing nature of her first date.

She glanced over her shoulder toward Chris.

He had come through for her.

Dara and Avi finished picking a few apples and returned to the front of the barn. A long table, set up with a white tablecloth and tiny plates of honey, stretched out before them. Avi set about washing the apples in a large barrel of water set up at the side before slicing them with a knife. He poured some honey from a jar onto a plate. And then he said the words that every nice Jewish girl wants to hear.

"Should we do the blessing first?"

Dara sighed, dreamily. "I would love that."

Avi said the blessing over fruit and fruit juices. He was half-way through the prayer when the sound of something buzzing caught Dara off guard. Looking up, she saw a tiny bumble-bee hovering above her head. She attempted to wave it away. Once. Twice. A dozen times, before she realized that Avi was waiting with an apple slice drenched in honey.

"Oh," she said, taking it from him. "Thanks."

Before she could take a bite, the bee returned. She tried to swat it away again, but it kept buzzing around her damn head. Her anxiety worsened. She hated bugs. She especially hated bees. Though she had never been stung before, she was suddenly positive she was allergic. It wasn't a totally irrational fear. She was allergic to mango, after all.

"Jesus," Avi said, swatting at her face. "That bee really likes you."

She tossed the apple slice down. "Maybe if I just…"

"Stop moving so much."

Dara swatted and ducked again. The bee buzzed away from her eyes and dropped out of sight. Dara breathed a sigh of relief. "There," she said, shrugging happily, returning to her date. "All better. I thought it would never—"

The buzzing began again. But this time, the sound of its tiny wingspan was different. It seemed muted, even though it was still clearly floating above her head somewhere. She raised her eyes upward, searching for it. Her anxiety took over. She looked toward Avi, his face frozen in some sort of seismic-shifting honey-drenched horror.

"Where did it go?" she whispered.

"What?"

"Where did the bumblebee go!" she shouted at the top of her lungs.

Avi pointed with one finger to the top of her head. The

horrific truth confronted her with full and terrifying force. The bee was in her hair. Her beautiful black curls, styled like a poofy peach, had trapped the fluttering creature inside.

Dara completely freaked out.

"Get it out!" she screamed.

"How?" Avi screamed back.

"I don't know," she said, jumping up and down in place. "Just get it out!"

The rest happened in a torrent of flapping and flailing. Dara kept screaming. The camera kept rolling. Chris jumped into the scene. With all the calm of a man who had never had a bee stuck in his updo, he attempted to get her to stop moving. It was no use. There was too much hair spray. Too many bobby pins. Dara was going to get stung. Her mind quickly spun to the worst-case scenario. She was going to get stung and die of anaphylactic shock. *She was going to die on national television*.

"Are we sure it was a bee?" Chris asked.

"Of course it's a bee!"

"It could have been a murder hornet," Avi offered from the sideline.

"What?" Dara said, glancing between them.

He shrugged. "I'm just saying—"

"It's not a murder hornet," Chris said, meeting her eyes directly. "Okay? It's not a—"

It was too late. The words had settled as truth inside her mind.

Dara decided to save herself. Scanning the set, she searched for something to finally rid herself of the vicious creature. She saw Bucky. Some shofars. More apple slices and honey. Finally, her eyes landed on that barrel of water. The idea took shape in her feet before she had a chance to think it through.

Pushing Avi aside, she made her way to the barrel and dived headfirst into the water.

The sound of the production crew screaming faded alongside the fluttering of wings. The last thing she heard above the bubbles and water was the sound of Chris Steadfast delivering his signature closing line.

17

DARA'S RAGE ECHOED FROM THE FRONT LOBBY OF
the main building and snaked its way through the many miles
of orchards and beehives surrounding them. In response to her
screaming, most of the staff of *Good News* took cover, breaking down tents and loading up props before escaping back to
New York City. Only Chris—out of sheer desperation inter-
woven with concern—braved the onslaught.

"You think it's funny?" Dara said, gathering up her bags
while simultaneously tapping a message on her phone, "You
think I don't have better things to do with my time than go
on your stupid TV show?"

"I don't think it's funny," Chris said.

"You made a fool out of me!" she said, nearly chucking
her phone at his head. "You made me look like an idiot on
live television!"

"I had no idea that would happen. I don't control the bees!"

Dara spun away, pulling her damp hair into a scrunchie
at the top of her head, the top half of her maroon dress still
equally soaked. Chris tried not to stare at her nipples peeking through the satin material. Instead, and not sure if he was

overstepping his boundaries, he took his suit jacket off, holding it out to her.

"Here," he said.

"What?"

"You're clearly—" he kept his eyes on the ceiling "—cold."

It took her a minute. She glanced down at her breasts and, groaning aloud, took the jacket from him. "Jesus Christ," she said, twisting around in her spot to put the jacket over her clothes. "Like this day couldn't get any freaking worse."

She fumbled with the buttons before spinning back around to face him. Her tiny frame swam in his jacket.

Chris felt terrible about what had happened. He knew she was embarrassed. The last thing he wanted was for her date to go so badly.

Her phone buzzed to attention in her hand. Dara looked down. "My car is here."

She turned to leave. At the bottom of the steps, her limo was waiting to return her to Hoboken.

"Dara," he shouted, chasing her down the stairs. "Wait just a minute!"

She turned back at the car door.

Chris rubbed the back of his neck, unsure how to phrase the question. "Are we still on for Yom Kippur, then?"

Dara scoffed aloud. "Absolutely not!"

With that, she was off. The limousine snaked its way through the front gates of Willow Crest, heading back to Hoboken. Chris waited for it to disappear fully from view, his heart sinking, before heading for home himself.

By the time Chris returned to his apartment in Brooklyn, it was dark. Struggling with the keys to his apartment, he opened the front door. Mona, the new babysitter, was already waiting in the foyer with her jacket on and holding her bags.

"You're late," she said.

"I know," Chris said, scrambling to apologize. "I'm so sorry. I got caught up in—"

Mona tied her scarf around her neck but didn't really care to hear him finish. "Lacey has been fed and is dressed for bed. She hasn't brushed her teeth yet."

"Oh," Chris said. "Well, I appreciate that, Mona."

"I'll see you tomorrow."

Before he could explain what had happened at Willow Crest—or dig an additional twenty bucks out of his wallet to offset her anger—the woman was gone. Alone in the foyer, Chris took a moment to collect his thoughts. He could hear Lacey laughing hysterically from the living room. At first, he assumed she was immersed in yet another horror movie. But as he drew closer, he was surprised to find his daughter was watching *Good News*.

"Hey," Chris said, laying his keys on the kitchen counter. "You're watching my show?"

"Uh-huh."

The fact surprised him. Having been deemed *totally uncool* by his tween daughter about six months ago, Lacey wasn't exactly a fan of *Good News*. She never watched his show. Now, she had recorded today's episode on DVR and was watching the date.

"When is the next segment with Dara?" Lacey asked, twisting around.

"I'm not sure." Chris ran one hand through his hair. His daughter was quickly becoming the Queen of Uncomfortable Questions. "You didn't think our show today was a total disaster?"

"Of course it was a disaster!" she said, jumping up from her spot. "That's what made it so good! Jasmine wants to know if you're gonna set her on fire for the next date."

"Jasmine is watching the show, too?"

"Dad," Lacey said, placing both hands on her hips. "*Everybody* is watching your show."

Chris wasn't sure what to do with this information.

"Can I meet her?" Lacey asked.

He grimaced. Another impossible question from his daughter. He debated explaining to her that Dara was likely quitting. But admitting the truth aloud would mean having to confront the reality of *Good News* being canceled. It would mean having to tell his daughter that they would likely need to move from their home in New York City.

"I don't know, kiddo," Chris said. "Dara is super busy."

"But one day?" she asked eagerly.

"Maybe." Chris glanced down at his watch. "Come on, now, it's past your bedtime. Chop-chop and off to bed. Brush your teeth first."

For once, his kid actually obeyed without argument.

With Lacey in bed, Chris began cleaning up the living room. Picking up papers, her book bag, a tiny pink sweatshirt and the remote. He was just about to place it back on the coffee table when he was overcome with curiosity. Sitting down on the couch, he rewound Dara's segment back to the beginning.

Watching *Good News* from the vantage point of a viewer, he again saw what people liked about Dara. It wasn't just that she was beautiful, brilliant and tough. She was *authentic*. She was at ease with her vulnerabilities, even if she struggled to deal with the aftermath of them. Chris liked her, too. She made him laugh. She made him smile. She made him...*feel*. The numbness that had suffocated him over the last two years dissipated when she was near.

He wasn't sure what that meant, or how to handle it. He only knew that he desperately wanted to see Dara again. Despite the fact that it was late, and he really needed to get some sleep himself, Chris found himself watching her segment on repeat.

Dara breathed deeply as she entered her home. The comfort of her safe space, away from the nonstop noise of social media alerts and emails, beckoned. Tossing her bag down by the door, and still wearing Chris's jacket, she took stock of her lonely apartment.

The place was spotless. On her coffee table, carefully labeled with Post-it notes, were three binders full of options for food, flowers and table settings that Dara would need to peruse with her bubbe for her ninetieth birthday party.

In the kitchen, she was pleased to see indications that Naveah had gone to the store. In addition to fresh organic fruits and veggies for snacks, her meals for the next three days had been prepared and pre-portioned in healthy and perfect servings. Dara grabbed a biodegradable carton marked *Thursday* from the top shelf. Opening it up, she found a platter of baked tofu, quinoa and spinach from her favorite kosher vegan restaurant.

She was just about to grab a fork, when her eyes wandered to her desk. A green folder with a large sticker for the Center for Neuro-Oncology on the front.

Dara immediately lost her appetite.

Putting her food away, she headed over to her desk, opening the folder. She was not a doctor, but over the last six months, she had become adept at sifting through the complicated language of her grandmother's medical records. Taking a deep breath, her eyes scanned the words.

Digital images of contrast enhanced MRI taken at Center for Neuro-Oncology find that there is a well-defined mass mea-

suring 3.5 cm x 2.2 cm x 6.4 cm in the superior cortex. Since prior scan dated four months ago shows the same lesion measuring 3.2 cm x 1.9 cm x 5.4 cm, findings indicate that tumor has been unresponsive to treatment.

A cry escaped her lips. Feeling sick to her stomach, Dara fell into her desk chair. The tumor in her grandmother's brain had grown. Tossing the file down, not wanting to confront the reality of terminal illness, the in-between place beckoned her once again.

What would she do without her beloved bubbe? What would she do when her grandmother had passed, and she was all alone…terribly alone…in her quiet and pristine apartment, with no one there to hold her hand, or help her to move beyond her fears?

The thought terrified her more than bridges.

More than dating, even.

Leaving the file, her hands still shaking from the news—from the realization that tomorrow, she would have to ask Naveah to start looking into hospice options—she went upstairs. She went through the motions, getting undressed, washing her face, brushing her teeth.

Back in her bedroom, in just her bra and panties, she caught sight of herself in the full-length mirror. Cocking her head sideways, staring at her near-naked body, she analyzed her form. Her small breasts, the bones in her hips. Her eyes wandered back to her bed, where she had laid Chris's jacket.

Dara couldn't help herself. She put his jacket back on.

It smelled like him.

Delicious.

Closing her eyes, she imagined his strong and supportive arms wrapping around her. She heard his voice, promising her that everything would be okay. *I promise, Dara. I'll be with you...every step of the way.*

She gave in to the ridiculous fantasy. She imagined his lips pressing against her own. She saw his hands running down the length of her body as her fingers stroked the same places. She ran her hands down the center of her breasts, edging past her belly button, landing at the waistband of her lilac panties.

Opening her eyes, she stopped. Catching her reflection in the mirror, she sighed, annoyed. She wanted to hate Chris. It would have been easier for her to blame him for today's dating disaster. Alas, Dara could see everything he'd done for her at Willow Crest. His efforts on her behalf, his attempt at finding her the perfect Jewish husband, were genuine.

It wasn't his fault she had a panic attack over a bumblebee.

Or that it happened on live national television.

Sitting back down on the bed, she considered her options. She could give in to the anxiety pressing against her chest. She could be done with Chris and this ridiculous experiment, give up on dating forever, but where would she be a month from now? A year from now? Providing her dating disasters were not adversely affecting J-Mate, then what was the harm in continuing forward?

The world would learn that Dara Rabinowitz was not perfect.

But maybe that was a good thing...

Of course, what Dara was not willing to admit aloud to herself was that beyond the practical necessity of what he provided—someone to hold her hand while she went on dates, someone to be there while she confronted her very deepest fears—Dara liked being around Chris. She had enjoyed her morning with him, their banter in the golf cart. She especially liked being the Rosh Hashanah apple of his eye.

She didn't want to lose him.

Her decision made, Dara went back downstairs to her computer. And then, still wearing his jacket, the scent of the man filling up her nostrils, Dara jotted out an email to all the members of her executive staff.

Hi Team,

Please double-check the subscription numbers for J-Mate. Providing we have not taken a hit after today's live event on *Good News*, please send an email to Chris (and Eleanor) to let him know that we are still on for a Yom Kippur segment. But no more live shoots.

I'm around if you have questions.

Best,
Dara

Yom Kippur

18

YOM KIPPUR, LITERALLY TRANSLATED TO MEAN THE day of covering, was the most holy day of the Jewish lunar year.

Like all Jewish holidays, it began in the evening and stretched twenty-five hours until the following night. In contrast to Rosh Hashanah, which celebrated the birth of the world, Yom Kippur was a serious affair. A day of atonement, when Jews were expected to repent for their wrongdoing, taking stock of their lives and making *teshuva*, changing as necessary. As such, the day was marked by a twenty-five-hour fast, and oodles of time spent reflecting in synagogue.

Dara arrived at Temple Emanuel in Hoboken to see throngs of Jews—families with baby carriages, little kids playing games on the ramps—spilling out onto the street. As one of Hoboken's most popular synagogues, it was a massive structure, with a Hebrew school and adult day care center attached. Marble columns interspersed with stained glass welcomed all visitors.

Dara took a deep breath. This was not her normal synagogue. Usually, she spent all of Yom Kippur with her bubbe and the ChallahBack Girls at a small shul across town. Indeed, she had spent the morning there. But after the *Yizkor* service—which Dara did in memory of her mother—it was agreed that she would leave Kehillah Tikvah and head across town to Temple Emanuel.

Chris had picked the location. Partly for its popularity, but also because it hosted one of the hottest Yom Kippur Break Fasts for singles in town.

Dara pushed one black curl behind her ear, and began her trek up the stairs. She hated the feeling of not knowing anybody. Her anxiety was made worse by the sight of a group of young men—all around her age and wearing kippot—whispering in her direction.

Dara squinted, confused. What the hell were they looking at her for?

She was just about to spin around on her ballet flats and head for home when a mirage appeared. Christopher Steadfast came bounding down the stairs, full of energy and pep. The man had clearly eaten.

"You're in a good mood," Dara said.

"You're—" Chris cocked his head sideways "—not."

She sighed. She did not mean to sound so damn annoyed with him, but she always struggled with fasting on Yom Kippur.

"I'm sorry," she said, shaking off her hanger. "I've just spent the last six hours in shul with my bubbe. I'm starving, and thirsty, and if you really want to know the truth… I'm thinking about eating your shoes."

Chris laughed. Though Dara wasn't actually joking.

Yom Kippur always kind of went the same way for Dara. The night, like the morning in services, always started out promising. Dara would awake full of confidence, certain that she was capable of surviving yet another fast. By early afternoon, and the start of *Yizkor* services, however, she would find her willpower faltering.

"Well," Chris said, touching her on the arm. "I promise. This date should be easy."

"I wish you would stop using adjectives."

"I'm serious, Dara," he said, his laid-back nature ever apparent. "This time, there won't be any honey or murder hornets. I haven't planned anything extravagant. It's just Yom Kippur Break Fast at Hoboken's most popular synagogue for young Jewish singles. You've been to dozens of Break Fasts before, right?"

Dara wasn't paying attention. Instead, she was keenly aware of the sun beating down on her neck. Like always, it was hot as hell. It was like some sort of great cosmic joke played on the Jewish people every year. No matter what Gregorian date the holiday of Yom Kippur fell on, the fall weather would suddenly abate, and turn into a heat wave. Just like it would switch to freezing or even a freak winter storm over the holiday of Sukkot.

Dara tried to remind herself of the positive. She had made it to *Neilah*, the afternoon service. She had survived more than twenty hours so far without food and water. Just a few more hours of suffering to go, and she would be able to eat and drink again during the sacred Jewish tradition known as Break Fast.

She looked back at Chris, ready to snap at the man to move it along, when the strangest thing happened. It must have been her hunger, or the dehydration, but the light of that September sun suddenly shifted. The voices on the street, and on the stairs surrounding them, faded into nothing. Chris was looking at her.

Not just looking at her, she realized, but falling into her eyes. She became acutely aware of the way his gray eyes twinkled, and the juxtaposition of his body, his hips angled in her direction. Their feet were almost touching. He had a glint in his eye that made her feel, just for a moment, that he was interested in her.

Chris cleared his throat. "Should I show you what we're planning for tonight?"

Dara brushed the thought away. "That would be great."

Chris led her away from the crowds. Heading up the stairs, they made their way through the front entrance, where security was checking IDs and tickets. "She's with me," Chris said, ushering Dara straight through. Not surprisingly, the foyer was even more packed than the outside. Bumping elbows and ducking under arms, Dara followed Chris, the sound of the rabbi's voice—the high-holiday *nusach*, or melodies—following them as they walked.

It was only when they were a little space away from the entrance, where the crowds thinned out and the groups of adults verged into tiny semicircles of kids and teens hiding from their parents, that she brought up the concern that had been sitting on her chest since arriving at Temple Emanuel.

"Am I losing my mind?" she asked.

"What?"

She shook her head at the thought. "I feel like people are talking about me."

"Oh," Chris said, considering her words. "Well, they probably recognize you."

"Recognize me?" Dara didn't understand.

"We've been getting a lot of great feedback on your series," Chris explained. "Our ratings have been going up, too. I wouldn't be surprised if most of the people here know who you are, given the Jewish interest angle, and that you live in Hoboken. I've been experiencing something similar on the subway, too."

"Wait," Dara said, twisting in place. "Does this mean they're not canceling your show?"

"I don't know," Chris admitted. "But we're fighting hard, aren't we?"

Dara smiled softly. "We are."

They walked through a courtyard, where the first brackets and bolts of a sukkah were being built, before heading down a long set of stairs. Arriving at a large room in the basement, they saw tables still in the process of being put out.

"This is where they're going to be doing Break Fast," Chris said, nodding toward a section of the room where three cameramen were working hard at testing the lighting of a corner. "We'll have you meet your date right there. This is going to be a look live, where we film it to look like it's live even though it's not. That being said, to give it the feeling of on-air tension, everything will take place in one shoot."

"One shoot?"

"A five-minute package from start to finish. We'll cut when it's over."

"Why does that make me even more nervous?"

Chris laughed. "You're gonna be great, Dara."

She wanted to believe him. She wanted to stay with him, too.

Alas, it was still Yom Kippur. Jews all around the world were offering up their last penances, hoping to be sealed for a good year in the *Book of Life*. What would God think, or write into her story, if she spent her afternoon musing with Christopher Steadfast instead of atoning? Especially considering the state of her beloved bubbe's health, she did not want to take any chances.

"I should probably go back to services," Dara said. "*Neilah* is kind of important."

"Of course." Chris stepped away from her. "I should actually make sure everything is in order with production, too. The rabbi here had all sorts of rules about our filming tonight.

Eleanor will meet you upstairs in a bit. Give you the final run-down and answer any questions you may have."

Dara nodded. "Great."

"And I'm always here if you need me."

Neilah was the last of the five Yom Kippur services. It began in the late afternoon, and was considered one of the most sacred services of the Jewish tradition. As such, and given the themes of Yom Kippur, it was a solemn affair. The ark was open, and for the majority of the final hours, Jews were required to stand.

Dara entered the main sanctuary of Temple Emanuel. Not surprisingly, it was packed. Slinking into a back pew, she found a seat but remained on her feet. The familiar *nusach*, or melodies, of Yom Kippur floated throughout the sanctuary. Dara couldn't help herself. Even though she had just arrived at services, she glanced down at her watch.

It was only 5:15.

She still had two hours to go.

Dara sighed and opened her siddur, or prayer book. It was around this time every year that Dara cursed being born Jewish. She hated Yom Kippur. She hated everything it represented, and being hungry, and the way it caused her boundless angst with its texts of terror about being written into the *Book of Life*.

Oh sure, she knew that Yom Kippur had *reasons* for its commanded suffering. It was supposed to remind you of your death, hence why it was called the day of covering—a gentle nod to the Jewish tradition of throwing dirt upon a grave. Like blowing the shofar, or ram's horn, through the month of Elul, it was supposed to shake you, and wake you, from a life of spiritual sleepwalking.

Still, it seemed easier to just push a goat off a mountain.

"Well, Dara," said a voice beside her. "You finally got me into services for the High Holidays."

Dara glanced over to see Eleanor Cohen, executive producer for *Good News*. Dressed in a pair of blue jeans, paired with hiking boots and a tight cotton T-shirt, with a black wire wrapped around her waist that traveled up to her ear, she stood out among the room full of calf-length skirts and business suits paired with kippot.

"You're Jewish?" Dara asked.

"Jew-*ish*."

"That's...not a thing."

"Whatever," Eleanor said, shrugging her shoulders. "Anyway, once you're done with this...this thing of yours, Eli will be waiting for you just beyond the doors. After he gets you miked up, he'll move you downstairs for hair and makeup. We'll call you when we're ready to start filming. Any questions?"

"I guess not."

"Great."

With that, Eleanor escaped services through a side door.

Dara stood in her spot, siddur pressed up against her chest, her hunger and thirst creeping back. She thought of the way Eleanor wore blue jeans on the holiest day of the year. The electronics snaked around her waist, when Dara wouldn't even deign to carry a cell phone. The word she used to describe her faith. *Jew-ish*. Dara didn't like the term. Even though she knew exactly what Eleanor meant by the phrasing.

Eleanor was the type of Jewish woman who worked on Yom Kippur. She didn't care about the folkways and traditions of her people. She didn't feel bound up by Jewish law. She ate shrimp and traveled on Shabbat without thinking twice. And then, through the windows of the main sanctuary, Dara's eyes landed on Chris. He was talking to Eli.

She watched him intently, folding into the strong shape of his shoulders. She loved his smile, the dimple that always appeared on the right side above his lips. It was fascinating how her own heart had shifted with getting to know him. When she had first met Chris, she had been starstruck, completely nervous. Now her entire body fell into ease whenever he came close. She didn't understand how someone so foreign to her everyday realities could make her feel so perfectly at home. But there was something about Chris that transcended logic.

For one brief moment, she found herself imagining what it would be like to be like Eleanor. To break the chain. To not care. To admit attraction, acknowledge her own desire and want, even though it stood in stark juxtaposition to all she believed. Almost as quickly, she forced the thought away.

No. Absolutely not. It could never happen.

People like Eleanor fell in love with non-Jews. People like Eleanor intermarried, and raised their children outside the faith, putting up Christmas trees every December. Not people like Dara. Not someone committed to, and deeply invested in, her faith. Her heart would never falter in such a way.

Taking a deep breath, she dug her ballet flats into the pink carpet beneath her feet, finding her footing.

19

FOOD. WATER. SUSTENANCE. IT BECAME ALL DARA could think about in those final moments of services, standing at the back of the synagogue, bouncing up and down in her flats.

Trying not to look at her watch, she cursed the Heavens above her. Despite a room full of starving people, the rabbi had the audacity to go over the 7:13 end time with his rousing—*oh, he is not pulling out the guitar*—rendition of *Aleinu*. Great. Dara had gone through all of Yom Kippur, atoning for transgressions, only to begin sinning the very second it ended by having homicidal thoughts about the clergy.

Ashamnu, indeed.

Dara rolled her eyes up toward the ceiling. She wondered if popcorn ceiling could be eaten. She dreamed of pipes bursting, water raining down, her tongue outstretched. She prayed for an ending to this nightmare. Until—*baruch Hashem*—a miracle. The shofar was blown. Yom Kippur was over. *Adon Olam* exploded from the bima as a wave of relief filled the room. Before the rabbi was even finished singing, half the congregants had already left.

"Dara?" Eli called out to her from the main doors of the sanctuary. "Over here!"

Dara elbowed her way toward the front entrance. With half the shul heading for the exits, and the other half heading down the stairs for Break Fast, the main lobby had become a kosher sardine can. Out of breath, dying for a drink, she touched her parched throat.

"Hey," Dara said. "Do you happen to have—"

Eli did not let her finish. Holding up a microphone in his hand, wires dangling like bracelets around his wrist, he glanced around the room.

"Any idea where we can get you set up?" Eli asked.

Dara huffed. She didn't need a freaking microphone. She needed a goddamn drink of water. Still, the quicker they got this over with, the quicker she could dive face-first into a lox platter. Taking Eli by the arm, she marched him down an empty hallway. He affixed the battery pack to the back of her skirt.

"All good?" she asked.

Eli tugged at the wires. "Seems right."

"Great." Dara sighed, searching the hallway for a water fountain. "Because I could really use a drink of—"

"Come on," Eli said, not letting her finish. "We need to get you to hair and makeup."

The room where Break Fast was being held was crammed full of people. A long line trailed out the back door and snaked its way around a buffet table. Throngs of young Jewish professionals stood in semicircles, shoving tuna fish sandwiches and marzipan rainbow cookies into their mouths. In the corner, set up in a spot with cameras and lights, was Chris.

"Do you mind if I just grab a cookie real quick?" Dara asked.

"No time," Eli said, pulling her into a side room.

The rest happened in a whirlwind of movement. Dara was

thrown into a chair, Sheila moving quickly to get her ready, switching it up between palettes and brushes before nearly asphyxiating her with a giant bottle of hair spray. Once Sheila backed off, Eli returned. With the triumph of angels singing, they returned to the room where they were holding Break Fast.

Normally, this would be the part of her date where Dara would begin vibrating with nervousness. Alas, hunger seemed to be the kosher kryptonite to her generalized anxiety disorder. The only thing she could think about was food and water. The only thing she could imagine was shoving one of those delicious-looking tuna sandwiches into her starving belly.

She didn't even like tuna fish sandwiches.

"You ready?" Eli asked, one hand over his earpiece.

"Actually..." Dara was certain she was going to pass out. "I really need a drink of—"

"In five, four, three..."

The camera light turned red. Eli pushed Dara in the direction of the buffet table. Waving her forward, mouthing the words *just act natural*, and Dara took that as her cue.

Reaching for a plate, she grabbed the first item she could find. *Coleslaw.* She hated coleslaw. Despised the way the dressing reminded her of eating runny eggs. Alas, she was *totally* and *completely* dying of starvation. Quivering in her ballet flats, she piled her plate with the shredded cabbage salad and didn't wait to fill up the rest of her plate before taking a bite. *Sweet heavenly coleslaw.* It was the best damn coleslaw she had ever eaten.

Her taste buds zinged. Her esophagus parted for the oncoming onslaught. She began to gorge. An uncontrollable urge to fill her empty belly rose deep within her. Unable to stop, she ravaged that buffet table. She grabbed a tuna fish sandwich. Six rainbow cookies. She guzzled directly from the pitcher of iced tea. But nothing stopped the *need* inside of her. She was right in the middle of chomping on a cookie when the light of the camera turned her way.

"So, Dara," Chris said, clearly unaware that she needed a moment. "Tell us how you're feeling about things tonight?"

Crumbs fell from her mouth while she chewed. "Huh?"

"I know that your last date didn't go quite as expected," Chris said, "but I think tonight we've found a very special man to make your acquaintance."

Dara reached for a cheese *boureka* and mumbled, "Great." She bit into the pastry. Tiny flakes of phyllo dough, and an explosion of flavor—hints of the Mediterranean mixed with the *shuk* of Jerusalem—exploded in her mouth. She closed her eyes in ecstasy. In pleasure. The party in her mouth continued, rippling from the front of her tongue all the way down her throat.

"God, yes!" she moaned, throwing her head back in sheer delight. "This is what I needed. This is what I have waited my entire life for!"

"Dara?" Chris whispered.

Her eyes flew open. "What?"

"Little help here?"

She had forgotten where she was, and that she was supposed to be filming a look live for television. Dara wiped the tiny bits of phyllo dough away from her mouth, and shirt, returning to life. "I'm hoping to meet my future husband, of course!"

Chris took that as his cue. He started talking, going on and *on* about the traditions of the holiday. *God, he talked so much.* She bounced in frustration at his every wasted second where she could be eating. Couldn't he see she was dying of hunger? Reaching for a strawberry rugalach, she plunged it into her eager mouth, her stomach grumbling for more.

Chris turned to the camera. "Well, Dara…are you ready to meet the special man we've chosen for you today?"

Dara was still chewing. "Yeah. Awesome."

Chris moved to take her plate away.

Dara growled.

Chris gave up on taking her food and focused on filling in the dead air.

"And while you're eating," Chris grumbled in the direction of the camera, "let me tell you a bit about Max."

Max was an environmental lawyer who spoke four languages. He had a swimmer's body and no complications. Though he was under Dara's height requirements, he was a good-looking young Jewish man. Chris stepped off to the side as Max walked into the frame. Finding herself alone with him, and with three minutes of filming left to go, Dara told herself to get a grip. Putting her plate down, she focused on making polite conversation.

"So, Max," she said, determined to break the spell of Break Fast. "It's not often you meet someone who has dedicated their life to keeping our world beautiful. What made you want to become an environmental lawyer?"

Max wiped cookie crumbs from his lips with a napkin. "Puffins."

"Puffins?" Dara squinted curiously in the young man's direction. It was not the answer she was expecting.

"You see," he said, taking another bite of cookie, "I was twelve years old when the Toga Handle oil spill happened in Alaska. It was actually my Bar Mitzvah project to do a fundraiser for the puffins who were covered in gasoline."

Dara nodded. "I remember when that happened."

"I couldn't get over what those poor puffins had been through," Max said, genuinely. "The sight of them…their cute little black-and-white wings, covered in tar…the way they couldn't waddle over to their spouses and eggs. My Bar Mitzvah day came and went, but I never forgot those puffins. I knew from that moment on I was going to make puffin safety the center of my work."

Dara blinked. "That's beautiful."

"Thank you." He smiled. "Puffins are my life."

He continued chomping and speaking. Making love to a marzipan rainbow cookie he had grabbed. Dara watched as his two lips flapped up and down, the cookie dissolving into bits of wet crumbles beneath his teeth.

"Did you know," Max said, still chewing, "that a male puffin—"

All at once, Max stopped speaking. Dara was not sure what was happening. She glanced toward Chris. Chris glanced toward Eleanor. Dead air lingered in the space between them, and then Max reached up and grabbed his throat.

"Oh my God," someone screamed from the crowd. "He's choking!"

An uproar rose from the room. Voices began shouting for a doctor. Max, in a moment of sheer and rightful terror, panicked. With one hand on his throat, and the other searching for a lifeline, he began flailing about the room like...well, like a puffin.

People screamed. Max kept spinning. Dara attempted to help, trying to get the man to stand still so someone could perform the Heimlich maneuver. Instead, he responded in the way of all sea creatures struggling for their life, and bucked so hard she went flying.

Dara fell into the rabbi. In an attempt to find her footing, she inadvertently elbowed him in the nose. The middle-aged man in the kippah yelped and went stumbling back into the cantor, who, in a domino effect, went tumbling into one of the high-intensity studio lamps surrounding them. All three went crashing to the floor, taking half the buffet table with them.

"Oh my God," someone screamed. "The rabbi is bleeding!"

Dara looked up to see blood spurting from his nose. Quickly, she moved to get the poor man a napkin.

"I'm so sorry," she said, handing it to him. "Are you okay?"

He waved her concern away, pointing back to Max. "Save him."

The rabbi was right. But Max was still flailing, and nobody could get near him. Alas, the room was filled with Jews and many of them had no experience playing high-impact contact sports. Brain injuries, after all, were not conducive to getting one into a top-tier graduate school.

And then, a hero stepped forward.

Chris was kneeling down by the camera, hands outstretched in front of him, eyes focused on Max. She wasn't sure what he was doing, but the stance reminded her of a defensive linebacker in a football game.

Max spun and teetered like a human-sized dreidel, eventually twirling his way to a spot just inches from Chris. Chris made his move.

He grabbed Max by the waist. Thrusting with great and heaving effort, he pushed hard on the spot below his sternum. The entire room gasped and fell into silence. Chris pumped, grunting with all his manly effort, while Dara waited with eager breath for a resolution to this nightmare.

Finally, on his fourth great and thrusting action, the cookie dislodged from Max's throat. Mushy bits of red and green went flying through the air, a veritable rainbow of color, before landing in a splatter of modern art all over Dara's face.

It took Dara a full ten seconds to realize what happened.

Dara screamed. "No!"

Max breathed deeply. Dara closed her eyes, masticated cookie dangling from her eyelashes, and immediately worried about pink eye. Eleanor made the sign for five seconds. Chris fumbled to the center of the room. Sucking back air, the room a disaster zone behind him, he wrapped the show with his signature line.

"I'm Chris Steadfast," he said, panting through heavy breaths. "Till next time, America... I'll be waiting for you."

20

IT WAS GETTING TO THE POINT WHERE EVERY DATE
ended with Dara soaking wet.

Chris waited for her in the hallway of Temple Emanuel,
rubbing out a tension headache from the center of his head.
Through the door, he could hear the sound of the sink running
water. It went on for several minutes, periodically interrupted
by the sound of Dara hiccuping—possibly also crying—inside. Chris began to get worried.

"Dara?" he asked, knocking gently on the door. "You
okay?"

Her answer was swift and furious. "Go away!"

"Come on," Chris said, and jiggled the door handle. "Let
me in."

She did not answer him.

Chris leaned his head against the door. What could he say
to her? She was right to be upset. It was yet another vast embarrassment under his watch.

After a few more moments, Dara finally emerged. Her
cheeks blushed red. Her makeup, along with any remaining
cookie, had been wiped clean from her face. He debated tell-

ing her that she missed a spot, that there was still a tiny bit of yellow cookie folded up into one of her black curls, but stopped himself. He could tell she had been crying.

"Dara," he said, "I'm really—"

She cut him off. "Can we reshoot it?"

Chris glanced down the hallway, where a lone custodian was just finishing up putting away tables and chairs. "I don't really see how," Chris said, genuinely. "Most everyone, including the production staff of *Good News*, has gone home already. There's no food left. They've already started putting away tables."

"Well, what about filming outside of Yom Kippur?"

Chris shifted in his spot. "When?"

"I don't know," she stammered nervously. "But surely we can figure something out."

Chris wanted to help. Problem was, it was nearly impossible to get Dara away for a day of filming during the High Holidays. With Sukkot coming up—and her date for that holiday already firmly organized—their options were limited.

He dug his hands into his pockets, trying to focus on the positive. "Dara," he said, thinking back to the ratings bonanza of the Rosh Hashanah episode. "I know this date didn't turn out how you expected, but I think people are going to love seeing what happened. You were natural, and funny, and real. Reshooting with Max would only come off as stilted."

She interrupted him. "It was a disaster, Chris."

"We'll get it right the next time."

"The next time?" she scoffed. "A man almost died, Chris! I gave the rabbi a bloody nose! I'm pretty sure this is a sign from God that I'm meant to stay single forever!"

"I don't know," Chris said, trying to keep it casual. "Nobody died. Nobody wound up in the hospital. Sure, it was a little messy, but I don't think ruining a Yom Kippur Break Fast is the absolute worst thing that can happen to you on a date."

"I'm glad to see we have such high expectations for my love life."

He remained calm and rational. He wanted her to be calm and rational, too. "All I'm saying is I don't think we can assume that God is intimately involved in your personal life... until someone is struck by lightning."

"Chas v'chalilah!" She placed one hand on his mouth to stop him. "Don't even put it out there."

He froze beneath the warmth of her touch. Her soft hand pressed against his lips sent sparks down his spine. He was suddenly aware of every passing second. The quiet in the hallway. The overhead light, stuttering on and off above them, daring them to find themselves alone and in the dark. But she was so close to him. He could smell the shampoo in her hair and rose soap lingering on her hands. Every urge that had been squelched since the death of his wife came rushing forward in one tumultuous wave of desire. He wanted her.

Dara pulled her hand away. Moments later, she was spinning. Twisting in her spot, turning away from him, her breath quickened. Her chest heaved up and down as her face turned bright red. Chris could tell that she was veering into a panic attack.

"Hey," he said. "It's okay."

"No," she spat out. "It's not!"

"Everything is fine, Dara."

"No! I'm dying!"

"You're not dying," he said calmly. "I wouldn't let you die, okay?"

Dara stopped spinning long enough to meet his eyes. "Do you have a phone?"

He squinted, surprised. "What?"

"I didn't bring mine," she explained. "Yom Kippur. I don't carry. Just...let me borrow your phone."

Chris obeyed, digging into his pocket. Tapping it on, he saw that there was a waiting text message from Lacey. Quickly, he swiped the message away and handed his cell phone over. Dara did not waste any time. She went right to his web browser, typing something into his keypad.

Moments later, he heard the familiar sound of a long beep, followed by the scratchy staccato of a radio. *"Three four one bravo this is ten-twelve for a drunk and disorderly, caller is an employee, says the suspect is naked, wearing a wolf mask…demanding chicken wings."*

"Roger that," another voice came through. *"We're on our way."*

Chris squinted. "Are you listening to a…police scanner?"

He knew the sounds better than anybody. He had spent the majority of his career with one running in his office nonstop.

Dara pressed the phone against her ear. "It relaxes me."

"Something about crackheads getting tased relaxes you?"

"It's healthier than binge drinking."

He shrugged. "Fair point."

For the next ten minutes, Chris sat with Dara in the hallway of Temple Emanuel, listening to the emergency scanner. It brought him back to the time before *Good News*, when he was still working as a broadcast journalist, doing the hard-hitting stuff at a Washington, DC, desk. Back then, he would have done anything for a good story. He was always the first on the scene, the journalist with the biggest scoop. And then, Claire died.

Dara's breathing slowed. The red in her cheeks flushed back to olive. Dara pulled the phone away from her ear and attempted to explain. "I know it sounds silly," she said quietly. "But when I hear all those voices—all those stories, happening at once—I know I'm not alone in this world."

"But a lot of those stories are bad. It doesn't stress you out… hearing everyone's sadness?"

"You're right." Dara considered his question thoughtfully. "A lot of the stuff on the scanner is terrible. There are heart attacks, and people committing crimes, and car accidents. Life is filled with terrible and hurtful things. But you know what always makes me feel better about that?"

He shook his head.

"Life goes on, anyway."

Chris swallowed a lump in his throat. Dara was really unlike anyone he had ever met.

A feeling welled up in his chest, familiar yet foreign. Life didn't feel as if it went on for Chris. It felt as if it stopped the night Claire died. But there were days where he wondered if they hadn't swapped places. If she were still alive in Virginia, and he was lying on some highway, police flares lining the street, camera crews gathering around.

"Are you okay?" Dara asked suddenly.

Chris returned from his thoughts. "Hmm?"

"You're just suddenly very quiet."

"I can't be quiet?"

"It's just weird for you," she said, shifting in her seat. "Usually you're plowing me with questions...or giving me stupid race car metaphors."

Chris bit back a smile. "I have more stupid race car metaphors if you like?"

"I think I'm good."

Chris nodded. And then, maybe because he wasn't a planner—or a thinker—he reached over and took her hand. Surprisingly, she let him. They sat for a few silent moments together. His secret comfort. Her secret sin. They held on to each other, sharing the empty space of a synagogue hallway together after the High Holidays, neither of them in a rush to move.

Outside Temple Emanuel, Chris searched for a cab. Flagging one down, he opened the door for Dara, helping her into the passenger side.

"So," Chris said, "I'll see you on Sukkot?"

"I'll be there," Dara said, before adding, "come rain or shine. Though, judging how my dates have been going… I'm pretty sure it will be raining."

Chris laughed.

He waited as her cab took off for Hoboken, making sure that she was safely on her way, when his phone vibrated in his pocket. He was expecting to see a message from Lacey. Instead, he was surprised to find a text message from Jensen. Opening it up, he smiled. Attached to the message was a photograph of Katie, clad in a hospital gown, holding a brand-new baby boy.

JENSEN ALVIREZ JR.
BORN 8 LBS AND 7 OUNCES

Chris smiled, rolling his eyes up to the Heavens. What perfectly imperfect timing for a baby to appear in the world. Alas, it seemed that Dara was correct. Life could be hard. It was filled with sadness, and bitterness, all manner of suffering—but life also found a way to go on, anyway. Perhaps Chris could find a way to move on, too.

With a new bounce in his step, Chris headed in the direction of the subway, toward Lacey and home. He had a long night ahead of him, after all…planning Dara's date for the Jewish holiday of Sukkot.

Sukkot

21

SUKKOT BEGAN SHORTLY AFTER YOM KIPPUR, AND commemorated the Jewish exodus from Egypt. In remembrance of the tiny tabernacles the Israelites resided in during their wandering, Jews were commanded to build roofless huts, or sukkot, in their schools, restaurants and backyards. Turning their permanent home temporary, and vice versa, they were also expected to eat and sleep in the sukkah for eight days.

As Dara exited the cab on the Upper West Side, she could see four large sukkot, in a diagonal pattern, centered inside the expansive courtyard beyond the front doors of the elegant kosher restaurant known as Shulchan Aruch.

Whatever anxiety she had been feeling about her third date faded with the sight. Sukkot was one of her favorite holidays. Just seeing the large wooden structure brought back a thousand pleasant memories of her childhood. She recalled cracking her teeth on caramel apples while making construction paper decorations in her Jewish day school.

She could spend hours alone there, staring up at the stars through the *s'cach*, the leaves and branches that made up the roof. She never felt alone in the sukkah. It was like her emergency scanner app in this way. The holiday always reminded her that she was a part of something bigger.

"Dara!" Chris said, appearing as he always did to greet her arrival. "You made it."

"I made it." Dara beamed.

Chris pointed toward the sukkah. "What do you think? I scoured the whole city to find the very best sukkah for your third date. It's pretty romantic, isn't it?"

Dara sighed dreamily. "It's perfect."

"Right?" he said, placing his hand on the small of her back. "Come on. Let's get you over to hair and makeup."

Chris led Dara through the courtyard. Inside, surrounded by bales of hay, was a pop-up makeup studio being overseen by Sheila. They followed the usual pattern: Dara took a seat in front of the ring light while Chris explained what they would be doing for her third date.

"This date is going to be really easy. No murder hornets this time. No Heimlich maneuver, either. You're going to meet your suitor for dinner in the sukkah."

"Just dinner, huh?"

"Nice and simple."

Otherwise, Dara knew the drill. It was another look live. A one-shot take meant to give the feeling and intensity of being shot in real time.

Dara had thought that her two previous dating disasters would have made her some sort of Jewish-world social pariah. Instead, it was the opposite. She received oodles of emails offering up love and support. Sometimes she would even get stopped on the street, where devoted fans would want to snap her picture.

As it turned out, the world related to her dating disasters. If someone like Dara—a rich, beautiful and powerful *match-*

maker—could have trouble finding her perfect match, it meant no one was alone in their dating struggles.

Indeed, none of her worst fears about dating—or being on television—had come true. Oh, sure. She had the occasional troll. You couldn't be Jewish, and in the public eye, without a hearty dose of anonymous internet antisemitism directed your way. But mainly, the good of the public reaction far outweighed any bad. Over time, her irrational fears dampened.

She was getting used to the cameras. She was getting used to the nonstop attention, too. Plus, it gave her a reason to keep spending time with Chris. She really enjoyed getting to know him over their shoots.

"And don't worry," Chris said, leaning in closer. "I picked out a great guy for you. He checks nearly every item on your perfect Jewish husband list."

Dara forced a smile. "Perfect."

One hour later, the hubbub of cameras and lights were set in motion. Sitting at a dinner table inside the sukkah, decorated with gold-and-blue tablecloths, Chris introduced their segment.

"We're here on the Upper West Side for the first night of Sukkot. Tonight, Jews all around the world are celebrating this holiday by eating and sleeping in sukkot, the structures you see behind me. But at the kosher restaurant known as Shulchan Aruch, one lucky bachelor is hoping to turn an evening beneath the stars…into a lifetime of romance."

A young man appeared. Chris introduced him as Yonatan. Dara instantly felt her cheeks get hot. He was super cute, with short brown hair that curled in the most delightful way around his ears. Whether or not he had a swimmer's body beneath his sensible blue sweater, she could not be certain. Still, he was fit and pleasing to the eye.

"Wow," Yonatan said, sliding down in the seat across from her. "You're even more beautiful in person."

Dara blushed. "Thank you."

His eyes trailed down to her feet. "I like your shoes."

"Oh." Dara was taken aback. "Thank you."

It was strange, obviously. The way he so casually noticed—and then mentioned—her feet. But she could understand getting flustered before a camera crew better than anyone.

Dara shrugged it off. It was a beautiful night. Yonatan was pleasant. Her mind wandered to the potential of romance as the waitress appeared with dinner. Normally, there would be four courses to celebrate the holiday, but Dara and Yonatan would only be filming during the entrée. Limited time, and all that.

Dara took the first few moments to get to know the young Jewish bachelor. He had no children or previous marriages. He worked as a podiatrist, which, while not all that exciting, was still technically a doctor. He was polite, saying thank you when the waitstaff arrived with their plates. There was nothing overtly weird about him...except for the fact that he kept stepping on her shoes.

At first, she thought he had done it by accident. But after the sixth time, feeling his black loafers creeping up against her brown ballet flats, she was getting uncomfortable.

"I'm sorry," Yonatan said, turning red with embarrassment, trying to explain himself. "When I get nervous, I have a tendency to move around a lot."

"Oh," Dara said, understanding anxiety better than anyone. "I totally get that."

"I keep kicking you beneath the table."

He was staring at his plate, looking so very sad about his quirky behavior. Dara couldn't help but feel for the man. "It's okay," she said, and genuinely meant it. "I have a few quirks of my own that come up when I get nervous."

"You know," Yonatan offered, "if you want, you can put your feet up here?"

Dara squinted, confused. "Up where?"

"Here." He tapped on his thighs. "You can just put your feet up on my lap. Relax a bit while you eat. I don't mind. You're a size eight, right?"

"What?"

"I just…" He licked his lower lip. "I love size eights. Size eights are like…my favorite size ever."

Yonatan was leaning across the table, smiling wide. Dara felt that weird slowing of time.

She had nothing against foot fetishes, of course. As a third-generation matchmaker—and the daughter of a sex-positive cognitive behavioral therapist—she had been raised with a firm belief that there was a lid for every pot. Plus, as someone whose own mother helped floundering marriages, she knew that being honest with a partner about sexual needs was important to a healthy relationship. Plenty of men, and women, with fetishes of all types fell in love and had successful marriages.

It's just…well, feet were not her thing. She also couldn't help but think that Yonatan would have been better off saving that information for their third date. Alas, Dara was rather old-fashioned when it came to love. She believed that handcuffs, like spankings, should be reserved for people with established safe words.

He seemed perfectly nice, otherwise. No doubt he would find the size eight sole mate of his dreams.

The date was over. Dara knew it. Even if her suitor, drooling dreamily over her flats, did not. She glanced over to Chris, unsure of what to do next. They were on camera. In the middle of shooting a look live. Dara brushed away her disappointment and focused on eating her dinner.

When Yonatan's eyes locked on her ankles beneath the tablecloth, and he let his gaze linger there for an inappropriate amount of time, she kicked him in the shin. He sprang back to life. "Sorry!" he said, before picking up his fork to finally eat his damn meal.

Thankfully, dinner was delicious. The stuffing was a glorious combination of seasoned rice mixed with berries and sweet potatoes. Hints of cranberry and citrus exploded on her tongue. It was a surprising blend of flavors, given the fall vegetables it accompanied, but it worked together beautifully. Dara had only taken a few bites, and was enjoying her meal immensely, when a strange tingling sensation began on her tongue.

"And you said—" Dara cleared her throat, reaching for a glass of water "—your sister called in to the show?"

"That's correct," he beamed.

"Do you—" Dara gulped back the glass, but it did little to squelch that strange itchy feeling now spearing down the center of her throat. She cleared her throat again before reaching to pour herself another glass of water. "Do you have... any other... siblings?"

Yonatan began talking about his family. She was grateful for the respite. On instinct, she found herself pulling at the top of her collar. When she realized her microphone was there, she stopped tugging. But something was wrong in her chest. She could feel it. She was certain of it. That tingling sensation—that terrifying knowledge you were dying—taking over every inch of her body.

No. She willed the intrusive thoughts away. This was just an anxiety attack. This was just her panicking, like always. She was obviously not dying.

Dara reminded herself of these facts. What had she even eaten? A tiny chicken stuffed with rice and berries? Some water and a bite of egg challah? The only thing Dara was even remotely allergic to was mango. Mango wasn't on the Ashkenazi Jewish flavor palate. She shook off her fear.

"So, Yonatan," she said, putting down her water, taking another bite of chicken. "What made you decide that you wanted to—"

Her voice went hoarse. The food she was masticating rested in the back of her throat. Carefully, and still fully telling herself she was having a panic attack, she put down her fork. Spit the tiny bit of food into a napkin beneath the table. She could not swallow. Like her mouth had suddenly been dropped by her brain, she couldn't get service. But that tingling in her mouth and throat was now forming into an itch.

Yonatan put down his fork. "Dara, are you okay?"

"I'm feeling…"

"Have some water?" he said, pushing a glass her way.

She fanned her chest.

"Maybe if you took your shoes off?"

Dara squinted. "What?"

"I'm just saying." He leaned across the table. "You might feel better without shoes on. Are you wearing nail polish?"

Dara didn't have enough time to correct him. Shaking her head, she caught a passing waitress. "I'm sorry," Dara said, her voice raspy and difficult to find. "What's in this chicken?"

"The capon?" the waitress asked, like there was any other meal they were eating.

"Yes," Dara said, forcing out the words. "What is it made with?"

The young girl put one finger on her chin and considered the question. "Jasmine rice, sweet potato, dried cranberry, chicken stock. You don't have a gluten or peanut allergy, do you?"

"No."

Dara couldn't help but feel relieved. It was just her anxiety playing tricks on her. It most certainly wasn't her throat closing up, and her mouth getting itchy, because she was about to die of anaphylactic shock. Dara was being ridiculous…like always.

The waitress turned to leave. She was halfway to the exit of the sukkah, standing between two couples and many barrels of hay, when she twisted around on her sneakers. "Oh," she said, snapping her fingers at the realization. "It's also got a fruit glaze on it."

"Fruit?" Dara squinted, her anxiety spiraling for real now. "What kind of fruit?"

"A mango and rosemary mixture."

The words moved in slow motion. *Mango.* There was mango in her meal. She wasn't having an anxiety attack. Dara was *actually full-on dying.*

"Help!" Dara popped up from the bench. "Now!"

The courtyard devolved into full-blown chaos. Chris jumped into the scene. Visitors lifted up from their chairs and cried aloud in sheer terror.

"My bag," Dara said, pointing toward where her hair and makeup had been done. "There's an EpiPen. In my bag. Hurry!"

She was aware that she was falling. The feeling of being laid back on the grass, dew seeping through the back of her pants, leaving large green stains all over her expensive new blouse. She could hear words. *Ambulance. Allergy.* And then, someone opening a box. Chris apologizing as he tugged on her jeans, pulling down the material to reveal one hip bone, fingers fumbling nervously.

If she wasn't dying, she might have enjoyed the feeling.

The stars in the sky faded from her view. She felt the familiar sting of the EpiPen piercing her flesh. Chris wrapped a protective arm around her, safe and loving, before Dara made one final request.

"Chris," she whispered, pulling him close. "Don't let him take off my shoes."

22

THE AMBULANCE RACED DOWN FDR DRIVE WITH
sirens blaring. Chris found himself veering with each divot
and turn of the emergency vehicle. Anxiety. Desperation.
Longing. He was not the type of man to fall on his knees in
prayer, but sitting beside Dara on the way to Mount Sinai, his
heart aching, he considered it.

He had almost lost her.

Dara, however, was having the time of her life. Lying flat
on a stretcher between him and an EMT, her head bobbed
from side to side. He was relieved that she was okay, that she
was still awake and communicating. Even if she could no longer discern her indoor voice from her outdoor one.

"Chris!" Dara said, tapping him on the arm. "Chris!"

"I'm right here," he said, squeezing her hand. "You don't
need to scream, Dara."

She nuzzled her head into his wrist. "You're amazing, Chris!"

He smiled. "I appreciate the compliment."

Dara groaned, and then rolled onto her belly, nearly falling off the stretcher in the process. Chris whoa-ed, grabbing

her and pulling her back to safety. She didn't seem to realize that she had almost fallen.

"You're so pretty," Dara said, clutching his elbow. "Do you know how pretty you are? You're like...the sky! The bright blue sky!" She considered the thought before her eyeballs rolled back into her head.

Chris glanced over to the EMT. "Is she high?"

"Not exactly," he explained, fiddling with her IV. "It's more like she's dreaming. The meds we gave her in tandem with the EpiPen kind of whack you out."

"Chris." Dara began tapping on his arm again. "I like you."

"I like you, too," Chris said. The EMT went back to his monitoring of her vital signs.

"You're, like, *sooooooooooooo* pretty."

He laughed. "So you keep telling me."

"Are we friends?" she asked, her head twisting back and forth like it was struggling to remain affixed to her neck. "I want to be your friend."

"Of course we're friends."

"Nooooooo." She wagged one finger at him. "We're *work* friends. We're *ca-leagues*. I don't know anything—" she hiccuped "—about you. You're like your shoulders."

"My shoulders?"

"Squared. Guarded. Nobody wants to see—" she waved her hands around like she was making a potion "—all that. You know why you ask so many questions, Chris?"

"I suppose you're going to tell me."

"Because—" she jabbed one finger toward his eye "—you don't want to talk about yourself. It's easier...to point the camera at somebody else."

Chris leaned back in his seat, surprised at her analysis of him. Dara had pegged him perfectly. He was just about to defend himself—or, at the very least, explain that he had good reason for being so guarded about his personal life—when her eyelids began to close.

"I'm so tired," she said. A dollop of drool ran down the side of her mouth.

At her words, the EMT sprang into action. All at once, he was putting something into her IV before pressing a few buttons and double-checking her vitals once again.

"Is she okay?" Chris asked, the anxiety in his chest returning.

"She's stable," he said. "But it's better if she can stay awake until we get her to the ER. The doctors will want her to be able to answer some questions."

Chris nodded. Still holding her hand, he kept her talking and conscious.

"You're gonna be okay, Dara." Chris spoke gently. He had an urge to stroke her hair, to run his fingers over the spot above her ear, pushing through her tangles.

"I wish we were married!" Dara said, suddenly.

"You want to get married?"

"Would you marry me, Chris?"

"I think you're on a lot of very strong drugs."

"I LOVE DRUGS!" she screamed, popping up like some possessed character from *The Exorcist*, before flopping back down to her bed. "I can't marry you," she said, with an exaggerated frown. "You're not...*sssshhhe*-wish."

"Sssshe-wish?"

She booped him on the nose, before cackling in hysterics. "You don't even know what a mezuzah is!"

"I know what a mezuzah is," he defended himself.

"Oh yeah!" She snapped her fingers in his face. "Well, you don't even know what a *hatafat dam* is!"

Chris considered the accusation. "You're right. I don't know what that is."

"Well," she said, moving to sit up once again. The EMT,

experienced with these things, pushed her back down to the bed with one latex-covered hand. Dara, unfazed, continued on. "If you knew what it was…trust me, you wouldn't want one."

They pulled up to the hospital, and the doors to the ambulance were flung open. A dozen hands were soon upon her, unloading her from the vehicle. Dara, still in some semi-aware dream state, waved like a beauty queen parading through the state fair.

The EMTs followed behind her. Chris waited for a moment, giving them all space to do their jobs, before stepping out of the ambulance himself.

He took a deep breath. Standing at the entrance to the emergency room, the sign above him glowing in neon lights, he was inundated with a rush of emotion. He closed his eyes, willing the memory of Claire away.

Two cars pulled up to the entrance. Chris recognized the first one, a beat-up old jalopy with a *Nobody Loves Staten Island* bumper sticker, as belonging to Eleanor. The second was a van for *Good News New York*. Chris barely had time to register the sight of both vehicles, and what they were doing at the hospital, when the production team for *Good News* streamed onto the street around him.

As the crew pulled out cameras and set up lighting, Eleanor began barking orders. "Let's get some B-roll of the hospital. Chris, I want you in front of the entrance. We'll run a few takes on your closing, get a few sound bites for the audience… use it as a tease to the at-home viewing audience."

"No."

Eleanor placed her hands on her hips. "What do you mean, *no*?"

"I mean, no!" He said it again, his anger growing. "Dara almost died tonight. She almost died, Eleanor! And all you care about is getting a sound bite? Did you even ask if she

225

would be okay? Or is that just another opportunity to boost the ratings?"

The entire production crew fell silent. Chris was not the type of man to lose his temper, but he was suddenly transported back in time. His rage misplaced, the feelings from the night Claire died mingling with his present, he spun around in his spot. Marching toward the waiting room of the ER, he disappeared inside without another word.

Four hours later, Chris had still not received an update on Dara. He sat in the waiting room beside a dozen other strangers, CNN blaring in the background. Visitors came and left. Down the hallway, a young woman folded her head into her hands and burst into tears. Chris shifted in his seat and tried not to think about Claire.

He pulled out his cell phone and checked the time. It was 10:00 p.m. Lacey's babysitter would need to be going home. He debated next steps.

He could text Jensen and Katie, ask them to watch Lacey for the rest of the evening. But Katie had just had a baby, and the last thing Chris wanted to do was add to what was probably already an exhausting week and a difficult sleeping schedule. He considered leaving the ER, letting Eleanor or Eli deal with Dara, but he felt a personal responsibility to remain behind.

He had promised to be with Dara every step of the way, after all. He couldn't just abandon the poor woman in the ER of a Manhattan hospital when she had almost died. He needed to be there for her. Finally, he settled on the only decent option left to him. Chris texted Mona.

I'm gonna be here a little longer. Would you be able to stay late tonight?

How much later?

Not sure.

I don't think so, Chris. I got to
get home to my own kids.

He hated doing it, but he felt that he had no choice. For as
brave as his daughter was regarding killer clowns, he knew
she would get scared being left alone at night. He texted
Mona back:

**Can you bring her here before you go
home? I'll pay for an Uber.**

Give me an hour.

Chris glanced up at the clock. It worried him that it was
taking forever. His eyes wandered back to the other families
in the waiting room, the looks of worry and concern across
their faces.

"I'm sorry," Eleanor said, taking a seat next to him.

Chris nodded. Since she was offering a mea culpa, he felt
the need to ask for forgiveness, too. "And I'm sorry," he said,
genuinely. "I shouldn't have lost my temper. It wasn't actually
about you. It's just, I was reminded of..."

Eleanor nodded. "I know."

A moment of silence stretched between them.

"Look," Eleanor said, clasping her hands in front of her. "I
know who I am, okay? I'm driven. I'm tough. There's nothing I want more in life than to get moved to a top-rated show
on prime time. Sometimes, I'm a hard-ass because of it. But I

know what I want, Chris. I'm not gonna apologize for going after it. So I guess my question for you is…what do you want?"

He knew what she was asking. Did he really want this show? Was he willing to do the things necessary to get to prime time alongside her?

Chris wasn't certain. His passion for news had taken a serious hit many years ago, then dipped into nonexistence after Claire. He felt stuck, like he was constantly spinning in circles. He had been on the journalistic path since college. Giving that up now would basically mean starting over. He didn't have the luxury of beginning again. He had a kid.

Still, he couldn't help but sit with her question. What did he really want for his life? He thought back on the last few weeks, the way his heart had shifted since meeting Dara, his fear at watching her pass out, riding with her to the hospital. He hadn't been able to leave her behind. And then, suddenly, he had his answer.

He wanted Dara.

The realization surprised him.

Eleanor said her good-nights and took off. But Chris was still swirling.

Nearly losing Dara tonight had confirmed the feelings that he had been trying to bury. More than liking her, he realized, she had made him rethink the trajectory of his own life. Pulling out his phone, he googled the words *converting to Judaism*.

Quickly, he scanned the top few sources. Classes, learning languages and prayers. He would have to find a rabbi. Converting to Judaism seemed hella complicated. In the faith he was raised, you just showed up at the door, claimed your intention to become a Baptist and got dunked in water. Easy peasy.

His eyes caught a phrase that he recognized from his ambulance ride with Dara: *Hatafat Dam Brit*. Curious, he clicked on the link. He began reading the article. In order to convert to Judaism, males needed to be circumcised.

At least that wouldn't be a problem. He was American, after all. It was standard practice to circumcise males right after birth in pretty much every major hospital. But then, leaning in closer, he read the fine print:

"The mohel pricks the foreskin of the convert with a pin in the place where circumcision would have occurred. Blood is drawn and collected on a strip of gauze. The evidence of the conversion is then displayed to the rabbinic court. In this way, the halachic, or Jewish legal commandment, of the Brit Milah, or covenant of circumcision, is performed."

Chris shifted in his seat. You had to really love a woman if you were willing to get your *schlong* pricked for her. Maybe that was the point, though. Judaism was a religion that didn't believe in proselytizing.

A commotion at the front of the waiting area drew his attention. Chris glanced up to see Mona arriving with Lacey. His heart sank at the sight of his poor kid, in pajama pants and a pink coat, being dragged along by an equally exhausted babysitter. Quickly, Chris clicked off his phone and rose to greet them.

"Hey, you," Chris said, bending down to kiss Lacey on the cheek, before turning his attention to Mona. "I really appreciate this, Mona."

"Hmm," she said, and twisted back around toward the door.

She did not look happy as she left. Chris couldn't help but wonder if he would still have a babysitter tomorrow. He made a mental note to give her a raise. Otherwise, he focused all his energy on taking care of his kid. Grabbing a pillow and blanket from the nurses' station, he created a makeshift bed for his daughter in the waiting room.

"Here you go," Chris said, laying it all out. "Almost as good as home."

Lacey blinked in his direction. "Is Dara dead?"

"What?" he asked, surprised. "Of course not."

"Then why are we at the hospital?"

Lacey had become quite the fan of his show since Dara's arrival. Ever since what she called *the murder hornet incident*, his daughter had never missed an episode. She even watched all the in-between segments, the fillers meant to drive up interest—interviews with friends, family and potential suitors.

Chris tried to assuage her fears. "Dara is fine. She just had an accident."

"People go to the hospital to die."

"People go to the hospital for all sorts of reasons," Chris explained. "Most of them come out alive."

"Well, what about Mom?"

"Mom didn't die in a hospital."

The words fell from his lips before he had a chance to stop himself. Right away, he realized his mistake. Lacey didn't know the full story of how Claire died. She was only nine years old when it happened, after all. He had made a conscious decision to spare her from the worst of the details.

"But you went to the hospital," Lacey said, confused. "After she died."

He went to the morgue. He went to the funeral home. He went to the police station to collect items and sign paperwork. But Claire had died on the side of I-95. She had died alone, too. The thought always bothered him.

"Lacey—" Chris said, getting flustered.

"Where did she die, then?"

"Look," he said, trying to change the topic. "We'll talk about it later, okay?"

"No, we won't. You never want to talk about it."

"Please," he said, pointing to his makeshift bed. "Just try

to get some sleep. I'll make this up to you tomorrow with all the ice cream you could possibly want to eat."

Lacey huffed her annoyance, but eventually acquiesced. As she drifted off to sleep, Chris watched over her, his mind wandering.

Of course, the decision to convert to Judaism wouldn't only affect him. He had a daughter, after all. Would Lacey need to convert, too? He couldn't imagine her being amenable to giving up Christmas, the Easter Bunny and pork.

He returned to Google. As it turned out, children could be converted by their parents before the age of thirteen, after which they were considered an adult under Jewish law and thus had to reaffirm their commitment to Judaism. Otherwise, and for a female, the only requirement for conversion was immersion in the *mikvah*, or ritual bath.

He glanced at his daughter, sleeping peacefully beside him.

Lacey didn't even like taking showers.

Finally, a nurse's voice rang out from the doorway. "Anyone here for Dara Rabinowitz?"

Chris raised his hand. "Me."

"She is waiting for you in room 18," she directed him. "If you like, you can go in and see her now."

"Thank you."

The nurse took off. Chris stirred his daughter awake. "Hey, kiddo," he said, and explained the situation. "I'm gonna go check on Dara, alright? I'll be right down the hallway, in room 18."

"Can I come with you?"

"Not now."

"But—" she whined. "I've always wanted to meet her."

"Another time, okay? For now, I just need you to wait here."

She blinked her sleepy eyes in his direction. "Okay."

★ ★ ★

Chris found Dara sitting up on a bed, wearing a hospital gown. His heart leaped at the sight of her, safe and alive. Throwing his arms around her in a tight embrace, he pressed her against his chest.

"Hey," he said. "How are you feeling?"

"Better."

The hug lingered between them for longer than necessary. Finally, Chris released her.

In the distance, he could hear the sound of beeping machines. Nurses shouting in the hallways. And yet, for the first time since he had met her, he let himself acknowledge the overwhelming sensation of want prickling through his chest.

"Maybe I'm not supposed to find anyone," she said, quietly.

"Dara—"

"No," she cut him off. "I'm a disaster, Chris. I'm, honestly, the most unlucky person in the world when it comes to love. Every date…every single date I go on turns out *worse* than the one before it. Clearly, it's a sign. Clearly, the universe is trying to tell me that I'm meant to be single forever."

Chris sat down on the bed beside her.

"I try so hard," she said sadly. "I try so hard to get everything right, to get everything perfect, and it all falls apart anyway."

He considered the statement. "Maybe that's the issue."

She wrinkled her nose in his direction. "What?"

"Love isn't careful. It's messy…and confusing. You put yourself out there, knowing that it may end in disaster. But you show up anyway. That's what people see in you. That's why people love you, too. You think you're the only person in the world who has had terrible dates, but everyone has been there."

"Everybody has not almost died in a sukkah."

Chris couldn't help but laugh at that one.

"True." He smiled, nudging her shoulder a little. "You do have a knack for the dramatic."

Thankfully, Dara laughed, too. Their cheeks blushing and elbows touching, they folded into another awkward moment of silence. And yet, Dara didn't pull away. The heat of her body sparking the passion in his own. He found himself drawn to her, staring at the lines and angles in her delicate neck. All he could think about was pushing her thick hair behind one ear and trailing his tongue along her skin.

"Dad?" Lacey said, peeking her head inside.

"Lace—" Chris jumped. His heart sank at the sound of her tiny voice at the door. Sprinting to the threshold, kneeling down in front of her, he was simultaneously concerned about his daughter while wondering what Dara would think.

"What's up, kiddo?" he whispered.

"I'm thirsty," Lacey said dramatically. "Can I have some money for a soda? There's a vending machine at the end of the hall."

Normally, he would not let his daughter drink soda before bedtime. Or after, in this case. But considering he had dragged her to Manhattan to the ER of a hospital, it seemed fair to make an exception. Chris dug into his pocket, pulling out a few dollars.

"Knock yourself out," he said.

"Thanks."

"And, Lacey," Chris called out to her before she departed. "As soon as you're done getting a soda, please go right back to the waiting room. I don't want you wandering about the hospital, okay?"

Lacey disappeared from view. Chris turned back around to find Dara staring, her lower lip now planted on the floor. "You have...a daughter?"

Chris rubbed the back of his neck. "Yeah."

"Lacey—" she closed her eyes over the words "—isn't your girlfriend?"

"No."

"I don't...understand."

Chris had kept the truth about Lacey—and Claire—under wraps since he'd started at *Good News*. But he didn't feel right lying to Dara. He wanted her to know him.

"I was married...for ten years."

"Oh. Wow," she said, almost to herself. "I had no idea." She swallowed. "That's a long time. You...divorced?"

"No," he said quietly. "She...died."

There. He had said it. Someone else in this world knew his truth.

He went on. He explained how it was a typical afternoon in September when Claire died. Lacey had just started school. Claire had complained about a headache that morning, but otherwise, everything seemed fine. She took some Advil and Chris went off to work.

"She was on her way to pick up Lacey from dance practice in Alexandria," he said. "She was driving on I-95, when suddenly, she veered off the road. Turned out it was an aneurysm. Nobody's fault. One minute she was here, and then she wasn't. She died on that road, all alone...before I got there."

He didn't say the part about how he blamed himself. *If only I had been the person to pick up Lacey that afternoon. If only I had insisted Claire go to the doctor for that headache, or stayed home to be with her.* It was unfounded guilt. Claire always got headaches. Claire always picked up Lacey from extracurricular activities. What happened to her that afternoon was simply a random and senseless tragedy.

Grief wasn't logical. It was the only thing he knew for certain about his pain. It whispered terrible things to him at night—told him that he wasn't good enough, told him that he should have done more. Perhaps, in some way, it was why he could always relate to Dara's anxiety. He understood being overwhelmed by your own irrational thoughts. It *felt* reasonable, even when you *factually* knew that it wasn't.

"You found her?" Dara asked.

He nodded. "I was always the first reporter on the scene."

"Oh, Chris," Dara said, laying one hand on his wrist. "I'm so sorry."

"After Claire died," he explained, "my whole world collapsed. Everything reminded me of the loss. The neighbors. My family. Our church. One day, I went to the grocery store, and just stood in the same aisle for hours, unable to choose a box of macaroni and cheese. Unable to move, or process... I just sort of spun out. Two days later, I accepted a position at *Good News New York*. I changed my broadcasting name from Chris Steed to Christopher Steadfast, and never looked back."

"You could have told me," Dara said, finally. "About Lacey, especially. I would have understood."

"I know." He sighed, trying to explain his rationale. "It wasn't that I was trying to hide her from you, either. It's just... I've found it easier to keep that part of my life private. Beyond the fact that I don't want my daughter in the public eye, television is a jealous lover. My job requires long hours and near constant devotion. Executives don't have space in their budgets for head anchors who have to race home and deal with kids."

"But you love it, right?" Dara asked. "*Good News*. Making television. Telling stories?"

"I don't know." Chris sighed. "I used to love it. I used to want nothing more than to be a reporter. But now, all I really want is to be a good father to Lacey. I just want to be able to give her some stability, and happiness, after everything she's been through."

"That's why you were so desperate to save your show," Dara said, suddenly putting it together. "For Lacey."

"Everything I do," he said, genuinely. "*Everything* has been for her."

Dara stared down at the cup of water between her hands.

"You're suddenly very quiet," Chris said.

"I'm just…" She shook off whatever she was thinking. "Taking it all in."

"What?" he asked, deflecting with a joke. "You don't meet a lot of widowed single dads?"

"It's not that," she said. He noted she did not laugh. "It's just…well, I thought you were someone different. I also thought Lacey was your girlfriend."

"Really?"

She nodded. "I envisioned her as a leggy blonde with a penchant for bodycon dresses."

Chris laughed. "Sorry to disappoint you."

Her heart-shaped lips angled up in his direction. "I'm not."

Chris couldn't pull himself away. He had almost lost Dara tonight. The realization had stirred awake long-buried feelings. He had resisted her since their first meeting, but now, he accepted the truth. He needed her. He longed to tangle himself up in her perfect lists and messy locks.

Chris inched closer. Dara did the same. Her lips parted, wet and tender, in his direction.

And then, a knock at the door pulled them apart.

23

THE KNOCK AT THE DOOR CAUGHT HER OFF GUARD.
Dara jumped, accidentally smacking Chris in the nose on accident. By the time she realized what she had done—that she had almost kissed the handsome and totally not-Jewish reporter—she had, thankfully, returned to her senses.

Catching her breath, shaking off any lingering feelings of attraction, she turned in the direction of the doorway. Standing on the threshold, wearing a stethoscope and a kippah, was the most handsome Jewish doctor she had ever laid eyes on.

Baruch Hashem, indeed.

"I'm Dr. Daniel Evans," he said. "I'm the attending physician here at Mount Sinai." Heading over to the wall, he grabbed Dara's medical chart.

Dara could not speak. There was something about the young man that felt familiar. Like she had known him all her life. Or maybe…it was something much simpler. Dr. Daniel was quickly ticking off every item on her perfect Jewish husband list.

He was the perfect height, coming in at a respectable five foot eleven. He had dark hair and eyes, and what could only be described as a swimmer's body. But what really got her kugel cooking was the yarmulke he was wearing. It was made up of quilted materials, and Dara recognized it immediately as a design from the online company Eco-Jew. Based in Seattle, Eco-Jew used recycled materials to create artisan Judaica.

Suddenly, Daniel looked up from her file. Glancing over to Dara, back to the chart, his eyes bugged out of his head. "Oh my God!" he said. "You're Dara Rabinowitz. From *Good News New York*?"

Dara touched her heart, surprised to be recognized. "I am."

"Wow!" He shook her hand with great enthusiasm. "I'm, like...a huge fan."

"Really?"

"I watch all your segments!" Daniel blushed, and began rambling. "Well, when I can. Obviously, I'm at the hospital much of the time...and then, on the weekends I volunteer at a medical clinic. But I record all your segments and watch it on my time off."

"Really?" Dara turned bright red. "That's so sweet!"

"You're pretty much the highlight of my entire week."

It was then that Dara realized where she knew him from.

"Oh my God," Dara shouted, covering her mouth with both hands. "You're on J-Mate!"

He blushed, sheepishly. "Well, I just moved to the city."

"No, I mean—" Dara shook her head in disbelief "—you're YourMomWillLoveMe? I almost wrote you a few weeks back."

"Really?"

"Yeah." She smiled. "I was going to, but then...well, it's a long story."

They went on sharing their mutual admiration of each other for several minutes. Dr. Daniel doling out compliments. Dara giggling like a schoolgirl, playing with one curl while he spoke. In truth, she was so enamored with the young physician, she completely forgot that Chris was still in the room.

"Did you just say that you only recently moved to the city?" Dara asked, curiously.

"About three months ago," Daniel said.

"Wait, you wouldn't happen to be cousins with Elissa Spitzman?"

"How…how did you know that?"

"Do you have J-eography set up on your J-Mate?"

"Do I?" He laughed, pulling out his phone.

Seconds later, and with both their apps open, they began comparing notes. There was more laughter as Dara realized that Dr. Daniel Evans was, indeed, the young physician that her own sister, Shana—along with Elissa Spitzman from Camp Ahava—had tried to set her up with during a casual Shabbat *shidduch* only a month prior.

"Wait," Dr. Daniel said, blinking a bit. "So you're Shana Rabinowitz's sister?"

"I am."

"I can't believe I didn't put that together!"

Dara pointed to her corkscrews. "The hair didn't give it away?"

He had just burst out laughing when Chris decided to interject.

"I'm sorry," Chris snapped. Dara was surprised by the tone in his voice. His words came out clipped and sharp. "If you two don't mind hurrying this up, it's late. I need to get home. Is it safe to say that Dara is getting discharged?"

"Oh." Daniel smiled, his head swiveling between them. "Right. I had completely forgotten that we're here for a reason."

Daniel went to wash his hands in the sink. Dara squinted in Chris's direction, and mouthed the words, *What's wrong?*

Chris mouthed back, *I have a kid, remember?*

She supposed that made sense. Still, she had not met anyone as perfect as Dr. Daniel since beginning her search for the perfect Jewish husband. The least Chris could do was give her five minutes.

Daniel finished washing his hands. "To think, we could have met a month ago."

"Like kismet," she said.

"Or *bashert*." He winked at her.

Daniel brought his hands up to her neck and gently palpated the muscles. "I'm just checking for any more swelling," he explained. "Making sure there are no lingering aftereffects. It's mango you're allergic to, right?"

"Yes."

"Well," he said as he pulled his hands away from her. "Mango is now officially my least favorite fruit."

Chris scoffed aloud.

Dara ignored him, turning her attention back to Daniel.

"So that's it?" she asked. "I'm free to go?"

"Actually," Daniel said, pulling his prescription pad and a pen out of the front pocket of his white doctor's coat, "I'm afraid I'm going to need to schedule a follow-up with you."

"A follow-up?" Dara asked, concerned. "Is there something wrong?"

"I'm afraid so." He frowned. "But thankfully, I have the perfect prescription."

Daniel tore off the page, handing it to Dara.

Reading it, she broke into a wide smile. "Yes."

"Really?"

"I'd love to."

She was still giddy with delight when a voice rang out over the loudspeaker. A code red had arrived. All doctors on staff were needed. Dr. Daniel placed his pen back into his pocket and apologized for having to leave her so abruptly.

"Of course," Dara said, understanding. "Lives to save and all."

"But we'll talk tomorrow?" Daniel asked.

"Definitely," she promised.

Daniel disappeared from the room. Dara beamed happily from the bed, waiting for Chris to squeal in excitement along with her. Instead, he folded his arms across his chest.

"I'm not sure I understand what's going on," he said, clearly perturbed. "Are you getting discharged from the hospital or not?"

She held up the piece of paper. "Dr. Daniel asked me out!"

"What?"

He grabbed the note from her hand. On it, Dr. Daniel had written a prescription for:

An evening on the town with a very handsome Jewish doctor.

"I'm sorry," Chris said, tossing the note back to her. "This can't happen."

"What do you mean *this can't happen*?" Dara said. "He asked me out, and I accepted. I don't think you have any ability to stop us."

"Well, what about the show?" He was pacing around the room, growing more agitated.

Dara considered his question seriously. "We can just wrap him into the next date," she explained. "Simchat Torah is coming up, and I know an amazing place—"

"Absolutely not."

"Why not?"

"Because," Chris said, clearly annoyed. "It won't feel natural!"

Dara shifted in her seat. "I don't think any of my dates have felt *natural*."

"Dara, we haven't even vetted the man. He could be a ma-

241

niac. He could be a serial killer! He could be after you for your money!"

"Really, Chris?" Dara crossed her arms against her chest. "The man volunteers at a free clinic on the weekends. He was wearing an Eco-Jew kippah. He's the attending physician in a major Manhattan hospital. I think it's fair to say we'll be safe on one date. Besides, you'll be there with your cameras."

"Well, what if he doesn't want to do it?"

"I'm sure you can persuade him with your charming Southern ways."

"Well, what if he loves sports?"

"Chris!" She laughed outright at his objection. "I don't understand why you're being so weird about this."

"I'm not..." he stammered. "I'm not being weird."

"Look," she said, uncrossing her arms, "he's Jewish. He's a doctor. He knows my sister. He's totally perfect! And isn't that the whole point of this series? To find *me* my Mr. Perfect on Paper? Well, this is the closest anybody has gotten."

She was beaming ear to ear as she spoke. The potential of Dr. Daniel—the realization that he wanted to date her, too—bringing with it a thousand floating butterflies. Dara was happy.

Alas, Chris looked downright miserable.

She looked away from him, willing him not to say the words aloud. After all, the kiss they had almost shared was completely irrelevant. Christopher Steadfast was not Jewish. It didn't matter if her heart leaped whenever he was near. It didn't matter if she *occasionally* slept in the suit jacket she had yet to give back. They were two people who were not looking in the same direction. A marriage between them was not in the cards.

"This feels right, Chris," she said.

He was quiet for a long time. "Fine," he said finally, throwing his hands up into the air. "Okay. Your next date will be with Dr. Daniel."

Dara squealed aloud. Shooting up from the bed, she wrapped her arms tightly around his neck in a warm embrace. She had to stand on her tippy-toes to do it. "Thank you, Chris."

"Yeah, yeah," he said, patting her on the back. "I know. But—" He pulled away from her, meeting her eyes directly. "If he winds up murdering you and wearing your skin around as a person suit, don't say I didn't warn you. This one was your terrible idea."

Simchat Torah

24

CHRIS HAD NEVER BEEN TO A PARTY QUITE LIKE THE one being held at Congregation B'nei Sarah on the Upper West Side. Young Jewish singles, intermingled with families and the elderly, passed out tiny shots of schnapps. An emphatic mixture of music, klezmer intertwined with violin in G-sharp, floated through the air.

Simchat Torah, literally meaning "rejoicing with the Torah," followed immediately after the Festival of Sukkot, and celebrated the conclusion of the annual cycle of Torah reading. It was tradition on Simchat Torah to remove each Torah scroll from the arc where it normally rested, and parade it with great and joyous exuberance around the main sanctuary of the synagogue. In this way, it recalled the great joy and exuberance that the ancient Israelites must have felt upon receiving the Torah at Mount Sinai.

Inside the main sanctuary, Chris watched a large group of Jews dancing together. Skirts and tzitzit wildly waving, hands interlocked as the participants kicked up their feet in raucous and unbridled energy. He found the explosion of joy surrounding him infectious. Bopping his head to the music, he almost missed Dara spinning in her own *hakafah* beside Dr. Daniel.

"Hey," she said, suddenly spinning her way over to greet him. "You're here!"

Chris blushed. "I'm here."

"Did you have any trouble getting here?" she asked, screaming over the crowd.

Normally, Chris was the person who arrived early to their filming locations. But something about Dr. Daniel—*perfect Dr. Daniel, with his stupid freaking medical degree*—had changed Dara's pattern. She had come to synagogue early. Much to his chagrin, she had started her date early, too.

"No," Chris said, screaming back. "But I'm surprised you're here already."

"Oh. Is that okay?"

"Yeah, it's just..." Chris couldn't help himself. He was suddenly looking for reasons to tear them apart. "I don't want you to look sweaty."

"What?" she screamed, cupping her ear.

"Sweaty!" he repeated. "I don't want you to look—"

It was too late. Before he could explain his *totally logical* rationale, Dr. Daniel grabbed her by the hand. "Come on," Daniel shouted, pulling Dara into another round of circle dancing. "It's no fun without you!"

Chris watched Dara disappear into the crowd. His stomach twisted. His heart ached. And then, he forced himself to get a goddamn grip. Dara was happy. She had found someone she liked. More important, considering her last few dates, she hadn't broken an ankle or wound up in hospital. The least Chris could do was be happy for her.

Moments later, Eleanor appeared at his side.

"She seems to like this one," she said curiously.

"Yeah."

"We might need to rethink the trajectory of her segment. Maybe we wrap sooner than we expected."

Chris didn't like the thought. "She just met him, Eleanor."

"Yeah, but—"

"I mean—" Chris was suddenly adamant in his dismissal of the possibility "—she doesn't even know this guy. And look at him, all smiling and happy, dancing with a Torah in a large and doting circle while Dara squeals and fawns over the man like some adolescent schoolgirl. It's horrible. We really should put a stop to this."

Eleanor squinted. "What the hell has gotten your panties in a ruffle?"

"Nothing." He swallowed the words he wanted to say. "I just want the best for her."

"Sure," Eleanor said, raising a brow. "The best for her."

Eleanor headed off to check on sound. Chris resolved to get a grip. After all, nothing had happened. All Dara and Daniel were doing was circle dancing. Still, watching them together, he couldn't help but direct a twinge of animosity toward Mr. Perfect on Paper.

Two hours later, Congregation B'nei Sarah was on their third *hakafah*—or round of circle dancing around the synagogue—and Dara was officially out of breath.

"Are you having a good time?" Daniel shouted over the music.

"The best," she admitted.

"Me, too."

Dara fell into his eyes as the lights of the camera following after them grew brighter. Though she had never inherited her grandmother's talent for dance, she could manage a proper Jewish circle dance with the best of them.

"Are you good for another round?" Dara asked, shouting over the music.

"Actually—" Daniel stepped in closer to her "—I was wondering if you would like to take a break together? Perhaps get something to drink. Talk a bit. I'm excited to get to know you better, Dara."

Her heart pattered inside her chest. "I'd love that."

She followed him outside. As they walked in the direction of Riverside Park down by the water, the music from Congregation B'nei Sarah dimmed. Before long, the only people on the street were Dara, Daniel and the cameras trailing them. Dara and Daniel spoke about their families, their careers, their hopes and wishes for the future…until finally, Dara got right down to business.

"Do you watch any sports?"

Daniel smiled, knowingly. "I hate sports."

"You're kidding me."

"Honestly. I can't think of a worse thing to spend my time doing during the weekend. Sitting around, watching a football game, drinking beer? Sorry…hard pass. I much prefer volunteering, spending my free time giving back to my community. I take very seriously the Jewish mandate of *tikun olam*, making the world a better place."

"Wow."

A cool breeze wrapped around their shoulders. Romance was in the air.

"And do you have any hobbies?" Dara asked, dreamily.

"You mean, when I'm not volunteering at the clinic?"

She laughed. "Yeah."

"It's kind of embarrassing to admit," he said, blushing, "but I love going outlet shopping. Not as much for myself, of course…but I love finding some great deal on a blouse or a bag for my mom or my sister."

Dara swallowed. "I do the same thing for my bubbe."

Suddenly, she caught sight of a string of lights hanging from two trees. Beneath it, a picnic blanket was laid out and waiting. Food and champagne rested beside a bouquet of three dozen roses. Dara was so caught up in the moment, she completely forgot about the camera crew still circling around them. She also forgot about Chris. Looking over, she was surprised to find him watching patiently from the sidelines.

Dara turned back to Daniel, surprised. "What is all this?"

"This is for you," he said, leading her to the blanket. "I know that some of your dates have been less than stellar, so I wanted to rectify that. I hope everything is to your liking."

"You planned all this yourself?"

"I worked with Eleanor on the details," he explained, sitting down beside her. "But it was important to me that our first real date be...well, ours."

Dara sighed. "It's lovely."

"Just so you know—" Daniel picked up a plate of chocolate-covered strawberries "—there's no mango in anything."

She laughed aloud. "I appreciate that."

He fed her a chocolate strawberry, then poured two very tall glasses of bubbly. After a few moments of indulging in the delicious fizz and sweetness of the moment, Daniel put down his plate of food.

"Look, Dara," Daniel said, meeting her eyes directly. "I like you, but I want to be up front here. I'm thirty-six years old. My medical career is firmly established. I own my own apartment. I'm not saying these things to brag, but rather, so that you understand where I'm coming from. I'm not dating to mess around. I'm searching for my future wife. Also, God willing, the mother of my children. I hope that you're looking for the same thing."

Dara nodded, solemnly. "I am."

"Good," Daniel said, taking her hand. "Because I can't help but feel that we are absolutely perfect for each other."

Dara felt light-headed. She wasn't sure if her dizziness stemmed from the way Dr. Daniel was edging closer to her, or the half glass of champagne she had just downed, but the pounding in her chest refused to abate.

She envisioned a thousand happy holidays together. Passover dinners and Shabbat lunches, entertaining friends. Standing beneath the huppah, their children getting Bar and Bat Mitzvah, trips to Israel—a committed Jewish family.

Dara had always been taught not to kiss on first dates, but Dr. Daniel edged closer to her on the blanket. Cupping her chin with three soft fingers, he spoke words of romance, telling her she was beautiful, describing all the elaborate ways he loved the curl in her corkscrews. Dara couldn't help herself. She swooned over each flawless sentiment.

What would one little kiss hurt?

There was a good chance this man was going to be her future husband. Shouldn't they seal the deal, let the at-home viewing audience know that fairy tales were possible? Despite the ridiculousness of her lists—the careful way she organized her life to manage all her fears—Dara had found Mr. Perfect on Paper. Love was in the air.

Closing her eyes, and parting her lips, she gave in to the spinning in her chest.

Chris took his cue.

Stepping in front of the camera, he began to wrap their Simchat Torah segment.

"That's all the time we have for today," he said, "but tune in next week when we find out if Dr. Daniel and Dara will indeed be heading on to a second date. I'm Christopher Steadfast with *Good News New York*—"

He was just about to wrap their segment with his signature line when a sight on the picnic blanket made his stomach drop. Dara and Daniel were kissing. Full on, hands and tongues tangled up in each other, eating each other's faces.

Chris couldn't breathe. He couldn't think. Something about Dara kissing Daniel threw him completely off his game. For the first time in his life, Chris flubbed his line.

"Till next time, America," he said, choking on his tongue, "*whoa.*"

Mid-October

(OTHERWISE KNOWN AS
THE END OF THE
JEWISH HIGH HOLIDAYS)

25

CHRIS TAPPED HIS PEN REPEATEDLY AGAINST THE PALM of his hand.

Sitting in his office, watching Dara's segment on *Good News* for the umpteenth time, he couldn't deny that the couple on the screen before him made great television. Better yet, and for once, everything had gone according to plan.

Dara didn't get attacked by a roving band of vicious insects. Daniel hadn't asked her to take off her shoes. Even the location, shots of happy dancing juxtaposed against the quiet of their picnic together, worked beautifully. Chris felt invited into their journey, and yet, something was off.

He couldn't quite place the unsettled feeling that rolled around the bottom of his belly, but it felt like stale coffee. Like something gross eating away at his guts. He tried to disregard the feeling, settle it with one of Lacey's snack-sized bags of pretzels paired with antacids, but it was no use. The more he watched Dara kissing Dr. Daniel on the television screen in his office, the more he felt like vomiting.

He was losing her.

Chris glanced up at the sound of a knock on the door to see

Eleanor standing on the threshold. She was holding a bottle of Veuve Clicquot in her right hand, a slim folder tucked under her arm. Two plastic cups, clearly stolen from the watercooler down the hall, dangled from her left hand.

"Good morning!" She beamed.

Chris squinted. It was weird to see Eleanor smiling.

"Morning…" Chris said suspiciously. "You're in a chipper mood this morning. What's with the champagne?"

Plopping into the chair across from him, she allowed a few moments of silence to settle between them, increasing the tension in the room. Finally, she leaned back and, resting both of her stilettos against the edge of his desk, tossed the folder in his direction.

"Read it and weep." The sound of joy in her voice was both shocking and immeasurable. "We have *officially* beaten *Good Day* in the ratings."

Chris could hardly contain the speed with which his fingers raced to pull open the pages. "*What?* We're number one in our time slot?"

"Not just number one in our time slot," she explained, working to open up the bottle. "We're number one in the *entire* morning and afternoon lineup. *Good News* is currently the highest-rated daytime show on cable television."

The champagne cork popped. Eleanor set about pouring two plastic cups of bubbly. Pushing one across the desk, she lifted her own up into the air, readying herself for a toast. Chris, however, had no interest in drinking. He was still too busy choking on her words.

"So—" He needed to make sure he heard her correctly. "We're not getting canceled?"

"Nope."

"I can stay in New York?"

"You and the kid. How's that for a happy morning, *Papa*?"

Chris leaned back in his chair. Dara and Dr. Daniel had saved his show. He was not the type of man to get emotional, but he found himself folding his forehead into the palm of his hand, a wave of relief crashing over him.

"Wow," he said.

"I know!"

"So what does that mean for us?"

Eleanor took that as her cue. She quickly ran through the logistics of the next several shoots. "Obviously we need to start thinking about next steps. I checked in with all the focus groups, and they love Dr. Daniel. People want to see him and Dara together. So what I'm thinking is we keep following them through their courtship. Maybe wrap in the bubbe and the family, too. Milk this for everything we can! Do whatever it takes to keep those numbers coming…"

"And if the numbers keep coming?"

She leaned over to whisper. "What I heard last from the upper floor executives is there's a place open in prime time. Big brass is looking to replace John McKenzie of *Daily Break*. This could be our chance, Chris! This could be the opportunity to move on from *Good News* and make a name for ourselves in this business permanently!"

Chris considered her words. *Daily Break* was an award-winning show in a prime-time slot, focused on hard-hitting investigative journalism. Back in the old days, Chris would have jumped at the opportunity. Now, two dichotomous feelings rose up inside him. A bubble of excitement—of being a stable provider for his young daughter—alongside incomparable dread.

"What's the matter?" Eleanor asked.

Chris returned from his thoughts. "I'm just thinking it through."

"You're also not drinking any champagne."

"It's 9:00 a.m."

Eleanor squinted, swallowing a glug. "So?"

Chris ran one hand through his hair. "You don't think he's a little weird?"

"Who?"

"Dr. Daniel."

Eleanor laughed aloud. Then, completely flabbergasted by the suggestion, she began pointing out all the ways that Dr. Daniel surpassed the basic expectations of the male species. "The man is a heroic ER doctor. He's freaking gorgeous. He volunteers at a free clinic on weekends and makes excellent life choices. I mean…he makes *way* better life choices than you!"

"Thanks."

"Did you know he calls his mother every day?"

"Of course he does."

"I mean, not for nothing, I interviewed the man. I interviewed his family, his friends and the girl he dated in high school. Hell, I even called up the rabbi who circumcised him. Not one person has a bad thing to say about him."

Chris couldn't help himself. "But don't you think he's just a little too perfect?"

"Well, duh!" Eleanor scoffed aloud. "That's the whole point of him, Chris! That's why Dara likes him, and the focus groups adore him. Hell, I might even be falling for the man. Dara is getting exactly what she wanted. What a lot of people following her story wanted for her, too. She's getting her happy ending. She's making us all believe that there's some Dr. Daniel rainbow waiting at the end of our dating shinoozle-storms."

Chris shifted in his seat. He couldn't deny that everything Eleanor was saying was true.

"Look." She softened. "I know how you get about ethics in journalism, and not overstepping boundaries in telling stories, but we're not forcing anything here. Dara and Daniel like each other. Even without our cameras, even without our help setting up dates, they would still continue seeing each other, right?"

"Right."

"All we're doing is documenting it."

Chris took a deep breath. "It's just news."

"It's better than news." Eleanor grinned. "It's *Good News*."

26

THAT AFTERNOON, IN THE CONFERENCE ROOM OF
a luxury hotel in Hoboken, Dara was thinking about the future. Surrounded by twenty-four members of her executive
team—a plate of sugar cookies shaped like the J-Mate logo
laid out between them—she was deep in day four of their
quarterly meeting.

"So, as you will see," Janet said, turning toward a large
PowerPoint presentation projected on the wall. "Subscriptions
for J-Mate are at the highest they have ever been."

Dara glanced over to see Naveah furiously taking notes.
Though her company was almost entirely remote, once every
quarter she flew her executive team in to Hoboken for an
all-hands-on-deck meeting. She would put everyone up at
a luxury hotel on the waterfront, and then, after long hours
in a conference room spent discussing marketing, sales and
forecasts, she would treat her team to fabulous meals and special events.

It was a fiscally responsible and increasingly common way
for tech companies to manage their ever-growing staff of remote employees. Their once-a-quarter meet and greets al-

lowed everyone on Dara's team to get on the same page and speak with one voice.

It also served as their makeshift office watercooler—a time away for her staff to get to know each other—without Dara having to pay exorbitant fees for expensive commercial real estate. Plus, her employees appreciated being able to work together. It was a win-win situation for everyone involved.

Janet continued with her presentation. Moving to another slide, she spoke rapidly, running her hand along a red line graph that moved steadily upward. "Numbers have increased since your first appearance on *Good News* with your grandmother," she explained, "and then risen substantially with the appearance of Dr. Daniel."

Dara was surprised by this new revelation. It had been a few days since their kiss had aired on national television, but the response to Dara finding Mr. Perfect on Paper had been swift. She'd needed to turn off her phone. Thankfully, she had a team of highly paid professional staff willing to manage the onslaught.

"People love him," Janet said.

"Adore him," Diego, head of sales, interjected.

Naveah sighed aloud. "He really is Mr. Perfect."

Dara did not say anything. Like any good CEO, she was taking it all in—listening to the feedback.

"If you're interested in pursuing him," Janet said nervously, "we could continue making it work with *Good News*. Change the concept from you dating different men to following the developing relationship with Daniel."

The entire room fell silent. All eyes now fixed firmly upon Dara, they were waiting for her to say something.

Of course, she knew what she was supposed to say. *Yes! Of course! I can't wait to go on more dates with Dr. Daniel.* After all, the man was perfect. Everyone seemed to love him.

There was only one problem: the kiss.

It hadn't felt right. Or rather, the kiss hadn't *tasted* right.

"And you've spoken with *Good News* about this?" she asked.

"Of course." Janet beamed. "Eleanor is thrilled—"

"And Chris?" Dara asked, interrupting her. "Did anyone talk to Chris yet?"

"As far as we know, Chris is all in."

The words stung. Still, she reasoned away any hurt feelings with sound logic. If Chris was happy, then it likely meant that the ratings for *Good News* were doing better. Perhaps she would not have to give up her favorite show on daytime television, after all.

"And Dr. Daniel?" Dara asked, suspiciously. "Has anyone spoken to him about filming more of our dates? The man is a busy ER doctor, after all. I highly doubt he has time to be tramping all over the city, going on fabulous dates with me, filming every second of—"

"Actually," Naveah interrupted, "I already spoke to Daniel about it, and he said—" she pulled up an email on her tablet to quote from directly "—'I would do anything to spend more time with Dara.'"

The response to this revelation was immediate. The entire room devolved into wistful sighs, touching their hearts.

"So, I'm the last person you asked?" Dara said, somewhat perturbed.

"We wanted to have everything in order," Janet explained, glancing around the room, "before presenting our next marketing campaign to you..."

"Your next campaign?"

Dara squinted in the direction of her staff. She could tell by the way their cheeks blushed, and they smiled at each other, that they had been working on something for a few weeks now. It only made Dara feel more nervous. Reaching for a logo-shaped cookie, she bit the *J* off the *Mate*.

Janet flicked to a new image. Dara tried not to scream aloud at the sight.

Projected on the wall in front of her—at least six feet tall and spruced up via Photoshop—was an image of her and Daniel from their first date. Dara sat on the red-and-white-checkered picnic blanket. Daniel cupped the bottom of her chin, moving forward to kiss her. Fireworks burst in the sky. The trees of Riverside Park watched over them.

Her eyes scrolled down to the bottom of the image, where dramatic white cursive reminiscent of wedding invitations read:

Find Your Perfect Match At J-Mate

Janet clapped both hands together. "What do you think?"

"There weren't fireworks," Dara said succinctly.

"I know." Janet laughed. "But it gives a pop of color to the night sky! Plus, we ran it by six different focus groups, both Jewish singles and their Jewish parents, and everybody wanted the fireworks. I'm telling you, Dara, this is the way to go!"

Dara shifted in her seat. "But we didn't get together via J-Mate."

"But you're both on it." Janet was ready for the argument. "You saw him on there. You would have messaged him if it weren't for…you know."

"Generalized anxiety disorder," she said, definitively.

Janet turned back to the image. "People relate to you, Dara," she said, gazing up with starry eyes at the oversized image. "They see themselves in you. Why not let them see that, because of J-Mate, they can also find their happy ending?"

Her head of marketing and publicity wasn't wrong. J-Mate was not just about cultural, religious and family obligations. At its heart and soul, they were selling a story. Dara and Dr. Daniel had quickly become part of the fantasy they were promising.

Dara knew that they were waiting for an answer. If she was going to be pursuing a relationship with Dr. Daniel, why not continue filming it on camera? Her mother had been on television, after all. It hadn't destroyed her career or professional reputation. And Dr. Daniel ticked every box on her perfect Jewish husband list. The chances of it working out between them were good. Better than good, in fact. They were two people gazing in the same direction.

Alas, sitting inside that conference room with her executive team, staring at an image of their most intimate moment together, she couldn't help but recoil. How could he be so perfect if his kiss didn't taste right? It was like their saliva didn't match. When he touched her, when he placed those perfect lips gently upon her own, it felt like something was missing.

It made no logical sense. On paper, they worked. In terms of the algorithm—the same algorithm Dara had created for J-Mate—they were compatible. They should have been a perfect match. And yet, Dara was hesitating.

"When do you need to know by?" she asked.

"As soon as possible would be ideal," Janet admitted.

Dara nodded. Executive leadership often required making difficult decisions.

"It's fine," Dara said, finally.

"Really?"

"I think you've all done a tremendous job this quarter."

The room quickly sprang into smiles, followed by open expressions of gratitude. Dara smiled along with them. Until finally—with some large measure of relief—she realized she was overthinking. She had a tendency to take a good thing and roll it around in her head until it became awful.

After all, it had been forever since she kissed somebody. There had been cameras following her every move. Even the most courageous of women would have had trouble feeling romantic under such troublesome circumstances. It was not a problem with Dr. Daniel, or their courtship. It was simply the way her brain worked.

She reasoned away any disconnect she felt. It was just her anxiety.

November

27

"KAAAAAAAAATIE!"

The scream that rolled across the Bryant Park ice-skating rink in Manhattan caused several heads to turn, and two poodles nearby to begin barking.

Chris looked up from the table he was sitting at to see Lacey attempting to sprint away on a pair of white skates. Clutching a railing, struggling to maneuver her blades across the short pink carpet, she made a valiant but futile effort.

Jensen and Katie were approaching, a baby carrier swinging between them. Like all new parents, they were loaded down with stuff.

"Oh my God!" Lacey screamed. "Is that the baby?"

"Gentle!" Chris shouted, rising from the table. "New baby!"

It was no use. Lacey was far too excited to calm down. Despite the skates, his daughter began jumping up and down like she had a pogo stick wedged beneath her legs.

Thankfully, Katie didn't seem to mind the tiny hands flailing about her face. Katie handed the baby off to Jensen, before bending down to Lacey, giving her the biggest and longest hug. Chris warmed at the sight. He was grateful to have Katie and Jensen—and now, Jensen Jr.—in their lives. He could never repay them for their kindness.

"Sorry we're late," Jensen said, approaching the table Chris had safeguarded for their Saturday afternoon catch-up together. Around mugs of hot chocolate and plates of Christmas-themed cookies, Jensen dropped his bags. "Ms. We-Should-Follow-Rules-And-All wouldn't let me take the fire truck."

"Um, okay." Katie laughed, plopping down beside him. Settling the carrier on the seat beside her, she gently fussed with the baby's blankets. "Last I checked, there's a reason why *someone* here is no longer allowed to play with the siren."

"Just because there's been some noise complaints…"

"Some?" Katie raised an eyebrow in his direction. "Gunther is gonna have you doing probie work and sleeping on the sofa until Jensen Jr. has children of his own."

Chris raised one eyebrow knowingly toward his best friend. "You getting a little spoiled with those lights?"

"Hey, now!" Jensen defended himself. "I risk my life on the daily for this city. I think given how many times I have bravely rushed into a fire, flexing these big and beautiful muscles to save someone's life, there's nothing wrong with taking the truck to avoid New York City traffic."

"Is he serious?" Chris asked Katie.

"Oh, he's serious," Katie said.

Chris couldn't help but smile. "Care to introduce us to the newest member of the Alvirez family?"

Katie removed the infant from the carrier, lifting him up to show him off. Even though they had seen the baby in passing, Chris had been careful to give the new family their space. This would be the first time that they were officially hanging out.

"Everybody," Katie said, turning his sweet little face upward, "meet Jensen Alvirez Jr."

He was beautiful. Chris took the tiny wonder in his arms.

He smelled like new baby. Like innocence, and possibility, all wrapped up in chunky ankles and the most adorable over-sized belly. He could have held that baby forever, but the child begun fussing.

Chris gave the baby back to Katie, who propped the child up on her chest, rocking him gently. Lacey took a spot beside Katie, shaking a tiny rattle in both their faces. Jensen Jr. responded by drifting back to sleep.

"He doesn't do much," Lacey said.

Katie laughed. "He's still very little."

Lacey turned around with a huff. "Boring!"

Chris frowned at her. "Be nice, okay?"

She crossed her arms against her chest, refusing to make eye contact with any of them. Lacey had recently been getting into moods. Chris knew it was part of her age. His baby girl was growing up. Still, it felt like yet another thing in her young life that he was incapable of helping her through.

Thankfully, Katie was there. Springing into action, she handed Jensen Jr. off to his father. "Hey, how about you come with me to get some ice skates?"

Lacey grumbled, "Are you bringing the baby?"

"Nope," Katie said, standing up. "Just me and you."

This seemed to make Lacey happy. She popped up from the table, leaving her hot chocolate and Santa-Claus-shaped sugar cookie. Hand in hand, they headed toward the ice skate rental booth. Chris watched them depart before turning his attention back to Jensen.

"I appreciate you guys doing this," Chris said. "I know how busy you must be with the new baby, and holidays coming up. But Lacey... Lacey has really missed Katie."

"Of course," Jensen said, rocking his new son gently. "It's our pleasure, man. Besides, and being completely honest here, it feels good to get out of the house. It can get a little stir-crazy

273

otherwise, you know? Just sitting around, managing feedings and sleep schedules when you're not sleeping yourself. Man, parenthood is exhausting!"

Chris nodded. He remembered those days well.

"You got any advice?" Jensen said.

"Me?" He laughed. "You don't want advice from me."

"Of course I do," Jensen said, seriously. "You're a great dad."

Chris faltered. Though he knew Jensen was being genuine, the words stung. Most days, he didn't feel like a great dad. Usually, he felt like a failure on every conceivable level. But it was nice—after struggling so hard—to be recognized for his efforts.

"So?" Jensen prodded him again. "You got any advice?"

Chris considered the question for a few moments. "Show up for Katie."

"For Katie?"

"Yeah," Chris said. "I know it sounds antithetical, but if you want to be a good father, start by being a good husband first. Don't let Katie handle all the emotional labor in the relationship. Help her with cleaning, childcare, laundry, dishes. Be the person who schedules doctor's appointments and looks up summer camps. Bring home flowers just because, and ask how she's doing. Tell her she looks beautiful. You do all those things…you'll be a good dad."

The baby began to cry. Katie looked back from the ice skate rental booth. Moments later, she was charging up the hill in their direction. "Aw," Katie said, taking the child from her husband, "my poor little man! You must be so hungry!" Taking a spot by Jensen beneath the tree, she wrapped a cloth around her neck and began breastfeeding.

Lacey came huffing over. "What are you doing?"

"Feeding the baby," Katie said.

"But we're supposed to go ice-skating!" Lacey stomped one foot.

"Hey!" Chris immediately moved to correct her. "That's not nice. Katie is a mommy now, and that means she has other responsibilities, okay?"

Lacey crossed her arms against her chest. "Stupid baby!" She huffed back down to the ice.

Chris rubbed out a slowly developing headache from the center of his forehead. "I'm so sorry. I don't know what's gotten into her—"

Katie interrupted. "She's jealous, Chris."

He nodded. "I know."

Katie continued feeding the baby. Nobody said it aloud, of course, but Chris knew what his young daughter was feeling. He could be all types of things to his daughter, but he could never be her mom.

"Also," Katie said, raising one eyebrow in his direction. "She needs a bra."

Chris groaned. "She mentioned that to you?"

"She didn't need to."

Katie nodded toward his daughter, throwing a silent tantrum down by the rink. Even from his vantage point, he could see the outline of development beneath her pink jacket. His friend was right. As much as it pained him to admit it, his little girl was growing up.

"Ugh." Chris dropped his head into his hands. "She brought it up right before you went on maternity leave. I haven't had time to deal with it yet. Maybe I was secretly hoping it would go away."

Katie smiled. "I don't think it's going away, Chris."

"Probably not."

"Seriously," Jensen said, shaking his head. "You don't want her to be that kid."

"What kid?"

"The kid with the floppies."

Katie rolled her eyes. "Don't call them that."

"Hey!" Jensen defended himself. "Pretty much every sixth-grade fantasy I had was about a girl with floppies."

She grimaced. "You're disgusting."

"And I adore you," Jensen said, moving in for a kiss. "You, and your floppies."

Katie blushed, before swatting him playfully away. Soon, their teasing morphed into comfortable, loving quiet.

Watching them, seeing how happy they were, Chris was suddenly confronted by his own loneliness. Lacey was not alone in her pain. He wanted what Katie and Jensen had. He missed having a partner. He longed for a best friend to share the journey with, someone to collapse into, breathe in like comfort, on his very worst days.

His mind wandered to Dara. A smile crossed his face. He wondered what she was doing right now. It was Saturday. Knowing Dara, she was likely off at synagogue, or visiting her grandmother. He envisioned her—lists in hand, plans in place—stomping all over Hoboken. That woman had a list for everything. Until she didn't. But he found the messy parts of her far more compelling than the carefully constructed image she projected to the world.

"What are you smiling about?" Katie asked, quizzically.

Chris returned from his thoughts. "Hmm?"

"You are beaming ear to ear."

"Oh," Chris said, rubbing the back of his neck. "Nothing. Just thinking about work…"

Jensen raised one eyebrow in his direction. "That's going pretty well for you, nowadays?"

"Highest ratings yet. Even Lacey watches the show."

"We watch it every day in the firehouse," Jensen admitted.

"Wow," Katie said. "So it looks like you'll be staying in Manhattan?"

Chris nodded. "It appears so."

"Awesome." She pointed with her chin toward Lacey. "Because we are going to be in need of a babysitter in the coming years."

Chris laughed. "I think Lacey would love that."

The baby finished eating. A few burps and gurgles later, Jensen Jr. was returned to his carrier. Chris looked toward his daughter. She was down by the ice-skating rink, her ire forgotten, practically vibrating with excitement.

"Katie!" Lacey called. "Can we go ice-skating now?"

Katie rose from her spot. "I'm coming!"

As Katie headed toward the ice, Chris fell into the sounds around him. Jensen Jr., so sweet and perfect, making adorable little baby noises in the carrier across from him. The voices of children and their parents spinning in circles down on the ice below. Normally, Chris wasn't particularly into the holidays. But this year, something about the Christmas music playing happily on the speakers above him filled him with an indescribable sense of hope.

Jensen ordered a beer. "So, it sounds like everything is going great with your show."

"It is," Chris said. "Dara has really turned my life around."

"Has she, now?"

"She's amazing, you know? Funny, smart… I don't know if it comes across on camera, but she's really the most remarkable person I have ever met. I admire her. The way she shows up for people, and for herself. She really is…something special."

"It sounds like you really like this woman."

"I do," he said. "We've become good friends over the last few months."

"Just friends, huh?" Jensen took a swig of his beer. "Not to point out the obvious here, my man, but you don't talk about her like a friend. You talk about her like you have a hard-core and serious crush."

It was the first time someone had said the words aloud. Chris shifted in his seat, looking toward the ice-skating rink. Lacey and Katie were tumbling all over each other. Chris couldn't help but think back over their last few weeks getting to know each other.

He wanted Dara, obviously. Ever since he had nearly lost her over Sukkot, and he realized that she had awakened some long-buried feeling inside of him. And yet, he respected her too much to interrupt what she had with Dr. Daniel. Dara was happy. Unless she gave him some sort of clear sign otherwise, he had no intention of ruining the bliss she had found.

"Just friends," he confirmed.

28

THE MORNING OF HER NEXT TELEVISED DATE WITH
Dr. Daniel, Dara felt jumpy. Perhaps it was because Chris had
promised her some sort of epic surprise. Maybe it was because,
having finally met her Mr. Perfect on Paper, she felt the pressure that came with dating for marriage. But sitting in the
limo, knowing that she was rolling along like a matzah ball
toward her future, all she wanted to do was throw up.

The car slowed. The location of her date came into view.
Dara squinted, trying to figure out where she was. It was a pier
of some sort, with a large warehouse attached. And then, Dara
knew what Chris was planning. Next to the water, near a camera crew still in the process of getting set up, was a helicopter.

Chris knew that something was wrong the minute he arrived at City View Helicopter Tours. Normally, arriving to
an on-location shoot for *Good News* meant he would find the
place buzzing. Instead, looking past the helicopter and a romantic table set up with flowers, he found the lot empty.

"Hey," Chris said, tracking down an intern. "Where is everybody?"

"Inside the main building."

Chris squinted. "Why?"

"Some sort of problem with Dara." The kid shrugged.

"*Oy.*"

Chris made his way over to the airplane hangar.

It was your typical warehouse for these types of things. Main office in the front. A large room with blue chairs for waiting visitors. A restroom in the back. The majority of the space, however, was used to house the helicopters and small aircraft owned by the company and not currently in use.

Chris followed the sound of voices arguing, eventually coming upon Dara. She sat in a metal chair with her arms crossed against her chest, Dr. Daniel kneeling lovingly at her side. The entire production crew wrapped around them in a semicircle and gave the impression that she was in the middle of being interrogated.

"Can't you write her a prescription or something?" Eleanor asked Daniel.

"I told you," Dara snapped back, "I don't want to take anything!"

"What about alcohol?" Eli offered up. "We have like ten cases of champagne in the back of the truck."

"Would you like a glass of champagne, darling?" Daniel asked.

"At this point," Eleanor grumbled, "just give her the damn bottle!"

Chris had heard enough. Plastering on a wide smile, he moved to intervene. "Everything okay here?"

All at once, everyone twisted in their spot...and began yelling at him.

Eleanor bemoaned all the wasted money. Dara wondered aloud how Chris could have been *so idiotic* as to book a helicopter ride. Even Dr. Daniel seemed frustrated. He defended

Dara's honor, demanding that they change all plans immediately. Chris took all their "constructive criticism" in before wondering if he couldn't get that drink himself.

Finally, after what felt like an eternity of everyone pointing out his failures, he got the gist of what was going on. Dara's generalized anxiety disorder was once again spinning out of control. She didn't want to fly in a helicopter. Nobody in the production crew knew what to do.

"You know what?" Chris said, interrupting them all. "Could I maybe talk to Dara alone?"

After another round of upset, the group agreed. Everyone moved outside, leaving Chris and Dara alone. Chris pulled up a metal chair, taking a seat beside her.

"You okay?" he asked softly.

"Of course I'm not okay!" she spat back. "A helicopter, Chris? A flying death trap with spinning blades? Do I look like someone who wants to go plunging into the Hudson today?"

Chris chewed on his lower lip. In truth, he'd known a helicopter might freak her out—but everything freaked Dara out. Bees. Dating. Going on television. Her fear had never stopped her before. Nor had he ever let it dictate his choices for her.

Yet the thing that struck Chris was that Dara was not moving. Despite her fear, she was still sitting in that metal chair. Chris recalled something his father always said. *People tell you who they are with their feet.* There was a part of her that wanted to get on that helicopter. She just needed help to do it.

"What do you need from me, Dara?" he asked.

She closed her eyes. "I don't know."

He thought back to everything he had learned about her over the last few months. And then, pulling out his phone, he opened the emergency scanner app he'd downloaded. The sound of beeps, static and voices echoed through the empty hangar. After several minutes, Chris dared a glance at her. Tears were rolling down her cheeks.

"Oh, God," he said, searching his pockets for a tissue. "I didn't mean to make you cry."

"No," she said, wiping away the wet spots. "It's the good type of tears."

He rolled that concept around in his head. Not all tears were bad. Some hurts deserved to roll freely down your cheeks, without shame or embarrassment. A quiet moment settled between them. Dara took a deep breath, appearing more relaxed.

"Are you feeling any better?" Chris asked.

"A little," Dara said.

"But still anxious?"

"Honestly," she said, as if annoyed with herself, "I've been anxious all morning. No reason for it, really. It just sometimes happens that way. Anyway, once it gets going…it's hard to stop. The helicopter just put me over the edge, I guess. I'm sorry for completely freaking out on everybody."

"You have no reason to apologize." He meant it.

She nodded.

"Look," he said, wanting to be extremely clear about offering an alternative. "If you want, we don't have to do the helicopter. We can just shoot some B-roll with you sitting on the thing, and then drinking champagne or whatever…"

"Won't that look…anticlimactic?"

"Probably." He shrugged. "But I'm not gonna force you to do anything you're not comfortable with. I think you can handle the helicopter ride, of course. I think you may even like riding in the helicopter, once you get up there, and you see New York City, and the setting sun." He nudged her playfully. "Once Dr. Daniel is taking your hand, making everything feel romantic and magical…"

She blushed. "That does sound kind of nice."

He cleared his throat. "The point is, don't do it for me. Don't do it for Dr. Daniel, either. Do it for yourself. Do it because...deep down inside, you want to get on that helicopter and go on this adventure."

He could see her thinking it over, musing on all the positives alongside the worries.

"Maybe we could try it?"

"How do you mean?"

"Well," she said, coming up with the solution herself, "we could go up into the air, and if it gets too scary for me, if my anxiety really can't handle it, we could come right back down?"

"I don't think that would be a problem."

She quieted, thinking through her answer. Chris waited, like always, by her side. He didn't need to rush her. He knew Dara. He knew all the things she was capable of. He knew what her answer would be even before she spoke the words aloud.

"Okay," she said. "Let's do this thing."

"You doing okay, Dara?" Chris asked, smiling comfortably, from the seat facing hers in the back of the helicopter. The cameraman sat by his side, with the two pilots in the front seat behind them. She tried to remind herself that everyone else in this airborne death trap was having a pleasant experience.

"Fine!" she called back out to him.

Realizing that the camera lens was pointed in her direction, she removed her left palm from the interior wall of the vehicle. The other hand, as it turned out, was being firmly gripped by Dr. Daniel. In an attempt to alleviate her anxiety, he had taken it on the ride up, refusing to let it go.

"Look," he said, leaning over her lap to point to a figure in the distance. "The Statue of Liberty!"

Dara smiled politely, and returned her attention to Chris. "How much longer?"

Chris checked with the pilots. "Fifteen minutes."

"Fifteen minutes," she repeated quietly under her breath.

It was definitely not the easy-breezy and fun-filled date Chris had envisioned for her. Her anxiety made sure of that, after all. It was ever present. Even with a pep talk—and Chris sitting calmly across from her, reminding her that things would be okay—she was far too much of a worrier to ever really enjoy taking a helicopter tour around Manhattan. But she was able to find some enjoyable moments.

The way the sun looked, pink and purple, setting over Manhattan. Seeing Ellis Island from above, wondering what her great-grandmothers would be thinking, seeing all she had accomplished in the generations after their arrival. Plus, there was a very cool moment near the Empire State Building where all the tourists on the observation deck began waving at them.

She was glad she had gotten on that helicopter.

The only thing she didn't enjoy was the feeling of Dr. Daniel's hands wrapped around hers. She tried to tell herself she was being ridiculous. The man was simply trying to be supportive. The problem was that his hands were warm and sweaty. In the already crammed helicopter, with the light of the camera beating down upon her, his touch felt intolerable.

She wanted to shake him off her.

Still, sweaty palms and an acquiescing nature were no reason to end an otherwise perfect relationship. Thankfully, Dara was a pro at talking herself out of nonsensical thoughts.

As the helicopter returned to the landing pad, she reasoned away those feelings. This was just her anxiety, spiraling out of control. This was just her brain, preparing for some tragedy that would never come true. Just like with the helicopter, Dara had a tendency to see problems where there were none.

Her feelings could not be trusted.

The helicopter landed. The camera crew swept around to the front to get a better view. Dr. Daniel appeared at the door and aided Dara down the steps, leading her toward a table where champagne and desserts were waiting. He poured two glasses of bubbly, handing her one.

"Dara," he said, "I hope you and I continue to reach new heights together."

He leaned in for a kiss.

Dara closed her eyes. This was it. Her second chance at romance.

His lips met hers. She felt heat, the softness of his tongue dipping into her mouth, saliva intermingling with the sweet taste of expensive champagne. His technique was perfect. There was nothing wrong with his touch, the gentle way he caressed the bottom of her chin. It should have been perfect.

And yet—she couldn't help but think it—the kiss still didn't taste right.

29

OVER THE NEXT FEW WEEKS, DARA THREW HERSELF into her relationship with Dr. Daniel. She was determined to make it work, to prove to herself that she could push through any fears and have a successful relationship with her very own Mr. Perfect.

She allowed herself to get caught up in the whirl of a new televised courtship. There were trips to outlets, followed by dinner at one of Manhattan's most exclusive kosher steak restaurants. There was an afternoon spent on a chartered yacht, circling downtown Manhattan. They even spent an evening with a graffiti artist, learning how to spray-paint their names— *Dara and Daniel*—in looping letters and neon colors.

"It looks like a wedding invitation," Daniel had commented.

Dara, of course, had agreed.

Indeed, Dara had been so busy with Dr. Daniel—and the wild success of J-Mate following the marketing campaign touting their new relationship—that she was spending far less time visiting her grandmother. On the first Saturday that Dr. Daniel was on call, she moved to rectify that situation.

Dara arrived at Kehillah Tikvah just as Torah reading was

beginning. The small population of attendees who had been there for the Jewish High Holidays was now cut in half. Only her bubbe, the ChallahBack Girls and a few faces she recognized lined the pews.

At this point, the synagogue was nothing more than an old stomping ground. A place to recall memories and catch up with friends before shutting the doors completely. Life didn't move on here. It didn't break out into "Od Yeshama" beneath a huppah, or echo with the cries of newborn babies. Kehillah Tikvah was a synagogue that was dying.

Still, it was the shul that Dara had grown up in. The synagogue she had stood on the pulpit of as a young girl, donning a tallis, or prayer shawl, when she had turned thirteen and become a Bat Mitzvah. It was the place where they had held the funeral for her mother.

Despite the fact that everyone she had grown up with, including Shana, had moved on to other shuls—bigger shuls with more active families and vibrant Hebrew schools—Dara spent extraordinary amounts of money to keep the *ner tamid*, or eternal flame, perched above the ark burning.

She paid for the lights, the maintenance, even the shaky old rabbi chanting Torah at the front of the room. Perhaps it was futile, trying to hold on to something that was dying, but Dara loved the traditions she was raised with. She felt a personal responsibility to protect the things, and the people, she valued. But beyond all these things—beyond the guilt of feeling personally responsible for keeping this version of Judaism alive—walking through the doors of Kehillah Tikvah always felt like coming home.

She loved this place. She loved these people. It would be a loss unnoticed by most of the world. But it would be a loss just the same.

Dara slunk down next to her grandmother. In response to

her arrival, the other three ChallahBack Girls leaned over in their pews and waved.

Dara was happy to see them. There were hugs and hand squeezes followed by lots of unnecessary compliments. Thankfully, the rabbi on the bima—like most of the audience in attendance—was one decibel away from being fully deaf. Despite the zealous energy with which all four women greeted her, their conversation did little to disturb the services at hand.

"We saw the last date!" Arlene said in an extremely loud whisper.

"He's so handsome," Shira added.

"And romantic," Ruth said.

"Do you like him, Dara?" Arlene asked.

"Yes," Dara said, genuinely. "He's a wonderful man."

All of the ChallahBack Girls squealed in simultaneous delight.

Dara blushed beneath their accolades. Dr. Daniel was perfect. He checked every box on her perfect Jewish husband list. He went out of his way for her, planning romantic dates, being up front in his own wants and feelings. He never played games with her heart. He was Jewish, and committed, and kindhearted. He acquiesced to her every whim and demand. He would make a wonderful husband and father. There was only one problem...

The kiss never tasted right.

It was something Dara was desperately trying to work through. And so, she made it a point to kiss Daniel on every single date.

She kissed him before he ate and after he ate, analyzing the feeling that arose deep within herself. When that didn't help, she offered him vanilla ice cream, mint bubble gum and cherry-flavored sucking candies. Still, and despite the sweet flavors lingering on his tongue, there was no change in her reaction.

It wasn't that he tasted *bad*. There was nothing, technically, wrong with the man's flavor. He was gentle, sweet. He didn't give her a mucocele by sucking on her lower lip, causing permanent injury. (It had happened to Shana.) But every time Dr. Daniel started kissing her, she found herself counting the seconds until he stopped.

At kiddush luncheon after services, the conversation had veered from Dara's latest date to a full-on discussion of their wedding.

"Oh, please!" Ruth said, biting into her bagel laden with egg salad. "Obviously, the wedding will be in Manhattan! Far more options for venues that can handle kosher food."

Dara debated reminding the ChallahBack Girls that she and Daniel had only been dating for a few weeks. She didn't even know his middle name. Still, the women were so excited, talking about all the details of her wedding. Even her bubbe—clearly having a bad day—seemed pleased.

Dara glanced over to Miriam's plate of uneaten lox.

"Bubbe?" she whispered beneath her breath. "You're not hungry?"

Miriam tapped her on the hand. "Not today, Rose."

Rose was her mother's name. Dara would have burst into tears right then and there had it not been for the ChallahBack Girls. "Miriam!" Ruth said, with absolutely no finesse. "You *alter cocker*. Don't you know your own granddaughter Dara?"

Miriam returned from that faraway place. "Of course. Dara."

Dara began cutting the lox on her grandmother's plate into smaller pieces. "Please eat something, Bubbe."

"It's fine, Dara," Arlene said, touching her gently on the

hand. "We'll make sure she gets something to eat when we get home."

Dara nodded. She knew she could always rely on the ChallahBack Girls to protect, and love, her grandmother. Still, the guilt tore at her, that ugly in-between place where she lived returned with a pressing weight upon her chest. "Maybe," Dara stuttered, glancing around the table, "maybe I'm spending too much time with Dr. Daniel."

"Nonsense!" Shira said, shaking her head.

"Bupkes!" Ruth agreed.

"*Du farkirst mir di yorn,*" Miriam sighed.

Dara shrank in her seat. Was she going to be the death of her grandmother? Despite her own hesitation at the relationship, everyone she cared about was rooting for it to work out.

"You need to have pigs in the blanket," Shira said, wagging two fingers at Dara so she would pay attention to her over the other chattering yentas. "Nobody likes a wedding without those little hot dogs."

"It's true." Ruth nodded. "My nephew's wedding…it had everything. A pasta station. A mashed potato bar. Rack of lamb!" Everybody salivated and nodded. "But you know what everybody kept talking about? There were no pigs in the blanket!"

"A *shanda*!" Shira said, shaking her head. "A disgrace."

"The younger Jews are very fancy nowadays," Arlene attempted to explain to the two women. "They want all the fancy things they see on the Instagram. Do you know what my grandson served as an appetizer during Passover dinner last year? Raw fish! He called it tuna tartare. He said it was better than gefilte fish. Can you believe it?"

"Sounds terrible," Shira said, and dived face-first into her plate of whitefish before picking out a bone from her teeth.

"You're planning on having pigs in the blanket at Miriam's birthday party on the last night of Hanukkah, right?"

"Of course," Dara assured them. She quickly made a mental note to have Naveah call the caterer on Monday.

Personally, she was not a fan of the tiny kosher hot dogs wrapped up in puff pastry and dipped into mustard. Given the extraordinary cost of kosher caterers, it made sense that modern-day Jews chose a pasta station over pigs in the blanket. Like all things in life, the world was changing. Judaism was changing with it.

"The important thing about Dr. Daniel—" Ruth said, breaking through the chatter "—is not to waste time."

"Hear! Hear!" Shira said, lifting her glass of water.

"He seems like a very nice young man," Arlene offered up.

"He is," Dara agreed. "He's positively lovely."

"And how many dates have you been on now?" Ruth inquired.

Dara shifted in her seat. "Six."

"Six." The whole table shook their heads over her words. She could feel the judgment lingering alongside their shocked expressions.

Dara knew the implication. She was already thirty-four. Daniel was thirty-six. They had spent their most fertile years, like many American Jews, getting educated and building their careers. Dating was put off until one was established, capable of supporting a growing family, mature enough to handle the ups and downs of life that came with it.

Now, like so many women in her age bracket, she found herself in a conundrum. She was successful. She had established herself and her career first. But her options for starting a family were quickly closing down.

If Dr. Daniel was not the one—if they weren't both heading toward marriage—there was no point in messing around.

There was no time for it, either. Everyone knew that after the age of thirty-five, having children was more difficult for women. What was the point of struggling so hard to find a proper Jewish match if not to create future Jewish generations?

It took time to plan a wedding. They would also need time as a married couple to get to know one another, to travel and live together, before bringing in children. How much time would they waste simply getting to the point of an engagement?

"Really, Dara!" Arlene said, laying one hand on hers in an outward show of support. "If you like this one, and he likes you, there's no time to waste. Just get right to it."

Ruth nodded. "Make the *shidduch*."

"Much better than my Morty," Shira offered up.

"A legless donkey would have been better than your Morty," Ruth snapped back, before turning her attention to Dara. "Dr. Daniel, however, is perfect."

The ChallahBack Girls leaned forward, eager for an explanation. Instead, it was Miriam who broke the silence. Putting her fork down, she fixed Dara with a serious frown.

"So, what is the holdup?" Miriam asked.

"The holdup?" Dara squeaked out.

"You tell us he's perfect," Miriam said, simply. "You tell us he checks every box on your perfect Jewish husband list…but still, you don't sound like you want to marry him."

On the subject of Dara, and marriage, the old woman was completely coherent.

Dara debated telling them all the truth. That every kiss with Daniel tasted wrong. That no matter how hard she tried, no matter how much she wanted this to work—for her grandmother, for her people, for her business, for Chris and his show—she felt like she was shoving a square tongue into a round mouth.

"Actually," Dara said, shifting in her seat, "I do have some news on the *shidduch* front." Dara took a deep breath. It was now or never. "Daniel and I were thinking that it might be nice for all of you to meet. We were thinking that maybe we could all get together for Bubbe's final dress fitting before her ninetieth birthday party. I'll have Naveah and crew make it extra special…and then, we could meet up with his parents for dinner afterward. I was thinking we could check out Halav, that new kosher Italian restaurant on the Upper West Side?"

Dara realized she was rambling. Quickly, she snapped her lips closed, just in time to see Arlene practically bouncing in her seat with excitement.

"Dara-la!" she squealed, leaning over to squeeze her hand. "Does this mean what I think it does?"

Dara said it definitively: "Daniel and I have decided that it's time for the *machatunim* to meet."

December

30

DATE NUMBER SEVEN FOR DARA WAS LESS ABOUT romance and more of a joint errand. Bubbe Miriam was having her final dress fitting for her birthday bash at Zelman's Bridal Couture on Sixth Avenue.

Like always, Chris stood off to the side during the filming of the look live, trying to remember the names of everyone in boisterous and noisy attendance. The entire Rabinowitz clan had taken over the expansive shop known for extravagant bridal and evening wear. Apparently, the *machatunim* were meeting this evening at some kosher Italian restaurant.

Machatunim. Chris had learned that there wasn't an equivalent word in English. Though the simplest explanation would be co-in-laws. It spoke to the unwritten idea in Jewish tradition that, when you married a person, you married their family.

Chris scanned the room for this new and emerging family unit. There was Dara and Daniel, sitting front and center on a pink couch. To the other side were three elderly women—Shira, Arlene and Ruth—whom Dara called the ChallahBack Girls, and who lived at Adath Israel with Bubbe Miriam. On the other side of the couple was Dara's older sister, Shana, and the four small children that always seemed to accompany her.

Circling the crew, and not to be outdone, were all three of Dara's assistants, Naveah, Cameron and Alexa. With tablets in hand, and helping to pass out glasses of champagne and circular platters of cheese and crackers, they made sure that every whim of Dara's, and her family's, was answered for immediately.

With the inclusion of Eleanor, Eli, three camera teams from *Good News* and six different associates from Zelman's—including the owner—the space had morphed into straight *balagan*.

The cameras circled, zooming in closer. There were the obvious shots, of course. Close-ups of Dara and Dr. Daniel holding hands. Shots of Shana—her daughter Tzippy on her lap—sipping kosher champagne while talking to one of the ChallahBack Girls. Until finally, the noisy crowd fell into silence.

The cameras turned in the direction of the dressing room. Bubbe Miriam emerged from the back and, sashaying her hips in a light dance, displayed her epic gown.

"Oh, Miriam!" Arlene gasped, rising to her feet. "You're stunning!"

"She looks thirty years younger!" Ruth said.

"Is it comfortable, Bubbe?" Dara asked. "Do you love it?"

"Oh, Dara-la!" Miriam swooned, taking a spot in front of a three-way mirror. "How could I not love it? The dress is a dream!"

The entire room applauded. Even Chris had to agree with the sentiment. It was clear to him that Dara had spared no expense on the gown. It was a deep purple and made of sequins, with drapes of fine black silk cascading down the arms.

A sales attendant stepped forward and, pulling at the sides and straps, declared that her dress was perfectly fitted. Bubbe

Miriam returned to the dressing room, and the eager chatter of their large group began again.

"Your grandmother looks amazing," Daniel said genuinely.

"The artistry on that dress," Arlene said, touching her heart. "Just stunning."

"I want a dress like Bubbe!" Tzippy whined aloud.

The room devolved into laughter. Shana explained to her youngest daughter how the most special dresses go to the most special people at a party.

"Like when Auntie Dara gets married," Shana continued, glancing between Dara and Daniel. "And when you get married, too," she said to her daughter. "You'll wear a beautiful white dress, and everybody will come to celebrate your most special day."

"I can't wait to get married," Tzippy sighed, longingly.

The cameras zoomed back in on Dara, sitting on the couch beside Dr. Daniel, their hands interlaced. Hoping for more footage to work with in the editing room, Eleanor waved them into conversation. Daniel took his cue, turning to Dara.

"You are an amazing granddaughter," he said.

"Thank you."

"I wish my grandparents were still here," he said, blushing slightly. "But I'm so grateful I've had the chance to meet your bubbe and her best friends."

"Me, too."

Daniel moved in for a kiss. The cameras angled in closer.

All at once, Chris felt his normally stable stomach tumble.

And then, most surprisingly, Dara popped up from her seat. "I'm just gonna—" she said, glancing around the room. "I'm just gonna look around, okay?"

"Of—of course," Daniel said, leaning back in his seat.

Dara smiled politely, and took off.

She spent the next several minutes perusing the evening

gowns of Zelman's. The cameras followed her until eventually she came to a section full of mannequins displaying wedding dresses. Chris watched the footage on a monitor as she meandered toward one style in particular. A long white dress, with three-quarter-length lace sleeves, and a spectacular beaded bodice.

"Would you like to try one on?"

Dara turned around to see an eager Zelman's sales attendant standing there, all smiles.

"Oh," Dara said, waving away her curiosity like an afterthought. "I was just looking."

It was too late. At the prospect of Dara trying on a wedding dress, the whole room burst into peer pressure.

"Nonsense!" Shira said.

"We're all here, after all," Shana said, bouncing Tzippy on her lap.

"No time like the present," Arlene said.

Poor Dara. Even from his vantage point—out of the way of her family, friends and Dr. Daniel—he could see how uncomfortable she was. Her shoulders shrank. Her cheeks turned beet red.

Chris had never intervened in one of her shoots before. He had to stay on the sidelines and wait for his cue before wrapping the segment.

"Come now," Dara said, firm in her resolve. "This is Bubbe's big day. I don't want to ruin it—"

"What would you be ruining?" Miriam emerged from the dressing room. Her final fitting complete, she had removed her party dress and was back in her street clothes. "I would love to see you in a wedding gown. Who knows if I'll ever get the chance again?"

Dara's lower lip quivered. "But what about Daniel?" she squeaked out.

"I'll step out," he said, politely.

"But—"

"Please," he said. "Take this opportunity. I should probably be going over to the restaurant to meet my parents, anyway. Besides, my hope is that one day soon... I'll get the chance to see the real thing in person."

At his words, Shana sighed aloud. The ChallahBack Girls squealed in simultaneous excitement. And then, Daniel kissed her. The cameras moved in closer as his tongue dived in and out of her mouth for far longer than was really necessary.

Chris resisted the urge to throw up all over his loafers.

Otherwise, he tried to take a cue from Dara, and focus on the positive. His friend was happy. She enjoyed being with Dr. Daniel. She enjoyed the sensation of his tongue attacking her uvula like he was personally trying to discover a new way to perform a tonsillectomy.

Beyond all these things, even Chris couldn't deny that they were making great television.

Eleanor stood across from him, beaming with excitement. Wedding dresses and the prospect of a happy ending with Mr. Perfect on Paper would certainly keep *Good News* enjoying their ratings gangbuster. It would be good for everybody.

"Okay." Dara smiled, sheepishly. "I suppose trying on one dress wouldn't hurt."

"Fabulous!" the sales attendant said.

Dara took Miriam's place in the dressing room. Miriam took Dara's spot on the couch. Dr. Daniel left the premises. Chris stood off to the side and waited. It was no big deal. Dara, finding her Mr. Perfect. Dara, getting married.

And then, Dara emerged from the dressing room, a vision in white. Chris nearly choked on the sight.

She was beautiful. An angel, floating down the runway, making him believe in happy endings. No—he shook the thought away. Not an angel. Not a princess, either. But Dara. Black hair set against porcelain satin. A beautiful, brilliant, sometimes even fearless and one-of-a-kind woman. With her quirks, and her emergency scanner app, she saw the world differently than most folks. Being able to share her worldview over the last few months, seeing life through her lens, had changed him.

"Oh, Dara!" Miriam blinked back tears. "You look so beautiful! You have no idea…no idea how happy the thought of you getting married makes me."

"Bubbe," Dara said, beginning to cry, as well. "Please don't cry."

"Oh, God!" Shana began to bawl. "I'm just so happy for you, Dara."

Before long, everybody in the damn place was crying. Shana, the ChallahBack Girls, all three assistants. Even Eleanor, he realized, was attempting to suck back a tear.

Chris shifted in his spot, annoyed. He suddenly wasn't sure if he was attending a dress fitting or a funeral.

With the cliff-hanger established, Eleanor made the sign for Chris to wrap. Stepping in front of the camera, he delivered his signature line. "I'm Chris Steadfast. Till next time, America"…*blah, blah, blah*. This time, however, he couldn't even fake a smile.

Inside the dressing room of Zelman's, the sales attendant worked to unbutton and unzip Dara from the ten-thousand-dollar wedding gown she was wearing. Staring at herself in the mirror, Dara didn't understand why the sight of herself wearing a wedding dress made her feel nauseous. But she couldn't help this terrible sensation spinning around in her chest. She was certain that somehow, in some way, she was making a terrible mistake.

Naveah stuck her head inside the dressing room.

"Dara," she said, tablet in hand. "I've paid for your grandmother's dress and arranged for Cameron to pick it up three days before the party. Should I start getting everybody moved over to the restaurant?"

"That would be great," Dara said.

"Anything else I can get you right now?"

"No."

Naveah left Dara to finish getting dressed. The sounds of the once busy bridal shop shifted into quiet. With Daniel already at the restaurant and waiting with his parents, the production crew disappeared. Naveah finished wrangling Dara's family into waiting cars. Dara was grateful to find herself alone. She needed a quiet moment to collect her thoughts.

Sitting down on one of the plush velvet chairs in the dressing room, she sighed heavily. Trying on that wedding gown, she should have felt...she wasn't sure, exactly. Different? More excited? Less nervous?

Then again, she had never been married before. Maybe wanting to dive headfirst into a vat of benzos was the normal reaction to falling in love.

Grabbing her bag, she headed for the front door. She was just about to exit the premises when she heard the strangest sound coming from one of the dressing rooms. Twisting around on the teal carpet, she craned one ear curiously in the direction of the noise. Dara would recognize that pattern of beeps, static and voices anywhere.

Following the sound, she made her way down the hall. Pushing open the door of the last dressing room in Zelman's, she came across the most peculiar sight. Chris was inside, sitting on one of their pink velvet chairs, cell phone pressed up against his ear. He was listening to the emergency services app.

"Chris?" Dara asked, surprised.

He turned around and, seeing her, forced a smile. "Hey."

"What are you doing?"

"Just, uh…" he stammered.

"Listening to the emergency scanner app?"

Chris pursed his lips, caught. He seemed hesitant to reveal any secrets about what was going on inside of him. Still, they were friends. She had gotten to know him pretty well over the last few months. If Chris was using one of her coping mechanisms, there had to be a reason. She leaned against the door of his dressing room.

"Is it helping?" she asked softly.

"A little bit. Not really."

Dara laughed. "I suppose it's not for everybody."

He nodded, falling into silence again.

Dara didn't want to leave him. She couldn't remember a single time since their meeting—except maybe talking about his wife, Claire, in the hospital—where he had looked so damn sad. It made her feel bad for him. It also made her wonder what was wrong.

Stepping inside the dressing room, she took a chair beside him. Eye level now, hip to hip, she did what Chris always did for her. She was present for him, giving him space to find his words, letting him know that she was near.

"Is everything okay?" she asked.

"I don't want to bother you with it."

She reached over, taking his hand. "We're friends. Whatever you have to tell me won't be a bother. I'm here for you, okay?"

She could see him hesitating, debating the question.

"I… I…" Chris stuttered, and stopped—a staccato of missed opportunities—before finally spitting out the words. "I need a bra."

Dara squinted. "What?"

He backtracked. "Not for me. For Lacey. Lacey needs a

bra." He began rambling. "She's been asking for months, and I've just been hesitating on it forever. I tried going on Amazon, but there are like…ten million different types of bras, and Katie is on maternity leave, and now, I'm the negligent father of the motherless child who is gonna be the only sixth grader in the entire world walking around with floppies."

It took Dara a minute to figure out what he was talking about. When she finally realized that Chris was dealing with Lacey hitting puberty, she almost had to laugh. Clearly, for all his confidence and swagger, there were still aspects of life that terrified him.

Fortunately, Dara did not have *these* anxieties. She was Jewish, and therefore saw human sex and sexuality in a positive light. She was the daughter of a cognitive behavioral therapist, with a specialty in marriage and family development, and a subspecialty in women's sexual health. She had been raised by and alongside strong women—not just her mother, but Miriam, Shana and the ChallahBack Girls. If there was anyone on the planet who knew the importance of celebrating the achievements of womanhood, it was Dara.

"Well," she said easily, "I can help you."

"With what?"

"The bra."

"Oh. Really?"

"I mean, I'm not a parent. I also don't know anything about being a parent, but I know about being a woman, and all those super important firsts that come with growing up female." Now Dara was the one rambling. "So yeah…if you want my help, if you think Lacey won't mind me tagging along on your first bra-shopping trip—"

"Lacey will love you," he said quickly. "I mean… Lacey will love having you there."

Dara smiled. "Then I'll be there."

A long pause stretched between them. She could see that Chris was overwhelmed. But it was nice—for once—being the person to hold someone else's hand through the things that scared them.

31

CHRIS WAS, YET AGAIN, DESTROYING BREAKFAST.

Standing in his kitchen, he shook a plate of bacon back and forth, just as the pancakes he was making on the griddle began to burn. Smoke billowed into the air, causing the fire alarm to begin blaring. By the time he realized what was happening, put down the bacon and stood on a chair to turn off the alarm, it was too late. The pancakes were totally ruined.

"Great," he said, staring down at two black moons.

He debated throwing them out and starting over, but as usual, they didn't have time. Glancing down at his watch, he went with the next best option. He flipped them over to the side that was still pristine and loaded them onto a plate. Chris was determined to make today special for Lacey.

"Oh, God," Lacey moaned, coming down the hall. "Why do you even bother cooking?"

She was still in her pajamas, crease marks from her blankets pocking the sides of her cheeks. She squeezed into a seat and slumped her chin into the palm of her hand, staring at the mounds of food—eggs, bacon, pancakes, oatmeal and fruit—that Chris had laid out.

"I bother because I'm your dad, and I love you, and this breakfast is for your very special day!"

She lifted up one pancake, unimpressed. "My special day?"

"We're going shopping."

It took Lacey a minute to realize what was happening. When she did, she exploded from her chair, throwing her arms around him in a tight embrace. Chris barely had time to hug her back before she was already on her feet and racing back to her bedroom.

"Hey!" he said, his heart warming to see her so excited. "Have some breakfast first. We're not meeting Dara till ten o'clock."

"Dara?" Lacey cocked her head. "From the show?"

"Yeah."

"She's coming with?"

Chris shifted in his seat. It wasn't like it was a date or anything. Dara was simply a friend. No different than Katie. Still, the question felt loaded. "Is that okay?" he asked, carefully. "I just figured it would be useful to have a woman there. Of course, if you're not comfortable with her being there, we can try to figure it out on our own."

Lacey considered the question. "Nah," she said, shrugging her shoulders. "I mean, having a woman there makes sense. Plus, I always wanted to meet Dara."

With that, Lacey sat down at the table and began scarfing breakfast.

Chris couldn't help but feel relieved.

Chris was a jumble of nerves that morning. Standing outside Nordstrom in midtown Manhattan, waiting for Dara to appear, he tried his best to act normal for his young daughter.

"So," he said, digging his hands into his pockets. "You excited for today?"

Lacey grimaced. "Seriously?"

"What?"

"Dad," she said, annoyed. "You're totally embarrassing me right now!"

"Sorry."

"Just be cool, okay?"

"I'm literally just standing here."

Lacey groaned aloud. Apparently, just standing next to his daughter on a public street was the absolute worst thing he could do as a parent. Chris had no idea how he would survive the next seven years of adolescence.

Fortunately, Lacey had none of the same hesitations regarding Dara. Seeing the young tech executive walking down the block, his daughter broke into a wide smile.

"Dara," Lacey called, jumping up and down. "Over here!"

Dara responded with a little wave. As she drew closer, Chris felt his heart skip. God, she looked beautiful. He loved the way her black curls cascaded from beneath a white knitted hat. He also couldn't help but notice that the blue scarf she was wearing was embroidered with tiny gold menorahs. She looked like a dream. Like some Hanukkah fantasy come to life. Chris found himself spinning like a dreidel.

"Oh my God," Lacey said, awestruck. "I can't believe it's you!"

"It's me." Dara laughed before bending down to greet his daughter. "And you must be Lacey. Your dad has told me so much about you."

Lacey blushed.

"Thank you for coming," Chris said.

"My pleasure," Dara said, genuinely, before turning back to his daughter. "Now, are you ready to do some damage on your dad's credit card?"

"Totally."

"I love shopping." Dara sighed, heading for the front entrance.

"I know," Lacey gabbed, like they were two old friends. "I watch your show."

Inside the lingerie department of Nordstrom, Chris was met with what could only be described as a menagerie of underwear. Hanging from the walls, displayed on mannequins and neatly tucked into drawers. He was—as expected—completely out of his element. Thankfully, Dara was incredible. As they walked around the store, Dara engaged in an hour-long bra tutorial while Lacey trailed behind her, eager to learn.

Chris couldn't help but feel both impressed and relieved. Giving them space, but keeping one eye on the lesson, he learned a lot about women's underwear. Lace versus cotton. Underwire woven beneath the cup. Different colors and cup styles that one would have to change depending on the style of the blouse it was worn beneath. It was completely different than his underwear, which came in a bag, and was marked as one of four sizes.

"See?" Dara said, leaning down to show Lacey two options. "This works really well under a T-shirt, but this is better for playing sports."

Finally, Dara and his daughter—along with a sales attendant—disappeared into a back room to try on styles.

Left alone, he walked around the store, scoping out items for himself, trying not to look like some creepy old pervert. Still, it had been some time since he had seen a woman in lingerie.

On instinct, he found himself mesmerized by a wall of bras with the biggest cups he had ever seen in his whole life. Bigger than his head, really, with lilac lace that arched into a delicate V-shape at the front. He pulled it off, noting the size. 36G. He had no idea what that meant, but he liked the lace. The color, too. It would suit Dara.

He envisioned the lilac lace against her olive skin. The way her long black hair would cascade over it. He imagined himself running his fingers over her nipples, feeling her body react to the sensation of his touch. His own body twitched pleasurably in return.

"I don't think it's your size," a voice said behind him.

"Oh!" Chris jumped, turning to see Dara standing there. "No. I know... I mean..."

She laughed. "Relax, Chris. I'm just kidding."

"Right." He breathed a sigh of relief. "I knew that."

She cocked her head, still smiling warmly at him. God, he loved her smile. He also felt incredibly guilty for being unable to control his attraction to her. She was dating another man, after all. She was heading toward marriage with that man, too.

He focused all his thoughts on being her friend, and the practicality of her help in buying his daughter a bra.

"Where's Lacey?" he asked.

"Fitting room." Dara squeezed his arm. "You are really nervous!"

"It's just, uh," he stammered, "not my comfort zone."

"Well, Chris," she teased him, "don't look at the wall—focus on the goal."

He laughed. "I deserve that."

Two hours later, Chris was handing over his credit card for two giant shopping bags' worth of bras for his young daughter. Maybe it was overkill. But seeing the smile on his kiddo's face, knowing that he had done right by her, made all the months of trepidation feel worth it.

Outside Nordstrom, the early-afternoon sun was shining. The Manhattan streets crowded with holiday shoppers. Their shopping done for the day, Dara and Chris awkwardly negotiated next steps. He knew she was a busy professional. She probably needed to get home. Still, he couldn't help but notice that her feet were hesitating.

"You got big plans tonight?" Chris asked.

"Oh," she said, shrugging her shoulders. "Not really."

"What about Dr. Daniel?"

"On call," she explained. "I suppose we could meet up for dinner, me being in the city and all...but why ruin a good thing, right?"

The words hung in the air like a chill. *Why ruin a good thing?*

"So," Chris said it carefully, "you're just gonna go home, then?"

"I have some work to catch up on," she admitted. "Plus, my bubbe and the ChallahBack Girls are getting together for trivia."

"Sounds like a wild night."

"Hey, now," Dara warned him. "You've never seen Arlene at trivia night. That woman is ruthless."

Chris laughed. "I have no doubt."

Another awkward moment stretched between them.

"And you?" Dara asked.

"Well, I was planning on taking Lacey to her favorite ice cream place." He glanced over to his daughter, now flossing beside a hot dog vendor. "Because clearly she needs more sugar."

"Clearly."

"You should come with us!" Lacey returned, grabbing Dara by the hand. "MilkShAXEs is *soooooooo* much fun. You throw axes! And eat ice cream, and...and...it's really fun. We can even team up against my dad!"

"Ice cream and axes, huh?"

"I admit it," Chris said. "I'm a terrible parent."

Dara smiled. "The worst."

"He also lets me watch horror movies," Lacey said, before

beginning to full-on whine. "Please! Please! *Puh-leaze*, come with us!"

Normally, Chris would tell Lacey to knock it off at this point. But truth be told, he wanted Dara to come with them. It seemed a waste, walking away from each other so soon.

"You really don't need to," Chris said, trying to give her an out. "Plus, it's all the way in Brooklyn."

He was waiting for Dara to politely decline. Instead, she surprised him.

"You know what? Ice cream and axe throwing sounds great."

32

LACEY SENT ONE AXE ZIPPING THROUGH THE AIR.
For a skinny thing, she had arms that could rival any Major
League pitcher. It went sailing past the attendant watching
nearby, and landed with one great thump in the center of the
target. The throw was enough to win the game.

"Yes!" Lacey screamed. "We did it!"

"You did it!" Dara said, squealing in delight.

Throwing high fives and victory wiggles in each other's
direction, they made sure to spend as much time as possible
teasing Chris about the loss. Alas, he had put up a good fight.
But after three rounds of axe throwing, and one banana split
shared between them, the handsome head anchor of *Good
News* had no choice but to admit defeat.

"Alright," he said, touching his heart at the tragedy. "It's
official. You and Dara have fully kicked my butt."

Lacey responded to his downfall with song and dance.
"Kickin' your butt!" she repeated. "Kickin' your butt! Pooh-
pooh, yeah-yeah, butt-kickers forever!"

Dara couldn't help herself. She joined in her song and dance.
Chris broke into hysterics watching them.

Obviously, Dara was not usually the type of person to devolve into such juvenile antics. Especially in public, and given her role as a brand representative, but there was something about Chris, and his daughter, that seemed to put her at ease. She could not recall a time in her life when she'd had so much fun, or felt so *carefree*.

Dara crossed her arms and leaned against the cage of the axe throwing lane casually. "So, what do we win?" she teased him.

Chris considered the question. "How about dinner?"

"I would love that."

"Do you mind pizza at my place?" he asked, before glancing at Lacey. "It's a school night."

"Pizza sounds perfect."

Chris only lived a few blocks from MilkShAXEs, but the walk back to his apartment allowed Dara to take in the sights of his neighborhood. The tiny stretch of apartments and townhomes intertwined with hipster restaurants and long-standing bodegas. A feeling of life thumped and breathed in this neighborhood, a messiness she enjoyed, with its hodgepodge of delightful characters. It was nothing like the pristine condos and high-rises that lined the Hoboken waterfront.

They came to a quaint-looking town house. Lacey raced up the stairs and inside. Dara took a moment to survey the place where Chris and his daughter lived. She wasn't sure what she was expecting. But once again, he surprised her.

When Dara had first met Chris, she envisioned him living in some fancy high-rise in Manhattan. A bachelor pad with expansive views of the city, black leather couches and overpriced neon-lit artwork. But this place was rather sensible for a man and his family. With delicate archways and art deco tiles beyond the staircase, and a school halfway down the block.

The only thing that wasn't sensible, of course, was the firehouse it was attached to.

"You live next to a firehouse?" Dara asked, surprised.

"Yeah."

"Isn't that…noisy?"

He cocked his head, as if he had never once considered the question. "You know, now that you mention it… I always wondered why I got such a good deal on the apartment."

Dara laughed. "Yeah. Probably not the hottest property on the block."

Their apartment was on the first floor. Lacey raced ahead, making her way inside and disappearing straight into her bedroom. Meanwhile, Chris was firmly focused on making a pathway through the tiny hallway inside, picking up bits of clothing, moving backpacks and bags out of the way.

He turned back to Dara sheepishly. "It's a bit of a mess."

"It's lovely," Dara said, honestly. "You have a beautiful home."

Chris didn't need to be embarrassed. Dara took in the space where he lived. If anything, she loved the way his house looked. Unlike her three-bedroom loft apartment, with its dangerous staircase and sterile finishes, Chris's home was designed for a family. It was lived in. Things were out of place, and messy, but the chaos only felt like a proclamation of love.

"So," Chris said, pulling a take-out menu from the drawer. "It's pretty standard Italian fare for around here, but if you want something else…salad or pasta…"

"Cheese pizza is fine."

Chris nodded. "One cheese pizza, coming right up."

Lacey flew back down the hall in her socks, coming to a messy stop right before crashing into the table. "Dara!" she said, tugging on her sleeve. "Come see my bedroom."

"Do you mind?" Dara asked, glancing toward Chris.

"I don't think I could stop either of you if I wanted."

Dara followed Lacey to her bedroom. Holding her hand while they walked, Lacey set about giving her the grand tour. Stepping over laundry, she pointed out her collection of killer clown memorabilia, arts and crafts she had made in school, her favorite pink bedding. Finally, she came to her nightstand. Grabbing the photo off the top, she handed it to Dara.

"This is my mommy," she said. "She died two years ago."

Dara took a seat on her bed. Staring down at the image of the woman with strawberry blond hair, her heart broke for Chris. And Lacey. "She's beautiful," Dara said, genuinely. "You look a lot like her, you know?"

"I know," Lacey said. "Is your mom still alive?"

"No," Dara said. "My mommy died ten years ago."

"Do you miss her?"

"Every day."

"I miss my mommy, too," Lacey said. "My dad never talks about her, though. It's hard because, sometimes… I forget her, you know? Like what she looked like. I think I remember, but then… I realize all I remember is this picture. I've never met someone else whose mommy died before. Everyone in my school has both parents alive. Some people even have two moms. I know one girl…she has, like, four moms."

"Well," Dara said, smiling, "anytime you want to talk about your mommy, or how it feels to have lost your mommy… I'm happy to listen."

Lacey responded to this by giving Dara the biggest hug possible. Dara returned the affection with all the love she could muster. She felt for this child. She also related to her.

Eventually, the sound of Chris clearing his throat at the door drew her attention away.

"Sorry to interrupt," Chris said. "Pizza is here."

Dara and Lacey returned to the living room. Chris began

putting out plates before angling two boxes of pizza in the center of the table. The first box was exactly what Dara had ordered. A very safe, and also kosher, cheese pizza. But glancing down at the second box, she was certain that the restaurant must have gotten their order wrong.

"*What* is that?" Dara asked, aghast.

"That," Chris said, picking up a slice of pie loaded down with jalapeños and pineapples, "is the stuff dreams are made of." He took one giant bite.

Lacey reached over and did the same. "It's the perfect blend of spicy and sweet!" she explained.

"Want to try it?" Chris asked.

Dara stared down at the Indigestion Pie. Normally, she would have declined the offer. She wasn't really a fan of pineapple, and though she liked a good kick to her food, she had never thought to put jalapeños on her Italian food.

It was just outside of her comfort zone. Something she wasn't entirely used to, and therefore, had a tendency to avoid. Still, there was something about being in Brooklyn, with Chris and Lacey, that made Dara feel adventurous.

"You know what?" she said, reaching over to grab a slice. "I think I will try that pizza, after all."

Dara took a bite. Her taste buds exploded with sheer delight. Sweetness, followed by fire. It tingled on her tongue, only to be followed by the salty richness of mozzarella cheese layered with thick red sauce.

"Oh my gosh," she said, still chewing, "that is amazing!"

"Told you," Lacey said. "So much better than plain."

Chris smiled at her from across the table. She was fully outside the limits of any plan now…but she loved it. She loved being with Chris. She loved being with Lacey. It felt right, being with them, sharing a table full of surprises.

"Dara," Lacey said, curiously, her mouth full of pizza. "Why do you keep kosher?"

Dara put down her slice. "Well, a lot of reasons. For one, it's part of Jewish law—part of our tradition as Jewish people—and I try to live my life as Jewishly as possible because it gives me meaning. Secondly, it was how I was raised. I've never had a ham-and-cheese sandwich, for instance."

"You've never had a ham-and-cheese sandwich?" Lacey asked, amazed.

"Nope."

"Not even a pork roll?"

Dara bit back a smile. "I'm afraid not."

"Whoa." Lacey was clearly trying to wrap her head around this news.

"But also," Dara added, "I like keeping kosher. Keeping kosher means that every time I eat, I think about something bigger than myself. I think about God, and my history, and the traditions of the Jewish people...and I like that. Keeping kosher forces me to live in the present, while connecting me to the past."

Lacey stopped chewing. Dara could see by the way she squished up her lips all the way to one side that she was thinking *most seriously* about this thing. "That's really cool," Lacey said, and took another bite of pizza. "I think I would like being Jewish. It's like...you get to be a time traveler!"

Both Dara and Chris laughed at the sentiment.

The conversation for the next half hour flowed smoothly and easily. Lacey moved away from the topic of Judaism to express an interest in computers, and learning to code. Dara promised to send along some materials to help her with developing that talent. Chris talked about Virginia, his family back home and how they should get back for a visit soon.

Dara rested her chin on her hand, mesmerized by the melodic lull of his perfect voice. It was the strangest thing, really. No matter what Chris talked about, she found him interesting. It had always been that way, even before she met him in person. She would have liked to stay in this apartment, in his presence, forever.

Finally, when the pineapple-and-jalapeño pizza was nothing but bits of crust in an empty cardboard box, Chris glanced over to Lacey. "Alright, kiddo, it's bedtime. You know the drill."

The whining began immediately. "But I'm not even tired!"

"Now," Chris said, fixing his daughter with a stare. Lacey stormed off down the hall.

"Sorry about that," he said.

"It's okay. I already knew you're the worst dad in the world."

Chris laughed. "Exactly."

Lacey stomped back out of her bedroom, towels and pajamas in hand, before slamming the door to the bathroom behind her. Chris waited for the sound of the shower to start running before returning to his conversation with Dara.

"I heard you talking to Lacey," he said. "About her mother."

Dara nodded. "Why don't you have more pictures of her?"

"How do you mean?"

"The only picture of Claire is in Lacey's bedroom."

The sound of water dinging and pinging against tiles echoed in the background. "It's hard," he said, clearing his throat before continuing. "Remembering."

"I know," she said, sympathetically. "But you have to put those pictures out. For Lacey. It's not fair to her. She deserves to know who her mother was."

Chris was quiet for a long time. "Your mother died ten years ago, right?"

Dara nodded.

"Does it ever…go away?"

"No."

She said it simply. Honestly.

"You always feel the absence," she continued, gently. "Every Mother's Day. Every birthday. Every holiday, putting out place settings on a table, staring at an empty seat. Sometimes it's not even the big events. Sometimes you're just sitting in your living room, drinking coffee, and the shifting light reminds you of this silly thing they did when you were a kid…so, you go to pick up the phone to call them, and then, you remember. They're gone. You can't call them, or talk to them. You can't ask them for a hug…and it feels like losing them all over again."

She could see the hurt in his eyes. She could feel the hurt, lingering in the space—on the family, too.

"But," Dara said, thoughtfully, "you learn to live with it. The sadness never goes away. Maybe it never gets smaller, either. But after a time, you learn to hold both. You learn that joy still exists…there's still laughter, and falling in love, and—" she smiled, glancing down at the crumbs of her pizza "—there's still jalapeño-and-pineapple pizza. You learn that good things still happen. You meet someone. You fall in love. Maybe you even get married. And when you walk down that aisle, you hold both. You hold the joy of the moment alongside your sadness for the one who can't be there."

Chris swallowed. "You really are something else, Dara Rabinowitz."

"I'm just good at overthinking."

"No," he said, meeting her eyes directly. "You are so much more than that."

A few seconds of thoughtful silence wedged their way between them, before her lips curled into a smile.

Moments later, the sound of the water turned off. The door to the bathroom flew open. Lacey emerged, wearing nothing but a towel. "Sorry! Sorry!" Lacey said, sprinting back to her bedroom. "I forgot my underwear!"

Both Chris and Dara laughed before taking that as their cue.

Chris rose from his seat and began cleaning dishes. Dara did the same. Grabbing her own plate, she moved to the kitchen to help him clean up. It was then that she realized the poor man didn't even have a dishwasher.

"You don't need to do that," Chris said, taking the plate away from her.

"I don't mind," she said, bumping elbows with him. His kitchen was small. Far smaller than the rest of his apartment. "Don't you know I enjoy cleaning?"

"Why does that not surprise me?"

"Because I'm a perfectionist," she reminded him with a self-deprecating grin. "With obsessive compulsive tendencies."

"By all means, then," Chris teased her, their hips touching at the sink, "come over and clean up anytime."

"Let's not go too far now."

The red in his cheeks had returned, along with that soft and sweet crinkle she adored around his gray eyes. God, he was handsome. Her eyes focused on a wet spot in the center of his perfect lips. What would it be like to kiss Christopher Steadfast? Would it feel different than kissing Dr. Daniel? Her chest rose in excited anticipation at the thought.

"And I appreciate you buying me dinner," she said, handing him another plate.

"Come on," he said, taking it from her. "After everything you've done for me today, I owe you a lifetime of pineapple-and-jalapeño pizza."

She couldn't help herself. She gave in to the fantasy. The idea of a lifetime of pineapple-and-jalapeño pizza with Chris sounded nice.

He bumped her arm again. "Sorry."

"Your kitchen is too small!"

"You want me to move?"

"Possibly." She grinned. "How does Hoboken sound?"

"Where is that again?"

"Oh, please."

"Besides," Chris reminded her, "it's usually only one in here."

He reached over, grabbing another dish. Their hands touched. She was just about to pull away when she realized that his fingers were still lingering there. And then, Chris ran both his thumbs over her knuckles. Every sensation in her body went into overdrive. And yet, she didn't pull away. She couldn't pull away.

Instead, her breathing quickened. Chris took that as approval. His fingers moved from her knuckles to her wrist. Wrapping his hands around her, he pulled her closer, nuzzling his nose into her neck, her back flat against the refrigerator.

"Chris," she moaned.

"Yeah," he whispered.

"We should stop."

"You're right," he said, still holding her. "You're totally right."

The space between her legs ached. The sound of him breathing in her ear merged with her own need. A sigh escaped her lips, hot and intense. She gave in to her want, arching her hips upward.

She wanted to kiss him. She knew by the way he pressed his body harder against hers that he wanted the same.

The stubble of his five-o'clock shadow tingled against her neck. He responded to her pleas of open desire, his hands moving from the bottom of her shirt, dancing up the back. Pulling at her blouse, his breath growing heavy, his hands met her bare skin underneath. A shiver ran up her spine. The thought crossed her mind that she should stop—that this was wrong, and had no good outcomes—but she was far too overwhelmed by the longing coursing through her belly.

She forced away any intrusive thoughts, giving in to the sensation of his hands. Joining him in exploration, she ran her fingertips over the edge of his belt. His body responded to her touch. He groaned, pressing himself against her belly, the stiff form beneath his jeans driving her wild. God, how she wanted him. She wanted him to take her, right here, against his refrigerator.

"Dad?" Lacey said.

They jumped apart. Embarrassed, adjusting their clothing and hair in a flurry of excuses, they were like two teenagers caught in the act.

Chris stammered. "We were just—"

"My earring," Dara said, touching one lobe.

"Right." Chris twisted in his spot. "Did you find it?"

"Yep," she said, too quickly. "Right here!"

"Oh, good." Chris turned back to his daughter. "I was just helping Dara find her earring."

As Lacey stood there in a pair of carnival-themed paja-mas with her arms crossed against her chest, her entire face morphed into straight disgust. She was not buying it.

"Ew," Lacey said.

Chris cleared his throat. "What do you need, kiddo?"

"The toilet's not flushing," she said.

"Ugh." Chris met Dara with apologetic eyes. "Let me just... deal with that."

Chris headed off to help Lacey. Dara used the space to get a hold of her senses. Pushing her hair out of her eyes, breathing oxygen into her flushed cheeks, she wondered what the hell had just happened. It had to be madness, an endorphin rush brought on by pineapple-and-jalapeño pizza. Leaning over the sink, she tried to understand what her reaction to his touch meant. Until finally, still spinning from their near kiss, she settled on her favorite way of dealing with stressful situations.

She returned her attention to cleaning up from dinner. Grabbing what was left of the cheese pizza, she wrapped up the remaining slices in aluminum foil, moving to place all the items in the fridge.

It was there, in the blinking haze of the automatic light, that her hands went still. Her feet became unsteady as shock overtook all sensible thought. Holding the door open, staring into the cold and icy grip of Christopher Steadfast's refrigerator, she was confronted with a terrifying sight.

There was... So. Much. Ham.

It was like all six shelves just exploded with *treif.* Like Chris had gone out, killed Wilbur himself, before churning him into a thousand different by-products. Everywhere she looked— every shelf her eyes landed on—it was there, threatening to attack her, overpowering her senses, greeting her kosher sensibilities with outright horror.

On the shelf in front of her was uncooked bacon. In the tray to her left were three different types of sliced ham. Even the store-bought salad dressing had bacon bits in it. But the worst thing of all, the thing that was the final nail in the relationship coffin between them, was the way the package of cheddar cheese slices was placed in the same drawer as the salami. There was no separation of meat and milk.

Dara slammed shut the door to the refrigerator, wishing she had never seen inside it. Alas, it was too late. In those few brief seconds of oink-filled horror, the realization of who he was—who Chris was without her—confronted her full force.

What was she doing in this place? What was she doing with Chris? How could she have been so naive to think that anything could be possible between them? She shook off the feelings, the madness, the intense sexual longing…when Chris returned to the living room.

"Sorry about that." Chris smiled. "Toilet has been giving us trouble lately."

"It's fine," Dara said, nervously. "I should get going, anyway. It's late and—and I have a big meeting early in the morning."

"Oh." Chris sounded disappointed. "I mean…of course."

He moved to grab her coat. Always the gentleman, he helped her into it. Dara slunk her arms through the sleeves, twisting around. Their eyes met again.

"So, I'll—" He cleared his throat. "I'll see you at our next shoot?"

Dara swallowed hard. "Sounds perfect."

Grabbing her bag, she raced from his apartment, sprinting down his front stoop two steps at a time, like some sort of modern-day Yiderella, opting to wait for an Uber back to Hoboken alone.

Hanukkah

(THE FIRST NIGHT)

33

CHRIS WAS IN A GOOD MOOD ON WEDNESDAY morning. Floating into work with six boxes full of powdered jelly doughnuts stacked up inside his arms, he handed out free breakfast to security guards and television execs alike. Exiting the elevator, he landed on the fifth-floor hallway, bumping into Eli.

"You're chipper this morning," Eli said.

"What's not to be happy about?" Chris said, practically singing. "It's December. The holidays are coming. Everybody loves the holidays, right?"

Eli eyed him suspiciously. "Right."

Chris angled his box at the young man. *"Sufganiyot?"*

"What the hell is that?"

"It's a special word for a jelly doughnut," he explained, "In *Hebrew*. You're supposed to eat them on Hanukkah."

Eli shrugged and, reaching into the box, took one.

Of course, Chris's chipper mood could have had something to do with the strange almost-kiss he had enjoyed with Dara the previous Sunday. Granted, with his kid walking in on their near kiss, and Dara needing to get home for an early-morning meeting, their first time making out didn't go as well as one would have hoped. Still, the event had solidified in his mind a simple truth. Dara wanted him. She wanted him…just as much as he wanted her.

Whatever passion she was sharing with Dr. Daniel, Chris felt keenly that he now had a chance. Perhaps he would take Jensen's advice, and admit his feelings. Maybe he would even ask Dara if she wanted to come hang out with him and Lacey on Christmas. What else would she be doing, right?

Chris rounded a corner, heading toward his office. And then, his smile faded. Eleanor and Daniel were sitting inside.

"Chris!" Eleanor said, rising from his seat. "Just the man we were waiting for."

Chris hesitated in the hallway. He had a sinking feeling in his stomach, and an urge to run away. Unfortunately, he had no choice. Making his way inside, he took a seat beside Daniel.

"I'll let you tell him the good news," Eleanor said.

Dr. Daniel beamed. "I've decided to ask Dara to marry me!"

Chris felt his mouth go dry. "Excuse me?"

His cheery holiday season attitude quickly sloughed off. He knew that there were words he should be saying—*congratulations, how wonderful for you both, mazel tov*—but despite all his years working without scripts, he felt incapable of pulling out the words. Congratulations wouldn't stop the aching, scrambling feeling rising in his chest.

They couldn't get married. They just *couldn't*.

"Marriage?" Chris choked out, loosening his tie. "Don't you think…that's a little soon?"

Dr. Daniel laughed at the sentiment. "We're both in our midthirties."

"Plenty of time!" Chris clapped him on the back.

Daniel squinted in his direction, confused. "I'm sorry," he

said. "I think you're misunderstanding. I'm *going* to ask Dara to marry me."

"Daniel and I have been working out all the details," Eleanor said excitedly.

Chris tugged at his tie once again. Damn. It was hot. The stupid thing suddenly seemed hell-bent on strangling him.

"The details?" he choked out.

He still didn't understand what was going on.

Eleanor, however, could barely contain her excitement. She paced around them, talking with her hands as she unveiled the details of her master plan.

"I've worked it all out with the big brass on the upper floors," she explained. "Dara's bubbe is having her ninetieth birthday on the last night of Hanukkah. That's one week from tonight. So what we're all thinking is—given this amazing news and the ratings bonanza it is sure to generate—we turn Bubbe Miriam's party into a live one-hour special event!"

"Live," Chris stammered.

"There's music!" Eleanor exclaimed. "There's dancing!"

"Don't forget the unicorns," Daniel interjected.

"Don't interrupt me while I'm speaking, Daniel."

Daniel sank in his seat. "Sorry."

"Anyway," Eleanor continued, "we got the whole *mishpacha* there—Bubbe, the old broads from the nursing home, the siblings and their families—and then, bam! Daniel pops the question. God, it will be brilliant. Magical. *Perfection!* The audience will freaking love it."

Eleanor returned to Chris's desk, taking his seat. Daniel used the break in the conversation to politely raise his hand. "May I speak now?"

Eleanor waved him forward. "Go ahead."

"I know she really likes Bucky, the vegan golden retriever," he said, glancing between them both. "I think it would be great if Bucky could be there in some way."

"Goddamn it, Daniel!" Eleanor slammed one hand down on Chris's desk, causing the whole room to quiver in response. "This is why I like you. You're almost as brilliant as me."

Daniel blushed. "I like you, too, Eleanor."

Chris could feel the second hand on the clock ticking forward. It was unreal. It was all so soon. The couple had only known each other a few weeks. But mainly, there was this thought weighing him down. Once Dara got engaged—once she sealed the deal with Mr. Perfect on Paper—there would be no reason to keep meeting up to film.

Chris would lose her.

Eleanor raised one pert eyebrow at him. "You gonna say something, Chris?"

"I just—I don't think it's a good idea."

Eleanor blinked, but said nothing. Moments later, she was leading Daniel to the door with a thousand hearty mazel tovs.

"This is such wonderful news," she said, ushering the man out. "You don't worry about a thing, Daniel. We'll handle all the details, okay? Dara is going to have the best engagement of her life!"

"Hopefully, the only one," Daniel joked, nervously.

"Whatever." Eleanor shrugged. "So I'll call you later to start hashing out a game plan."

He blushed. "I'd love that."

Eleanor waited for Dr. Daniel to disappear from view before shutting the door to the office. Returning to her seat at the desk, she confronted Chris directly.

"What's going on?" she demanded.

"Nothing," Chris lied.

"Then what the hell is your problem?"

Chris began scrambling for words, for excuses, for time.

"Well, what about the show?" he asked. "People love seeing Daniel and Dara. People love following their adventures together. They get married now, who's gonna be pulling in our numbers? We'll be back to getting our balls busted by *Good Day*! We need to keep this Daniel and Dara thing going. We need to milk this courtship for as long as humanly possible."

Eleanor considered his words, and then broke into a wide smile. "That's just it, Chris," she said. "We don't."

"I...I don't understand."

She met his eyes directly. "Prime time."

"What?"

"Prime time, Chris," she squealed, balling both fists up at her face. "Come the New Year, we're getting moved over." She didn't give the news any time to sink in before continuing. "I wasn't originally going to mention anything to you until we had a contract—you know how fickle bigwigs at the upper levels can be—but they're impressed with you, Chris. You saw a click-banger and you ran with it. You've proven you have what it takes to pull in the big numbers! Now, it's not talk anymore—it's really happening. You're moving over to John McKenzie's position on *Daily Break*...and I'm coming with you."

"Jesus." Chris rubbed the back of his neck. "Really?"

"Really."

"Well, how long is the contract?"

He had to ask. One of the issues with *Good News* was that he was constantly under threat of termination.

Eleanor smiled. "Three years."

"Three years?"

"How's that for stability, huh?" Eleanor grinned, leaning back in her seat again. "Hell, I might even feel secure enough in my position to take a vacation. An expensive one, too."

Chris collapsed in one of the guest chairs. It wasn't just the accolades, and security…a prime-time show meant money. Enough money to buy Lacey all the bras she wanted. Enough money to afford a zillion nannies to help her get fitted for them. He could keep his daughter in New York. But there were also downsides to this news. A prime-time show meant he would be working evenings. It meant longer hours, more pressure from the big brass on the upper floors and even less time spent devoted to his daughter.

He should have been happy. But his heart was racked with uncertainty.

And then, a horrible and sinking feeling landed in his gut. Beyond all these things, beyond the practicalities of being a single and working parent, was the realization that he was going to lose Dara. Dara, who made him laugh again after a thousand terrible nights. Dara, with her weeping-willow hair, and ridiculous lists, and an emergency scanner app pressed up to her ear. Dara—she made life go on.

"I'm sorry," Chris said, rising from his seat. "I need to go."

34

INSIDE HER HOBOKEN APARTMENT, DARA SLUMPED over her desk. Chin in one hand, the other on her mouse, she was pretending to listen in on the sales and subscriptions meeting being held over Zoom for J-Mate.

"In New York," Janet said, continuing her presentation, "our numbers are into the double digits. For every six people who identify as single and Jewish in the city, at least three of them are on J-Mate and utilizing the J-eography update. Our new marketing campaign featuring Dara and Dr. Daniel has solidified J-Mate as a leader in the space."

Her staff reacted to news of these numbers with exuberant applause. Dara did the same.

She tried to stay focused, but found it hard to pay attention. Dr. Daniel had sent her an email earlier with options for engagement rings. She wasn't surprised to receive it. Now that they had confirmed their intentions of marriage—and their families had met—there was no logical reason to wait.

She clicked absentmindedly through each photograph, trying to find a favorite. There was a lovely blue sapphire in a vintage style. A solitaire in a Tiffany setting. A princess cut with a band in rose gold. Each one was more exquisite than the last, yet none of the rings felt right.

Suddenly, there was a knock at the door. Dara excused herself from the meeting and headed to the entryway, checking though the peephole.

Her heart leaped at the sight of Chris in her hallway, then sank with dread. She still wasn't sure what to do about their near kiss in his apartment last Sunday. The way she had so recklessly given in to nonsensical feelings, before bolting completely for home. Pulling the edges of her cardigan closed tight, she gathered her courage, opening the door.

"Chris," Dara said upon seeing him, "What are you—"

Chris interrupted her. "Can I come in?"

She could tell something was wrong. She could see it in his eyes, red and wet, and the prescient way he kept one hand on the lintel of her doorway. Despite all her better instincts, she opened the door to her apartment, welcoming Chris inside.

"Can I get you something to drink?" Dara asked, heading toward the kitchen.

Chris stood in the foyer of Dara's apartment, the bubbles in his chest quickly rising. He couldn't help feeling overwhelmed. Not just because he was here, ready to confess his feelings, but because he had never actually been inside Dara's apartment before.

Gazing around him, he couldn't help but feel intimidated. He knew Dara was rich—running her own technology company, all that—but an apartment like hers, with floor-to-ceiling windows overlooking the water and Manhattan, must have cost well into the millions.

And yet, it was such a clear reflection of her personality. Spotless. Perfect. Everything neatly organized, in proper little stacks and in their places. One menorah, ready for the first night of Hanukkah, sat on the coffee table, waiting to be lit this evening. Chris looked past the pristine quartz countertops and stainless steel appliances—with their lack of streaks or fingerprints—to see her opening a cabinet in the kitchen.

"I have coffee," Dara said, running through options, "tea, juice, water—"

"Water is fine," he said.

She turned to pour him a glass. Meanwhile, Chris took a seat on her couch. Leaning over his knees, breathing through the tension in his chest, he searched for the words.

"It must be important," Dara said, setting the water down on the coffee table and taking a seat beside him.

Her voice brought him back. "What?"

"For you to come out here in the morning," she said. "I know you're usually busy getting ready for your show at this time of day." She gave him a warm smile.

God, she was beautiful.

Maybe they were different people. Maybe when they met, they were looking in completely different directions…but they were standing toe-to-toe with each other now. He had to tell her what was in his heart.

"I love you."

Dara straightened. Her eyes went wide.

"I'm dating Dr. Daniel! We're talking about marriage!"

"Call it off." He said it directly. "Call it off…and be with me."

"You don't even know me!"

"I know you," he said, the words falling from his lips. "I know you visit your grandmother damn near every day. I know you keep kosher, and eat hot dairy in restaurants, and that, before last night, you had never tried jalapeño-and-pineapple pizza."

"Chris—"

"I know you're allergic to mango," he continued, "and that you know everything there is to know about bras, and that you are the type of woman...the type of person...who will go out of your way for an eleven-year-old girl because she doesn't have a mom."

"Please," she whispered.

"And I know that you're afraid of bridges, and bumble-bees, and helicopter rides...but you fight so hard anyway. Just like I know that you love listening to your emergency scanner app because it calms you down when you're edging into a panic attack, and it reminds you that life goes on. Life goes on, Dara...no matter what."

He took her hands gently in his, pulling her toward him.

"Go on with me," he said, meeting her dark eyes directly. "Let's build something beautiful together."

For one brief moment, she hesitated. Her lower lip quivered. She did not pull away. Chris believed that his words, spoken from the very depth of his heart, had made an impression on her. She met his own intensity with longing eyes. Yes, she wanted him. All the feelings rumbling in his belly were there in hers, too. Chris leaned in to kiss her.

"Stop," Dara said.

Chris stopped. "Dara—"

"No." She pulled away from him. "Stop this, Chris. Stop this nonsense."

"It's not nonsense!" he defended himself. "What we have together, what we feel—"

She closed her eyes, shaking her head. "You're not Jewish!"

"What?" Chris said.

"You're not Jewish, Chris."

Chris felt his stomach sink.

Okay, they had different religions. He knew her Judaism was important to her, but didn't love surpass all things? Couldn't they find a way to work something out?

"Do you love me, Dara?"

"It doesn't matter."

"Of course it matters!" he said.

"No." Her voice softened, her sadness evident. "It doesn't."

She sighed heavily. Chris felt his heart pounding. He had a sense where this was heading.

"Well, what if someone converts?"

She shook her head. "Chris—"

"I mean, I know you don't want someone who converts for marriage, but I've been learning, Dara. I'm even fine with getting the whole *hatafat dam* thingy...and I could talk with Lacey, too. I could see how she feels about—"

"It won't work."

"Why not?"

"Because," she snapped back at him, "being Jewish is more than a label for me, Chris. It's more than eating some brisket on Rosh Hashanah, or going to synagogue for a few hours on Yom Kippur. It's keeping kosher, and observing the Sabbath, and maybe even wearing a wig when I get married."

"You would do that?"

"I don't know," she said, honestly. "But the point is, I want a husband who is willing to have the conversation with me. I want a partner as committed to my faith as I am, because living between two worlds...having to make those choices on the daily...is really freaking hard."

Chris swallowed. "I'm used to hard things, Dara."

"Not like this," she said. "It's too hard for someone who doesn't already live it. And if you don't believe me, try being Jewish for a week. Stop eating un-kosher food. Turn off all your computers and phones on Shabbat. Wear a yarmulke on the subway. And after that week…tell me if you can live your entire life that way."

Chris shifted in his seat. He couldn't help but agree that she had a point. Still, he was annoyed. Dara wasn't even giving their relationship a chance. She wasn't even willing to consider, or talk about, the possibility of compromise.

She also hadn't spoken one word about love. It struck him as painfully obvious. She was heading toward marriage with Dr. Daniel—giving Chris a thousand different reasons why they couldn't be together—and not one of them boiled down to the passions of her heart.

"Do you love him, Dara?" Chris asked.

"He's a good man."

"You didn't answer my question."

Dara sighed, staring down at her lap.

It annoyed him. She was so willing to give up on her feelings. On Chris.

She was so black-and-white. Like her hair, onyx corkscrews pressed up against porcelain skin. There had to be some happy medium that they could find. There had to be some version of gray.

Lots of people had successful interfaith relationships. Lots of people married folks who converted, too. Chris was certain that her avoidance of the question, her inability to even entertain the possibility, was tied to a deeper fear.

"You know what I think, Dara?" Chris said, finally. "I think you're afraid."

"Afraid?" she balked. "Of what?"

"I think that love—real love, the type of love where you lose control of yourself completely—scares the hell out of you."

"Oh, please."

"I think it's easier for you to marry someone you don't care about, someone who's safe and appropriate, someone who doesn't challenge your carefully constructed boundaries, than to risk getting hurt."

"Because you're suddenly the expert now?"

"I have more experience in that department than you."

She gasped. Her lower lip fell open, insulted.

"Falling in love is a risk, Dara," he said, confronting her directly. "It's messy, and hard, and complicated. There's no such thing as a perfect person, and there's *always* the chance of getting hurt. But when you fall in love with the right person...it's worth all that. Because marrying someone you don't love, even when they check every box on one of your ridiculous lists, will never make you happy."

Dara did not blink. "Get out."

"Dara—"

"Get the hell out of my apartment *now*."

Chris hesitated. He did not want this conversation, or their friendship, to end this way. The delay gave Dara just the amount of ammunition she needed.

"Fine," she huffed, the words exploding from her lips. "You want to talk about fear? Let's talk about fear! You moved to New York, and left your entire family and career behind, because you've never been able to deal with what happened to you. You don't have any pictures of Claire up in your house— even though you spent over a decade with that woman, even though she is the mother of your child—because you're incapable of facing your own pain. You point the camera at everyone else, plow them with questions, all so you can avoid telling one single truth about yourself. *You've never moved on.* You just run further and further away. Hell, maybe becoming Jewish is just another way for you to escape!"

"I'm not converting to run away."

"Are you so sure?" she snapped back at him. "How do you even know what you want for your future when you haven't even begun to deal with your past? But you're right, Chris. Maybe I am afraid of falling in love. Maybe I am a control freak who needs to wrap everything up in perfect lists, and perfect systems…but at least I deal with my crap."

It was done. Whatever possibility there was for a relationship between them faded with their final words.

Digging his hands into his pockets, Chris headed for the door, leaving Dara behind forever.

Hanukkah

(THE LAST NIGHT)

35

CHRIS THREW ONE PUNCH DEEP INTO THE HEAVY
bag. Despite a brutal seventy-five-minute workout with Jensen in the firehouse, he couldn't squelch the upset in his belly. Finishing his round, he glanced over to his phone on the counter and picked it up.

"Dude," Jensen said, wiping the back of his neck with a towel. "If you look at that phone one more time, I'm taking it away from you."

"I know, I know," Chris said, tossing it down. "I just... have a lot on my mind."

Jensen raised an eyebrow suspiciously. "No doubt."

Chris sighed and, grabbing his bottle of water, chugged it back. He was out of sorts and in a terrible mood. Switching places with Jensen, leaning against a locker full of equipment, he ran through his to-do list for the day. It was the last night of Hanukkah. Bubbe Miriam's ninetieth birthday bash was being held tonight, and with it, Chris had been given the opportunity to host his first ever live prime-time event.

It was a chance for him to prove to the network bigwigs that he was capable of handling a prime-time slot, and say goodbye to the world of daytime television forever. He should have been happy, but there were tensions afoot.

For one, Dr. Daniel was going to be asking Dara to marry him. The very thought filled him with jealous fury.

But the bigger issue was that he hadn't spoken with Dara since their fight a week ago. Instead, it had been radio silence between the two of them.

"Why don't you just call her, man?" Jensen said.

Chris shook his head. "You weren't there."

"Okay," Jensen said, casual as always. "So you had a blow-out. Katie and I have blowouts all the time. Blowouts are a normal part of relationships. Now you get to the good part… making out."

"You mean, making up?"

"Yeah." Jensen punched him in the arm. "Exactly."

Chris rubbed the fleshy bit where he had been hit. "Ow."

Of course, he wanted to call her. He wanted to talk about what had happened, and make sure she was okay. He wanted to find some way to salvage their friendship. But every time he went to pick up the phone, he stopped himself.

Dara hadn't been wrong in the things she had said.

Chris finished his bottle of water, and his workout with Jensen, and returned upstairs. The apartment was quiet. It being a Thursday morning, Lacey was at school. Tossing his sweaty clothes to the floor at his side, he stepped into the shower, allowing the scalding water to pour down his naked neck.

Dara. He couldn't stop thinking about her. He couldn't stop thinking about how tonight, she would be making the biggest mistake of her life.

How could she marry Daniel? How could Chris put a smile on his face and pretend she hadn't once stood in his kitchen, pressed up against his refrigerator, her fingers trailing around his waist?

Chris turned off the water and grabbed a towel, heading back to his bedroom. Hanging on his closet was the tuxedo that Eleanor had arranged for him to wear tonight. Sitting down on his bed, he debated his options. And then, finally, after far too much time counting minutes and seconds, he picked up the phone.

"What's up?" Eleanor said on the other end of the line.

In the background, he could hear New York City traffic. She was already in her car, heading into the city and Pier 15, to make the final preparations for tonight's event.

Chris began to ramble. He explained that he wasn't feeling good, that it was a school night for Lacey and that he had a fight with Dara. Finally, Eleanor just demanded he cut through the bull and get down to the point.

"I can't do it, Eleanor."

"What!"

"Put Lisa on as head anchor tonight."

She spent the next fifteen minutes screaming at him through the phone. Chris didn't fight her on it. There was no worse crime in television than for your talent to bail on you at the very last minute. Even if you had the stomach flu, even if you had to sprint off camera every time they called cut to go puke in a can, you showed up for the people who relied on you.

"Look," Chris said, finally interrupting her diatribe, "I understand if you're pissed. I understand if you can't cover for me, either—"

Eleanor interrupted him. "Of course I'm going to cover for you! What kind of executive producer do you think I am? What kind of *friend* do you think I am? I'll make up some excuse that will keep you from getting straight-up fired by the head brass."

"Thanks, Eleanor."

"But seriously, Chris." She tried to reason with him one last time. "Are you positive this is what you want to do? I mean, this is your chance. Your big opportunity. The network execs want to see that you can handle a prime-time slot. They're interested in you now, but you know how fickle those idiots on the seventh floor are. They see Lisa tonight on that screen instead of you, and what do you think's gonna happen? They'll move her into the prime-time slot, and you'll be stuck in the dregs of daytime television for the rest of your natural life. Is that really what you want, Chris? *Good News*. Forever."

"I know what I want," Chris said, "which is why I can't do the show tonight. But I'll be watching, okay?"

"Yeah," she scoffed. "Lot of good that will do me."

"I appreciate this, Eleanor."

"Whatever," she said. "I hate you."

"You're the best."

Eleanor hung up the phone. The decision made, Chris settled into the silence of his apartment, debating what to do next.

He hadn't had a day off to himself, and without a kid, in what felt like years. Considering the state of the house, and knowing it was about to be Christmas, he decided to take a cue from Dara's pristine living quarters, and focused on cleaning up.

After getting dressed, he texted Mona that she could have the day off. Then, he started in the kitchen. He cleaned up the plates in the sink, wiped down the counters and table, threw out any old food from the fridge. He vacuumed the hallways and straightened up his bedroom, before scrubbing the bathroom. Finally, he made his way to Lacey's room.

It was one step away from being a full-fledged horror movie. Picking up dirty clothing from the floor, collecting it in a hamper, he made his way down to the laundry in the shared basement.

Dumping her items into the washer, he waited to hear the sound of the water rushing through the pipes before turning back to head upstairs. It was then that an image, locked up behind a grate, caught his eye. Putting his hamper down, he moved closer. He had forgotten about the mountain of boxes he had left downstairs from his move to New York two years ago. They were the boxes he had never unpacked. The boxes he had shoved into storage after moving in.

They were the boxes that held items from his life in Virginia with Claire.

Dara's words echoed in his brain.

And then, digging inside the pocket of his jeans to find his keychain, he opened the storage space. Wiping away dust, running his fingers over packing tape to find the scribble of permanent marker, he came across a box labeled *Christmas*. With all the strength he could muster, Chris hoisted it onto one shoulder and brought it upstairs.

36

DARA AWOKE THE MORNING OF MIRIAM'S NINETI-
eth birthday feeling worse than a burnt kugel. Her stomach
was in shambles. Her head ached. She felt like she hadn't slept
properly in years. Then again, Dara hadn't been sleeping well.
Ever since her fight with Chris, she had been racked by per-
sistent anxiety, constantly worried that she was making a mistake with Dr. Daniel.

"Just one more bobby pin," Simi said, sticking it into her
head.

Dara stared back at her reflection in the mirror. Her black
hair was tied up into a tightly wound coif of braids and curls.
Her makeup, a sweeping palette of deep purples and blacks,
made her look thoughtful and exotic. She looked perfect. Everything had been designed—from her dress, to the lighting,
to the gift bags and the purple carpet—to match the theme
and colors of the party. But despite everything going to plan,
it felt wrong.

"Dara," Naveah said, appearing with her tablet. "I wanted
to give you a status update."

Her lovely assistant was decked out in a light violet color, her blond dreadlocks now highlighted with little white gemstones. Dara waved her forward, while Simi applied one more round of gloss to her lips, and Cameron finished steaming her evening wear.

"The ChallahBack Girls and your bubbe are just finishing up at the spa," she said. "They're heading back to the suite at the Mandarin Oriental now. They'll take lunch in their suite, and then hair and makeup will arrive to get them all fabulous. I've also confirmed the cars for Shana and yourself. Your limo should be here with Dr. Daniel at four o'clock precisely."

"Excellent," Dara said. "You've taken care of everything."

"Almost." She smiled. "But if you're done with me here, I'll leave you in the capable hands of Simi and Bobbi and Cameron, and head over to Pier 15 myself. I want to run through some things with the party planner and caterer before you arrive."

"Of course. I won't keep you any longer."

Naveah turned to leave.

"Oh, Naveah," Dara called out. "Have you heard anything else from *Good News*?"

"How do you mean?"

"Well, I know we're making this a special one-hour live event," she said, cautiously. "I was just wondering if there is anything I need to do specifically. I mean, I usually hear from Chris…or Eleanor, or Eli, or somebody…but it's been weirdly quiet. I would imagine, with such a big show coming up, there's something I should be worrying about, right?"

All the members of her support staff cast sideways glances at each other. Dara had the distinct impression that everyone was in on some secret. Naveah played off the question innocently.

"Oh," she said, waving away Dara's concern. "No. Nothing you need to be doing. In fact, tonight is all about your bubbe

Miriam having the most epic ninetieth birthday ever! You just show up, have fun and let us handle everything."

Naveah flittered away. Dara sank down into her chair, the pressing anxiety on her chest returning.

37

THE FIRST BOX WAS THE HARDEST.

Chris tore open the packing tape and stared down at the hodgepodge of hastily thrown in Christmas toys and trinkets. It was amazing how quickly two years could pass. How he both simultaneously remembered and forgot every detail of their life together.

One by one, he pulled out items. There was the box of Christmas ornaments Claire loved. The Santa figurine, six tiny reindeer pulling a red sled, which used to sit front and center on their fireplace mantel.

Chris took every item out. By the fourth box, he had found a rhythm. It got less difficult, and more enjoyable. Every now and then, he would well up with sadness. Some memory would come, surprising him, and his heart would ache at the loss. A photo of him and Claire, arms linked together, at prom. A bottle of her favorite French perfume, the one crafted specifically for her on their ten-year anniversary, with some of the scent still left inside.

Then, almost as quickly, he would stumble onto some new trinket or item that shifted his hurt into laughter. A silly pig figurine she had given him the week before their wedding. A photo of them dressed up like kosher pickles and a jar for Halloween.

Finally, after several hours, he was finished sorting through the boxes. As he hung the very last photo on the long wall of the apartment hallway that separated the kitchen from the bathroom, he heard the sound of a key turning in the door. Taking the nail out of his mouth, he put the last framed photo and his hammer safely down on the floor.

Lacey stepped inside, her pink backpack slung over one shoulder. Her feet came to a standstill in their foyer, her mouth falling open.

"What the—"

"Hey, kiddo." Chris beamed.

She looked at him. "You're home?"

"I'm home," he said, throwing his hands up. "So, what do you think?"

She was overwhelmed. In Virginia, they had lived in a modest three-bedroom, two-bathroom ranch inside the interior beltway of Fairfax County. What would barely make a dent in their old living room now took over every square inch of space in their tiny two-bedroom, one-bathroom apartment in Brooklyn. And yet, despite being crammed wall-to-wall, window-to-window with sparkle and tinsel, the whole space felt magical.

Claire had always loved the holidays.

"Where did you get all this stuff?"

"You don't remember?"

Lacey took tiny steps toward the kitchen table. Running her fingers over the Santa figurine, her little voice squeaked out with surprise. "This is from our old house?"

Since moving to New York, Christmas in their house had been rather uneventful. He still put up decorations—left a million presents under the tree for Lacey—but all the Christmas decorations were purchased last-minute in bulk from Amazon. They had no sentimental value. They had no memories attached to them, either.

Chris sucked air into his chest. "I was doing laundry," he explained. "I guess I had completely forgotten all this stuff was downstairs. Anyway, I thought…why not? It's almost Christmas. So I brought it up. Started putting them out. Once I was done with Christmas, I got started on the boxes with all our old photos."

She wasn't listening. Instead, her tiny toes moved in the direction of the hallway. She scanned the long line of photographs that Chris had now decorated their home with. They were everywhere. Photos of Claire when she was younger. Photos of Chris and Claire together. Photos of them, in Virginia and together, living as a family.

Lacey stopped at a photograph of her and her mother visiting Yosemite. Lacey was only a toddler, but she sat on Claire's lap while snowcapped mountains and gray shifting clouds peeked overhead. Lacey lifted one hand to the photograph, touching the edge of the frame. And then, spinning around on her sneakers, she raced toward Chris, throwing her arms around his waist. Chris hugged her back.

Some things didn't need words. His little girl. His almost woman. She deserved to grow up knowing her mom.

He knelt down to her. "I wanted to apologize to you."

"To me?" she asked.

He nodded. "I should have brought this stuff out of storage a long time ago."

She stared at the floor. "It's okay."

"No," he said. "It's not. But from this point on, we're gonna do things differently. I'm not gonna be afraid to talk about Mom anymore. We'll put up as many pictures as you want.

And anything you want to ask me about her, anything you want me to tell you about her, I will. I'll do my best...to tell you the truth about everything."

For the next three hours, Chris and Lacey went through their tiny two-bedroom apartment. He pointed out every decoration and trinket and photograph, attaching whatever memory he could find to go with it. Until their house was a Museum of Claire. Until both he and his daughter were falling over in hysterics, laughing at all the good memories they had shared together.

Chris came across a photograph of him and Claire sitting in the stands of a JMU football game, wearing matching face paint. Lacey wanted to know where it was taken.

"This one," Chris explained, "we were in college."

"You and Mommy knew each other for a long time."

"We did."

"How did you meet?"

"I never told you the story?"

"I don't remember it," she said sadly.

Chris brought Lacey over to the couch, taking a seat. "So, in fourth grade, there was this group of boys, and they would get together during recess and find as many ladybugs as they could, collecting them up...and then they would stomp on them with their sneakers."

"That's awful."

"Yeah," he said. "Your mom didn't like it, either. So anyway, your mom—she had such a big heart, you know? And she got really mad about this. She ran over to those boys demanding they let those ladybugs go. And, of course, they wanted your mom to back down. Which she didn't because your mom...your mom wasn't scared of anybody. So anyway, this bully, I don't even remember his name, he pushed your mom. And I saw it, and I didn't like it…so I jumped in and pushed him back."

"And you kicked his butt?"

"Actually, the opposite. He kicked my butt. The kid was in sixth grade. We all got suspended for three days. But you know what, Lace…it was totally worth it, because I met your mom. And we became good friends. And we spent the rest of the year sitting on the jungle gym together, protecting lady-bugs from bullies."

Lacey fingered the edges of the photograph. "Mom sounds brave."

"She was."

"You sound kind of dorky, though."

Chris smiled. "I was cool in my own way."

"Dad," she said, squinting up at him. "I have another question."

"Shoot."

"Did you and Dara break up?"

The question surprised him. "We weren't dating, kiddo."

"Daaaad." She cut him off with a major tween eye roll.

"What?" he said, genuinely. "Dara and I were just friends."

"Come on," she said, crossing her arms. "I'm not an idiot." Lacey proceeded to explain it to him. "First off, you looked at each other all starry-eyed. She came bra shopping with us, and went axe throwing with us, and came over to the house for dinner. And then… I saw you in the kitchen. *Gross*."

Chris shifted uncomfortably in his seat. He really did not want to ever have a conversation about his sex life with his daughter.

"And now," Lacey continued, emphatically, "you're not even talking! You're home even though tonight is the big live event to end all her segments with Dr. Daniel. I'm not stupid,

Dad. I'm eleven *and a half* years old. I know you liked her. You don't have to hide it from me."

Damn. His kid was insightful. Clearly she could see they were far more than simply friends, or colleagues.

"Okay," he said. "You're right. I did have feelings for Dara."

"Told you."

"And Dara." He sighed. "I think she did have feelings for me, too…but there are complications."

Her nose wrinkled. "Complications?"

"It's hard to explain. It's grown-up stuff."

"Like blow jobs?"

"Uh, *no*…" Chris said, feeling his heart race. "Also, who taught you that?"

Lacey shrugged. She was not about to start snitching on her friends. Chris closed his eyes, and bit back the deepening sense of foreboding. *Just talk to her.*

Taking a deep breath, he decided to try a new tactic with his daughter. Being open.

"Dara is Jewish," he said, meeting her eyes directly. "To be with someone like Dara, I'd have to convert—change religions. That means I'd have to become Jewish. *We'd* have to become Jewish."

The news made her gasp with excitement. "Does that mean I can have a Bat Mitzvah?"

"Wait—what?"

"Oh my God," she continued, "Jasmine is going to be *soooooo* jealous. I can't wait to become Jewish! I'm gonna be the most popular kid in seventh grade!"

Chris couldn't help but laugh. Leave it to an eleven-year-old to boil life down to popularity contests and parties.

"You know, Lace," he said, wanting to be clear. "It's not just having a Bat Mitzvah. Converting might mean you have to give up stuff, too. Like no more Christmas, or Easter Bunny… no more bacon, either."

"No more bacon?"

"That's right. No more bacon. No more ham-and-cheese sandwiches, or pork rolls, or anything with pork products."

"Well, can I still watch horror movies?"

Chris smiled. "I think that would be okay."

Lacey sighed heavily before considering the implications of conversion. "I don't know if I want to give up bacon," she said, honestly, "even for a Bat Mitzvah. But can't you figure all that stuff out at a later time?"

"How do you mean?"

"I mean, maybe you and Dara celebrate Hanukkah, but I still have a Christmas tree. Or maybe, we don't eat bacon in the house, but I can have bacon when we go out to breakfast. Like the way Amerpreet has his own shelf of food at the firehouse, or my friend Jasmine can't eat peanuts."

Chris tousled her hair. "You're a really smart kid, you know that?"

"I know."

It was good advice. Not that it mattered. His relationship with Dara was over. Still, he was surprised at how well Lacey was handling the news.

"And you're not upset that I had feelings for someone… who wasn't Mom?"

Lacey got quiet. "You were always sad after Mom died. Even when we moved to New York, even when you were smiling, you were always sad. And then, Dara was on your show, and suddenly, you were smiling for real. We were going out for ice cream, just because. I don't know, but I feel like…if someone makes you want to eat ice cream, you should probably keep them around. I want you to be happy, Daddy. I want us both to be happy."

Chris swallowed. "I love you, Lace."

"I love you, too, Daddy."

The sound of Brooklyn traffic swelled outside his window. The lights of the Christmas trees flickered back at them. With the sun setting outside, the whole world felt wrapped up in the promise of the holidays.

"Tell you what," Chris said, looking down at his daughter. "Why don't you go put your school stuff away, throw on some comfy clothes. I'll finish cleaning up in here, and then we'll go out to the store, buy more ice cream than is humanly possible to eat, and come back and watch the show together."

Lacey jumped up from the couch excitedly. "That is the best idea you've had all day!"

Chris laughed. Lacey sprinted toward her bedroom. He waited for the door to close behind her before returning to his tasks.

He finished hanging the last framed photo in the hallway. He cleaned up bubble wrap and empty boxes, bringing them back to the storage locker downstairs. He bent to plug in the lights of the Christmas tree, digging through branches, when his hand bumped into something.

Pulling it out, he found a small box covered in green crushed velvet. Chris analyzed it curiously. It must have fallen out, shuffled its way beneath the tree when he was unpacking boxes. He opened it. Inside, there was a tiny silver frame, a photograph that Claire had turned into a Christmas ornament.

A red ribbon dangled in a loop from the top. Two purple flowers decorated the sides. In the center, a large yellow butterfly spread its wings and lifted into flight.

It was not an expensive ornament. Chris recalled Claire buying it on sale at some arts and crafts store after they were first married. But inside the flimsy metal frame was a picture of all three of them, taken on the day Lacey was born, while they were still at the hospital.

A wave of feelings crashed over him. Hurt and sadness. But sitting beside his grief was also joy. He found the goodness from that day.

The way Claire looked, exhausted but happy, rocking Lacey in her arms. The promise of a new life, the feeling of being witness to a miracle, meeting his daughter for the first time. It was love at first sight for all of them.

Chris pulled the ornament from the box and found a spot on the tree to hang it from.

Lacey returned to the living room in a tornado of excitement. "Okay, I'm ready!"

"Well, come on, then," Chris said, grabbing their coats. "Last one to the store has to eat pistachio ice cream with pineapple sauce!"

"Ewwwwww," Lacey squealed, taking off down the stairs.

Chris glanced back at his apartment. At the Christmas decor, all their memories of home, past and present, intertwined together. At the photographs, joy and pain, lining the walls. And then, leaving Claire dangling from the branch of an evergreen tree, he moved on.

38

DARA WAS FULL-ON VIBRATING.

Sitting in the limo beside Dr. Daniel on their way to Pier 15 on the Hudson River, she busied her shaking hands by checking herself one last time in her compact mirror. Despite the fact that everything was going according to plan, Dara was having a conniption.

Her anxiety swelled to epic proportions. Beads of sweat appeared on her neck. She was certain that at any minute she would be screaming at the driver to pull over, retching and heaving her guts all over the six-inch stiletto heels that Cameron had picked out for her to wear this evening.

It was the last thing she wanted to deal with. But as she had already taken her limit on both daily antianxieties and only-as-needed rescues, she searched for some other way to take her mind off the inevitable. Glancing over to Dr. Daniel, she waited for him to notice that she was about ten seconds away from devolving into a full-blown panic attack. Instead, the man was in a bubble, totally unaware of what she was going through.

Dara sighed, loudly. Daniel did not notice. She tried again, fanning herself, breathing heavily. Still nothing. Finally, she decided to speak up.

"I'm nervous," she said.

"Oh." Daniel took her hand. "Well, don't be nervous, darling."

She grimaced. "It doesn't work that way."

"What?"

"Anxiety," she said. "You can't just tell someone who's nervous not to be nervous."

"Well, of course not." He smiled again. "All I meant to say is, there's nothing to be nervous about. Everything has been handled by Naveah and the event planners and the production crew of *Good News New York*. All you need to do now is show up to your bubbe's party and have a wonderful time."

Right.

His words were epically unhelpful.

It bothered her. She disliked the way he called her *darling*. She disliked how he felt so at ease telling her to calm down. She despised the way he used placations, instead of having a conversation with her, like Chris would do. Chris would prod her with questions. Chris would annoy her to no end with his curious nature and charming smile. Chris would want to know what was on her mind, and how he could help her feel better.

God, how she missed Chris right now.

"It's just…" Dara said, twisting in her seat. "Chris and I kind of got into a huge fight. I'm just worried…it's going to be awkward around him."

"Well," he said, considering her statement. "You're a big girl. I'm sure you two can hash it out when we get there, and if you don't, I doubt it really matters. After tonight, you won't be seeing him anymore anyway. Big finale, and all."

"Of course," she said. "You're right."

Daniel turned his attention to looking out the window. Dara sank back into her seat.

She had a good idea what was coming tonight. She knew the moment that Eleanor—and Daniel, and Janet, and Naveah—had approached her, all bubbling over with excitement about the idea of shooting a live one-hour special of *Good News New York*. A proposal was in the works. She didn't know how, or the exact details, but she knew it was coming.

That terrible twisting sensation started pulling at her guts again. She shook the feeling away. It was all in her head. It was her anxiety, playing tricks on her heart, messing with her feelings. Daniel was perfect. Her perfect Jewish future husband. She just needed to relax.

Scrambling for her bag, she pulled out her phone, turning on her emergency scanner app.

"What are you doing?"

"Oh." Dara laughed a little and attempted to explain. "Sometimes when I get nervous, I listen to the emergency services scanner app on my phone."

"You what?" He looked confused.

"It helps with my anxiety. I know it sounds strange, but something about hearing all those stories, all those sad events happening at once and simultaneously—"

He did not understand. She could see it in his eyes. The way he squinted at her, mouth all funny, one step short of disapproval. She stopped trying to explain herself to him, falling into silence instead.

"Hmm," Daniel said, seriously. "Well, we can work on that later."

"Work on what?"

"Getting you on the right medication," he said, simply. "Obviously, whatever you've been doing all these years hasn't been working."

Dara turned off her emergency scanner app, putting her phone away. He didn't get it. Worse yet, he didn't even let her explain all the reasons she found it helpful.

Chris would never have responded that way.

The limousine arrived at Pier 15 on the Hudson. Lights twinkled down the pier. A giant menorah—all eight lights burning brightly—greeted their arrival. A string quartet began playing music. The driver opened the door, and a pathway of purple carpet appeared before her.

39

DR. DANIEL EMERGED FROM THE LIMOUSINE FIRST.
He offered Dara a hand, and she stepped out on the carpet.

Pier 15 was fully decked out for the occasion. The entire venue was lit up in colors of violet and white. A string quartet played swing music from Miriam's dance hall days, while two waiters in tuxedos offered tiny glasses of champagne. Down the street, parked out of view from the main event, were three production vans from NBS-7 Studios.

Dara and Daniel had arranged to arrive early to the party. Dara to check in with Naveah, making sure that everything would be perfect for her grandmother. Daniel because he wanted to run through some last-minute details with Eleanor.

But stepping onto the carpet, Dara quickly realized that checking in was all for naught. Naveah—with assistance from both Cameron and Alexa, plus two party planners hired especially for this event—had everything in order. Tablet in hand, Naveah stood at the front entrance, directing the caterers, animal handlers and dance crew. Around her, in busy pockets of buzzing energy, was the production team of *Good News New York*.

"Dara! Daniel!" Naveah called, racing over to greet them. "Well, what do you think?"

"It's perfect," Dara admitted freely.

"You've outdone yourself," Daniel said, wrapping one hand around Dara's waist.

She couldn't help herself. On instinct, she found herself stepping away from him.

"My grandmother is going to love this," Dara said.

"Well, that's the point!" Naveah beamed between them. "Making Miriam feel like the queen she is. And like I told you earlier, there is absolutely nothing for you to worry about. I have handled every detail to perfection." She smiled in the direction of Dr. Daniel—like they were sharing some secret between them—before shrugging happily once more in Dara's direction. "So, would you like the grand tour?"

"We would—"

"Actually," Daniel interrupted her. "If you don't mind, I need to talk to Eleanor for a moment." He nodded down the deck, where Eleanor was speaking to three of her production crew. "Could I catch up with you both later?"

"Of course," Dara said. "Take all the time you—"

He was already halfway to Eleanor—and full-on gliding in his approach—before she could finish her thought.

"So?" Naveah asked, drawing Dara's attention back. "Would you like a tour now, or should we wait for him?"

Dara glanced back to Daniel. He was laughing with Eleanor over some shared secret, turning bright red in the process. "You know what," she said, not wanting to interrupt them, "let's just do this part ourselves."

Naveah smiled. "Great."

The inside of Pier 15 was even more fabulous in design, decked out in the theme of winter wonderland meets dance hall from the forties. Naveah took Dara on a grand tour, pointing out each station and detail.

Dara had spared no expense in the creation of this party, and it was evident in every carefully thought-out, prearranged detail. Along with a kosher sushi and smoked salmon bar, there would be pigs in the blanket. The band would play a medley of swing music, interspersed with klezmer and pop. A large acrylic menorah—the same menorah that had been used during the infamous Matzah Ball Max—sat at the back of a stage, waiting to be lit for the last night of Hanukkah.

Spinning white-and-purple lights circled the dance floor as the fifteen-piece band finished setting up on risers. Dara glanced down to see she was stepping on her grandmother's initials in Hebrew. A mem and resh delicately drawn in careful calligraphy spun alongside black-and-white photos from Miriam's youth.

"And the horses?" Dara asked.

"You mean the unicorns?" Naveah asked jokingly.

"Yes, the unicorns."

"They're outside," she confirmed. "Hidden from view."

Dara sighed. Not one detail was out of place. Not one thing she had wanted, or instructed Naveah to get, was left out from the planning. And yet, something felt wrong. Or rather, Dara couldn't help but think—someone was missing.

Naveah excused herself to go check on one of the vendors.

Alone on the dance floor, Dara felt her anxiety return. The spinning lights suddenly made her nauseous.

She was certain that her life was ending, that she could not handle tonight. She stroked one arm nervously, attempting to self-soothe. She ran through all her self-talk, whispering that she could handle anything, but her anxiety would not abate. Her eyes wandered over to the side of the room. Eli was bent over one of the tables, camera in hand, filming shots of decor and lighting.

"Hey," Dara said, walking over to him. "You're doing B-roll now?"

"Oh," he said, shrugging happily. "Yeah. I got promoted."

"That's amazing!"

"Thanks," he smiled genuinely. "I've been working hard for it, and I guess, well…things are changing. All the staff is moving around, actually. Turns out, it's gonna be a really great New Year's for *Good News*, after all."

He returned to getting his footage. Dara debated leaving him to it, then on second thought, scratched that idea. She had a right to know, after all. Tapping him on the shoulder, she interrupted the young man in his task once again.

"Do you know where Chris is?" she asked, trying to sound casual.

"Chris?"

"He usually greets me on shoots, but I haven't seen him."

"Yeah." Eli grimaced. "It's no big deal. I think Eleanor was going to talk to you about it, but… Chris isn't filming tonight's event."

"What?" Dara shook her head. "I don't understand."

"To tell you the truth, I don't really, either. All I know is Lisa is taking over the segment for tonight. Chris won't be here."

She couldn't believe what she was hearing. Dara stared down at her shoes. Chris wasn't coming. He wouldn't be by her side on what was shaping up to be one of the most important nights of her life.

She had never felt more alone.

Eli attempted to make her feel better. "But really, Dara," he said, putting his camera down. "Don't worry about it. Lisa is a total professional. She has just as much experience as Chris. She'll make sure everything tonight goes perfect."

She forced a smile. "Perfect, huh?"

"Without a single hitch."

Dara nodded. *Perfect* seemed to be the word of the evening. And yet, standing alone on that dance floor, the irony struck her particularly hard. Perfect was suddenly the last thing in the world she wanted.

40

THE PARTY FOR BUBBE MIRIAM WAS IN FULL SWING.

The guests had eaten their fill from sixteen stations' worth of kosher delights. The open bars had been fully taken advantage of. Even Shana—her opinionated big sister—couldn't find one single complaint to lob in Dara's direction. The crowd gathered around the dance floor, waiting for Bubbe Miriam to make her grand entrance.

"Are we all ready to celebrate the person we're here for?" the master of ceremonies asked.

The guests responded with unanimous cheers. The music softened. Lisa and the camera crews for *Good News New York* moved into position. And then, the doors parted. The entire room gasped.

Miriam, decked out in her elegant purple gown, was sitting atop a chariot, being ushered into her party by two white horses transformed into unicorns, their manes dyed a rainbow of colors, golden horns affixed to masks on their heads. Miriam waved in the direction of the crowd.

Yet, even with mythical creatures announcing her arrival, nothing could top her shoes. Adorned in silver gemstones with large tulle flowers decorating the front. Miriam kicked up her heels from atop the chariot. The crowd cheered fervently as the jewels on her shoes shimmered in the lights.

The master of ceremonies continued. "Let's give a big round of applause to Bubbe Miriam! *Yom Holodet Sameach*, Bubbe Miriam! We wish you many more good years of life, happiness and blessings!"

The music exploded once more. *Hava Nagilla* swept over the room. The guests clasped hands together, forming a circle, surrounding Miriam in a hora. Dara found herself squelched between Shana and Daniel.

"Isn't this wonderful?" Daniel shouted over the music.

"Great!"

She didn't understand why her response felt like a lie. Glancing around the room, seeing the joy on her grandmother's face, she knew things were going perfectly. And yet, every time Dara searched the crowds, looked past Dr. Daniel to the crews of *Good News New York*, her heart sank.

Why wasn't Chris here?

Four strong men appeared to help Miriam off the chariot. The horses were taken back outside, and she was led to a golden throne.

"Well, Miriam," the master of ceremonies said, "I hope you're ready for some surprises, because your family and friends have gone all out to make sure that this is the most epic birthday party that New York has ever seen!"

The ChallahBack Girls appeared from the side. Wearing pink feathers and sequined flapper gowns, they strutted to the center of the room, before breaking out into a flash mob. At the sight of the octogenarians doing a synchronized dance, the room broke into wild applause. Miriam clapped along, delighted.

"But what would a ninetieth birthday be," the master of

ceremonies said, as their performance drew to a close, "without remembering a lifetime of good deeds."

The music fell into a soft hum. The doors opened again. And then, the room flooded with children. A parade of tiny beings—all wearing clothes in the exact shade of purple as Miriam—entered the room. Holding one white rose apiece, the children presented them to Miriam, before taking their positions at the side with their parents.

"Each of these children," the master of ceremonies explained, "is a product of a match that you made."

Miriam's eyes flooded with tears. Soon, she was inundated with white roses. Her lifetime of good deeds. Her legacy of love, tied up and intertwined with the Jewish people.

Her memory would always be a blessing.

With the surprises done for the time being, the music began again. Dara found herself in another hora. Circling the room, the music sweeping her up in the feeling of spinning, she glanced over to Daniel and saw Eleanor give him a thumbs-up. Dara felt sick.

As she turned around, heading for the door, Shana called out to her. "Where are you going?"

"I just..." Dara searched for an excuse. "I need a moment."

She took off. Leaving Daniel and her sister behind, she pushed past the throngs of guests to find the party suite. Normally reserved for brides, Dara was using it as a space for her grandmother and the ChallahBack Girls to recoup if necessary.

Closing the door behind her, she collapsed onto a couch. In the privacy of that room, Dara exploded into tears. They came fast and furious, a wellspring of unbridled emotion. She reached for a tissue, wiping her eyes, but it was no use. The sadness she felt was overwhelming.

"Dara?" Her grandmother appeared at the door.

Quickly, Dara sat up. Sucking back any tears, she dug her

dirty tissue into a fold in the couch. This was her grandmother's big night, after all. She did not want to ruin it by acting foolish.

"Are you okay?" Miriam asked, stepping inside.

"I'm fine," Dara lied. "Just something…in my eye."

Miriam was not buying it. She closed the door behind her. "Dara-la," Miriam said softly, taking a seat beside her granddaughter on the couch. "Talk to me."

The tears began again. "It's just," Dara stammered, giving over to the moment, "this whole time, I've been searching for Mr. Perfect on Paper…and I thought that was what I wanted, Bubbe! All the correct things, all the things I care about, perfectly arranged and lined up for my future life. And Dr. Daniel, he is perfect, he's perfect in every single way…but he's not—"

"Chris," her grandmother finished the sentence for her. "He's not Chris."

Dara swallowed hard, shaking her head. "You knew?"

"I've suspected."

"Since when?"

"Since that first day at *Good News*."

"The first day?" Dara said, shocked. "But how?"

Miriam shrugged toward Heaven. "Some things have no explanation."

She was waiting for her grandmother to point out the obvious. That she could always demand Chris convert. That, according to Jewish law and matrilineal descent, their children would be Jewish. That falling in love with him would set her apart from her community, leave her open to scorn and judgment. That she was betraying six thousand years of Jewish history. But her grandmother didn't say anything. She just sat, silently, taking it all in.

"What do I do, Bubbe?"

"What do you want to do?"

"It's against Jewish law," Dara said.

"So is eating shrimp," Miriam reminded her. "Yet Arlene has never met a shellfish platter she didn't like."

"Shana will never forgive me."

"Shana is not living your life," she said, before adding, "Besides, I know Shana. She'll forgive you the minute another nanny quits and she needs a babysitter."

"He'll never be able to lead a Passover Seder."

"So you'll run it," she said simply. "Why else did your parents pay all that money for Jewish day school?"

"He has a daughter."

She nodded thoughtfully. "That is a complication," she admitted. "But you're a smart girl. If you two love each other… you'll figure it out."

"And what about the Jewish people? What about my responsibility to our history, and our culture?"

She sighed. "Intermarriage gets blamed for many of the faults of Jewish life. Do I wish you had fallen in love with someone Jewish? Of course. I would be lying if I told you otherwise. There will be lots of people who don't agree with your relationship. Lots of people who shirk your family, who make you feel less than welcomed, in both Jewish and non-Jewish communities."

Tears streamed down her cheeks. She didn't understand why it had to be so hard.

"I'm an old woman," Miriam sighed, "and I'm dying. When I think about where I'm going, when I think about what I want for you when I'm gone… I don't think about the legacy of the Jewish people. I don't think about where Judaism will be in another six thousand years. I think about *you*. I think about my beloved granddaughter—my most special *shayna madela*—being safe and happy. That's all I want for you, Dara. That's all I've ever truly wanted for you."

Dara shook her head, struggling to make sense of her grandmother's words. It was the last thing she expected to hear from a woman whose entire life had been formed around Jewish matrimony. But even if her grandmother could accept a relationship with Chris, it wouldn't change one simple fact. Dara loved being Jewish. She didn't know if she could compromise on her faith. But she wasn't sure she wanted to give up on her heart, either.

"What if I make the wrong choice?" Dara asked.

"You may," Miriam said honestly. "We never fully know if the path we're walking is the right one. Maybe Chris will work out. Maybe he won't. Maybe you'll be happier with Dr. Daniel. Maybe you won't. But that's life, Dara-la. No guarantees. Not everyone's a winner. We do the best we can, with the information we're given."

A knock on the door drew her attention away. Dara sucked back tears just in time to see Eli sticking his head inside.

"Sorry to interrupt," he said, glancing between the two women. "But I was wondering if we could see you both outside for an interview?"

Dara nodded. She knew what was coming.

Eli closed the door behind him as he left. Miriam didn't need to say anything else. Dara helped her grandmother up, and they walked together with shaky steps back outside. Dara's anxiety spiraled as she approached the dance floor. She clutched her grandmother's wrist tighter. A purple carpet, littered with rose petals, met her feet. At the end, surrounded by flowers and a string quartet playing a soft tune, was Dr. Daniel.

Miriam walked Dara halfway.

And then, her bubbe let go of her hand.

Making the rest of her way down the carpet, Dara took slow and steady breaths. Fake snow drifted down around her as the cameras moved in closer to capture a better angle. Despite the fact that they were surrounded by people—both her immediate family and his—it felt eerily quiet. She could hear the sound of waves lapping up against the pier as she arrived beside him.

Daniel smiled. "Dara."

"Daniel," she said, swallowing hard. "What is all this?"

He took a deep breath. The cameras swung around again. Eleanor nodded in Daniel's direction, and he continued, taking both her hands inside his.

"Dara," he repeated. "The day you came rolling into my emergency room was one of the best days of my life. You're beautiful and brilliant. You're committed to your family, and your faith. I enjoy every minute I get to spend with you."

Dara nodded. This was it. It was happening. She looked back toward her family. Her bubbe, and her sister. Her brother-in-law and her nieces and nephews. The ChallahBack Girls, clutching each other's arms, smiling in her direction. These people loved her, didn't they? But love in her world came with certain expectations.

Dr. Daniel wasn't wrong. They could have a beautiful, and appropriate, life together.

Shana wiped away a tear from her eye. Dara turned back to Dr. Daniel and heard a loud *bark-bark-roooooooo* erupt from the end of the carpet. She turned to find Bucky, the vegan golden retriever, wearing a little blue tallis, along with a matching blue kippah, holding a tiny blue-and-gold gift bag in his mouth.

"Bucky!" she squealed in delight.

"I know how much you love him," Daniel said, proudly.

Bucky came prancing down the aisle, his tail waving happily, that bag swinging from his giant lips. She bent down to kiss him all over. "Oh, Bucky." She nuzzled into his furry face to whisper, "I'm so glad you're here."

Daniel took the bag from Bucky. With one more bark, and a few hearty chuckles from the attending audience, her favorite television golden retriever retired in a good-boy sit at the side.

Dara knew what was coming next.

Daniel removed a small box from the bag and got down on one knee. Opening it up, he presented her the sapphire-and-diamond engagement ring that she had picked out. The crowd gasped at the sheer size, and obvious expense, of that tiny piece of jewelry. Dr. Daniel, the Perfect Jewish Husband, had gone all out.

"Dara," Daniel said, beaming in her direction. "You and I have begun this journey together. But a few weeks, a few months...they aren't enough. I want to spend the rest of my life with you. Will you do me the pleasure, and honor, of being my wife?"

Dara fingered the navy blue velvet edges of that box.

She found herself getting caught up in the fantasy. The handsome Jewish doctor, on one knee, asking for her hand in marriage. Her loving family, so proud and hopeful, standing beside her. Hell, even Bucky was here to send her off into engaged bliss. The whole world was rooting for them.

But when she glanced back at the camera crew, when she scanned the eager and waiting faces of Eleanor and Eli, Lisa and Sheila, standing nearby—she missed Chris. She missed Lacey, and killer clowns, and jalapeño-and-pineapple pizza. She missed their surprises, and their messiness, and the totally unexpected joy they had brought into her life.

With everything she ever wanted right there in her reach, she realized that it was never Daniel she was excited to see on her dates. It was never Daniel that made her heart race on approach. It was Chris. Always Chris. The easygoing, charming and totally not-Jewish reporter had completely stolen her heart.

She pulled her fingers away from that velvet box.

"Daniel," she said, as the waters crashed in the distance. "You are a wonderful man. You're thoughtful, and kind. You're an incredible doctor. I know everyone here agrees with me when I say that you are, without a doubt, a real-life Mr. Perfect on Paper...but you are not perfect for me."

A gasp went up from the crowd. Shana screamed outright, before huffing in Hebrew under her breath. She knew that Eleanor was having a conniption. And Daniel—poor Dr. Daniel—looked completely lost.

"I'm sorry, Daniel," she said, genuinely. "I'm so incredibly sorry...but I can't marry you. The answer is no."

41

"THE ANSWER IS NO."

Chris blinked, dumbfounded. Over half-eaten bowls of ice cream and discarded paper plates lined with pizza crust, his mouth went dry. His heart rate sped up as he leaned forward on the couch beside Lacey, staring in confusion at the television screen.

He couldn't have heard her correctly. Did Dara really just turn down Mr. Perfect on Paper on national television?

And then, finally, he made sense of what was happening.

"Holy shiiiiii—" Chris jumped from the couch.

"Dad!" Lacey interrupted him, pulling on his sleeve. "In this house, we say *shinoozle*."

"Right," he said, simultaneous panic—and excitement—welling up inside his chest. Trying to figure out how to handle the situation, he began pacing like a madman. "What do we do? How do I handle this?"

"What do you mean?" Lacey said, jumping up from the couch beside him. She looked at her father like he was the biggest idiot on the planet. "We go get her, Dad!"

His eyes wandered down to his young daughter. His daughter—who looked so much like Claire. She was so wise, and brave, and...freaking brilliant.

In a flurry of movement, they were off. Grabbing their winter coats, their feet rolling like thunder down the stairs. Chris scrambled to find a taxi, but it was Thursday night on a cold December evening in the city. Finding a cab into Manhattan would be next to impossible.

He was seized by a growing freneticism. Dara had anxiety, after all. What she did—standing on that pier in front of an entire country—took courage. There would be a backlash. Whether she loved him or not right now almost felt irrelevant. He needed to be there for her.

Chris started to lead Lacey toward the closest subway when he saw Jensen on the sidewalk. Standing behind him was the night crew of Engine 46. In the fire station behind them, a television set blared the live episode of *Good News*. Dara was still on camera, talking. Although, at this point, he couldn't hear what she was saying.

"Dude," Jensen said, scratching the back of his head. "Everything okay?"

Chris yelled, "I don't have time to explain!"

"Okay," Jensen said, placing both hands on his chest. "But you seem really flustered, man. Maybe sit down for a second. Tell us what's going on——"

"We're going to get Dara!" Lacey interrupted, jumping up and down in her spot. With all the intensity of a precocious tween, she described the situation, with no concern for social mores. "She's in love with my dad, and my dad is in love with her, but neither of them are going to live happily ever after, eating ice cream for all eternity, unless we get to her tonight!"

Lacey waited for the grown-ups in her life to respond appropriately. Jensen did the honors.

"So you're telling me," he said, putting one finger on the

center of his chin, "that your dad is rushing into the city to confess his true and undying love to Dara Rabinowitz—the same Dara Rabinowitz who just walked away from Mr. Perfect on Paper on national television?"

"Uh-huh." Lacey nodded. "We have to get there right away!"

"Get where?" Lilliana frowned. "Traffic will be a nightmare into Manhattan at this time of the evening." She nodded toward a line of cars packing their cross-street.

"I'm taking the subway," Chris explained.

Amerpreet spoke up. "Aren't they doing construction on the Q line?"

Reese crossed their arms. "Yep. I tried to get into the city yesterday and it took me damn well over six hours."

Don couldn't help but concur. "You'll be moving at a snail's pace no matter how you get into the city."

"Your best bet is to talk to her tomorrow," Jensen suggested.

"I *can't* talk to her tomorrow," Chris said urgently. "She needs me!"

"She needs you, huh?" Jensen said, glancing knowingly toward his friends.

"Kind of like...an emergency?" Amerpreet asked.

Chris squinted. "What?"

"Because if it's an emergency..." Gunther stepped forward, arms crossed against his green shirt, chest hair spilling out from the top. The old man did not play around when it came to that word. "Then I guess we have no choice but to pull out the trucks."

Chris finally got the drift. "Yes!" he shouted, looking at his friends. "Yes! It's an emergency!"

Jensen smiled. "Well, took you long enough."

In a groundswell of movement, the crew of Engine 46 was off. Opening garages, getting on the horn, pulling out the fire trucks. Chris barely had time to swallow, let alone express his gratitude, when Jensen drove that long red sleigh into the driveway.

"Well, come on," Jensen said, waving Chris and Lacey forward.

Chris helped Lacey into the seat beside him. When they were all situated safely in the front, he turned to his best friend. "I appreciate this. You have no idea."

"I love you, too, man."

Lacey groaned at their bromance. "Can we go already? I'm gonna be a thousand years old by the time we get there!"

Chris laughed. Jensen grinned mischievously. And then, with all the glee of a six-year-old hitting an elevator button, Jensen leaned over and pulled a lever. The siren rang out above them. "God." Jensen threw his head back. "That right there… that alone is worth the cost of admission!"

The engine revved forward. The fire truck pushed its way through Brooklyn, while the taxicabs and late-night revelers did their best to steer clear. On the horn, Chris could hear someone speaking. Gunther—otherwise known as Rudolph— was letting other ladders know that Engine 46 was on their way into Manhattan.

Chris took a deep breath. His daughter by his side, his future in the distance, he swore he could smell the scent of lavender and citrus—the perfume Claire always wore—as they raced off together in the night. Chris had spent the last two years of his life running away, but tonight, he was running toward something.

42

DARA HEARD AN AUDIBLE GASP GO UP FROM THE crowd. The camera crew stood shocked, unsure of what to do next, before Eleanor motioned that they should keep rolling. Dr. Daniel blinked, confused, and the cameras panned in, moving closer. She wanted to make this right. She knew she needed to explain herself and what had happened.

"You deserve someone who loves you, Daniel," Dara said. "You deserve someone who sets your heart on fire, and makes you excited to get out of bed each morning. And I know that's not me. I know that you feel it, too."

"But…" Daniel stammered. "We both want the same things."

"We do," she admitted. "But what I learned from this journey, from finding my real-life Mr. Perfect on Paper, is that love isn't something that can be quantified on a list. Love is messy. And terrifying. It shows up when you least expect it, and complicates your life in every way. But it's also…safe. And comforting. It allows you to be yourself completely, without judgment or fear, and it feels right. I don't know how something so incredibly scary can also feel right, but I need to give this inkling in my heart—in my soul—a chance."

"You're in love with someone else?"

"I am."

"Why didn't you tell me—" he glanced in the direction of the camera "—sooner?"

"I guess I just wanted to make this work. I wanted it so bad, I was willing to squelch all those feelings. And you were so wonderful to me. You *are* so wonderful. I thought it was my mind playing tricks on me. And I wanted to make my sister and my bubbe and both our families happy. But making everyone else happy was making me miserable."

She looked over to her family. She loved them so much.

"I don't know what will happen in the future," she said, turning back to him. "But it would be wrong to marry you, Daniel. I think we might find a way to be content, but we would never truly be happy. And we both deserve to be happy. We both deserve to find people who scare us…and change us, and are imperfect, and messy…but are worth the risk, anyway."

Dr. Daniel did not say anything. She imagined he was a jumble of emotions, anger being at the forefront of them. Still, her decision had been made. There was nothing left to say. For now, she just needed to get away from the cameras. She turned to leave.

"Dara." Dr. Daniel reached for her hand, stopping her. "I wish you all the best."

She cupped his cheek. "You really are perfect."

With no more discussion—or apologies—she pushed through the crowd of onlookers. The cameras followed her out as she made her way down the pier. Naveah chased after her with her coat and bag. Dara thanked her, pulling it over her shoulders as a gentle flurry began. It was freezing out, and her entire world was in shambles, but she breathed a small sigh of relief.

Finally, she was walking alone.

No cameras. No family. No audience. She strolled along the water's edge, until she could no longer hear the sound of music from her grandmother's party.

She leaned against the railing of the pier. Breathing in the scent of sea salt, she could see the lights of New Jersey. Somewhere just beyond the water were the Statue of Liberty and Ellis Island. The place where her great-grandparents had arrived in the early twentieth century, seeking an escape from religious persecution. Seeking a new country in which to live freely, expressing their Jewish identity. Had she betrayed them?

The cold air bristled against her skin. The sound of cars rushing by mingled with laughter coming from bars and restaurants. New York City never slept. You could disappear into the sounds of a million other lives, a million other experiences, and never spend a minute reflecting on your own.

Her phone buzzed in her pocket. She raced to pull it out, hoping it was from Chris, but no such luck. Instead, she saw a text from Janet.

Whatever you do, do not check social media.

Dara rolled her eyes. Really? This was what her friend was going to lead with? Of course she was going to check social media *now*. She tapped open Twitter. Not surprisingly, she was trending. Sadly, it was under the hashtag #cancelJMate.

She scrolled through the top comments.

I'm canceling my J-Mate subscription right now.

What a horrible person!

She didn't deserve Dr. Daniel!

I HOPE SHE GETS IMPALED BY A UNICORN!

Ouch.

Dara closed out of Twitter. It was a public relations nightmare. But what was the alternative option? Marry Dr. Daniel. Live unhappily ever after for the rest of their natural lives.

Television didn't tell the whole story of a person. She had learned that lesson well by meeting Chris.

Her heart ached at the thought. Where was he tonight?

She took a deep breath. Her hands shook from the cold as she attempted to call Chris. She tried three times, letting it ring until voice mail picked up, before giving up completely.

Of course he was still mad at her. Or maybe he had simply come to agree with her about the impossibility of their relationship ever working out.

Sucking back her sadness, she settled on comforting herself with the only thing that ever really helped. Opening her emergency scanner app, she placed it to her ear, closing her eyes. She drifted into all those familiar voices. The hum of codes, and static, before the dispatcher muted everyone into silence. No matter what was happening in New York City—all the good and bad of it, mushed up together like potato latkes on Hanukkah—life would go on.

Suddenly, a voice rang out through the radio.

"Dara," he said, speaking directly through the speaker. "It's me. Chris. I forgot my phone at home. Listen, if you're hearing this… I'm on my way, okay?"

"Me, too!" Lacey said.

"Me, three!" another voice said.

"Us, too!" rang out a chorus in the background.

Dara laughed, the tears coming fully now.

"I hope this isn't a mistake," Chris mumbled.

"It's not! Chris! Chris! I'm right here!" she screamed into the phone, before realizing that she was talking to no one. Chris could not hear her. Her phone was not a two-way radio. She spun around with only one thought on her mind. She needed to get to him.

She made her way back toward Pier 15—until disaster struck.

"We're stuck in traffic," Chris said.

"Heading toward the Brooklyn Bridge," Lacey added.

"The bridge." She shook her head, looking toward the water.

Brooklyn Bridge was so far away, on the opposite side of the city, and downtown. She glanced down at her feet, forlorn that she was wearing totally improper shoes for racing across Manhattan. Undeterred, she attempted to find a cab. But it was no use. It was a freezing night in December. Also, the last night of Hanukkah. All the yellow taxis were taken. She was just about to give up, and deal with whatever blisters were waiting for her, when a sound drew her attention upward.

Down the pier, with great noise and fanfare, the Challah-Back Girls were riding a golf cart, swerving between lampposts and trash cans.

"Out of the way!" Shira said, coming to a full stop in front of Dara.

"What the—" Dara glanced between the three women. "Did you steal a golf cart?"

"She's drunk!" Ruth said, outing her friend.

"I'm not drunk," Shira said, before leaning over to add, "Though what I did drink...may not be mixing well with my medication?"

"Oh, for Heaven's sake," Ruth said. "Let me drive!"

Shira slapped away her hand. "You snooze, you lose, *grandma*."

"That new hip is going to your brain!"

Dara's heart swelled, watching them bicker. She had thought that turning down Dr. Daniel would disappoint her beloved makeshift family. Instead, and quite the opposite, they had stolen a golf cart for her.

"Wait," Dara said. "You're not angry at me?"

Ruth squinted in her direction. "Why would we be angry with you?"

"Well, I...I turned down Dr. Daniel."

The old women looked at each other.

"Dara-la," Arlene said, shaking her head, "we only ever supported the relationship because we thought that's what you wanted!"

"I always thought he was totally wrong for you," Shira sighed.

"You did the right thing." Ruth nodded. "The hard thing—but the right thing."

Nothing else needed to be said. Even when she walked alone, she would always be lifted up and supported by the people who loved her. Dara blinked away tears. "But that still doesn't explain why you're here with a golf cart."

"Well, it's all over Facebook!" Ruth explained, holding up her phone.

On the page for *Good News*, right below a five-minute clip of Dara dumping Dr. Daniel, was a message from the account of one Christopher Steadfast.

This is Christopher Steadfast, head anchor for Good News. I'm using my friend's phone. If someone could get a message to Dara Rabinowitz, please tell her I am on my way. Please...tell her to wait for me.

More surprising, it had been liked one thousand two hundred thirty-six times.

Shira beamed. "He's coming."

"In a fire truck!" Arlene added.

"I know," Dara said, holding her phone. "He's stuck in Brooklyn...by the bridge!"

"We know!" they said at the same time. "Hurry! Get in!"

Dara climbed into the back of the vehicle. With a roar of the engine, they were off. Her odds of dying in this golf cart, in particular, seemed better than most. But Dara didn't care. Whatever anxiety she felt was stifled by this driving desire, this incomprehensible need. Her feelings were not irrational. If anything, she knew exactly who she was. And maybe, for the first time in her life, she knew exactly what she wanted, too.

She had never been so certain about something in her entire life. There was no hesitation in her heart. No desperate lingering with her finger over some button. Chris had taught her something valuable in that regard. All the best things happened when she threw away her plans.

"Left!" Dara shouted, directing Ruth. "Right! Watch out for that... Never mind." They tumbled over a plastic bag filled with... Dara didn't exactly know. But it sounded crunchy and caused the entire golf cart to bounce upward three inches.

Finally, she saw the Brooklyn Bridge in the distance. Chris was there. Somewhere out there...

"Oy veis meir," Arlene said, pointing with fury at the cars in front of her. "Look at this traffic!"

"Thursday night in Manhattan," Shira agreed, shaking her head.

"The young people certainly like to drink."

Dara rose from her seat. She had never walked across any bridge before. Bridges terrified her. The heights. The wind. The chance of a 10.4-Richter-scale earthquake bringing the whole thing down, and her crashing to her death with it, beneath the waters. Improbable, obviously. But still…a thought very much there in her head.

"Dara." His voice came over the emergency services scanner again. "Oh, God… Dara. I just have so much I want to say to you, so much I need to explain to you…but I want you to know…before I met you, I was afraid to smile. I was afraid of everything. Of life, and being happy, and taking a chance on love again. And then I met you and…you brought me back to myself."

She laughed, tears falling again. "Me, too."

"I know you think…because you have anxiety, that you're not brave. But that's not true. I've been thinking about it a lot, actually, and here's what I want to tell you. Courage isn't about jumping out of airplanes or building businesses from scratch. Real courage is showing up, even when you're afraid. Real courage is putting yourself out there, even when you fail—especially when you fail. Courage is saying, this is who I am, standing up, allowing yourself to be vulnerable. And you are brave, Dara. You're the bravest person I have ever met."

"Chris…"

"God," he said, almost in a whisper. "I hope you're listening."

She was.

An idea formed inside her brain. Quickly, she scrambled, opening Facebook and finding the page for *Good News New York*. Her nerves frayed, her heart pounding inside her chest, she typed out a reply to his comment:

Chris, I'm on the other side of the Brooklyn Bridge. I'm coming.

She hoped that the likes of her viewing audience, along with those pesky algorithms, would carry her message to the top of his notifications. Only time would tell. Chris was on the other side of that bridge. She took a deep breath and, spurred on by love and adrenaline, tossed her cell toward Arlene.

"Hold my phone," she said, full of grit.

Dara hoisted her evening gown up around her calves and began walking forward. The cold air blew as she took her first steps onto the pedestrian walkway.

It was as terrifying as she imagined. Cars zipped by on the median. Walkers brushed past, indifferent to her terror. Indeed, in the ball gown she was wearing, it felt particularly dangerous. As if the hoop skirt would lift her up like an umbrella, whisking her to her death. Or worse, she would stumble in her heels, falling to her death in the murky waters below.

She debated taking off her shoes, but that seemed just as dangerous in New York City—so she settled on the next best option. She kept her eyes forward. She took one step after another in six-inch stilettos, reminding herself with every terrified but determined breath that she was one step closer to Chris.

"Dara!" someone shouted in the distance. "Can you hear me?"

Her heart fluttered. Her soul lifted as her fears faded. She knew right away that it was him. Chris was no longer speaking through the radio. He was standing on the other side of the bridge.

"Chris!" she shouted, jumping up in her spot. "It's me! I'm coming!"

She began to run, stumbling in her heels, her heart pounding madly inside her chest. And then, she saw him, the emergency lights of the fire truck flashing a kaleidoscope behind him. He was out of breath. All sweaty. Totally inappropriately dressed for the weather. But he had met her—literally and figuratively—halfway.

Chris drew closer. She did the same. Meeting in the middle, finding each other, they stopped stammering and hesitating over their feelings. Chris took her in his arms and placed his lips upon hers.

All at once, Dara melted. She gave in to the feeling of his touch, the heat of his mouth, the pressure from his hands and the throbbing, aching passion of her heart.

She wanted him. She loved him. *She just knew.*

As they pulled apart, Chris blinked back disbelief before glancing over the side of the bridge. The waters were crashing down below. Shaking his head at the sight, laughing a little at words that didn't need to be said. Dara laughed, too. Yes, she had done it. She had crossed a bridge for him. She had faced her most profound and ridiculous fears for a chance at love. She had no idea what would happen between them, or what their future would look like...

But love would be their starting place.

Christopher Steadfast was not perfect. He didn't fill one single box on her Jewish husband list. He came with baggage, and complications, and surprises aplenty. But when she gazed into his eyes, she felt safe. The whole world could quake, and roar, and none of it would matter. She knew who she was, and what she believed. More important, she knew who she wanted.

Dara uttered the first words that came to mind. "I've been waiting for you."

EPILOGUE

one year later

Dr. Daniel Evans brought his black loafer down onto the glass cup surrounded in white silk.

It was tradition in Judaism to mark every happy occasion with a little bit of sadness. Even at a wedding as surprising, and happy, as that of Dr. Daniel Evans and Eleanor Cohen, the broken glass was a reminder of the fragility of human life.

"Mazel tov!" the crowd shouted, and the couple departed down the aisle.

Chris and Dara were still sitting in their seats at the back of the ceremony hall as the crowd dispersed. "Wait," Chris said, confused. "There's no kiss?"

Dara laughed. "Not in a traditional Jewish ceremony. You break the glass, and then the couple goes off to the *yichud* room."

"The *yee-chood* room?" Chris repeated the word. Over the last year, he had been working hard at learning more about the traditions that Dara loved.

"In the old days," Dara said, leaning in to whisper, "the

yichud room was where a couple went to…well, seal the deal. But nowadays, it's where a couple spends their first few minutes alone together as husband and wife."

Chris smiled thoughtfully in her direction. Though he had not said it aloud, she got the feeling he was taking notes.

"Eleanor looked so happy," Dara said, thinking back to the way the hard-nosed executive producer beamed during the ceremony. "And Daniel…did you hear how he got choked up during *kiddushin*?"

He nodded. "It was an incredibly moving ceremony."

Dara agreed. "It's a good match."

Chris took her hand, squeezing it tightly. "It is."

She warmed at the feeling of his touch. Love was in the air. The joy in the room felt contagious as Chris and Dara walked toward a lounge where appetizers and drinks were being served. They made the rounds, saying hello to people from *Good News* and the Jewish community they recognized, before finding the lox station. Three different types of smoked salmon were carved and presented on their plates.

Eleanor and Daniel returned from the *yichud* room.

"Dara!" Eleanor said, throwing her arms around Dara.

"Mazel tov!" Dara said, and genuinely meant it. "You look so beautiful."

"This old thing?" Eleanor waved off the compliment before clapping Chris hard on the arm. "And Chris! How the hell have you been?"

"Good." He smiled before nodding toward Dr. Daniel. "Congratulations to you, as well."

"Thank you," Daniel said.

Daniel's face was still red as he beamed in their direction. Dara couldn't help but notice that he kept one hand around the small of Eleanor's back. And Eleanor—perhaps even more telling—seemed to truly enjoy it.

Eleanor shook her head. "Dara, I have been thinking about you for months."

Dara touched her heart. "Me?"

"If you hadn't broken Daniel's heart," she explained, fully animated, "I might still be single! Who would have thought it, huh? You dumping Daniel on national television was the best thing to ever happen to me. I got a new show on prime time *and* a new husband! I can't thank you enough."

Daniel grinned. "Me, either."

"I'm so happy for you both," Dara said, and genuinely meant it.

"And Chris." Eleanor turned her attention on him. "Sure I can't lure you back to television?"

Chris released the lox sandwich he was in the middle of scarfing. He had quit *Good News* shortly after getting together with Dara. With her help—and in fairness, more than a little seed money—he had started his own podcast out of his living room. His show, which he called *Life Goes On*, focused on healing after tragedy. Helping others through their grief aligned perfectly with his values. The work fulfilled him immensely. And the schedule allowed him to spend more time at home with his growing daughter. Over the last month, his show had hit one million subscribers.

Chris let Eleanor down gently. "I'm afraid not."

"Well." Eleanor huffed a little. "I suppose I understand that. The hours in prime time are as bad as medicine...right, honey?"

Daniel nodded. "Right, darling."

"But hell—" she smacked Daniel on the back "—we both love what we do, right?"

Their eyes met, and they kissed, their tongues leaving little room for modesty. Dara averted her eyes.

"God," Eleanor said, pulling away from Daniel. "I freaking love you!"

Eleanor left to greet some guests at another table. Dara found herself standing between Daniel and Chris. A few awkward moments of silence followed before Chris took the hint. Reaching for his pocket, he pulled out his phone.

"You know what," Chris said, "I'm just gonna go check on Lacey. Do you mind, honey?"

"No," Dara said, touching his wrist gently. "I'm good."

Chris took off to call his daughter. For the first time in over a year, Dara found herself standing alone with Dr. Daniel.

"I'm really glad you could make it," he said finally.

"Oh, Daniel. I wouldn't have missed this wedding for the world."

"I wasn't sure...with your grandmother, and all."

Dara nodded. Miriam had died less than a month ago. The loss was still incredibly raw. But she and Shana and the ChallahBack Girls had sat by her side right until the end. Up until that final day when Dara held her hand and whispered in her ear that she could let go.

"I'll always miss her," she said, glancing down to the red-and-white oxford heels she was wearing. "But I know that she's with me. She's always guiding my steps...whether I know it or not."

Daniel nodded. "She was a force of nature."

"She was."

"And Chris?" Daniel glanced over to the door, where Chris was speaking on the phone. "You two have been together for a long time?"

"We have."

"Are you two—" he hesitated on the question "—talking about marriage?"

"We are," she admitted. "But we're also taking it slow. We still have some things we need to work through...but we love each other, and Lacey, and we're determined to make it work."

"Good." Daniel squeezed her arm. "I'm happy for you, Dara."

"Thank you."

"Daniel!" Eleanor screamed from across the banquet hall. "Get your *tuches* over here! I want you to meet my best friends from college!"

"Excuse me," he said, taking off toward a table where Eleanor was surrounded by women just as bold, loud and bawdy as her.

Dara found herself alone once more. She drifted into the music and the people surrounding her.

"Has anyone ever told you," Chris said, sneaking up behind her and whispering in her ear, "you look like someone from television?"

Dara laughed. Spinning around to face him, she melted into the soft and familiar features of his face once more. He was holding two plates of food. "You brought me kosher rack of lamb?" she squealed, delighted.

"I know how much you like it."

She sighed. It was not on her list, of course. But Chris was most excellent at surprises.

The doors to the main reception opened. Music began floating through the halls. G-sharp, a mixture of modern pop and old-world-style klezmer, as couples grabbed hands and raced toward the dance floor. Chris gestured with a slight bow. Dara put down her plate and took his hand, following after them.

The room was crammed full of revelers. But in that moment, in that music, it felt like they were the only people in the world.

"I love you, Dara."

"I love you, too," she said, leaning her head on his shoulder.

"Od Yeshama," a traditional song for Jewish weddings, began playing in the background. The crowd around them broke into an enthusiastic round of horas, or circle dancing. The guests parted in the middle, making room for shtick, entertaining the bride and groom like the king and queen they were, before the bringing out of chairs. Daniel and Eleanor were lifted into the air in an enthusiastic celebration of love and mazel.

Alas, Chris and Dara were oblivious. They missed the chairs, circle dancing, shtick and another round of food. The whole world spun on around them as they continued slow-dancing off to the side.

Chris twirled Dara around. She twisted and dipped, a move she had learned once from her beloved bubbe. Lifting her bubbe's oxford heels into the air, she floated freely, back arched, eyes pointed up toward the Heavens. She knew it was a sin, wearing her shoes, showing them off on her own feet without any concern for tradition—but she was happy. She was risking it all, letting go of her lists and her plans, re-envisioning her future.

Chris brought her back safely to the ground. In the process, his satin blue kippah almost fell to the floor.

Dara reached up, saving it just in time. She readjusted it to the correct position on his head. Chris pulled her closer. Her arms wrapped around his neck, his piercing gray eyes gazing into her own, until she couldn't resist the temptation any longer. She kissed him, long and hard, deep and passionate, falling into the warmth of his lips.

He tasted absolutely right.

★ ★ ★ ★ ★

ACKNOWLEDGMENTS

This book exists because of the love, support and encouragement of countless people.

Thank you to Emily Ohanjanians, my incredible editor at MIRA, who once again drew out all the depth of this story with her brilliant and insightful editorial eye. Emily—thank you for saying *yes*, for championing my work, for the gentle way you exist in the world and for your on-point feedback. Thank you for being someone who lives out their values through their actions. It has been an honor to work with you, and learn from you, over the last year.

My gratitude forever to my two amazing literary agents from Transatlantic Literary Agency, Carolyn Forde and Marilyn Biderman. Carolyn Forde, when do you sleep?!? Marilyn Biderman, thank you for your wisdom, witticisms and recipes. Your advice and support through this process has been invaluable. No matter where we go next, I am grateful that I have you two brilliant women by my side.

My continued thanks to Addison Duffy and Jasmine Lake, my film and television agents at UTA. My gratitude also goes out to all my foreign publishers, who work so hard to bring my stories to readers across the world.

Thank you to everyone at MIRA for giving this book the most extraordinary home. Thank you to Nicole Brebner and Dina Davis for championing this book. Thank you to Lia Ferrone, publicist extraordinaire, for fielding the never-ending barrage of emails, event requests and questions. My gratitude also goes out to Gigi Lau, Laci Ann and the Harlequin art department for their amazing cover art. Thank you also to Jennifer Stimson and Bonnie Lo for their excellent copyeditor skills.

Thank you to everyone at MIRA, Harlequin and Harper-Collins—all the production staff, rights people, marketing teams, sales folks and more. Many of them I unfortunately will not be able to name at the time of writing these acknowledgments, but I know they work so darn hard to make sure this book lines your shelves.

This book could not have been written without the help of Michael Chesney. Michael—thank you for taking the time to tell me about your experiences in broadcast journalism, for sharing so many deeply intimate parts of your own story and for fielding random text messages at all hours of the day. This book exists thanks to your knowledge and support.

My gratitude also goes out to Rabbi Aviva Fellman, who served as my *maira datra* and *rav* on this book. Thank you for answering any questions I had while writing this book, for your overwhelming excitement about my stories and just being an incredible friend. Everything has been easier with you by my side.

As always, my gratitude to my family. To my sisters, Evelyn Meltzer and Dr. Danielle Meltzer Chesney—I love you two more than anything in the world! Thank you for always being around to take phone calls, give your advice and just be an incredible support system no matter what is going on in my life. To my parents, Drs. Leslie and Jeffrey Meltzer, thank you for being the first people I call whenever I have good news.

My thanks, especially, to my husband, Xhevair Maskuli. Our entire lives changed when I became a working writer on deadline. Thank you for stepping up, getting dinner every night, driving me to a thousand bookstores, serving as my caretaker on business trips, cleaning the house so I could have rest days, running the dog and just being willing to share your wife (and our time) with the rest of the world. Your goodness forms the basis of every hero I write.

Finally, my gratitude to all the readers, booksellers, librarians, book bloggers, bookstagrammers and more who have shouted about my books from every social media profile and bookstore rooftop. Thank you to everyone—friends and family, writers and publishing professionals, reviewers and readers—for your constant and never-wavering support.

MR. PERFECT
ON PAPER

JEAN MELTZER

Reader's Guide

PIATKUS

1. What did you think of Dara's list for "The Perfect Jewish Husband"? Do you think the qualities she outlined are important in a partner?

2. Dara has generalized anxiety disorder. How has this condition affected her life? Do you know anyone who lives—or do you yourself live—with GAD? How does it affect their/your life?

3. If you had to create your own "Mr. Perfect on Paper," what qualities would be on your list?

4. Dara insists she could never be with a non-Jewish man. But she can't help falling for Chris. What do you think draws her to him?

5. Have you ever experienced the same kind of attraction to a person outside of your faith/culture/expected pool of suitors?

6. Do you believe love conquers all when it comes to relationships? Or do you believe it's more important for

two people to be "looking in the same direction," as Dara says of Jewish coupling?

7. Are you Team Chris or Team Dr. Daniel? Who did you want Dara to end up with? Why?

8. One major theme in the story is learning to face your fears in order to move ahead with your life. Do you agree with this assessment? Is there a time in your life when you had to do this?

9. What was your favorite scene in *Mr. Perfect on Paper*? Why?

10. If there were a movie based on the book, who would you cast as the characters?

Want more Jean Meltzer?

Don't miss the hilarious, and
heart-warming *The Matzah Ball*.

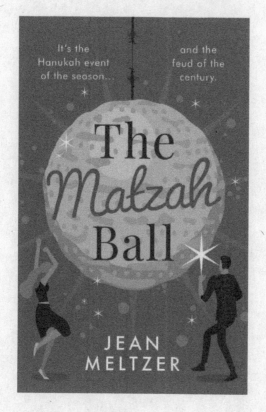

Available now from

PIATKUS

Do you love contemporary romance?

Want the chance to hear news about your favourite authors (and the chance to win free books)?

Kristen Ashley
Meg Cabot
Olivia Dade
Rosie Danan
J. Daniels
Farah Heron
Talia Hibbert
Sarah Hogle
Helena Hunting
Abby Jimenez
Elle Kennedy
Christina Lauren
Alisha Rai
Sally Thorne
Denise Williams
Meryl Wilsner
Samantha Young

Then visit the Piatkus website
www.yourswithlove.co.uk

And follow us on Facebook and Instagram
www.facebook.com/yourswithlovex | @yourswithlovex

PIATKUS